The Road Back Home

Amelia Vale

Published by Amelia Vale, 2024.

THE ROAD BACK HOME

First edition. October 7, 2024.

Copyright © 2024 Amelia Vale.

ISBN: 979-8227353429

Written by Amelia Vale.

Chapter 1: Homecoming

The door swung open with a groan, revealing the familiar chaos of a home that had long been neglected. Dust motes danced in the dim light filtering through the windows, and I felt a pang in my chest as I took in the remnants of my childhood. The living room was a tapestry of memories—each faded photograph and worn-out sofa spoke of laughter and tears, moments frozen in time. My mother's favorite quilt, a riot of colors, draped haphazardly over the back of the couch, its edges fraying like the strings of my heart.

"Welcome back to the land of dust and bad decisions," I muttered to myself, a nervous laugh escaping my lips. The echo of my voice felt foreign in the vast silence. No one was here to greet me, no jovial shout of "Hey, stranger!" or the comforting aroma of my mother's infamous chili bubbling on the stove. Instead, all I heard was the faint creak of the floorboards, a haunting reminder that I was alone.

I shuffled into the kitchen, the heart of the home that had once been my sanctuary. It was here that I learned the art of cooking, standing on a stool beside my father as he deftly sliced vegetables for his famous gumbo. I could still hear his voice, rich and deep, explaining the importance of seasoning. "Cooking is like life, sweetheart," he used to say, "You have to taste as you go." But tasting felt so much harder now, as if every morsel I'd ever known had turned bitter with grief.

As I opened the cupboard, the hinges creaked, and I was greeted by an army of mismatched plates and chipped mugs, relics of my parents' attempts to build a life together. I reached for a glass, its cool surface comforting in my hand, and poured myself some water from the tap, wincing at the metallic taste. I could have sworn I heard the echoes of laughter in the background—my parents teasing each other over who made the best pie or who'd left the dishes in the sink yet again.

I wandered outside, the sun now a molten ball sinking behind the horizon, painting the sky in hues of lavender and fiery orange. I could see the old barn in the distance, its once vibrant red paint now a tired pink, flaking like the memories it housed. The fields of wheat danced in the evening breeze, whispering secrets I was too weary to decipher. As a child, I had spent endless summers running through those golden stalks, imagining myself as an intrepid explorer charting new territories. Now, those same fields felt like a prison, trapping me in the weight of loss.

Just then, a sharp bark pulled me from my reverie, and I turned to see Daisy, my childhood dog, bounding toward me with unrestrained joy. Her gray muzzle had become flecked with white, but her spirit was as vibrant as ever. "You old mutt!" I laughed, kneeling to embrace her as she jumped against me, her tail wagging with the kind of enthusiasm only a dog can muster. I buried my face in her fur, inhaling the familiar scent that mingled with the earthy smell of the soil. "Looks like it's just you and me now."

With Daisy by my side, I made my way toward the barn, the wooden door creaking in protest as I pulled it open. The inside was a trove of forgotten memories—a rusted tractor, an array of tools, and my father's old fishing rods hung like relics from another life. I could almost hear him telling me how to cast a line, his voice warm with patience. The weight of his absence settled heavily in the air, like a thick fog obscuring the path ahead.

I found a dusty old crate in the corner and sat down, Daisy nestling at my feet. A mix of emotions churned within me—grief, nostalgia, and an unsettling sense of purpose. The farm had always been my refuge, a place where I could find solace among the chaos of the world. But now, it felt like a weight I couldn't bear. My parents had built a life here, and it was a life I had walked away from, chasing dreams in the bustling streets of Chicago, the scent of spices and the clamor of pots and pans drowning out the silence of loss.

"Maybe you should have come back sooner," I whispered to Daisy, who looked up at me with her soulful brown eyes. I could almost hear her thoughts: "If you wanted to talk to me, you should have brought treats." The thought made me chuckle, breaking the tension that clung to my heart. I had taken so much for granted—the warmth of family, the grounding presence of home. It was easy to forget how essential it was until it was gone, like the last cookie in the jar that you thought you'd save for later.

The barn door swung slightly in the breeze, and I caught a glimpse of the fields beyond, illuminated by the last rays of sunlight. I could almost hear my father's voice again, echoing through time: "You've got to make a decision, kiddo. Do you want to chase the horizon, or do you want to plant your roots?" The question hung in the air like the scent of rain on dry earth.

In that moment, I realized that I had come home not just to mourn but to rediscover. It was time to confront the legacy that awaited me. As the stars began to twinkle overhead, I felt a flicker of hope spark within me, illuminating the shadows of doubt. With Daisy at my side, I was ready to embrace whatever came next, even if it meant facing the truths I had buried deep within my heart.

The evening deepened, and the stars began to blink into existence like shy children peeking out from behind the curtains of night. I lingered on the porch, taking in the sounds of Riverton—the distant call of a whippoorwill, the rustle of leaves in the gentle breeze, and the soft thump of Daisy's paws as she pattered around, chasing shadows and imaginary foes. It felt both comforting and unsettling, this mingling of familiar and foreign, as if time had conspired to hold still while I had hurried away into the whirlwind of city life.

With a determined sigh, I stepped inside the house, where the shadows lurked, and the air tasted of memories that hadn't quite settled. The kitchen, once a bustling hub of clattering pots and the rich aroma of herbs, felt hollow, each piece of furniture standing vigil like a soldier waiting for orders. The calendar hung askew on the wall, its last entries frozen in time, reminders of birthdays and anniversaries that had been celebrated with joy—now mere echoes in a house of mourning.

As I opened the fridge, hoping for a miracle of leftovers, I was greeted by the stale scent of air that had long forgotten the taste of fresh food. Just a month ago, I could have sworn my mother had a tray of her legendary lasagna waiting inside, yet now there was nothing but a half-empty bottle of ketchup and a few questionable condiments. "I guess culinary magic isn't a thing when you're in mourning," I mused, shutting the door with a resigned thud.

Daisy nudged my leg, and I looked down to find her gazing up at me, her brown eyes wide and earnest. "Okay, okay," I relented, "let's salvage this evening." I rummaged through the cupboards and pulled out a packet of ramen noodles. Sure, it wasn't quite the homecoming feast I'd envisioned, but it was better than starving while wallowing in memories.

As the water boiled, I stood by the stove, contemplating the future that lay ahead. Was it truly possible to resurrect the legacy of my family's cooking without my father at the helm? I imagined my parents, back in their prime, hustling in the kitchen, laughter bubbling over like the pots on the stove. They had always encouraged me to follow my passion, but had I strayed too far from the roots that nourished my dreams?

Just as I was about to pour the noodles into the pot, a knock at the door sent a jolt through me. Startled, I almost dropped the packet. "Who on earth?" I muttered, glancing at the clock that read eight. Who visited at this hour?

I opened the door to reveal Jamie, my childhood best friend, standing on the porch with a nervous smile. Her hair, now a riot of purple and teal, framed her face like a vibrant halo, and her wide-brimmed hat looked like it belonged in a Parisian café rather than a Kansas farmhouse. "I thought it might be a good idea to welcome you home," she said, a lopsided grin making her look like a mischievous sprite.

"Welcome me home by giving me a heart attack?" I teased, stepping aside to let her in. "What if I had been wearing something less...um, appropriate?"

Jamie's laughter bubbled out, filling the room like a much-needed tonic. "Let's be real; you've always been more 'no pants, ramen noodles' than 'elegant hostess.'"

"Touché," I replied, chuckling as I turned back to the stove. "Just getting back into the swing of things. Care for some gourmet ramen?"

"Only if it's not the soggy kind." Jamie leaned against the counter, her arms crossed, observing me with an intensity that made my skin prickle. "How are you holding up? Really."

I hesitated, the weight of the question hanging between us like a thick fog. "I'm... figuring it out. It's strange being back, you know? The house feels both like a warm embrace and a tight noose."

She nodded, her expression softening. "You have every right to feel that way. Grief is a complicated beast. It shows up uninvited and wrecks everything in sight."

I poured the noodles into the pot, grateful for her understanding. "It feels like I'm supposed to carry on the family tradition, but I don't even know if I want to."

"Why not?" Jamie asked, raising an eyebrow. "You've got the talent. Your food blog was a sensation! Everyone in town was raving about your heirloom tomato salad recipe. I mean, you could've gotten famous!"

"Fame isn't everything," I countered, stirring the noodles with a vigor that mirrored my rising frustration. "I chased my dreams, and now I'm back here, wondering if I can live up to my parents' legacy without them."

"I think you should just do you. That's all anyone can ask." Jamie's voice was soothing, but her eyes held a glimmer of mischief. "Plus, you can't tell me you don't want to shake things up a bit. Riverton could use a culinary renaissance, don't you think?"

"Renaissance? In Riverton? The most exciting thing here is the annual cow pie festival!" I laughed, shaking my head. "What are you suggesting, a food truck selling gourmet hot dogs with avocado salsa?"

"Now you're onto something! Don't knock it until you try it. You could combine all your city smarts with this sleepy town's charm," she said, the excitement in her voice infectious. "Just think of the possibilities!"

I stirred the noodles again, a vision forming in my mind—a quirky little bistro, filled with the aroma of herbs and spices, laughter echoing off the walls, and the comfort of home baked into every dish. "Maybe it's time to put those culinary skills to use in a place where they could really shine," I mused, the idea blooming like a wildflower in spring.

Jamie clapped her hands, her enthusiasm palpable. "That's the spirit! But first, let's see what we're working with." She leaned over the pot, a teasing grin on her face. "Do you even know how to make proper ramen?"

"Please," I replied, rolling my eyes playfully. "I'm a professional."

"Sure you are, Chef Ramen," she quipped, leaning back against the counter, her arms crossed in mock skepticism.

The banter flowed easily, and with each laugh shared between us, the weight in my heart began to lift just a little. As we settled into a comfortable rhythm of teasing and reminiscing, I realized how much I had missed this—friendship that was as effortless as breathing. Maybe, just maybe, Riverton could be more than just a place of sorrow. It could also be a canvas for new beginnings, painted with flavors and friendships I had thought were lost.

The moon hung low in the sky, casting a silvery glow across the fields as I sat with Jamie at the kitchen table, our laughter mingling with the aroma of simmering ramen. We had traded the weight of grief for the lightness of nostalgia, sharing stories that felt like talismans against sorrow. Each laugh was a tiny rebellion against the heartache that lingered in the corners of the room.

"Remember that time we tried to make a three-tiered cake for the county fair?" Jamie chuckled, her eyes dancing with mischief. "We ended up with a pancake instead because you thought we could 'wing it' without measuring the flour."

I groaned, slumping against the table dramatically. "Let's not revisit the horror of my baking 'skills.' I still owe those poor judges an apology."

Jamie waved her hand dismissively. "They clearly didn't understand the genius of culinary improvisation. I mean, who knew pancakes could be a viable option for cake?"

"Only us," I shot back, laughing. It was nice to feel this spark of joy, even if it was temporarily masking the grief. Yet, in the back of my mind, a storm brewed—questions about my future loomed larger than the shadow of the barn outside.

As the steam from the pot of noodles curled lazily around us, I felt a flicker of determination ignite in my chest. "What if I actually did something? You know, create a space here where I could share my love of cooking?"

Jamie's face lit up like a lightbulb, her eyes sparkling with possibilities. "That's it! You should start a cooking class! Bring some of that city flair back home. Riverton needs a shake-up."

"A cooking class?" I considered the idea, tilting my head as I rolled the words over in my mouth. "That's certainly ambitious. I'd be the only person in town cooking spicy Pad Thai while everyone else is grilling burgers and baking pies."

"Exactly!" she exclaimed, as if I had just discovered fire. "You could introduce them to a whole new world of flavors. Plus, it'd be fun! You know everyone around here has been cooped up in their kitchens since... forever."

"Except for the annual cow pie festival," I quipped, eliciting another laugh from her. "But seriously, what if nobody shows up? What if they think I'm just some city girl who lost her marbles?"

"They'll show up," she assured me, leaning closer, her excitement palpable. "You're not just a 'city girl'; you're a culinary artist with real talent. Think of all the townsfolk who've missed your cooking. And if anyone dares to doubt you, I'll show up with my 'Riverton Defense Squad.' We can march on the town hall if need be!"

"Riverton Defense Squad?" I laughed, picturing a ragtag group of farmers and shopkeepers armed with spatulas and rolling pins. "I love it. Just what I need—an army of pie bakers ready to fight the good fight."

"Exactly! We'll demand gourmet tacos at every event. It'll be a revolution!"

We fell into a comfortable silence, the kind that fills spaces with unspoken hopes. The noodles were now swimming contentedly in their broth, and the kitchen began to feel more like a hub of potential than a tomb of lost dreams. My heart swelled with the possibility of reconnecting with my roots, infusing this small town with the flavors and vibrancy I had experienced in the city. Maybe I could share my love for food, stitch together the frayed edges of my life here, and honor my father's legacy in a way that felt right.

Just then, the door creaked open, and a gust of chilly night air swept into the kitchen, ruffling the pages of my mother's old cookbook that lay open on the counter. I turned to see my brother, Ethan, stepping inside. He had always been the more grounded of us, a rock in turbulent waters, but tonight, he looked like he had carried the weight of the world on his shoulders.

"Hey, Ethan," I said, trying to gauge his mood. "Join us for some ramen? It's a gourmet feast, courtesy of yours truly."

He offered a half-hearted smile but didn't move closer. "I'll pass. Just came by to see how things are going."

"Fine, fine! A tad lonely here without you," I replied, my voice laced with the kind of cheerful sarcasm I often used to mask discomfort. "You should've seen Jamie and me plotting to take over Riverton's culinary scene. We were this close to starting a cooking revolution."

"Revolution? In this town? Sounds ambitious," Ethan remarked dryly, but I could sense the glimmer of interest beneath his cool demeanor.

"It is! I'm thinking of hosting a cooking class. It'll be fun, and we could bring people together again," I said, my excitement bubbling over.

"That could work, I guess," he said, scratching his head. "But do you really think they'll be open to... different kinds of food? I mean, you know how stuck they can be in their ways."

I leaned against the counter, determination steeling my resolve. "What's wrong with a little change? You never know until you try. Besides, we need to move forward, don't we? For Dad."

Ethan's expression shifted, something in his eyes darkening. "Forward is one thing, but forgetting is another. This town has a long memory."

"What's that supposed to mean?" I challenged, irritation creeping into my voice. "Are you saying we should just let it all go to waste? Hide in our little shells and wallow?"

"Not hiding, just... respecting what's been," he said, his tone edged with frustration. "You can't just waltz in with your city ideas and expect everyone to embrace them. They're set in their ways for a reason."

I was taken aback by his response, the air thickening with tension. "What do you want me to do? Abandon everything I've worked for just to please them? We can't live in the past forever!"

"Maybe you should start by actually connecting with the people here instead of trying to change everything at once," Ethan snapped, his voice rising. "Maybe they need you to understand them before you try to teach them."

His words struck me like a lightning bolt, leaving me momentarily speechless. The flickering tension crackled in the air between us. "Understand them? I grew up here! I know Riverton like the back of my hand," I shot back, my heart racing.

"You know a version of it," he retorted. "The town has changed, and so have we. You can't just walk back in and expect everything to be the same. It doesn't work that way."

A heavy silence settled in the kitchen, thick as fog. Jamie glanced between us, sensing the shifting dynamics. I opened my mouth to respond, to defend my vision, but the words caught in my throat as a chill swept through the room.

Just then, a sharp knock echoed from the front door, cutting through the tension. It was a sound that echoed with a promise of change, and as we exchanged glances, the weight of the moment hung heavy. "Should I get that?" I asked, my heart pounding with an unsettling mix of anticipation and dread.

"Better see who it is," Ethan said, his expression shifting from annoyance to something more guarded.

As I walked to the door, a feeling of foreboding settled in my stomach. What awaited me on the other side? I hesitated for just a moment before swinging the door open, revealing a figure standing in the shadows, drenched in the moonlight's eerie glow. My breath caught in my throat, and I felt the ground shift beneath me as I met the gaze of someone I hadn't seen in years.

"Surprise," they said, a sly smile curling their lips.

Chapter 2: Unearthing Secrets

The smell of cedarwood mingled with the faint scent of mildew as I stepped deeper into the farmhouse, my fingers brushing against the cool, weathered walls. Dust motes danced in the shafts of sunlight filtering through the grimy windows, illuminating the past that seemed to echo with every creak of the old floorboards beneath my feet. This house, once vibrant with laughter and warmth, now sat in a state of suspended animation, a shrine to what once was. My heart ached at the memories tucked within the peeling paint and faded wallpaper; the family dinners, the board games sprawled across the coffee table, my father's booming laughter ringing through the air like a beloved song.

I moved toward the sitting room, where my father's armchair, its upholstery threadbare from years of use, sat facing the fireplace. It seemed to wait for him, to yearn for his presence as much as I did. I closed my eyes for a moment, imagining him there, the familiar blend of aftershave and sawdust clinging to his flannel shirt, a newspaper crumpled in his hands. My breath caught in my throat; the memory was so vivid it felt like he could walk in at any moment and throw his arm around my shoulder, asking how life was treating me. But that was the cruelest part of absence—it carved away at the edges of nostalgia, leaving behind a hollow ache.

I ventured to the kitchen, the heart of the home, where sunlight pooled in the corners, illuminating the remnants of meals shared. The wooden table bore the scars of family life, its surface etched with the marks of heated arguments and tender moments alike. I pulled open a drawer, hoping to find some remnants of my father's recipes, the ones he'd passed down to me in fits of laughter and flour fights. Instead, I found old utensils, their handles smooth from years of use, along with an envelope that felt oddly out of place.

The envelope was yellowed with age, a small hand-written note tucked inside. I unfolded it gingerly, a mix of excitement and trepidation flooding my senses. The note was a simple grocery list, but it bore my father's distinct scrawl, with items like "flour," "sugar," and then, oddly, "golden key." My mind raced as I read those two words again, the implications swirling like a summer storm. Had he been planning something? Or had this been a mere coincidence, a grocery list forgotten among the everyday chaos of life? A golden key? It felt like a piece of a puzzle I didn't yet have the rest of.

I dropped the note, my curiosity piqued, and continued my search. Every nook of the farmhouse seemed to whisper secrets long buried, and I found myself drawn to the stairs leading up to the attic. The staircase groaned beneath my weight, a symphony of creaks that echoed my mounting anxiety. What lay hidden in the shadows of that attic? As a child, I had imagined it a treasure trove, filled with forgotten memories and dusty toys. Now, it felt like a vault of uncertainties, waiting to reveal what had been kept from me.

Reaching the top, I pushed open the door, the hinges protesting loudly as I entered. Dust swirled in the muted light, and boxes loomed around me like giants, each one a monument to the past. I shuffled through them, the musty smell thick in the air. Old clothes, books with crumbling spines, and remnants of my childhood lay scattered like fallen leaves. I unearthed a faded quilt, its colors dulled by time, and a twinge of homesickness swept over me as I remembered the stories my father had spun beneath its warmth.

But it was the last box I opened that sent a jolt through me. Inside, I found a collection of letters tied with fraying twine. They looked old, their edges yellowed and delicate. I picked them up gingerly, feeling as if I were handling something sacred. The top letter bore my father's name, but the recipient was unfamiliar. My heart raced as I peeled it open, a wave of trepidation washing over me. The neat handwriting, feminine and flowing, spoke of love and longing, of moments stolen in secret.

As I read, a story unfolded—one I had never known. It detailed a relationship my father had had long before I was born, filled with promises and dreams, punctuated by heartbreak and unanswered questions. I could hardly breathe as I absorbed the words, each sentence unraveling a thread of my father's life I had never known existed. The depth of his hidden emotions was staggering, and I felt like an intruder in a private world.

"Just what are you getting yourself into?" I muttered under my breath, the attic walls closing in around me. My mind raced, swirling with questions. Who was this woman? What had happened between them? Did my father ever regret his choices? The weight of the letters in my hands felt heavier than I anticipated, and I tucked them back into the box, needing time to process this unexpected twist in the narrative of my father's life.

The sound of footsteps on the staircase jolted me from my reverie. My heart hammered in my chest as I spun around, half-expecting a ghostly figure from the past to materialize before me. Instead, it was my brother, Sam. His familiar silhouette framed by the dim light sent a jolt of both dread and hope through me. He hadn't changed much—still the same tall, lean figure with a tousled mess of dark hair, but the tension between us crackled like static electricity, a remnant of all the years lost.

"Fancy meeting you here," he said, his voice a mix of surprise and caution, as if he, too, had stepped into a world he wasn't sure he belonged to anymore. I opened my mouth to respond, to dive into the abyss of our shared history, but the words felt lodged in my throat. Instead, we stood there, two pieces of a broken puzzle, waiting to see if we could fit together again.

Sam stepped into the attic like an intruder in a museum of our shared past, his presence both familiar and alien. The silence stretched between us, thick and heavy, as if the years apart had woven a tapestry of unspoken words and unresolved feelings. His dark eyes, sharp as a hawk's, scanned the cluttered room, landing on me with a mixture of surprise and something deeper—was it guilt? Regret? The flicker of emotion crossed his face so quickly that I almost missed it.

"What are you doing here?" he asked, his voice low, laced with a tension that felt like a taut string ready to snap.

"I could ask you the same," I shot back, crossing my arms in an instinctive defense. It was a reflex, really, an echo of all those times we'd sparred in the past. But even as the words left my mouth, I regretted the edge in my tone. We were both navigating a minefield, and I wasn't sure where the traps lay.

"I came to see if there was anything left worth saving," he replied, his gaze shifting to the letters I had just found, still nestled in their box. I felt a rush of protectiveness for the fragile words, as if they could shatter under the weight of our conversation.

"Looks like you're not the only one hunting for remnants," I retorted, gesturing toward the disarray of old boxes and forgotten memories. "Or are you just here to stake your claim?"

He raised an eyebrow, a hint of a smile playing on his lips, the kind that reminded me of the teasing brother I had once known. "You think I'd fight you for a moldy quilt and a collection of dad's old fishing gear? No thanks. I'd rather be catching waves in California than tangled in this."

The corner of my mouth quirked up. "Moldy quilts have their charm. You just wouldn't understand."

His chuckle broke the tension, a sound that felt like a balm on old wounds. "Alright, Miss Nostalgia. What's next? You going to start talking to the walls?"

"I might as well. They've been here longer than either of us." I took a step closer, lowering my voice. "But really, Sam, why are you here? I didn't expect you back, not after..." The words trailed off, the air suddenly thick with the bitterness of our last argument, the words we hurled at each other like stones.

He sighed, rubbing the back of his neck, an old habit I recognized well. "I thought it was time. You know, after everything. I was tired of running. But I didn't expect you to come back either. Not like this."

"Yeah, well, neither did I," I said, my heart pounding with unspent frustration. "But I thought the farmhouse deserved better than to rot away in silence. And you?" I pressed, my curiosity getting the better of me. "What do you want? Is it the farm, or something more?"

He hesitated, his expression shifting from playful to serious. "Honestly? I thought maybe we could figure this out together. But..." He paused, glancing at the letters. "Seems like there's a lot we don't know about Dad. Maybe there's more to what we've both been running from."

The sincerity in his tone drew me closer. "You think I want to hash things out? We can barely stand being in the same room without igniting World War III."

"True, but perhaps it's time to stop hiding. You have to admit, there's a lot of unresolved baggage between us. And maybe it's not all about us, you know? Maybe it's about him too."

The weight of his words lingered, and I felt a pull to dig deeper. "You're saying you want to stick around? Help me sift through this mess?"

"Only if you promise not to bite my head off the second I disagree with you," he replied, half-smirking. "But sure, I'll give it a shot. If you're willing to let me back in, that is."

"Fine," I relented, though it felt more like a truce than a promise. "Let's see how this goes."

As we began to sort through the attic, I felt the tension ease, if only slightly. It was strange to be in such close proximity to Sam after all these years, the past still looming large between us, but I realized that the very act of working together felt like laying a fragile foundation. We unearthed memories—old toys, mismatched furniture, and photos—each item evoking stories, laughter, and, yes, even some lingering sadness.

"This one's ridiculous," Sam said, holding up a photo of me in a Halloween costume that resembled a banana. "Did you really think that was a good idea?"

I laughed, my cheeks flushing at the memory. "I was five! And I thought I looked amazing!"

"Five or not, it's a wonder Dad let you out of the house like that."

"Oh, please, like you weren't wearing that awful pirate costume with the eye patch that fell off halfway through the night!"

He threw his head back, laughter spilling from his lips, and for a moment, it felt like old times. "Touché."

Just as the laughter faded, I reached for a box labeled "Keepsakes" and paused. It was the one I'd been avoiding, the one that promised heartache wrapped in memories I wasn't ready to confront. With a determined breath, I lifted the lid. Inside lay a collection of my father's journals, their spines cracked and pages yellowed with age. My fingers trembled as I pulled one out, the weight of it heavy in my hands.

"Is that what I think it is?" Sam's voice was low, almost reverent. "Dad's journals?"

"Yeah." I flipped through the pages, the familiar scrawl bringing back a flood of memories. "He wrote everything down. About the farm, about us."

"Us?" He leaned in closer, curiosity glinting in his eyes. "Are you thinking what I'm thinking? That maybe there's something in here that explains the why behind everything?"

I hesitated. "I don't know if I'm ready for that. What if it's just... painful?"

"Or what if it's enlightening? We won't know unless we look."

With a mixture of fear and anticipation, I opened to a random page. The handwriting flowed across the paper, each line a revelation waiting to be unearthed. My heart raced as I began to read, feeling the walls around us close in, not with dread, but with the promise of understanding.

As I absorbed the words in my father's journal, each line became a pulse in the silence of the attic, revealing a man whose heart had been intricately woven with both love and sorrow. The ink smudged in places where emotion had taken hold, spilling onto the pages like the tears he never shed. I felt Sam lean closer, his presence a comforting weight at my side, both of us drawn into this intimate glimpse of a man we thought we knew so well.

"Listen to this," I said, my voice barely above a whisper as I read aloud. "'Every day I wake up to the sounds of the farm, and it feels like I'm living in a dream. But the nights are a different story. I often find myself staring at the ceiling, wondering if I've made the right choices. My boys... they deserve so much more than I've given them.'"

Sam's expression shifted, the playfulness replaced with a seriousness that made my heart ache. "He wrote about us?"

"Not just us," I continued, my fingers trembling on the page. "He talks about the dreams he had, the life he wanted for us. There's a mention of someone named Clara... it's like he's torn between the love for his family and a life he never pursued."

"Clara? I've never heard that name before," Sam said, leaning in even closer, as if proximity could pull us further into our father's world. "What else does it say?"

I scanned the page for more context. "It's all very poetic. But there's also this shadow hanging over his words, like a storm cloud he can't escape. He mentions wanting to make things right, but he doesn't elaborate. It's maddening!"

"Sounds like our dad," Sam said, his voice laced with irony. "Always cryptic, even on paper."

I turned the page, feeling a pull of urgency. "Wait, there's more." I inhaled deeply, preparing to dive into the next section, my heart racing as if the pages might reveal secrets we were not meant to uncover. "He writes about a trip he planned to take, something big. He was going to tell us everything, but then..."

"But then what?" Sam prompted, his eyes glinting with curiosity.

"Then it just stops. The next entry is blank. It's like he was interrupted or... or something happened."

"Typical," Sam muttered, a hint of bitterness creeping into his tone. "He starts to open up, and then it goes silent. Just like everything else in our family."

I set the journal down, a mix of frustration and fear swirling inside me. "Do you think it was something he was hiding? Something that would have changed how we viewed him?"

"Or how we view each other," he countered, folding his arms. "There's a reason we haven't talked in years, you know."

"Because you left!" The words slipped out before I could stop them, a flare of the old resentment bubbling to the surface. "You turned your back when things got hard."

"Hey, I didn't leave because of you! It was—"

"Because of what? Because of Dad? Because of me?" I snapped, feeling the heat of the argument rise, a familiar dance of blame and hurt echoing through the attic. "You made it easy to forget, Sam. Easy to pretend we didn't exist."

He stepped closer, his voice low and intense. "And you made it easy to hold on to that anger. It's time we both let it go."

"Let go? So you can come in here and act like nothing happened?"

"Maybe I don't want to act anymore," he shot back, frustration simmering just below the surface. "Maybe I want to find the truth, whatever that is. You can't tell me you're not the least bit curious about what else he's written. What if we find out there's a reason behind everything? Behind our fights, his silence?"

My heart raced at the prospect, a mix of fear and longing igniting inside me. "You think these journals will give us answers?"

"I think they might help us understand," he said, the earnestness in his eyes cutting through my anger. "It's better than standing here, wrestling with ghosts."

I nodded slowly, the adrenaline of our argument receding, replaced by an urgency I hadn't felt before. "Okay. Let's keep looking. But if we're doing this, we need to be honest about what we find."

"Deal," he said, the tension between us beginning to thaw. "Just try not to lose your mind when you find out he wasn't the perfect dad you remember."

"Right back at you," I replied, taking another deep breath as I flipped through the pages.

As I delved deeper, the journal began to reveal more stories of our father's youth, tales of reckless dreams and romantic escapades, including a vivid account of a summer spent chasing fireflies with a girl named Clara. The nostalgia was intoxicating, painting my father not just as a parent, but as a young man with hopes, fears, and disappointments.

"Listen to this," I said, captivated. "'Clara is like the sun, bright and warm, but just out of reach. I wonder if she thinks of me when the sky dims.' It's so..."

"Romantic?" Sam suggested, a teasing grin breaking through his serious demeanor.

"Infuriating," I replied, rolling my eyes. "He spent so much time pining after this girl, and it feels like he never even told us. Did he love her? Did she choose someone else?"

"Maybe she's the reason he was never happy," Sam offered, his tone shifting. "Maybe she's the reason he stayed. The farm was just his consolation prize."

I frowned, chewing on that thought. "It feels so unfair that he kept all this from us. Why didn't he just tell us?"

"Maybe he thought we'd be better off without the burden of his choices," Sam suggested, his voice softening. "He might have thought he was protecting us."

"Or he was just afraid," I countered, my heart heavy with realization. "Afraid of us seeing him as human."

Just as we were about to dig into another page, a sudden crash echoed from below, jolting us both from our conversation. The sound reverberated through the attic, startling the dust from the rafters above. I exchanged a glance with Sam, a wave of uncertainty washing over us.

"What was that?" he asked, his brow furrowing as he glanced at the staircase.

"I have no idea," I replied, my stomach churning. "But it didn't sound good."

Before I could think it through, I set the journal aside and headed toward the attic door, heart racing. "Let's check it out."

Sam followed closely behind, the tension thick as we descended the stairs, each step amplifying the unease that had taken hold. We reached the ground floor and paused, listening intently for any signs of movement.

"Maybe it was just the wind," Sam suggested, though his tone lacked conviction.

"Yeah, right," I muttered, peering into the dimly lit living room. The shadows danced eerily, and the stillness was unnerving. Just as I turned to make a sarcastic comment, I caught sight of something out of the corner of my eye—a glimmer of light, moving fast, darting across the floorboards.

"What the hell is that?" Sam whispered, his voice a mixture of fear and curiosity.

Before I could answer, the light vanished, and in its place stood a figure, silhouetted in the doorway. My breath caught in my throat as I recognized the shape, the familiar outline that had haunted my childhood dreams and my adult nightmares.

"Dad?" I breathed, half-expecting him to dissolve like the memories we were just beginning to unravel. But the figure remained, solid and impossibly real, a ghost pulled from the depths of my imagination, waiting in the shadows of our shared past.

Chapter 3: The Rancher Next Door

The sound of the engine faded as quickly as it had approached, leaving only the echo of his words hanging in the air like the last notes of a familiar song. I couldn't help but smile back, a grin that felt slightly foolish yet entirely sincere. Luke Harrison had that effect on me, a man who could make the simplest greetings feel like the opening of a long-forgotten chapter in a beloved book. As I stepped outside, the sunlight embraced me, its warmth mingling with the cool autumn breeze that whispered promises of change.

"Hannah," he repeated, stepping closer, the porch creaking beneath his heavy boots. The scent of hay and leather clung to him, bringing a flood of memories rushing back—hot summer days spent chasing fireflies, nights filled with laughter and whispered dreams. "How was the city?" His voice had a hint of that playful teasing I remembered, the kind that could draw me in even when I tried to play it cool.

"Loud, chaotic, and far too much traffic for my taste," I replied, crossing my arms to fend off the sudden chill of vulnerability that crept in. "I think I prefer the silence of your ranch."

"Silence? On my ranch?" He chuckled, a sound like gravel crunching underfoot, deep and warm. "You must be forgetting my cattle's opinion on that. They tend to have very loud discussions at dawn."

I laughed, my heart racing as we fell into an easy banter, our words dancing around the unspoken tension that lingered just below the surface. It was the kind of back-and-forth that felt effortless, as though we'd never been apart, even after years of life's twists and turns that had pulled us in different directions. But the familiarity was also tinged with a newness, an electric undercurrent that hadn't been there before, a realization that perhaps there was more at play than I had dared to acknowledge.

"Are you still working at that advertising agency?" he asked, leaning against the porch railing, his broad shoulders relaxed but his gaze intent. I caught myself staring a moment too long at the way the afternoon sun caught the golden strands in his hair, the way it illuminated the strong lines of his jaw.

"Yep. Still working long hours to convince people they need the latest and greatest gadgets. It's a blast," I replied, sarcasm dripping from my tone. "You know, just fulfilling my lifelong dream of being a professional persuader."

"Sounds like you're having fun," he said, his eyes glinting with amusement. "But I'd bet the quiet life on the ranch is a lot more appealing than dealing with... whatever it is people do in the city."

"I guess," I said, biting my lip, suddenly self-conscious. "But it's not all bad. I mean, there's a certain thrill in helping a brand become a household name. There's a rush in the chaos." I tried to sound convincing, but the truth was, I had been feeling hollow lately, like a shell of a person rolling through life without truly living.

Luke shifted, pushing off the railing and standing a little taller, the muscles in his arms flexing as he folded them across his chest. "What about the 'Hannah' I remember? The girl who could make a thousand dollar dress out of a trash bag and a roll of duct tape? Who wasn't afraid to stand up for what she believed in?"

His words pulled me in deeper, nostalgia washing over me in waves. I thought about my teenage self, brimming with dreams and ideas, untainted by the harsh realities of adulthood. "I still have those ideas, you know," I replied, my voice a little softer. "They just seem less... important these days. I guess I got swept up in the chase for success, and somewhere along the line, I lost sight of what I really wanted."

His expression softened, and I could see the understanding in his eyes, a deep well of empathy that made my heart ache with longing. "It happens," he said, stepping closer, the space between us shrinking until it felt charged with possibility. "But you don't have to settle for a life that doesn't spark joy. Life's too short for that."

A sudden wind swept through, tousling my hair and the moment, but the warmth from his presence lingered, wrapping around me like a protective cocoon. I wanted to reach out, to tell him that his words stirred something within me, something that had lain dormant for far too long. But the unspoken fears wrapped tight around my heart, reminding me of the risks, the potential for heartbreak if I let myself fall too far.

"Have you thought about coming back? I mean, for good?" he asked, his voice dropping an octave, a low rumble that made my stomach flutter. "There's always room for a creative mind around here. I could use someone with your skills to help with the ranch. We could make it into something really special."

The offer hung in the air, tantalizing and terrifying all at once. I could feel the weight of his gaze, assessing and hopeful, but also wary. "You mean, like a marketing genius for cattle?" I laughed, trying to lighten the mood, but inside, my heart raced at the possibilities he hinted at.

"Hey, don't underestimate the potential of a well-branded herd," he shot back, his smile teasing. "But seriously, think about it. This place could be so much more than it is. And I can't help but think it would be better with you here."

In that moment, my mind was a whirl of conflicting emotions—fear, excitement, nostalgia—and I felt that familiar tug at my heartstrings, a call to adventure that I had suppressed for too long. What if I did come back? What if I took the leap? But the memories of city lights and the constant buzz of life held me back, leaving me suspended between two worlds, unsure which path to take.

"So, what do you say? Join me on the adventure?" Luke's question was hopeful, and I felt the weight of the unspoken promise in it, a future where we could rewrite our stories together.

The challenge of his proposition loomed large in the air between us, thick with possibility. I hesitated, caught in a web of thoughts, each strand pulling me in different directions. Luke watched me with those intense blue eyes, searching for an answer that I wasn't sure I was ready to give. A part of me wanted to leap into the unknown, to shake off the city's rigid expectations and immerse myself in the earthy chaos of ranch life. But another part, the cautious part, clung to the familiarity of my cubicle and the hum of urban life.

"I'm not sure I could just drop everything and start a new adventure," I replied, the words tumbling out before I could stop them. "I have responsibilities, a life I've built... or at least I'm trying to."

"Responsibilities?" he echoed, a teasing lilt in his voice. "You mean the endless stream of meetings and deadlines? Or the obligatory brunches with people who don't even know the difference between a cow and a horse? Sounds like paradise." His smirk was infuriatingly charming, and I felt the heat rise in my cheeks.

"You make it sound like I'm drowning in a sea of overpriced mimosas," I shot back, crossing my arms defensively, though I couldn't help but smile at his jab. "It's not that simple."

"I get that," he said, his tone suddenly serious, and the shift caught me off guard. "But sometimes simple is exactly what we need. You remember how it felt here—no pretense, no pressure. Just life, raw and real."

I did remember. The scent of fresh hay, the comforting rhythm of the seasons, and the way the stars blanketed the night sky like a cozy quilt. In those moments, I had felt alive. "It's tempting," I admitted, glancing away as the weight of my thoughts settled heavily on my chest. "But what if I fail? What if I can't adjust?"

Luke stepped closer, the heat radiating from him chasing away the chill of uncertainty. "Hannah, failure is just a stepping stone. I've had my share of setbacks. The barn I'm trying to rebuild? Let's just say the last storm didn't exactly play nice." He chuckled, and the sound warmed me from the inside out. "But that's part of it. We learn, we adapt, and then we get back up, maybe with a few new scars to show for it."

I couldn't help but admire his resilience, the way he seemed unflappable in the face of challenges. "You really think I could just pick up and leave everything behind?"

"I think you underestimate yourself," he said firmly, his voice unwavering. "You're not just some city girl lost in a world of deadlines. You're a creative force, a spark of inspiration. And if you let that light shine, it could make a world of difference around here." He motioned to the fields beyond, stretching out like an invitation. "This place has potential waiting to be unleashed, and I can't think of anyone better to help with that than you."

His confidence wrapped around me, and for a brief moment, I imagined what it would be like to take that leap—to trade boardroom meetings for barn chores, to replace the constant noise of the city with the symphony of nature. But doubts flooded my mind like an uninvited guest at a party, shoving aside the excitement that bubbled within me. "It's not just about me," I said quietly, my voice tinged with hesitation. "What would my parents think? What about my job? It's a secure path, a safety net."

Luke's expression softened, and he stepped back slightly, giving me space. "You have to live for yourself, Hannah, not for anyone else's expectations. Your parents want you to be happy, and I think deep down, they would support you if they knew how you felt. And as for your job, it might feel secure, but what's life without a little risk? Besides, you can't measure fulfillment by the weight of your paycheck alone."

His words sunk deep, swirling around in my mind like leaves caught in a gust of wind. I couldn't ignore the truth in them, the yearning for something more substantial than my current life. "It's just—what if it doesn't work out?" The fear of failure whispered its doubts, a haunting reminder of my city life's stability.

"What if it does?" Luke countered, leaning closer again, his eyes sparkling with an enthusiasm that made my heart race. "What if you discover something about yourself that you didn't even know was there? What if you find joy in the unexpected?"

The challenge hung between us, vibrant and charged, but the thought of stepping off that cliff—of leaving behind the life I had built—was both exhilarating and terrifying. But there was something undeniably tempting about the idea of being immersed in a world where the pace was slower, where the sun dipped low over the horizon, casting golden rays over the fields.

Just then, a loud "moo" interrupted my thoughts, breaking the moment like a dropped egg on the kitchen floor. We both turned to see Bessie, the most stubborn cow on the ranch, peering through the fence, her big brown eyes fixed on us as if she were in on the conversation.

"Looks like Bessie wants her say," Luke said, chuckling. "She's probably wondering when I'm going to get off my butt and bring her some hay."

I laughed, the tension in my chest easing slightly. "Bessie might have a point. You can't keep her waiting forever."

"Exactly," he replied, straightening up, a flicker of determination crossing his face. "And just like Bessie, you can't let the opportunity pass you by. So what do you say? How about we make this a working visit? Spend some time on the ranch, see how you feel?"

The offer hung in the air, tantalizing and terrifying. I was about to respond when my phone buzzed in my pocket, its shrill tone cutting through the moment. I fished it out, glancing at the screen. A message from my boss flashed brightly, demanding my attention.

"Duty calls," I said reluctantly, waving my phone like a white flag. "I guess this is what being an adult looks like."

"Or what it looks like to let life dictate your choices," Luke replied, his tone light but the meaning behind it clear. "You're not just an adult, Hannah. You're a woman with dreams, and it's time you chase them."

With that, he turned and walked toward the barn, his silhouette framed by the setting sun, and I was left standing on the porch, a whirlwind of emotions swirling inside me. The sun was dipping low, casting long shadows across the yard, and with every step he took, the notion of leaving everything I knew behind began to feel more like a possibility and less like a fantasy.

I watched Luke walk away, his figure blending into the shadows of the barn, and an unexpected longing washed over me. The idea of venturing into his world, surrounded by the sprawling fields and the symphony of nature, was intoxicating. My phone buzzed again, dragging me back to reality. I glanced at the screen, half-hoping it would be another chance to escape the impending demands of my job. Instead, it was a reminder of the meeting I had scheduled for later that evening, an urgent video call that felt like an anchor tethering me to the life I was desperately questioning.

"Great," I muttered under my breath, frustration bubbling just beneath the surface. It was hard to focus on anything when my thoughts were consumed by the possibilities of a different path. I took a deep breath, stepping off the porch and heading toward the barn. Maybe I could find Luke and have a word before my meeting. Maybe I could convince myself that exploring this new life didn't mean abandoning my responsibilities, merely reshaping them.

As I approached the barn, the sweet scent of hay and earth filled my senses, grounding me. Inside, the soft sounds of animals stirred; a gentle rustling mixed with the occasional lowing of cattle. Luke was bent over, sorting through bales of hay, his shirt sleeves rolled up to reveal tanned forearms dusted with bits of straw. He glanced up, his blue eyes catching mine, and a smile broke across his face like the first light of dawn.

"You came to help?" he teased, wiping his hands on his jeans, which were speckled with dirt and hay.

"Sure, I'm a professional hay mover now," I shot back, crossing my arms and leaning against the doorframe. "In a past life, of course. Or at least I will be if I decide to join your cattle wrangling empire."

His laughter filled the barn, rich and genuine, echoing off the wooden beams. "Trust me, you'd fit right in. But first, you need to learn how to throw a hay bale. It's a bit of an art form."

"Art form? You mean there's a technique to flinging hay like I'm launching a javelin?" I arched an eyebrow, fighting the urge to laugh at the mental image of me struggling with a bale.

He stepped closer, a playful grin tugging at the corners of his mouth. "More like a science. You wouldn't want to pull a muscle before the big meeting with the cattle, would you?"

I rolled my eyes but felt warmth creeping up my cheeks. "Oh, God forbid I pull a muscle before discussing the latest marketing trends over Zoom."

"Now that would be a tragedy." He grinned, the banter making the air around us crackle. "Come on, I'll show you the ropes."

Before I could overthink it, I followed him into the barn, the atmosphere thick with the scent of fresh hay and the soft murmur of the animals. As he demonstrated how to properly throw a hay bale, I felt the rhythm of his movements—easy, confident. There was something comforting about it, the way he spoke, his hands gesturing animatedly as he explained.

"See? It's all in the hips," he said, tossing a bale effortlessly, as if it weighed nothing. "You need to pivot just right, or else you end up looking like a flailing scarecrow."

I took a deep breath, channeling all the grace I could muster. I grabbed a bale and attempted to imitate his movements, my body twisting awkwardly. It flew from my hands, landing spectacularly short of the target, rolling gently across the barn floor like a sleepy tumbleweed.

Luke doubled over in laughter, the sound rich and infectious. "Scarecrow! Right on the money!"

"Alright, alright," I said, shaking my head, my laughter mingling with his. "I see your approach—comedy before agricultural prowess."

After a few more attempts, my muscles began to warm up, and my confidence surged. It was ridiculous how much fun I was having, how liberating it felt to laugh at myself. And as the sun dipped lower, casting warm rays through the barn's open doors, something shifted within me. This was the feeling I had been chasing, the pulse of life that surged through the air.

"See? You're a natural!" Luke exclaimed, clearly impressed with my newfound hay-flinging skills. The playful banter gave way to a softer moment as he looked at me, his expression changing. "I mean it, Hannah. You could make this work. I know you're scared, but look how easily you're adapting. You're meant for this kind of life."

His words hung in the air, heavy with promise. "Maybe," I replied, feeling a mix of hope and uncertainty. "But it's one thing to throw hay, and another to run a ranch."

He stepped closer, the space between us crackling with energy. "Running a ranch isn't just about managing cattle; it's about community, about building something that lasts. And you already know the heart of this place. You've been a part of it."

Before I could respond, my phone buzzed again, the shrill sound jarring us both back to reality. I fished it out of my pocket, eyeing the screen with a growing sense of dread. "It's my boss," I said, glancing at Luke, who wore a look of understanding mixed with disappointment.

"Take it," he said, his voice calm but laced with something deeper. "I'll be right here."

Reluctantly, I answered the call, my heart racing as the familiar voice of my boss filled the barn. We discussed deadlines, deliverables, and the upcoming project, but my mind drifted, focusing on Luke standing across from me, arms crossed, his expression inscrutable. I could feel the weight of his gaze, the tension building like a thick fog.

The call ended with the usual corporate pleasantries, but I could barely register it. "Everything okay?" Luke asked as I hung up, the corner of his mouth quirking up in a knowing smile.

"Just the usual," I replied, forcing a laugh that felt hollow. "You know, life in the fast lane."

"Sounds thrilling," he replied dryly. "So, what's the verdict? Are you staying or heading back to your whirlwind of a career?"

"I don't know," I admitted, feeling the stirrings of uncertainty clouding my mind again. "It's like I'm stuck in limbo. I love the idea of this life, but..."

"But?" Luke pressed, stepping closer, his eyes searching mine.

"I guess I'm scared," I said finally, the admission surprising even me. "Scared of failing, scared of losing everything I've built. What if I leave everything behind and it doesn't work?"

The air between us felt charged, filled with unspoken possibilities. "You won't know unless you try, Hannah. And I'll be here, supporting you, whatever you decide."

The sincerity in his voice melted something inside me, a flicker of hope igniting. But just as I opened my mouth to respond, a loud crash echoed from outside, rattling the barn and sending both of us jumping.

"What was that?" I asked, adrenaline rushing through my veins as I turned to the barn doors.

"Let's find out," Luke said, his tone shifting from playful to serious. He stepped ahead of me, pushing the doors open to reveal a scene that made my heart stop.

A flock of sheep was barreling toward us, bleating frantically, their shepherd nowhere in sight. But that wasn't the most alarming part. Just beyond the chaos, I spotted a figure standing near the fence, silhouetted against the dimming sky, a shadow moving ominously.

"Luke," I whispered, fear creeping into my voice as the figure turned, revealing a face I had not expected to see.

My heart raced as recognition hit like a tidal wave, and I knew in that moment that whatever comfort I had felt was about to be challenged in ways I had never anticipated.

Chapter 4: A Helping Hand

The sun rose each morning with a lazy stretch, spilling warm light across the fields that had long lain fallow. The once-vibrant colors of the farm were muted by neglect, but every day felt like a promise of revival. I would step out onto the creaking porch, a cup of coffee warming my palms, the rich scent of earth and growing things enveloping me like a familiar blanket. Luke arrived shortly after, his truck rattling into the gravel driveway, a cacophony of dust and laughter trailing behind him. There was a buoyancy to him, a kind of light that sparked against the drab backdrop of my grief-laden life.

"Ready to make this place look less like a scene from a horror movie?" he teased one morning, a grin split across his sun-kissed face. I couldn't help but chuckle, my heart doing a little somersault as he stepped out of the truck, his broad shoulders brushing against the doorframe. It was the first real laugh I'd managed since the world had shifted beneath me.

"Hey, I'll have you know this horror movie has its charms," I shot back, glancing around at the wildflowers stubbornly reclaiming their territory among the weeds. Each one was like a tiny testament to resilience, and I found myself wanting to be as brave as they were.

The days unfolded like a series of watercolor paintings, each filled with splashes of vibrant colors and the strokes of laughter. We worked side by side, a rhythm forming between us, weaving through our tasks with an ease that felt both thrilling and terrifying. Luke's hands were rough from years of labor, yet he handled the tools as if they were extensions of himself, his confidence contagious. I felt my own hands grow more adept, the soil and sweat mixing under my nails as I dug in, literally and figuratively.

"Are you always this serious?" he asked one afternoon, leaning against the fence post, his dark hair tousled by the wind. The way he tilted his head, curiosity gleaming in his eyes, made me want to share everything and nothing at the same time.

"I'm not serious," I protested, feigning indignation. "I'm just... contemplative."

"Contemplative? More like hiding behind that wall of yours." He pushed himself off the post and stepped closer, the space between us shrinking. "What are you thinking about? The state of your wildflower garden?"

His gaze was probing but playful, and I could feel the heat creeping up my neck. "I'm thinking about how I'd like to knock down that wall you keep mentioning, but it's more complicated than you think."

"Complicated's my middle name," he quipped, mischief dancing in his blue eyes.

"Really?" I laughed, the sound bubbling up unexpectedly. "I thought it was 'Luke.'"

"Only my mother calls me that," he replied, leaning closer, the air thick with unspoken things. "And I'll let you in on a secret—complicated usually comes with a good story."

For a moment, the world faded, and I could hear only the rustle of the leaves and the distant calls of birds weaving their songs. I was caught in the warmth of his presence, the magnetic pull of his earnestness stirring something deep within me. Just as quickly, however, the weight of my own solitude rushed back, and I took a step back, needing to breathe. "What about you, Luke? What's your story?"

He hesitated, the easy smile slipping for just a moment. "You first," he countered, a flicker of challenge igniting in his gaze.

I swallowed hard, the memory of my father's last days still raw, the grief like a phantom pain that wouldn't let go. "There's not much to tell. Just your average girl with an average family—until it wasn't."

The moment stretched between us, thick with anticipation. "Your turn. What's made you the person who's always so quick with a joke?"

He let out a breath, a gentle smile softening his features. "I guess I learned early on that laughter's the best way to break the ice... and the walls."

"Deep," I teased, my heart fluttering in response to the honesty threading through his words. "What happened? Did someone break your heart?"

"More like I broke my own heart. Chased the wrong dream for too long, ended up losing sight of what really mattered."

His revelation hung in the air, heavy yet strangely liberating. We shared a moment of silence, understanding woven between us like a fragile thread. Just then, the wind picked up, swirling around us, a playful reminder of the unpredictability of life.

Before I could reply, a sharp bark interrupted the moment. A scruffy dog appeared from behind the barn, tail wagging wildly, tongue lolling out in sheer joy. It was as if he had decided we'd forgotten the simplest joy of the day—unfettered companionship. Luke knelt, arms wide open, and the dog dove into his embrace, a chaotic whirlwind of fur and excitement.

"Meet Rufus," Luke said, laughter bubbling from his lips as the dog smothered him in slobbery kisses. "He's the real boss around here."

Rufus turned to me, as if inviting me into the fray. I knelt beside Luke, and the dog rolled onto his back, pleading for a belly rub. My heart softened further as I indulged him, laughter erupting from my lips. In that simple moment, the tension from before evaporated, and we found ourselves caught up in the innocent joy of this newfound friendship.

"I think Rufus approves," Luke said, his gaze lingering on me with a warmth that sent my heart racing.

"Does that mean I'm part of the team?" I asked, teasingly serious.

"Absolutely," he replied, eyes sparkling. "But I warn you, the initiation involves a lot of work and even more mud."

"Sounds perfect."

As the sun began to dip lower in the sky, casting golden light over the farm, I felt the walls I had built start to tremble, just a little. In that moment, as Rufus wriggled happily between us, I knew that maybe, just maybe, it was time to let a little light in.

The next morning unfurled with a kind of brilliance that felt almost surreal. The golden sun stretched its fingers across the land, coaxing vibrant colors from the dew-kissed flowers and breathing life back into the forgotten corners of the farm. I woke with the echo of laughter still swirling in my head, the memory of yesterday's easy camaraderie lingering like the scent of fresh coffee. Today felt charged with possibility, the air humming with the promise of something new.

Luke arrived with the same infectious enthusiasm, but this time he carried a wooden crate brimming with tools. "I've brought reinforcements!" he declared, setting it down with a triumphant thud. "Today, we conquer the orchard."

"Conquer?" I raised an eyebrow, crossing my arms as I leaned against the porch railing. "I thought we were just trying to keep it from looking like a scene from a bad zombie movie."

"Semantics," he replied, brushing off my playful jab with a grin. "But I assure you, with a little sweat and a lot of elbow grease, we'll have those trees producing apples fit for a king—or at least a very discerning squirrel."

I shook my head, unable to suppress my laughter. The way he wove humor into every moment made even the most mundane tasks feel exciting. We spent the morning clearing debris, pruning branches, and digging into the rich, dark earth. I watched him as he worked, the muscles in his arms flexing as he swung a pruning saw, the way he'd occasionally wipe the sweat from his brow with the back of his hand, revealing a glimpse of his playful nature beneath the rugged exterior.

"Do you ever stop talking?" I teased as he launched into another story, this one about the time he tried to impress a girl by baking a pie and ended up with an explosion of flour that coated his entire kitchen.

"Only when I'm busy thinking of you," he shot back, a mock-serious expression on his face.

I pretended to gag, holding my hand to my chest. "Flattery will get you nowhere."

"Good to know! I'll keep the compliments to myself, then." He chuckled, the sound a warm balm against the rising tension within me. Yet, I felt a flicker of something—an electric charge between us that sent my heart racing even as I tried to rein it in.

The afternoon dragged on, and despite the weight of the work, there was a buoyancy to the air that seemed to mirror the growing connection between us. Luke's laughter rang out, and I found myself eager to catch his eye, to share a smile or a playful jab. Each shared moment chipped away at the barriers I had so carefully constructed. Yet, lurking just beneath the surface was a reminder of why those walls existed.

As the sun began to dip below the horizon, painting the sky in swathes of pink and orange, we stood in the orchard, gazing at our handiwork. The trees looked more alive, the grass underneath our feet no longer a tangled mess. "We actually did it," I said, breathless from the effort and exhilaration.

"More than that," Luke replied, wiping his brow and stepping closer, his presence warm and inviting. "We've started something beautiful."

The air crackled with unspoken words, and for a moment, I felt as if the world around us faded, leaving only the two of us and the fragile connection that had blossomed. But just as quickly, a familiar shadow crept in, tightening my chest. The echo of my father's absence throbbed in my mind, a reminder of why I had retreated into my solitude. I stepped back, forcing myself to break the spell.

"Time to clean up," I said, the cheeriness in my voice a weak disguise for the tumult inside.

Luke looked at me, concern etched across his face. "Hey, what's going on? You were just—"

"Just tired," I interrupted, forcing a smile. "Long day."

He watched me for a moment, the air thick with questions he didn't voice. I appreciated his patience, but the walls I'd built were strong, and the thought of tearing them down felt overwhelming. I busied myself with gathering tools, the clatter a welcome distraction.

As the evening wore on, we headed inside, the cozy kitchen now filled with the scent of simmering stew. I stood at the stove, stirring absentmindedly while Luke cleaned up the mess we had made. "What's the plan for dinner?" he asked, peeking into the pot.

"Stew. Leftovers from last night." I tried to sound casual, but the thought of sharing a meal was laced with the anxiety of vulnerability.

"Ah, the famous 'I-can't-be-bothered-to-cook' stew," he teased, leaning against the counter with an easy smile. "You're lucky I'm not picky. My last roommate made a casserole that could've doubled as a doorstop."

"I won't be so forgiving if you give me a reason," I shot back, my playful tone masking the flutter of nerves in my stomach.

"Deal," he replied, his eyes glinting with mischief.

We settled at the small table, the warm glow from the overhead light creating a cocoon around us. As we ate, the conversation flowed easily, laughter punctuating our words as we traded stories about childhood mishaps and the absurdity of adulthood.

"So, you were really that kid who tried to climb a tree and ended up stuck for three hours?" Luke asked, incredulity painting his features.

"Hey! It was a very tall tree, and I was a very ambitious child," I protested, laughing at the memory. "Besides, I got down eventually. With a little help... and a very worried neighbor."

He shook his head, amusement lighting up his expression. "And here I thought I was the adventurous one."

"Adventurous? You mean reckless," I countered, winking at him.

As the evening wore on, however, an undercurrent of tension tugged at my thoughts. Each laugh felt like a double-edged sword, reminding me of how easily I was slipping into the comfort of his company. I realized I was treading dangerously close to a place I wasn't ready to revisit.

After dinner, Luke offered to help with the dishes, but I waved him off. "You've done enough. I can handle it."

"Are you sure? I make a mean dishwasher."

"Yeah, and I'm pretty sure that means letting all the suds overflow."

He chuckled, but I could see the concern creeping back into his eyes. "Just trying to be helpful here."

"Helpful is noted and appreciated, but I need some time to think."

His smile faltered slightly, the warmth in his gaze replaced with something softer, more contemplative. "Thinking's good, but don't think too much. Sometimes it gets in the way of what's right in front of you."

The weight of his words settled heavily in the air, and I felt the walls around my heart tighten, the familiar fear clawing its way back in. I turned away, focusing on the soapy dishes, but inside, I was battling a storm of emotion.

"I'll be right here if you want to talk," he said quietly, his voice wrapping around me like a gentle embrace.

I nodded, trying to push down the swell of uncertainty that threatened to swallow me whole. As I rinsed the last plate, I felt the tension ease slightly, yet the shadows lurking in the corners of my mind refused to fade. For every laugh we shared, a whisper of hesitation echoed within, reminding me that the heart was a delicate thing, easily bruised yet undeniably yearning for connection.

With the dishes done, I turned to Luke, my heart a mix of fear and hope. "Thank you for today. For everything."

He stepped closer, the space between us crackling with unspoken words. "Just remember, you don't have to do this alone. I'm not going anywhere."

His reassurance warmed me, a flicker of light in the encroaching darkness. Yet, even as the promise hung in the air, I felt the weight of my walls pressing down, unsure if I could truly let them crumble.

The days rolled on, each one draped in the soft glow of late summer light, infusing the air with warmth and possibility. Luke and I settled into a routine that felt as comforting as a favorite old song. Mornings were filled with laughter and banter, while afternoons saw us wrestling with the land, our teamwork forging an effortless connection. Yet, as our bond deepened, I felt an undercurrent of dread reminding me of the thin ice I was skating on.

One morning, as I surveyed the orchard, my fingers idly brushing against the rough bark of an ancient tree, Luke appeared beside me, a smudge of dirt on his cheek. "You know, I think we might actually have a future in this farm revival business," he said, gesturing grandly. "Next stop: Home and Garden magazine."

I snorted, unable to hold back my laughter. "Right, because our chaos is magazine-worthy. 'How Not to Garden: A Guide to Overgrown Weeds and Broken Dreams.'"

He feigned shock, placing a hand over his heart. "Ouch! You wound me. My dreams of fame and fortune are dashed."

I playfully rolled my eyes, but there was a part of me that reveled in the easy companionship we'd forged. Luke was like a light in the fog of my past, guiding me through memories I'd rather forget. Yet with each shared laugh, the walls I had so painstakingly built threatened to crumble, revealing the raw edges of my vulnerability.

"Okay, Mr. Future Gardener of the Year, what's the plan for today?" I asked, tilting my head to meet his gaze, heart racing at the flicker of something deeper that passed between us.

He grinned, an unmistakable twinkle in his eye. "I thought we could tackle the old barn. It's been waiting for a little love."

The barn loomed in the distance, its paint peeling and windows dusty, like a relic from another time. I nodded, swallowing the lump of hesitation in my throat. "Sure, why not? I'm all for bringing things back to life."

As we approached the barn, the scent of aged wood and wildflowers surrounded us, wrapping us in a nostalgia that felt both comforting and unsettling. I couldn't help but wonder how many secrets the barn had witnessed, how many stories had played out in its shadow.

"Just imagine the parties they must have thrown here," Luke mused, brushing away cobwebs with a playful flick of his wrist. "A dance floor, laughter echoing, maybe even a few romances igniting."

"Or a few heartaches," I replied, my voice softer. "This place has seen its share of ghosts."

Luke turned to me, his brow furrowing slightly. "You mean, like... actual ghosts?"

"More like the kind that linger in the memory." I sighed, feeling the weight of my past settle over me like a heavy blanket. "The ones that remind you of what you've lost."

He didn't respond immediately, his gaze searching mine. "You know, I think it's important to honor those memories, but you can't let them hold you hostage. You're still here, living and breathing. That's what counts."

His words resonated, both soothing and alarming. I wanted to believe him, to embrace the idea of moving forward, but the walls of my heart held strong. "Easier said than done, Luke."

"True," he conceded, stepping closer. "But what if you took it one small step at a time? Like reviving this barn?"

I chuckled lightly, trying to lighten the mood. "You mean, like turning it into a party venue? Sounds like a plan."

"Or a haunted house!" he quipped, a glint of mischief in his eyes. "We could charge admission."

"Right, because nothing screams 'haunted' quite like a couple of millennial farmhands."

Our banter was cut short as we stepped inside the barn, the light filtering through gaps in the wood, casting a warm glow on the dust motes dancing in the air. The interior felt both expansive and intimate, filled with remnants of the past. Old tools hung from the walls, and a dilapidated hayloft beckoned us to explore.

"What do you think?" Luke asked, surveying the space with an artist's eye. "A little elbow grease, some paint, and this place could be stunning."

"Or it could collapse under our weight," I replied, a teasing lilt to my voice, even as I felt the pull of possibility.

As we began clearing away debris, our laughter mingled with the rustling of hay and the soft creaks of the barn. I could feel my heart loosening its grip just a little, the humor between us weaving a comforting blanket over my lingering fears.

But as the sun sank lower in the sky, casting long shadows across the floor, an unexpected tension settled in the air. Luke paused, leaning against the wall, his expression suddenly serious. "Can I ask you something?"

"Sure. What's on your mind?"

"Why do you hold back? You're funny, smart, and clearly capable of so much more than you let on. I just... I don't understand why you seem so afraid to let people in."

The question hit me like a cold splash of water. My heart raced, caught between a desire to confide in him and the instinct to retreat. "It's complicated," I said, the words tumbling out as I searched for a way to shield myself. "I've just been through a lot."

"Life's complicated for everyone," he replied gently, stepping closer, his eyes earnest and probing. "But you don't have to face it alone. I'm here."

The sincerity in his voice threatened to breach the walls I had built, each word like a sledgehammer against the bricks I'd so carefully laid. I opened my mouth to respond, but before I could form the words, the sound of shuffling outside broke the moment.

We both turned, tension sparking anew as the barn door creaked open. Standing silhouetted in the golden light was a figure I hadn't expected to see—a tall, broad-shouldered man with a familiar air of authority. My breath caught in my throat as I recognized him instantly.

"Lucy," my brother Ethan's voice cut through the air, thick with a mix of surprise and concern. "What are you doing here?"

Luke's demeanor shifted subtly, tension flaring as he stepped protectively in front of me, as if sensing the weight of my brother's presence. "I thought you weren't coming back until next week," I managed, trying to mask the rush of emotions that threatened to overwhelm me.

Ethan's gaze flicked between us, the air charged with unspoken words and a tension I hadn't anticipated. "I had to check on the place. Mom was worried."

Luke opened his mouth, but before he could say anything, I interjected. "It's fine. We were just working on the barn."

Ethan's eyes narrowed slightly, and I could feel the scrutiny of his gaze, assessing the situation with the careful watchfulness of an older brother who had seen too much. "Working, huh? And who's this?"

"This is Luke," I said, forcing the introduction through a tight throat. "He's been helping me with the farm."

"Helping, is it?" Ethan's voice was calm, but there was an edge to it, a protective instinct I recognized all too well.

"Yeah, helping," Luke replied, his tone steady but laced with an unspoken challenge. "Just getting things back in shape."

The three of us stood there, a triangle of tension, the air thick with the weight of unspoken questions. I could feel the fragile equilibrium I had built with Luke beginning to crack under the scrutiny of my brother's watchful gaze.

"Look, I'm just trying to figure things out," I said, my voice rising slightly. "I can't keep hiding from everything."

Ethan softened slightly but didn't relent. "Just be careful, okay? You've been through a lot, and I don't want you to get hurt again."

In that moment, I realized just how far I'd come—and how far I still had to go. With Ethan's protective nature and Luke's warmth, I was caught between two worlds. My heart raced, not knowing how to navigate the growing tension that threatened to swallow me whole.

Before I could respond, Luke took a step back, creating distance, but the connection I felt with him lingered in the air like the scent of blooming flowers—sweet and intoxicating yet laced with uncertainty. "I get it," he said, his tone softening. "Family can be complicated."

Ethan's expression remained unreadable, his eyes darting between us, as if trying to piece together a puzzle that had suddenly shifted shapes. "Well, just remember you have people who care about you," he said finally, his voice steady yet layered with concern.

With those words hanging in the air, I felt the ground shift beneath me, the weight of decisions pressing down as I stood at a crossroads. Would I lean into the unexpected light that Luke offered, or retreat into the shadows of my past?

Just then, a distant rumble of thunder echoed across the sky, ominous and low. I glanced outside, and a shiver of unease crept up my spine as dark clouds began to gather on the horizon, swirling like a storm brewing just beyond our sight.

"Looks like trouble," Luke remarked, breaking the tense silence. "We should probably head back before it hits."

Ethan nodded, his protective instincts kicking in. "Yeah, let's move."

Chapter 5: Storm Clouds Gather

The day had been quiet, the kind of stillness that invites introspection and stirs the dust of forgotten memories. I stood at the kitchen sink, hands submerged in warm, soapy water, lost in thought as I gazed out at the fields stretching toward the horizon. The golden light of the late afternoon sun painted everything in a warm glow, the way nostalgia softens the hard edges of the past. I could almost hear the laughter of my younger self, racing through those same fields with wild abandon, unencumbered by the weight of adult responsibilities or the scars of familial discord. It was a fleeting peace, but one I craved deeply.

I was still savoring this rare moment of tranquility when the screech of tires on gravel tore through my reverie. I turned, wiping my hands on a dish towel, my heart beginning to race in rhythm with the thud of my pulse. The sun had dipped just low enough for shadows to stretch ominously, and I felt a prickling sensation crawl up my spine. The knot in my stomach tightened as I saw a familiar figure emerge from the driver's side of an old pickup truck.

Sam.

He strode toward the porch with a self-assured swagger, one hand shoved deep into his jeans pocket, the other casually brushing a stray lock of hair from his forehead. The sight of him ignited a rush of conflicting emotions: irritation, resentment, and a hint of disbelief. After all these years, had he really come back to disrupt the delicate balance I had painstakingly rebuilt? I gritted my teeth, steeling myself as he approached.

"Sam," I said, my voice steady despite the swirl of anxiety gripping my chest. "What are you doing here?"

His smirk widened, a blend of arrogance and familiarity that made me want to slap it off his face. "I'm here to claim what's mine, Hannah." The words dripped from his lips like honey, sweet yet laced with venom. He leaned against the porch railing, his posture casual, but the intensity of his gaze suggested a storm was brewing just beneath the surface.

"What you think is yours doesn't belong to you anymore," I shot back, crossing my arms in defiance. The warm air around us felt thick, charged with an energy that threatened to snap like a taut string. It was maddening how easily he could provoke me, as if my ire was the fuel he needed to ignite a firestorm of unresolved grievances.

"Really?" he scoffed, tilting his head in mock consideration. "You think you can just play house here, all alone with your little dreams of reviving the farm? You have no idea what you're up against." The words hung in the air, heavy with the weight of our shared history—one filled with betrayal and heartbreak.

I stepped closer, my heart racing with a mix of anger and indignation. "This isn't just some whim for me, Sam. I'm not just here to play pretend. This farm is my home, my inheritance. You don't get to waltz back in after all this time and pretend like you have any claim to it." Each word was a barrier I was erecting against him, a defense against the memories that threatened to drown me.

"Home?" He let out a harsh laugh that echoed against the weathered wood of the porch. "You think this broken-down place is your home? It's a relic of our failures, Hannah. A monument to what we couldn't save." His eyes narrowed, the smirk fading as he moved closer, invading my space. "And you think you can fix it? You think you can erase the past?"

His words pierced through me, raw and unforgiving. I felt the sting of tears, but I refused to let him see how deeply he had struck. Instead, I stood my ground, fueled by a mix of stubborn pride and defiance. "I'm not trying to erase anything. I'm trying to move forward, to breathe life back into this place. Something you wouldn't understand."

The air thickened with tension, and the wind picked up, rustling the leaves of the old oak tree standing sentinel over the yard. It felt as if nature itself was holding its breath, waiting for the next move in our little chess match. He stepped back, feigning a nonchalance that didn't quite reach his eyes. "And what about Luke?" he asked, his voice lowering, the smirk replaced by something darker. "You think he's going to just stand by while you're digging up ghosts?"

I felt my stomach drop at the mention of Luke. How had Sam even known about him? "That's none of your business," I snapped, the edge of my voice slicing through the thick air. But inside, a new layer of tension coiled tightly around my heart. The last thing I wanted was to drag Luke into this. He was my refuge, my ally in the battle to reclaim the farm, but now he felt like a pawn in this twisted game.

"Oh, but it is," Sam countered, his tone dripping with condescension. "He's a distraction, Hannah. A way to ignore the reality that's staring you in the face." He gestured toward the fields, the fading sun casting long shadows over the earth. "This isn't some romantic getaway. It's a sinking ship, and you're playing captain."

I clenched my jaw, fighting back the frustration that threatened to overflow. "And what do you propose I do? Abandon it all because it's hard? Just like you did?" The accusation hung between us, a challenge as sharp as glass.

"Maybe it's time you faced the truth," he said, his voice lowering to a conspiratorial whisper. "You can't win this fight alone, Hannah. You never could."

I wanted to scream that I wasn't alone, that I had Luke, who believed in me when I struggled to believe in myself. But the thought slipped away like sand through my fingers as Sam's words coiled around my heart, squeezing it painfully. The storm that had been brewing within me mirrored the gathering clouds above, dark and tumultuous. And just like that, I felt the fragile peace I had managed to hold onto begin to unravel, leaving me exposed in the gathering storm.

The wind howled like a banshee, throwing an unrelenting chill into the air as I took a deep breath, gathering my composure. Sam stood there, an unwelcome specter from my past, while I felt the walls of the house closing in around me, as if the very structure could sense the brewing confrontation. His words hung heavy between us, a noose tightening with every passing second. I couldn't let him reduce my hard-fought peace to mere rubble.

"You think this is easy for me?" I shot back, more forcefully than I intended. "I'm not trying to erase anything, but you're not helping." I tried to channel my inner warrior, even as my heart raced. I wouldn't let Sam dismantle the sanctuary I had painstakingly rebuilt.

"Helping?" Sam let out a bark of laughter that was anything but kind. "I'm here to provide a reality check, not a pep talk. You need to face it, Hannah: You're in over your head." The light from the dying sun caught the glint of something in his eyes—was it concern or something darker, more predatory?

"It's funny how you think you can just come in here and dictate my life," I said, crossing my arms tighter. "You don't know anything about what I'm capable of."

"Oh, I know plenty," he replied, his tone a caustic blend of mockery and history. "Like how you always want to play the hero, but when the chips are down, you run. Remember that summer when you decided it was easier to leave than to deal with the fallout? Some things never change."

I felt my breath hitch at the memory, a sharp pang of guilt twisting in my gut. How had we ended up here, trading barbs and dredging up the past as if it were a freshly opened wound? "You don't get to bring that up," I managed, anger flickering through my voice like lightning illuminating a dark sky. "You walked away too. You have no right to judge me."

The air between us crackled with tension, and I was acutely aware of the shadows lengthening around us, the dusk creeping in to envelop our argument in darkness. Just when I thought he might retreat, that he might choose to play the role of a distant brother instead of the adversary he had become, he stepped forward.

"Maybe it's time you learned to share the burden," he said, his voice lower, less taunting but no less challenging. "This farm isn't just yours. It never was. Our father made it clear before he died. You're not the only one who cares about this place, and I have just as much right to it as you do."

The words sent a jolt through me, a mix of anger and confusion swirling into a tempest of emotions I struggled to untangle. "So what? You think showing up after years of silence gives you some claim to it? This place is mine now, Sam. I'm not going to let you come in and rip it apart because you feel entitled." My voice wavered, but I stood firm, digging my heels into the ground as if I could anchor myself against the storm that raged within him.

"Entitled? It's called being a responsible adult," he shot back, his tone icy. "You're not even living in the real world. You've romanticized this farm, but it's a dying relic. Wake up, Hannah. There's more out there than this dusty old house and your dreams of a pastoral life."

And there it was—the core of my frustration: he didn't understand. I had spent countless nights dreaming of ways to revive this place, of turning it back into a sanctuary rather than a mausoleum of lost dreams. But he stood there, with all the arrogance of someone who had never truly fought for anything.

"You don't know what it means to fight for something," I spat, the bitterness creeping into my voice. "You think you can just swoop in and take what's mine without even trying to understand what it took to get here?"

He narrowed his eyes, anger flaring like wildfire. "And you think being stubborn will save you? That you can just wish it all back to life?"

The door creaked behind me, pulling my gaze momentarily. Luke stood in the doorway, eyebrows raised, a hint of confusion on his face. "What's going on?" he asked, stepping outside as if sensing the charged atmosphere.

I shot him a pleading look, my heart swelling with gratitude that he had come to check on me. "It's nothing, really," I began, but Sam interrupted.

"Just a family discussion," he said, his voice laced with sarcasm, a wolfish grin appearing again as he addressed Luke. "You're the knight in shining armor, aren't you? You're here to rescue her from the big bad brother?"

The air shifted, and Luke's posture stiffened, as if he could sense the friction between us. "What do you want, Sam?" he asked, the calm in his voice contrasting sharply with the tension surrounding us.

"I want what's rightfully mine," Sam declared, his gaze unwavering, as if he were the protagonist in some twisted morality tale.

Luke stepped forward, placing himself protectively between Sam and me. "And what would that be? To come here and bully Hannah? To rehash old grievances that should've stayed buried?"

"Oh, look at you, playing the hero," Sam sneered. "Let me guess, you're the one filling her head with fairy tales about fixing this place up, turning it into some quaint little escape? It's pathetic."

"That's enough," I interrupted, anger surging once more. I turned to Luke, who looked at me with a mix of concern and determination. "This is family business. You don't need to get involved."

"Family business?" Sam echoed, his laughter bitter. "More like a dysfunctional soap opera. Hannah, you're letting your heart rule your head again. Don't you see that you're headed for a disaster?"

The words hung in the air like an unwelcome guest, and I felt my resolve wavering. But then I looked at Luke, who had a fierce light in his eyes, a promise that we would face whatever came next together. In that moment, I found the strength to push back. "You think you can come here and tell me how to live my life? I won't let you dictate my choices or my future."

The atmosphere shifted again, the weight of unsaid things pressing down on us, and I realized then that this storm wasn't merely about the farm. It was about family ties, old wounds, and the painful truth that sometimes, blood doesn't guarantee loyalty. The shadows deepened around us, and as the first raindrops began to fall, I knew this confrontation was only the beginning.

The rain began to fall, gentle at first, a light drizzle that teased the parched earth. But as if sensing the tempest brewing between us, it picked up momentum, heavy droplets splattering against the porch, mirroring the chaos of our confrontation. Each drop felt like a punctuation mark, emphasizing the tension that crackled in the air. I could see Sam's annoyance flash as he pulled his collar tighter against the sudden chill, but the storm was only beginning, and I refused to back down.

"Let me remind you, Hannah," he said, his voice dripping with condescension, "you're not some plucky heroine in a feel-good movie. You're just a girl playing house, and this farm is a sinking ship."

I clenched my fists, fighting the urge to throw something at him—something heavy, like his ego. "Maybe you're just too scared to believe in anything," I retorted, my tone sharper than the rain that was now pouring down in earnest. "You'd rather watch it all fall apart than try to fix it."

Sam's face contorted, anger giving way to a mix of disbelief and disdain. "You think you're so brave, don't you? But the truth is, you're just avoiding reality. Why else would you cling to this place like it's your lifeboat?"

"Because it is my lifeboat," I said, stepping closer, my voice firm, "and if I drown, it won't be because I didn't try."

Luke, still standing protectively between us, shifted his weight, as if debating whether to step in further or let the storm rage on. "You both need to chill," he said, breaking the rising tension with an almost casual remark, yet his eyes danced between us, searching for a way to defuse the situation. "This is a family affair, and neither of you is going to walk away unscathed if you keep throwing around accusations."

"Family?" Sam scoffed, arms still crossed defiantly. "This family has been broken for a long time, Luke. You're just another interloper in this tragic play."

"Is that what you think?" Luke replied, his voice steady, though I could see the flicker of indignation in his eyes. "Hannah isn't just some character in your story. She's fighting for what she believes in. You need to understand that."

"Fighting?" Sam laughed, but it was empty, echoing hollowly against the backdrop of the pouring rain. "It's a losing battle, Luke. You should be the one looking out for her, not enabling her fantasies."

"Sam, you don't get it," I interjected, my voice breaking just a little. "I'm not dreaming. I'm doing. I'm putting in the work. Every day, I'm out there trying to breathe life into this farm. It's my legacy, not just a forgotten piece of land." The rain continued to fall, drenching the world around us, but the fire in my gut burned hotter.

The wind whipped through the trees, branches swaying as if caught in the debate. Sam's expression shifted, and for a moment, a flicker of something—regret, perhaps?—crossed his face. "You think you can save this place, but it's too far gone. You can't escape the truth. You're only holding on to a memory."

"Better to hold on to a memory than to live in a nightmare," I shot back, my breath coming faster. "You wouldn't know anything about that, would you? You left when things got tough."

"Maybe because I was tired of pretending everything was fine when it wasn't," he snapped, his voice rising above the rain. "You put on a brave face while everything around you is falling apart, and now you think you can fix it all by yourself?"

"Maybe you should stop pretending to care, then," I countered, matching his intensity. "You can't just come here, throw a tantrum, and expect me to hand over my dreams because you're feeling nostalgic."

The air hung heavy with unresolved feelings, and I could feel the storm inside me intensifying, mirroring the chaos outside. The skies darkened further, casting ominous shadows on the porch. Just then, a loud clap of thunder rolled across the sky, startling us both into silence.

Luke glanced up, eyes wide with concern. "We should head inside before we're all soaked," he suggested, but Sam waved him off, eyes blazing like two burning coals.

"No. I want this settled now," Sam said, determination etched on his face. "This isn't just about the farm; it's about what you think you can achieve here. You're fighting for a ghost."

"Stop it!" I shouted, the words bursting forth like a dam breaking. "Stop acting like you own this moment. You don't get to dictate my worth based on your perception of failure."

"Maybe you're right, but I'm not going to let you drag this family's name through the mud," Sam shot back, eyes narrowing. "You're not the only one with scars, Hannah. And if you can't see that, then you're more lost than I thought."

As the rain poured down, mingling with the emotion swirling between us, I could feel the tension vibrating in the air, an electric current that seemed to pulse around us. The truth he spoke pierced through my defenses, and for a moment, doubt crept in. What if I truly was fighting ghosts?

"Enough!" Luke intervened, stepping forward, a protective barrier between us. "Both of you need to take a step back and breathe. This isn't helping anyone."

But Sam wasn't done. "Maybe you should listen, Hannah. You can't outrun the past forever. It will catch up to you when you least expect it."

My heart raced as his words landed heavy, reverberating in the space between us. The very essence of what he said struck a chord, twisting the knife of self-doubt deeper. Did I have the strength to face not just the challenges of the farm but also the weight of my own history?

"Maybe it's time you learn to confront your ghosts," he continued, his voice dropping to a whisper, almost conspiratorial. "What if I told you I know something about Dad's last days that could change everything?"

The words hung in the air like a promise wrapped in a threat, chilling the already damp atmosphere. My breath caught in my throat, the realization dawning on me that this conversation was spiraling into uncharted territory. "What do you mean?" I demanded, my heart pounding, every ounce of defiance replaced by raw curiosity.

He leaned closer, a smirk returning to his lips, the rain cascading down like a curtain shielding whatever revelation lay behind his gaze. "Let's just say I have some information that could make you rethink everything you thought you knew about your precious legacy."

The storm raged on, and with every heartbeat, the tension thickened like the clouds above, dark and full of foreboding. The secrets of the past loomed larger than ever, and I suddenly felt the fragile thread of control slip from my fingers, as uncertainty settled in like the rain that soaked through our clothes. What lay ahead was murky, but one thing was clear: the storm was far from over.

Chapter 6: Heartfelt Confessions

The warmth of the porch wrapped around me like a well-worn blanket, the kind that held the scent of summer evenings and forgotten secrets. Luke sat next to me, his presence a comforting anchor amidst the tempest swirling in my heart. Fireflies danced around us, their soft glow punctuating the deepening dusk, each flicker a reminder of the fleeting beauty of the moment. I inhaled the familiar scent of freshly cut hay mingling with the cool evening air, grounding myself in the space we occupied—this haven we had carved out from the chaos of our lives.

I had always been one to wear my heart on my sleeve, but tonight, something about the stillness of the world urged me to peel back my layers, to reveal the fears that clawed at my insides like a feral animal desperate to escape. I stole a glance at Luke, his profile illuminated by the glow of the porch light, shadows dancing across his features in a way that made my heart race. He had this way of listening, as if he understood that sometimes silence was more eloquent than words. His brown eyes held a depth that promised understanding, a comforting balm to the raw edges of my thoughts.

"Do you ever think about what happens if we fail?" The words tumbled out of me, raw and unguarded. "The farm, I mean. It's not just land; it's Dad's legacy. Everything he built, every sacrifice he made—it's all at stake." I felt a tremor in my voice, betraying the strength I had tried to portray. Each word hung in the air between us, heavy with the weight of my fear.

Luke turned to me, the earnestness in his gaze almost palpable. "Hannah, you're not going to fail. You have more fight in you than anyone I know. Your dad saw that in you. It's why he trusted you with this place." His words wrapped around me like a protective shield, yet the nagging doubt didn't dissipate.

"Trust and I have a complicated relationship. Sometimes I feel like it's a one-way street." My voice wavered, and I bit my lip, willing back the sting of unshed tears. The last thing I wanted was to appear weak, but the truth was a fragile thing, and I felt it unraveling at the seams.

He reached out, brushing a stray lock of hair behind my ear, a gesture so intimate it sent a jolt through me. "You know I'm here for you, right? You're not in this alone." His voice was a soothing balm, each word wrapping around my heart like a promise.

In that moment, something shifted between us, the air crackling with an energy that felt both terrifying and exhilarating. My breath caught in my throat as I leaned closer, driven by a force I couldn't quite name. Our lips met, tentatively at first, a whisper of contact that ignited a spark within me. It was as if the universe conspired to fold our past experiences into this single moment, intertwining our fears, hopes, and dreams.

The kiss deepened, and for a brief instant, the world outside ceased to exist. Time suspended itself, allowing me to forget the burdens that had been gnawing at my soul. Luke's hands found my waist, pulling me closer as if he could fuse our spirits together. I melted against him, the warmth radiating from his body enveloping me in a cocoon of safety. I hadn't realized how starved I was for this connection until that very second.

But just as quickly as the magic ignited, a shadow flickered across my mind—the looming threat of the bank, the uncertainties swirling around the farm, and the specter of Sam, whose confrontational presence loomed like a storm cloud, ready to break. I pulled back, my heart racing not just from the kiss but from the flood of reality crashing in. "What if this complicates things?" I breathed, anxiety threading its way through my voice.

Luke's brow furrowed, his expression shifting from tenderness to concern. "What do you mean?"

"Us," I replied, my heart thudding in my chest. "If we—if I lean into this, and things go wrong, I don't want to lose you too. The stakes are high, Luke."

His gaze softened, a gentle understanding replacing the confusion. "You're worried about losing the farm, your family legacy, and now me too? Hannah, you're carrying too much. Let's not add to it by overthinking this. We're not just partners in the field; we're partners in life." His words sank in, and a flicker of hope ignited within me, battling against the shadows of doubt.

I chuckled softly, the sound tinged with irony. "So, what? We're like a sitcom couple now? 'Partners in Life: The Farming Edition'?"

Luke laughed, the sound rich and warm, dispelling some of the tension that had woven itself around us. "I think we could do a great pilot episode, actually. Lots of comedic relief from the cows. Maybe a cameo from the chicken that keeps escaping?"

Our laughter danced in the air, weaving a fragile thread of connection that felt more vital than ever. Yet beneath the levity lay an undercurrent of unease, a reminder that reality awaited us beyond the porch. I couldn't shake the feeling that our budding romance was a precarious balance—an intricate dance that could tip into chaos at any moment.

As the stars twinkled above, I found solace in Luke's presence, his warmth a beacon against the chill of uncertainty. There was a strength in vulnerability, a beauty in admitting my fears, and perhaps, just perhaps, a glimmer of hope waiting to unfold. But the night was still young, and as the fireflies flickered around us, I couldn't help but wonder what lay ahead in our entwined fates.

The next morning, the sun spilled into my bedroom like liquid gold, bathing everything in a warm glow. I blinked against the brightness, the remnants of last night still swirling in my mind. Luke's touch, the way he held me close, the easy laughter we shared—it was a balm for my worries, a flicker of light in an otherwise murky future. I rolled out of bed, my feet hitting the cool wooden floor with a soft thud, and made my way downstairs. The scent of freshly brewed coffee beckoned me, weaving through the house like a familiar tune.

As I entered the kitchen, my mom was already at the counter, her hair tied back in a loose bun, a faded apron draped over her shoulders. She was flipping pancakes, their edges crisping up nicely. The sizzle of batter meeting the hot skillet harmonized with the soft chatter of the radio in the background, the kind of music that makes you feel like everything is right in the world, even when it isn't.

"Morning, sleepyhead," she said, her voice warm and teasing, as she poured another round of batter. "You look like you've seen a ghost. Or maybe you just stayed up too late reading those romance novels again?" She shot me a knowing glance, one that made my cheeks flush.

"Mom, it was just a kiss," I replied, pouring myself a mug of coffee, the rich aroma filling the air. But the memory lingered, playing in my mind like a favorite song stuck on repeat. "And it was a pretty great kiss."

She raised an eyebrow, a smirk creeping onto her lips. "A kiss that has you blushing like a schoolgirl. It must have been more than just a 'great' kiss then."

I couldn't help but laugh, the sound light and buoyant, spilling into the space between us. "Okay, maybe it was monumental. But you know, it's complicated. With everything happening with the farm, it's like trying to keep a thousand juggling balls in the air while standing on one leg."

She paused, turning to face me, her expression shifting to one of understanding. "Life has a way of complicating things, doesn't it? But, sweetheart, you deserve happiness too. Don't forget that."

I poured a generous amount of syrup over my pancakes, the sticky sweetness almost too tempting. "I know, but what if happiness comes with a price? What if I lose everything trying to chase it?"

"Then you fight harder," she replied simply, her voice filled with conviction. "Sometimes, the most beautiful things require the most effort."

Her words lingered in my mind as I took a seat at the table, the sunlight streaming through the window illuminating the small space that felt so full of life and love. I couldn't shake the tension knotting in my stomach, a persistent reminder of the looming storm with Sam. If only I could compartmentalize my feelings for Luke and my obligations to the farm, but everything seemed to intertwine, as if fate were orchestrating some intricate dance I was ill-prepared for.

After breakfast, I headed out to the fields, the dew-kissed grass glistening like a million tiny diamonds in the early light. I reveled in the familiarity of the land—the gentle rustle of the leaves, the soft cooing of doves, and the far-off sound of a tractor humming along. Yet, today, my heart felt heavy, burdened with uncertainty.

As I wandered through the rows of corn, I spotted Luke, his silhouette framed against the vibrant green. He was talking to a few farmhands, gesturing animatedly as he explained something that had them all chuckling. I admired the way he moved, the confidence in his posture, and how easily he connected with everyone around him. It was a reminder of how much I valued his presence, how he managed to make the daunting tasks seem less overwhelming.

"Hey there, superstar," he called out, his voice cutting through my thoughts as he caught sight of me. "Care for a little help with the afternoon's crop inspection?"

"Only if you promise not to make me feel like a total amateur," I replied, playfully narrowing my eyes at him. "You know I'm still figuring this out."

He chuckled, a sound that sent warmth blooming in my chest. "Trust me, I've seen a lot worse. You'll be running this place single-handedly in no time."

The banter flowed easily, a playful rhythm that danced between us as we made our way toward the fields. But just as I felt the heaviness lift, the laughter began to fade. The sound of a truck engine revving nearby sent a shiver down my spine. My heart sank as I recognized the familiar red pickup.

"Speak of the devil," I muttered under my breath, watching as Sam climbed out, his expression a mix of arrogance and disdain. He strolled toward us, a swagger in his step that made my stomach twist.

"Thought I'd find you here, Hannah," he called out, his voice dripping with faux charm. "Still playing farmer, I see."

I bristled at his condescension. "And what brings you to my farm, Sam? Looking to lend a hand or just stir up trouble?"

Luke's body shifted slightly, an instinctual response that told me he was ready to step in if necessary. I appreciated his presence more than ever, my silent partner in this unfolding drama.

Sam laughed, a sound that grated on my nerves. "Oh, you know me. Just keeping an eye on my investments. You might need a little guidance." His gaze flicked between me and Luke, a smirk playing on his lips. "Especially with someone like him around."

"Luke is more capable than you'll ever be," I shot back, surprising myself with the ferocity of my words. The tension was palpable, and I could feel the air thickening around us, a storm brewing that threatened to spill over.

"Feisty. I like it," Sam replied, a glimmer of amusement in his eyes. "But let's not forget the reality of the situation. You're in over your head, Hannah. You can't keep this place running without support."

"I don't need your kind of support," I retorted, the steel in my voice surprising even me. "You're the last person I'd trust to help me save my father's legacy."

Luke shifted closer, a protective stance, and I could feel the strength radiating from him. The contrast between the two men was stark—one representing the weight of my past, the other embodying the promise of a brighter future.

"Just remember, Hannah, the clock's ticking," Sam said, his smile fading slightly. "You can't ignore the reality of this situation. If you can't find a way to make this work, it'll be too late."

With that, he turned on his heel and walked back toward his truck, leaving behind a lingering tension that hung like fog in the air. I could feel the weight of his words pressing down on me, threatening to drown out the hope that had flickered to life just the night before.

As Sam's truck rumbled away, Luke turned to me, concern etched across his features. "You okay?"

I took a deep breath, trying to shake off the unease that clung to me. "Yeah, just... you know how he is. He thrives on intimidation."

"Maybe we should stop letting him," Luke replied, his tone serious. "You've fought too hard to let him get under your skin."

His words resonated with me, igniting a fire in my belly. I realized then that I didn't have to face this battle alone. We could take on the world together, navigating the murky waters of uncertainty as partners.

"Let's show him what we're made of," I declared, newfound determination surging through me. "I'm done living in fear of what might happen."

With a nod of agreement, Luke and I stepped forward, united in purpose. The challenges ahead would be daunting, but the strength of our bond and the promise of the unknown ahead filled me with hope. Together, we could create a future that honored my father's legacy and our own dreams, pushing past the darkness that threatened to overwhelm us.

The days that followed Sam's unexpected visit felt like a tightrope walk, each step a careful balance between hope and anxiety. Morning sunrises turned into evenings soaked in golden hues, but beneath the beautiful façade, tension simmered just below the surface. Luke and I worked side by side, our hands engaged in the comforting rhythm of farm life, but the specter of uncertainty loomed large over us. It was like a shadow cast by the sun, an ever-present reminder of the challenges ahead.

One afternoon, as we were hauling crates of ripe tomatoes into the barn, I felt the weight of my thoughts pressing against my temples. Luke caught my eye, an understanding flicker passing between us as if he could sense the storm brewing in my mind. "What's on your mind?" he asked, wiping sweat from his brow with the back of his hand, a playful grin creasing his face.

"Just the usual," I replied, trying to sound nonchalant as I rearranged the crates to give myself a moment to gather my thoughts. "You know, worrying about how to keep this place afloat, dodging Sam's attempts at sabotage, and trying to avoid turning into a complete and utter basket case."

He chuckled, a sound that eased some of my tension. "Sounds like a classic Tuesday for you. But seriously, Hannah, you're putting too much pressure on yourself. What's the worst that could happen?"

I shot him a sidelong glance. "Well, let's see. I could lose the farm, disappoint my dad's memory, and end up working in a fast-food joint flipping burgers." I didn't mean to sound dramatic, but the words poured out before I could rein them in.

Luke leaned against the barn door, arms crossed, a teasing smirk on his lips. "You know, there's nothing wrong with a good burger. They say it's the perfect food. Have you ever tried a double cheeseburger topped with bacon and avocado?"

I rolled my eyes, but a smile crept onto my face. "You're ridiculous. I'm having an existential crisis here, and you want to talk about burgers?"

"Exactly," he said, his tone shifting to something softer. "Maybe the key to getting through it all is to find joy in the little things. We can't control everything, but we can choose to enjoy our time together."

His words struck a chord within me. Finding joy in the little things had always been my mother's mantra. Maybe it was time I started living by that principle again. "Okay, you're right," I admitted, pushing the lingering heaviness from my shoulders. "Let's have a burger night this week. We can even get fancy and grill them outside."

Luke's eyes sparkled with mischief. "Now you're speaking my language. But I warn you, if you burn the patties, I'm coming for your chef's hat."

"Chef's hat? I'll have you know I'm practically a culinary genius," I quipped, striking a pose as if I were on a cooking show.

"Sure, if we're talking about instant ramen," he shot back, laughter dancing in his eyes.

But just as the tension between us began to dissipate, the sound of gravel crunching under tires pierced the lighthearted moment. My heart sank as I recognized the noise of a familiar vehicle—Sam's truck, making its way down the winding dirt road toward the barn. "Great. Just what I needed," I muttered, half-heartedly trying to mask my annoyance.

"Want me to handle this?" Luke offered, his voice steady, but I could see the tension in his jaw.

"No," I said, shaking my head. "I can't keep running from him. This is my farm, and I need to stand my ground."

Luke nodded, respect flickering in his gaze, and I straightened my back, squaring my shoulders as Sam's truck came to a halt. The door swung open, and he emerged, all swagger and smugness, the sunlight catching the gleam in his eyes as if he were the hero of his own twisted story.

"Hello, Hannah," he said, a smug smile spreading across his face. "I hope I'm not interrupting anything important."

"Just enjoying some quality time on the farm," I replied, my tone icy as I refused to back down.

"I thought you might want to discuss that little arrangement we have," he said, his gaze flicking over to Luke, who stood protectively at my side.

"Sam, I've already told you I'm not interested in selling. This is my home." The words tasted bitter on my tongue, but I pushed through, determined to stand firm.

"Oh, but I think you'll change your mind once you see the bigger picture," he said, his tone slick like oil. "You do understand that the bank isn't just going to sit back and watch, right? They're getting impatient."

The air around us thickened with unspoken threats, and I could feel Luke's muscles tense beside me. "What exactly are you implying?" he challenged, his voice low and steady.

"Just that sometimes, letting go is the only option. You could save yourself a lot of trouble, Hannah." Sam took a step closer, invading our space, the confidence in his posture unnerving. "Think of the freedom. A fresh start, far away from this... burden."

I felt a surge of anger rise within me. "This is not a burden, Sam. It's my life. My family's legacy. I won't let you take that away."

"Fighting will only exhaust you," he replied, his tone dripping with faux sympathy. "You should know when you're outmatched."

With that, he turned to leave, but not before throwing a last parting shot over his shoulder. "Just remember, the clock is ticking. I'll be back soon to check on your progress."

The door slammed behind him, and the moment he was gone, the air around us felt lighter, as if a weight had been lifted. But my heart still raced, each thud echoing the fight that had just unfolded.

"What a charming fellow," Luke said, sarcasm dripping from his voice. "Did he take a course in villainy or is it just a natural talent?"

"More like a natural nuisance," I replied, letting out a shaky breath. "I can't believe he thinks I'll just roll over and give up the farm. Does he not understand the meaning of resilience?"

"Clearly not," Luke said, his gaze unwavering. "But Hannah, you need to have a plan. He's not going to back down just because you say no."

I nodded, biting my lip as the reality of the situation set in. "I know. It's just... everything feels so overwhelming. I thought once I started working with you, it would help me gain some clarity."

Luke stepped closer, his eyes searching mine. "We'll figure this out. Together. We're a team now, remember? You're not alone in this fight."

His words were a lifeline, pulling me back from the brink of despair. But even as I nodded, a flicker of doubt lingered in the back of my mind, gnawing at my confidence.

As the sun dipped lower in the sky, casting a warm glow across the fields, I felt a renewed sense of determination wash over me. The battle for the farm was far from over, but I wouldn't face it without a fight. I would protect my father's legacy with everything I had.

But as the shadows began to stretch across the land, a low rumble of thunder echoed in the distance, warning of a storm approaching. It was a reminder that while I was ready to stand my ground, the tumult of the future was brewing just beyond the horizon. And I couldn't shake the feeling that Sam would return, bringing with him the chaos I was desperately trying to avoid.

In that moment, I realized that the fight ahead wouldn't just be about the farm; it would be about my heart, my dreams, and the choices I had yet to make. The sun may have been setting on that day, but the battle for my life—and my future with Luke—was just beginning.

Chapter 7: Torn Between Two Worlds

The sun hung low in the sky, casting a golden hue over the fields as I stood on the porch of our old farmhouse, the wood creaking underfoot. The familiar scent of freshly cut grass mingled with the faint aroma of wildflowers, yet I felt as if I were trapped in a bittersweet memory. It should have been a moment of tranquility, a slice of life where I could lose myself in the beauty of the land my father had cherished, but Sam's return turned that serenity into a tempest.

I caught sight of him across the yard, leaning against the fence, a smug grin playing at the corners of his mouth. He always had that irritating ability to look perfectly at home in our lives, even when he was the storm threatening to uproot everything. With his tousled brown hair and a gaze that could slice through the thickest of atmospheres, he was a thorn in my side. I could almost hear the wheels turning in his mind as he concocted a plan to reclaim what he believed was rightfully his. It was a charade, a false narrative he spun with such ease that it made my stomach churn.

"Isn't it lovely, the way the sun sets?" Sam called out, his voice dripping with insincerity. "Almost as beautiful as the way you're ruining your father's legacy." The jab was delivered with such casual disdain that it sent a shiver through me. The easy charm that had once drawn me in now felt like a venomous snake coiled beneath the surface.

"Do you have to be such an ass, Sam?" I shot back, crossing my arms defensively. "Maybe if you spent less time trying to undermine me, you'd actually do something worthwhile."

"Touché," he replied, amusement dancing in his eyes. "But we both know I've always been more... efficient at this whole farm business." He motioned grandly to the sprawling fields around us.

"You might want to think twice before claiming ownership of this place. I hear rumors spread faster than wildfire in this town."

As his words settled like heavy stones in my chest, I felt the ground beneath me shift. The very thought of Sam wielding influence over my father's legacy sent me spiraling. This was my home, the place where every corner echoed with memories of laughter, sweat, and tears. But the shadows of doubt crept in, fueled by his malicious intent. What if he succeeded? What if I lost everything?

Just then, I heard a gentle voice break through my turmoil. "Don't let him get to you, Mia." Luke stepped onto the porch, his warm presence enveloping me like a well-worn blanket. He had a way of grounding me, of reminding me that even in chaos, there was a flicker of hope.

"I'm trying not to," I admitted, leaning against the wooden railing, grateful for his steady gaze. "But it's hard when he's hell-bent on making me look like the bad guy."

"He's just scared," Luke replied, his brow furrowed in thought. "He sees you stepping up, and he knows you have what it takes to run this place better than he ever could. That kind of power can be intimidating."

"Power? Is that what this is about?" I laughed bitterly, the sound echoing against the farmhouse. "I just want to honor my dad's memory. I'm not interested in power plays or petty arguments."

Luke's eyes softened, and he stepped closer, the warmth radiating from him like sunlight breaking through clouds. "I know. But sometimes, those who fear losing power will do anything to keep it. You need to be ready for that."

His words hung in the air, a lingering promise that somehow made everything feel heavier. I could see the flicker of concern in his eyes, a mixture of admiration and anxiety. I longed to reach out, to assure him that I would fight for this land, for my father's legacy, and for us. But with Sam's machinations threatening our fragile connection, the path forward felt perilous.

As the sun dipped lower, casting long shadows across the porch, I could feel the tension pulsing between us. It was a moment pregnant with unspoken words, and the distance seemed to widen as I wrestled with my conflicting emotions. The weight of expectation pressed down on me like the heavy summer air, suffocating and stifling.

"I wish things were different," I finally said, the honesty spilling out like the twilight spilling across the horizon. "I wish I could just focus on us without all this chaos."

Luke nodded, his expression mirroring my frustration. "Me too. But maybe we can turn this chaos into something positive. If we stand together, we can face whatever Sam throws our way."

His optimism was a beacon in the darkening landscape, and I found myself clinging to it, even as my heart trembled with uncertainty. "You really think so?"

"I know so," he replied, his voice firm and unwavering. "You're stronger than you realize, Mia. And I'm not going anywhere."

Just as I felt the warmth of his words seep into my bones, a sharp laugh cut through the air, sending icy tendrils down my spine. Sam was still lingering nearby, eavesdropping, relishing our moment of vulnerability. "Is this your grand plan? To hold hands and sing songs while I take over?"

I turned, my pulse quickening, ready to retaliate. But before I could formulate a response, Luke stepped in front of me, his presence like a shield. "Why don't you try focusing on your own life, Sam? You know, the one that doesn't revolve around ruining others?"

There was a shift in the air, a tangible energy crackling like the first hints of a summer storm. Sam's grin faltered for a moment, surprise flickering in his eyes before he quickly masked it with feigned indifference. "Oh, I'm just getting started. Enjoy your little fairy tale while it lasts."

As he sauntered away, I could feel the weight of the world hanging on my shoulders. My heart raced with the adrenaline of confrontation, but alongside that rush was a deep-seated fear. How could I possibly navigate the treacherous waters ahead? Torn between my past and the fragile promise of a future with Luke, I stood at the precipice of an impossible choice, aware that every step I took could either fortify or fracture everything I held dear.

The next morning broke with an uncharacteristically muted sunrise, as if even the sky sensed the heaviness that had settled over my heart. I poured a cup of coffee, the steam curling up like tendrils of hope, only to find that I couldn't muster any excitement for the day ahead. The usual rituals felt more like burdens than comforts, each sip a reminder of the precariousness of my situation. I could hear the roosters crowing outside, their calls echoing the chaotic soundtrack of my life—each crow a reminder of Sam's looming threats.

As I stepped onto the porch, I noticed the fields glistening with morning dew, the wheat swaying gently in the breeze like an ocean of gold. Yet, the beauty felt tainted by the shadows of uncertainty. I squinted into the distance, half expecting to see Sam striding toward me, his smirk plastered on his face as if he owned not just the farm, but my very soul.

"Morning, sleepyhead!" Luke's voice broke through my spiraling thoughts. He ambled up the path, his hair tousled and his eyes sparkling with mischief, a welcome sight against the backdrop of my turmoil. I felt a rush of warmth; even the mention of his name made my chest expand with a strange mixture of joy and anxiety.

"Are you always this cheerful, or is it just my misery that's putting you in a good mood?" I shot back, a teasing smile creeping onto my lips, grateful for the brief distraction.

"I could ask you the same," he replied, leaning against the porch railing. "You look like you've seen a ghost. Or maybe just the ghost of your father's legacy haunting you at night?"

"More like Sam playing a twisted game of Farm Monopoly. I just need to keep him from claiming Park Place." I chuckled, though my laughter felt brittle. "What's the strategy here? Do I need to buy more property or just hide the dice?"

"Maybe a little of both," he said, feigning contemplation. "But I'd say we need to roll with the punches. How about a morning of hard labor to distract us from our malevolent friend?"

"You mean actual work? You know I'm more of a 'watch the grass grow' kind of girl," I replied, wrinkling my nose playfully. "But I suppose it might beat wallowing in my worries."

"Great! Let's go then," Luke said, nudging me forward with a mock-seriousness that made me laugh again. "I'll even let you have the first pick on tools."

As we walked into the fields, the air filled with the sweet, earthy scent of soil and growth. We set to work, our laughter ringing out amidst the rustling wheat, a fleeting bubble of joy in an otherwise turbulent sea. With every swing of the hoe and pull of weeds, I could feel the tension in my muscles release, the rhythm of labor grounding me.

"See? You're not just a princess in a tower," Luke said, wiping sweat from his brow. "You can be a queen of the fields."

"Only if the crown is made of wheat," I replied, laughing. "Otherwise, I'll take a tiara made of coffee cups, thank you very much."

We worked side by side, the sun climbing higher and casting playful shadows as our banter flowed freely. I felt the warmth of his presence seep into the cracks of my worries, if only for a moment. But even as we laughed and shared stories, the specter of Sam loomed at the edges of my mind, a reminder that my peace was tenuous at best.

Just as we took a break, plopping down in the shade of an old oak tree, I heard a familiar, unwelcome voice cut through the serenity like a sharp knife. "What a lovely scene," Sam drawled, stepping into our makeshift haven, a devilish smirk on his face that immediately set my teeth on edge.

"What do you want, Sam?" I asked, frustration bubbling to the surface.

"Just admiring the view," he replied, his gaze flickering between Luke and me, a predatory glint in his eye. "I must say, Mia, I didn't take you for the type to waste your time on a farmhand. But then again, you always did prefer the charmingly unambitious."

Luke stiffened beside me, the air growing thick with unspoken tension. "I'm just helping Mia with the farm, Sam. Something you wouldn't understand, given your penchant for playing the victim."

"Ah, the classic defense mechanism: 'Let's just ignore the truth and play house in the dirt.'" Sam chuckled, as if he were the grandmaster of some twisted game. "But you'll need more than playful banter to keep this farm afloat. I've got the backing of the town, you know. They trust me, not you."

"You think I care about their trust?" I shot back, my heart pounding with a mix of anger and fear. "This is my home. I won't let you twist the narrative into something it's not."

"Good luck with that." He turned, casually tossing a final comment over his shoulder. "Just remember, Mia, stories have a way of getting out. And I have a particularly juicy one about a daughter who abandoned her father's farm for a boy."

As he walked away, I felt the weight of his words settle like a lead balloon in my stomach. I could see Luke's jaw clenching, his eyes darkening as he processed the threat that lingered like a storm cloud. "You don't have to let him get to you," he said quietly, his voice steady but laced with concern.

"I know, but he's right about one thing—he's good at spinning stories. And if he convinces the town I'm not capable, I could lose everything," I admitted, frustration spilling out in a rush. "I don't just want this farm; I need it to honor my dad. I can't let him win."

Luke leaned closer, his eyes locked onto mine, fierce determination etched in his features. "Then we fight back. Together."

The heat of his gaze ignited something inside me—a flicker of courage wrapped in a warm blanket of hope. "You really think we can?"

"Absolutely," he replied, his smile igniting a spark of belief. "We just need to show them who you are. You're not just your father's daughter; you're a force in your own right."

I couldn't help but smile back, the tension loosening slightly in my chest. "Okay, then. What's the plan?"

"First, we'll gather everyone who's ever relied on this farm—the workers, the neighbors, anyone who knows what this place means. Then, we'll make sure they all see you in action. They can't deny your passion once they see you fight for it."

I nodded, feeling a surge of determination swell within me. Maybe Sam had the upper hand for now, but with Luke by my side, I felt ready to claw my way back to the surface. We could turn the tide together, turning whispers into shouts and fears into fierce resolve.

As we stood under the shade of that old oak, I could almost hear the echoes of my father's laughter, urging me to rise to the challenge. The road ahead would be rocky, and Sam's machinations would continue to loom, but I refused to let fear dictate my destiny. I would fight not just for the farm, but for the love blossoming between us, fragile yet powerful, ready to bloom amidst the chaos.

The days that followed were an unpredictable whirlwind, each one more chaotic than the last. I found myself in a constant state of alertness, the weight of Sam's words echoing in my mind like a ghost haunting every corner of the farm. The once peaceful landscape was now a battlefield, and I was determined to arm myself with every ounce of strength I could muster.

Luke and I worked tirelessly, not just on the fields, but also on our plan to rally support from the community. Each afternoon, as the sun dipped low, we would spread word around town, gathering allies, both old and new, who understood the heart of this land. I discovered that people remembered my father fondly, his kindness a long-standing legacy. The thought brought a bittersweet comfort, as if he were watching over me, urging me forward.

"Tomorrow night's the town meeting," Luke said one evening as we finished stacking bales of hay. He wiped the sweat from his brow, his eyes sparkling with determination. "This is our chance. If we can show them that you're not just a daughter in distress but a woman ready to take charge, we'll flip this narrative right on its head."

"Flip it? More like turn it into a circus," I quipped, a smirk playing on my lips. "Are you sure you want to be my ringmaster?"

"Only if you promise to wear the sequined leotard," he shot back, chuckling. "I think it would really enhance the whole 'farm girl fighting for her legacy' vibe."

"Sequins and mud? A fashion statement waiting to happen." I laughed, the tension of the situation momentarily melting away. "But in all seriousness, do you really think we can convince them? What if they're already swayed by Sam?"

"I wouldn't underestimate you, Mia. You're stronger than you think. And besides, the truth has a funny way of coming to light, especially when you shine a spotlight on it."

His confidence was infectious, and I couldn't help but feel the embers of hope ignite within me. We spent the evening preparing, going over what I would say, practicing until our voices blended into the fading light of the sunset.

As we headed to town that night, I felt the weight of the community's eyes upon me, a mix of anxiety and determination swirling in my gut. The town hall was a familiar building, with its old wooden beams and creaky floorboards, yet it felt foreign as I entered, each face a reminder of what was at stake. I could see Sam leaning casually against the wall, arms crossed, a smug grin plastered across his face.

"Ah, the prodigal daughter returns," he sneered, the malice in his voice making my stomach twist. "Hope you've come prepared to admit you're out of your depth."

I took a deep breath, Luke beside me, his silent support steadying me. "You know, I used to think your arrogance was charming," I said, my voice unwavering. "Turns out it's just sad."

The meeting began, the atmosphere thick with anticipation. One by one, townsfolk shared their thoughts—some praising my father's legacy, while others, influenced by Sam's underhanded whispers, voiced doubts about my ability to run the farm. Each comment stung, but I kept my composure, allowing the simmering tension to fuel my resolve.

Finally, it was my turn to speak. The room quieted, and I stepped forward, my heart pounding in my chest. "Thank you all for being here," I began, my voice strong despite the anxiety coursing through me. "I know many of you have questions about my intentions with the farm. I want to assure you that my father's legacy means everything to me. This land is not just soil; it's filled with memories of laughter, hard work, and love."

I glanced at Sam, whose expression was now a mix of annoyance and disbelief. "I understand that my absence might have raised concerns," I continued, gathering momentum, "but my father raised me to be resilient. I've come back not to abandon the farm, but to breathe new life into it."

As I spoke, I saw nods of recognition from familiar faces, the glimmer of support igniting hope within me. The longer I spoke, the more I felt like I was stepping into my own power, shedding the weight of Sam's narrative. But just as I reached a crescendo, the door swung open, and in walked someone I hadn't expected—my mother.

Her presence felt like an unexpected gust of wind, blowing through the room and causing heads to turn. I hadn't seen her in months; the last I knew, she was in the city, buried in work and responsibilities that often felt too heavy for her. Her eyes met mine, and for a moment, time stood still. I could see the worry etched across her features, but behind it, a flicker of something—was it pride?

"Mia," she called, her voice cutting through the murmurs. "I should have been here sooner."

A wave of emotions crashed over me—relief, joy, confusion. I thought I had been fighting this battle alone, and now here she was, a force of her own, standing in solidarity.

"Mom," I breathed, my heart racing. "What are you doing here?"

"I came to see how you were doing, to support you," she replied, her eyes shining with sincerity. "I know we've had our differences, but I've always believed in you. This farm is your legacy too, and I won't let anyone take that from you, not even Sam."

My heart swelled, the adrenaline of the moment propelling me forward. "Thank you," I said, my voice cracking slightly. "I need all the support I can get right now."

The air shifted as murmurs of surprise rippled through the crowd. Sam's confident facade crumbled, his expression darkening as he realized he was losing control of the narrative.

With renewed vigor, I continued, "I refuse to let rumors define me or this place. I will fight for the legacy my father built and for the family that stands behind me." I turned to my mother, who nodded in encouragement.

But just as I thought the tide was turning in my favor, the unexpected happened. The mayor, a figure I had always respected, stood up with a grave expression. "Mia," he said, his voice heavy with concern. "I appreciate your passion, but there's something you need to understand."

The room fell silent, the atmosphere thick with anticipation. "Sam isn't just a voice in the wind. He has investors backing him. They're ready to put their money into a development plan that could transform this land into something... lucrative."

My stomach dropped, the weight of his words crashing down on me like a ton of bricks. "What are you saying?" I whispered, barely able to voice the fear that had taken root.

"They want to buy the farm from whoever has control. If you can't prove you're capable of running this place, they'll seize the opportunity," he finished, his gaze steady but full of sympathy.

The walls around me felt like they were closing in. I looked at Luke, whose face mirrored my shock, and then back at my mother, whose eyes were wide with disbelief.

"Is that true?" I demanded, my voice trembling. "You're going to let them take this place away?"

"Listen, Mia," Sam interjected, a smirk creeping back onto his face, "this could be your chance to step aside gracefully. You could save your family the trouble of fighting a losing battle."

The room felt like it was spinning, the implications of what the mayor had said swirling around me like a dark fog. I could see the townspeople glancing at each other, uncertainty clouding their faces. In that moment, I knew I had to fight—not just for my father's legacy, but for the very land that had raised me, the land that felt like a part of my soul.

Just as I was about to respond, the lights flickered ominously, plunging the room into darkness for just a heartbeat before the emergency lights kicked on, casting an eerie glow. I felt a cold chill run down my spine, the shadows in the corners of the room deepening.

And then, just as I was about to reclaim my voice, the emergency lights went out entirely, plunging us into an unexpected darkness. Confused whispers broke out, and I felt the panic rising like a tide.

"Luke?" I called, my voice echoing in the dark, fear creeping in. "Are you still there?"

Silence.

The air thickened with uncertainty, a sense of foreboding hanging heavy in the room. The darkness felt alive, and I could sense the tension rising as everyone shifted, searching for stability in a suddenly chaotic situation.

"Stay close to me," I whispered to no one in particular, my heart racing. I could feel the weight of the moment pressing in on me, the cliff's edge I was standing on suddenly more precarious than ever.

And then, just as my heart settled into a steady thrum of resolve, the lights flickered back on, illuminating a scene that sent a jolt of dread through my entire being. There, standing in the doorway, was a figure cloaked in shadows, the unmistakable outline of someone I thought I'd left behind.

The words I had prepared felt caught in my throat, the tension in the room electric, and I knew that nothing would ever be the same again.

Chapter 8: Revelations

The afternoon sun streamed through the tall windows of my father's study, casting warm, golden patches of light across the floor. The room felt like a museum, frozen in time, filled with books that smelled of aged leather and dusty memories. I could almost hear the whispers of the past swirling around me, urging me to delve deeper into this sanctuary of secrets. It was during one of those restless moments, when the weight of the world seemed to settle on my shoulders, that I stumbled upon it: a letter tucked behind an old, half-closed copy of The Grapes of Wrath. My heart raced as I pulled it out, the envelope yellowed and fragile, as if it were a treasure hidden away from prying eyes for decades.

With trembling fingers, I tore it open, the crisp crackle echoing in the stillness of the room. The handwriting was unmistakable; it was my father's—looping and elegant, each letter imbued with his unmistakable presence. I began to read, my heart pounding in sync with each word. The letter spoke of dreams he had nurtured for the farm, dreams he had woven into the very fabric of our family's history. He wrote of hope, of a future that included both Sam and me, the fields lush and vibrant under the summer sun, laughter echoing between the rows of corn. But beneath the surface of his words, a current of sorrow coursed through, hinting at the struggles Sam faced. My father had hoped for reconciliation before his untimely death, a bridge to be built from the remnants of our fractured relationship.

As I read on, my chest tightened with each revelation. The pain of knowing that my father had been aware of Sam's turmoil, yet felt powerless to mend our broken bond, filled me with a fierce longing for closure. The flicker of hope ignited within me, a small flame daring to challenge the encroaching darkness of grief and resentment. Could this be the catalyst for healing? Could we rewrite our story, turn the page on years of misunderstandings and silence? The thought was intoxicating, but uncertainty loomed larger than the expansive fields outside.

I found myself standing by the window, the vibrant greens of the farmland stretching out before me, as if the land itself was beckoning me to take action. Sam had always been a force of nature, strong-willed and stubborn as the wildflowers that sprouted between the cracks of the pavement. Confronting him would be no small feat, especially considering the chasm that had formed between us. My mind raced with memories of heated arguments, the sharp words exchanged in moments of anger that still lingered like a bitter aftertaste. But perhaps, just perhaps, the letter was the lifeline we both needed.

Gathering my courage, I ventured towards the barn, the heart of our family's legacy, where the scent of hay mingled with the earthy aroma of aged wood. Each step felt heavy with purpose, my heart a wild drum in my chest. I found Sam in the midst of his work, his broad shoulders hunched over as he meticulously checked the tractor. The sunlight danced across his tousled hair, illuminating the tension etched into his brow. I hesitated, the words forming a lump in my throat, but the urgency to bridge the distance between us pushed me forward.

"Sam," I called out, my voice breaking the stillness like the crack of a whip. He turned, surprise flashing in his eyes, quickly replaced by a guarded expression.

"What do you want, Mia?" His tone was sharp, a defensive wall erected between us, and for a moment, I regretted my decision to approach him. But the letter burned in my pocket, a reminder of the hope that had surged within me.

"I found something... something from Dad." My words hung in the air, heavy with unspoken emotions. I could see the flicker of curiosity in his eyes, but it was quickly buried under layers of resentment.

"Great, another one of his 'letters to my perfect children'?" Sam scoffed, wiping his hands on his worn jeans. "What's it going to be this time? More dreams that never came true?"

His bitterness cut deeper than I anticipated, and I took a breath, steeling myself against the sting of his words. "This isn't about that, Sam. It's about you, about us. Dad wanted us to reconcile."

"Reconcile?" he shot back, his voice rising. "What does that even mean anymore? He's gone, and it doesn't change anything. We can't pretend like he didn't die without us ever really talking."

I felt a wave of frustration rising within me, the memories of our past colliding with the weight of our current pain. "I know that! But he left me a letter. He wanted us to heal, to find a way back to each other."

For a heartbeat, silence enveloped us, heavy and palpable, as the tension crackled like electricity in the air. Sam's expression softened for just a moment, the barriers he had built seeming to waver as his defenses faltered. I pressed on, desperation creeping into my voice. "Can we at least read it together? You don't have to do this alone, Sam. I don't want to do this alone."

He hesitated, the conflict written all over his face. I could see the struggle beneath his exterior—the longing for connection battling against the urge to retreat. Finally, with a defeated sigh, he nodded, though the look in his eyes still held an edge of uncertainty.

"Fine," he muttered, leading me into the dimly lit barn. The scent of aged wood and fresh hay enveloped us, the atmosphere shifting as we took a seat on an old crate. I pulled the letter from my pocket, the paper crinkling softly as I unfolded it, the words alive with the weight of our father's hopes and dreams.

As I began to read aloud, I felt the walls between us start to crumble, each word a brick removed from the fortress we had both fortified over the years. And as I read, I realized that the path to healing was not as simple as I had hoped. It would be fraught with pain, vulnerability, and the rawness of emotions long buried. Yet, amid the uncertainty, I felt the flicker of possibility—a chance to forge a new bond from the ashes of our past.

As the last words of the letter faded into the warm air of the barn, an uncomfortable silence enveloped us, wrapping around our shoulders like an old blanket—one that was too scratchy to be comforting but familiar enough to elicit a shiver of recognition. Sam sat beside me, his expression inscrutable as he processed what I had just read. The words of our father hung between us, a fragile bridge over a chasm filled with years of unspoken grievances and shared grief.

"I can't believe he thought we could just... fix everything," Sam finally said, his voice barely above a whisper, laden with skepticism. He leaned back against the crate, the wood creaking beneath his weight, and stared at the wooden beams above us as if searching for answers in their splintered textures. "It's not that simple, Mia."

"Maybe it can be," I replied, surprising myself with the confidence in my voice. "We can't change the past, but we can try to move forward. Isn't that what he wanted?"

Sam's laughter was bitter, like the taste of burnt coffee. "What did Dad know about moving forward? He couldn't even get us to sit at the same dinner table without turning it into a battlefield. I can't believe you're hanging on to this idea that we can just become a family again."

The hurt in his tone was palpable, and for a moment, I felt the urge to pull away, to retreat into the safety of my own defenses. But as I looked at him—really looked at him—I saw the boy I had grown up with, the brother I had laughed with, fought with, and shared secrets under the stars. "Look, I'm not asking you to forget everything," I said, my voice steady despite the whirlpool of emotions stirring inside me. "But we have this chance to try. Dad wanted us to be a team. Can't we at least explore that?"

His expression softened for a moment, and I saw the flicker of hope I had felt earlier mirrored in his eyes, yet it was quickly doused by an overwhelming wave of doubt. "And if it doesn't work? What if it just ends up worse?"

I leaned forward, resting my elbows on my knees, my gaze fixed on the dirt-streaked floor, where shadows danced like playful spirits. "Then we'll figure it out together. At least we won't be doing it alone."

Sam's silence spoke volumes, a cacophony of conflict echoing in the spaces between us. I could almost hear the wheels turning in his mind, the struggle of weighing the risks against the potential for healing. I knew my brother well enough to understand that he had spent years shielding himself with cynicism, barricading his heart against disappointment. But this was our chance to break through those walls, to reforge our bond in the fires of honesty and vulnerability.

"Fine," he finally said, his tone begrudging but softer. "Let's say I'm willing to try. What does that even look like? You think we can just waltz into each other's lives and pretend everything's hunky-dory?"

A smile tugged at the corners of my mouth, warmed by the tiniest glimmer of triumph. "Hunky-dory? Who uses that term anymore? But yes, I think we can start by being honest about what we've been through and how it's affected us."

"I'm not a therapist, Mia," he shot back, his eyes narrowing playfully. "You want to talk feelings? I've got a long list of things I'd rather do. Like, I don't know, wrestling an alligator?"

"Very funny," I rolled my eyes, but the tension in my shoulders eased slightly. "Look, we can start small. What's the first thing that pops into your head when you think of Dad?"

He considered this for a moment, and I could see the gears turning in his mind. "His obsession with the weather," he finally said, a hint of a smile breaking through. "Always checking the forecast as if it would change the fact that the crops could still fail. Remember the year we lost everything to that freak hailstorm?"

"Yeah, he was convinced it was a sign from the universe trying to teach him a lesson." I chuckled, the memory of my father's earnest belief in cosmic signs flooding back. "I think he spent the whole summer talking about how he'd be a better farmer if only the universe would cooperate."

"Maybe it was less about him being a better farmer and more about the universe not wanting to hear his whining," Sam retorted, his voice lightening with the banter. "I mean, I've never seen someone throw such a tantrum over a weather report."

Laughter bubbled up between us, a sweet sound that broke through the tension like sunlight piercing through clouds. For the first time in a long while, I felt the air shift around us, charged with something hopeful, something that spoke of possibilities.

"See?" I said, grinning. "This isn't so hard. We just have to remember who we were before everything went to hell."

"Who we were, huh?" he mused, crossing his arms as he leaned back, a thoughtful look creeping onto his face. "We were pretty damn annoying."

"Speak for yourself," I shot back, nudging him playfully. "I was the perfect child. You were just jealous because I could still climb the tree in the backyard without breaking a bone."

"Perfect, my foot. You fell out of that tree more than anyone else I know."

"That's not the point!" I protested, the warmth of our laughter spilling over the shadows that had gathered in the corners of our hearts. "The point is, we had fun. We were a team, despite the bickering. We can get back there."

As we exchanged playful jabs, I felt the remnants of our childhood weaving through the air, reconnecting the threads of our shared history. The laughter felt like a lifeline, tugging at the edges of the darkness that had settled between us. Yet beneath the humor lingered the truth: the path ahead would not be easy. But in that moment, I felt the possibility of rebuilding, of rediscovering the bond that had once felt unbreakable.

"Okay, so what's next?" Sam asked, tilting his head as if he were considering whether to take a leap of faith or retreat back into his fortress of skepticism.

"Next, we tackle the heavy stuff," I replied, the gravity of the situation creeping back in. "We talk about what hurt us. We face the things we've avoided for too long."

"Sounds like fun," he replied, his tone half-sarcastic but also tinged with resignation. "Let's throw a party, invite all our trauma for a good time."

"Just don't expect a piñata," I shot back, trying to keep the lightness in my voice despite the seriousness of our task ahead. "But seriously, I think we owe it to ourselves to be honest."

"Right," he sighed, the bravado slipping slightly. "Honesty is the best policy. Until it gets uncomfortable, then it's all bets off."

"Agreed. But let's at least try, Sam. We owe it to Dad, and more importantly, to ourselves."

He met my gaze, and for a moment, the vulnerability in his expression mirrored my own. There was fear there, yes, but there was also the flicker of hope that had sparked in me earlier. "Alright, Mia. Let's do this," he said, his voice steadying. "But if this goes south, I'm blaming you."

"Fair enough," I replied, unable to suppress a grin. "But if it works, I'm taking all the credit."

With that, we set out on a journey neither of us had anticipated, stepping into the unknown with a mix of trepidation and resolve.

The air around us buzzed with possibility, the future stretching out like the vast, open fields surrounding the farm—ready for us to cultivate anew.

In the days that followed our tentative truce, the air in the barn shifted from heavy with unresolved tension to something more buoyant, a space where memories and laughter intertwined like the vines creeping up the weathered walls. We had agreed to face our past, but every day felt like we were tiptoeing through a minefield, the next misstep capable of detonating old wounds.

Sam and I fell into a new rhythm, a tentative dance of honesty layered with the familiar comfort of sibling banter. Our conversations oscillated between playful jabs and deeper explorations of our memories. It was cathartic, like finally taking a deep breath after holding it for too long. Yet, each laugh shared also carried an undercurrent of tension, as if we were both aware that beneath the surface lay unresolved issues waiting to resurface.

One afternoon, the sky hung low and gray, a perfect backdrop for introspection. The scent of rain wafted through the open barn doors, mingling with the musk of hay and the sharp tang of metal from the farm equipment. Sam and I sat perched on an old wooden beam, swinging our legs like children, gazing out at the sprawling fields beyond, the golden cornstalks bending slightly in the wind. I turned to him, feeling the weight of our conversations pressing on my chest.

"Do you remember the summer when we decided to build that treehouse?" I asked, a grin stretching across my face at the memory. "I swear we thought we could construct the next architectural marvel."

Sam chuckled, his eyes sparkling with nostalgia. "Yeah, with my master plan and your 'superior vision.' That thing was a death trap. I think I still have the scar from when you tried to use that rusty saw."

"You mean your 'I can do it all' bravado?" I shot back, laughing. "What was I supposed to do, just let you handle the power tools alone?"

"Please," he replied, rolling his eyes with mock exasperation. "I was the one who got us halfway up that tree before you decided to do a 'safety inspection' on the rickety ladder."

"That was an important job!" I retorted, though I could feel the warmth of embarrassment creeping into my cheeks. "You should have seen how it swayed. I was trying to save our lives!"

A silence fell between us, tinged with laughter that faded into a softer reminiscence. I could see Sam's gaze drifting into the distance, as if he were peering through the haze of time to that long-ago summer when we were blissfully unaware of the complexities waiting for us in adulthood.

"Those were the days," he finally murmured, his voice low. "When the biggest problem was whether we could get Mom to let us stay up past bedtime to finish that book series."

"Or whether you could convince me to share my candy stash," I added, a teasing lilt in my tone. "You had an uncanny way of making me feel guilty enough to give it up."

He shrugged, a half-smile breaking through the weight of our earlier conversations. "I learned from the best, didn't I? Manipulation 101 taught by Mia."

I nudged him playfully, but the lightness began to wane as reality crept back in. "But really, Sam, I think it's important we address what happened after... well, after everything fell apart." The gravity of my words hung in the air like the storm clouds brewing outside.

He turned to me, the humor fading from his expression. "You mean, how we went from building treehouses to avoiding each other like the plague?"

"Exactly." I swallowed hard, the knot in my stomach tightening. "We can't move forward if we keep sidestepping the truth. I think it's time we talk about the night Dad died."

His brow furrowed as the air thickened with the weight of unspoken words. "You think I've forgotten?"

"I don't think you can forget. None of us can. But it feels like we haven't faced it together, like we've both buried it under layers of anger and resentment."

Sam took a deep breath, the kind that seemed to shake him to his core. "What's there to say? He left us with a mess, and I wasn't equipped to handle it. I thought I was, but..." His voice trailed off, his eyes clouded with the memories of that night—an echo of our father's final moments, the urgency of that phone call, the suffocating fear that had gripped us both.

"I was scared, too," I admitted, my heart pounding in my chest. "I think we both were. But pushing each other away didn't help. It just made everything worse."

"What do you want me to say, Mia?" His frustration flickered like a match on the verge of going out. "Do you want an apology? Because I'm not sorry for trying to survive."

"No, it's not about that," I insisted, my voice firm yet gentle. "I want us to understand each other. To know we're still here, even if it feels like everything we knew is gone."

His jaw clenched as he processed my words. "I don't even know what to feel anymore. It's like being on a roller coaster where all the safety bars are gone and every turn makes me want to throw up."

"Let's at least take the ride together," I said, trying to inject a bit of lightness back into our conversation, though the underlying tension persisted like a fog. "If we crash, at least we'll crash as a team."

He let out a short laugh, and I could see him softening. "Okay, you're a little ridiculous. But maybe you have a point."

"Maybe?" I challenged, raising an eyebrow.

"Fine! You win this round," he grumbled, feigning defeat, though a spark of camaraderie flickered back into his eyes. "So, what do we do? Call in a therapist, or do we dive right into the deep end?"

"Let's just talk," I suggested, feeling the urge to push a little further, to unravel the layers between us. "No therapists, no filters. Just us."

"Alright," he sighed, leaning back against the beam, and for a moment, I thought we might truly be on the verge of breaking through.

The rain began to patter against the barn roof, a soft rhythm that echoed the increasing heartbeat of our conversation. I could feel the electricity in the air, a mix of uncertainty and anticipation. It was as if the storm outside mirrored the turmoil within us, swirling with the promise of revelation.

"Do you ever think about what Dad would say if he saw us like this?" Sam asked, his tone shifting. "Like, would he be disappointed or would he just be... angry?"

"I think he'd be frustrated," I replied, letting the thought settle. "He always believed in us, even when we couldn't see it ourselves. He'd want us to be stronger than the things that broke us."

"Stronger, huh?" Sam echoed, his voice barely above a whisper. "That's a tall order. Especially when I still feel like a failure."

I shifted closer to him, hoping to share the warmth that had been rekindled between us. "You're not a failure. You've carried the weight of this farm on your shoulders since he left. That's not something anyone can do alone."

"Maybe," he conceded, but there was still an edge to his words, a vulnerability lurking just beneath the surface.

As the rain intensified, the sound drummed louder above us, drowning out the noise of our thoughts for a moment. I closed my eyes, letting the rhythm wash over me, hoping it would cleanse away some of the pain we had carried for so long. But then, just as I felt the tension beginning to ease, a loud crash echoed through the barn, followed by the unmistakable sound of something breaking.

Startled, we both jumped to our feet, the moment of connection shattered like glass. "What the hell was that?" Sam's voice was sharp, his protective instincts kicking in.

"I don't know, but it sounded like it came from the back of the barn," I said, my heart racing as I exchanged a worried glance with him.

"We should check it out," he said, a flicker of determination igniting in his eyes.

We moved cautiously, the sound of our footsteps muted by the pattering rain, the atmosphere shifting from warmth to apprehension. As we rounded the corner of the barn, the light filtering through the windows revealed a scene that made my stomach drop: a large crate had toppled over, scattering its contents across the floor, but what caught my eye was not the spilled grain—it was the unmistakable glint of something metallic sticking out from the hay.

"Sam," I breathed, my voice barely a whisper as I knelt to investigate. My heart raced as I reached toward the object, every instinct telling me that whatever lay beneath the hay might alter everything.

Chapter 9: The Fight for Home

The wind whipped through the tall grass of the field, creating a gentle rustling that felt like whispers of the past. I stood on the threshold of the barn, the familiar scent of hay and old wood wrapping around me like a well-worn blanket. This place, once vibrant with laughter and dreams, now felt haunted by echoes of conflict. The golden light of late afternoon bathed everything in warmth, yet my heart was encased in a chill that refused to melt away.

As I took a step forward, the heavy wooden door creaked open, its hinges groaning in protest. There he was, Sam, framed in the doorway, his hands shoved deep into the pockets of his worn jeans. His disheveled hair caught the light just right, creating an almost ethereal halo that made him look both infuriatingly handsome and heartbreakingly distant. "You really think you can just waltz back in here and act like everything's fine?" His voice was low, the weight of his words settling over me like a heavy fog.

"I don't need to act!" I retorted, my voice ringing against the barn walls, bouncing back with a sharpness that echoed my frustration. "This place is part of me, Sam. You can't just lock me out because it suits you." The air between us crackled with unspoken words, the tension thick enough to cut with a knife. I could feel the fire within me igniting, the anger fueled by years of absence and regret, but it was also the fear of losing the one place I had always considered home.

His expression hardened, and for a moment, I saw a flash of something vulnerable in his eyes—hurt, perhaps. "You left, Mia. You chose Chicago over this," he shot back, each word dripping with bitterness. "How can I trust you now?"

The words stung more than I wanted to admit. "You think it was easy for me? You think I wanted to leave?" My voice trembled, but I pushed on, determined not to show weakness. "I had to figure out who I was without all this. I thought—" I paused, searching for the right words, "I thought that maybe by leaving, I could come back stronger. I could help save this place."

"Save it from what? From me?" His laugh was humorless, slicing through the air like a jagged blade. "You're here to save it? You didn't even want to be part of it anymore. You wanted the city lights and the fancy life."

"Don't you dare put that on me," I snapped, my heart racing as memories surged to the surface—nights spent dreaming of escape, days filled with the suffocating weight of expectations. "I wanted to find myself, but now I realize that part of me is here. This land, this family... it's where I belong."

Just as the silence threatened to swallow us whole, the distant sound of a truck engine rumbled toward us, cutting through the heaviness that had settled like a storm cloud. A flash of hope surged through me as I recognized the silhouette of Luke's pickup, his familiar blue truck coming to my rescue like a knight in dusty armor. I had always appreciated how he showed up when I needed him most, but this time felt different. This time, I was sure of my choice, and the reality of the situation pressed heavily upon me.

Luke stepped out, his presence grounding, a smile breaking across his face that always lit up the dimmest moments. "Hey! Hope I'm not interrupting," he called out, his voice cheerful and full of warmth, but I could see the tension in his shoulders as he assessed the scene unfolding before him.

"Perfect timing, as usual," I muttered, my eyes darting back to Sam, who stood rigid, arms crossed, an impenetrable wall of stubbornness. "We were just having a friendly chat."

Luke raised an eyebrow, glancing between us with that trademark blend of humor and concern. "Friendly, huh? Looks more like a duel to the death. Do I need to grab my sword?"

For a brief moment, the corners of my mouth twitched upwards, but the underlying tension remained. "No sword necessary," I replied, forcing a smile that felt both foreign and fragile. "But your presence is definitely appreciated."

"Just don't let him get under your skin," Luke said, his voice softening as he stepped closer to me, offering an anchor against the turbulent emotions swirling around us. "You know how stubborn he can be."

"Stubborn? I'm not the one who left," Sam interjected, his voice tinged with resentment, but I could sense a flicker of doubt in his stance. The storm raging within him was palpable, but maybe, just maybe, the winds were beginning to shift.

"I didn't leave you," I said quietly, my gaze steady on Sam, refusing to back down. "I left because I didn't know how to stay. But I'm here now, fighting for this place—fighting for us."

"Us?" Sam echoed, incredulity mixing with confusion. "You think there's still an 'us' left to fight for?"

"Maybe not the way you think," I said, my voice softening, a gentle truth spilling forth. "But there's something here, something worth saving. Not just the land but everything that it represents. Family, forgiveness, love."

The three of us stood there, suspended in a moment thick with unspoken words and unresolved feelings, the weight of the past looming over us like the shadows of the barn. My heart pounded, a fierce drumbeat echoing the hope that perhaps we could find common ground amid the debris of our shared history.

"Together," Luke said, his hand brushing against mine, a warm anchor in this storm. "We can face whatever comes next. You don't have to fight alone."

I looked at him, his strength steadying me, and then back to Sam, whose eyes shimmered with the pain of the unacknowledged. In that moment, I understood that love isn't always a grand gesture;

sometimes, it's simply standing side by side, facing the chaos of life together, ready to forge a new path through the wreckage of the old.

The silence that followed Luke's declaration hung in the air like a thick fog, wrapping around us and dampening the heat of our argument. I could see the tension in Sam's jaw tighten, the lines of frustration etched deep into his brow. The moment felt precarious, as if one wrong word could send everything crashing down. The world around us faded into a distant blur, the only reality being this triad of unspoken emotions, glaring truths, and unresolved pasts.

"Together," I echoed Luke's sentiment, willing my voice to steady as I turned back to Sam. "We can face this together, but you have to let me back in. I need you to understand that I didn't come back to undo the past; I came to help us rebuild."

"Rebuild what, exactly?" Sam shot back, crossing his arms defensively. "This isn't a Lego set, Mia. It's our lives." His eyes burned with a fierce intensity that matched the fiery sky above us, and I could sense the storm brewing within him.

"You think I don't know that?" I said, frustration spilling out like a tidal wave. "Every day I was gone, I felt that emptiness. This isn't just about the farm or the land—it's about all of us. It's about the laughter we shared, the dreams we built together in this very place. I want to find a way back to that."

"I don't think you understand how hard it is to just forget," Sam replied, his voice now softer, edged with something almost fragile. "It's not easy for any of us. You left, and in doing so, you changed everything."

"And you stayed," I countered gently. "You took on the burden of keeping it all together. I can't even begin to imagine how lonely that must have felt." The sincerity of my words hung between us like a lifeline. "But what if we could change it together? What if we could bring back the joy, the love? I'm not asking you to forget, but to find a way forward."

For a moment, the air thickened with possibility. Sam's expression shifted, the harsh lines of anger softening as uncertainty flickered across his face. Luke squeezed my hand, a reassuring gesture that tethered me to the moment.

"Do you really think we can go back to how things were?" Sam asked, his voice barely above a whisper. "Things aren't the same, Mia. They can't be."

"Maybe they can't be exactly the same," I admitted, my heart racing at the prospect of an uncertain future. "But they can be different. We can create something new, a stronger foundation. We owe it to ourselves to try."

Sam looked away, his gaze drifting toward the horizon, where the sun dipped low, painting the sky in hues of orange and lavender. The fleeting beauty of the moment stirred something deep within me, a longing for connection that felt both terrifying and exhilarating. I stepped closer, the warmth radiating from Luke's body amplifying my resolve. "You don't have to face this alone, Sam. Let me help."

"What do you even want from me?" he asked, the vulnerability in his tone cutting through the remnants of tension like a gentle breeze.

"I want you to be honest with me," I replied, my voice steady. "I want us to have real conversations, even the hard ones. I want you to let me in, Sam. I want to be a part of this."

Luke shifted beside me, his warmth a solid presence as I met Sam's gaze. "We're not here to make demands, but to offer support. We're on the same team, right?" he chimed in, attempting to diffuse the air thick with unacknowledged feelings.

Sam sighed heavily, a sound filled with the weight of years lost and memories tangled. "I just don't know if I can trust that you'll stay this time."

"It's fair to feel that way," I conceded, feeling a pang of regret for the past I had left behind. "But I'm not the same person who left. I've changed, and I hope you have too. We can be different together."

The silence that followed felt heavy, yet somehow hopeful. I could see the gears turning in Sam's mind, the barriers he had erected beginning to falter. Just as I felt a flicker of triumph, a loud clatter broke through the tranquility. A few goats, clearly intent on making their escape, dashed across the field, bleating in protest.

"Well, it looks like they're not interested in our heartfelt reunion," Luke said, his tone light as he chuckled at the chaos unfolding before us. "Should we wrangle them back? I think that's our calling."

"I can't believe they're still getting out," Sam grumbled, but a reluctant smile tugged at the corners of his mouth. "You'd think they'd learned their lesson after the last time."

As the three of us rushed into action, the absurdity of the moment shattered the tension like glass. We chased after the mischievous goats, laughter bubbling up from deep within me as I darted past Sam, feeling the thrill of the chase ignite my spirit. The goats zigzagged across the field, their unpredictable movements sending us into a flurry of chaos and camaraderie.

"Hey, that one's heading for the corn! Stop it!" Sam shouted, lunging forward in a futile attempt to corral the goat.

"I think it's a conspiracy against us," I panted, breathless and exhilarated, my heart racing not just from the sprint but from the sudden surge of lightness. "They want to test our unity!"

"More like test our sanity," Luke replied, his laughter mingling with the bleats as he sprinted after the goats. I couldn't help but laugh along, the sound bubbling up and spilling into the air, a mixture of joy and relief.

Finally, after what felt like a hilarious eternity, we managed to corral the errant goats back into their pen. We stood there, panting and leaning against the fence, our laughter still echoing through the fields. Sam's expression had shifted; the anger and resentment had ebbed, replaced by something softer.

"Maybe we're all a little lost," he said, glancing at me, his eyes sparkling with mischief and vulnerability. "But I think I could get used to having you back, even if it means chasing goats."

"Chasing goats might just be the highlight of my return," I shot back, the warmth blooming in my chest. "But seriously, we'll find our way, Sam. One goat at a time."

As we stood together, laughter still lingering in the air, I felt a sense of connection and hope blooming within me. It wasn't a perfect solution, and the road ahead would be challenging, but maybe we could forge a path forward that honored the past while embracing the potential of what was to come.

The goats settled back into their pen, their antics fading into a comical memory that hung in the air like the sweet scent of freshly cut grass. Luke leaned against the fence, his chest heaving from the effort and laughter, while Sam stood slightly apart, a smile lingering on his lips, albeit one touched with uncertainty. I felt the electricity of the moment still crackling around us, a palpable shift that promised new beginnings if only we dared to grasp it.

"So, what's next?" Luke asked, breaking the comfortable silence. His gaze flickered between Sam and me, sensing the unspoken conversations swirling in the air. "More goat wrangling? I'm sure they're plotting their next escape as we speak."

"Maybe we should set up a surveillance team," I quipped, nudging Sam playfully. "You know, to monitor goat behavior. It could be a new branch of farm management."

Sam chuckled, a genuine sound that sent a warm rush through me. "I'd rather manage actual crops than chase down these little escape artists. But hey, if it brings you back into my life, maybe it's worth it."

The sincerity in his voice made my heart flutter, the warmth of his words wrapping around me like a soft blanket. I knew then that we were standing on the precipice of something—something big, something important. But just as hope began to take root, a dark cloud rolled in, shadowing the sunlight that had been so bright just moments ago.

"I still have to talk to my parents," I said, glancing back toward the house, which stood tall and steadfast against the horizon. "They're probably wondering where I've been."

"Your parents are going to have a lot of questions," Sam replied, his tone turning serious. "They've been worried sick, especially since the farm has been struggling. They thought you were happy in Chicago."

"Happy?" I snorted, unable to hide the bitterness that seeped into my voice. "I was suffocating in my own skin. It was like being trapped in a world where everything was shiny and perfect on the outside but empty inside."

Luke placed a comforting hand on my shoulder, a steadying presence that calmed the tumult within me. "You don't have to face them alone. We can go together. They'll understand if we explain things."

The thought sent a jolt of anxiety through me. "What if they don't? What if they see my return as a failure?"

"Then you remind them that it takes courage to admit when you're lost," Sam said, his gaze unwavering. "They just want to see you happy, Mia. And honestly, I think they're probably too busy worrying about the farm to judge your life choices right now."

"Besides," Luke chimed in with a playful wink, "I'll just distract them with my charming personality."

"Oh, I wouldn't bet on that," Sam shot back, the teasing banter easing the tension in my chest.

"Seriously, Luke," I said, trying to sound stern while the corners of my mouth betrayed me, "you're going to have to be on your best behavior. No goat impressions at dinner."

He laughed, holding his hands up in mock surrender. "Alright, no goat impressions. But I can't promise I won't do a chicken dance."

"Definitely not," I said, shaking my head with a grin. "You might scare them off for good."

"Fine, but I'm keeping it in my back pocket for later," he replied, chuckling.

Just as the levity enveloped us like a warm embrace, a sharp shriek pierced the air. My heart raced as I turned toward the house, where I saw the figure of my mother standing on the porch, her hand over her mouth, her eyes wide with alarm. "Mia! Sam!" she called, panic lacing her voice. "Come quick! It's your father!"

All laughter evaporated in an instant, replaced by a thick fog of dread that settled in my stomach. I exchanged a look with Sam, his earlier ease replaced by worry, his expression now taut with urgency.

"Stay here!" I commanded Luke, even as I started toward the house, adrenaline propelling me forward. "Call the doctor!"

I sprinted up the porch steps, the wooden boards creaking beneath my feet, the sun's warm glow now replaced by a chilling shadow that hung over everything. My mother stood frozen, her face pale, her hands shaking as she pointed toward the living room.

"Mom, what happened?" I demanded, fear lacing my voice as I stepped inside, my heart pounding a wild rhythm against my ribs.

"It's your father," she whispered, tears spilling down her cheeks. "He... he collapsed."

Every instinct screamed for me to rush to him, but I hesitated, a lump forming in my throat. "Is he breathing? What did the doctor say?"

She shook her head, the anguish etched on her face making my chest constrict painfully. "I don't know. I just found him like this. Please, Mia... he needs you."

With a deep breath, I bolted toward the living room, my legs almost refusing to carry me as the weight of dread pulled me down. The air was thick with the scent of old wood and fading memories, the sunlight filtering through the curtains casting long shadows across the floor.

There he was, my father, sprawled on the floor, his face pale and lifeless against the wood. My heart plummeted into a pit of despair, a scream clawing its way up my throat. "Dad!" I cried, rushing to his side. "Wake up! Please, wake up!"

He lay there, unmoving, and as I knelt beside him, the world around me blurred into an indistinct haze, my mother's voice fading into the background. The only sound that remained was the pounding of my heart, frantic and wild.

"Mia, let me check his pulse," Sam said gently, kneeling beside me, his presence a lifeline in the storm of panic. I could barely nod, my focus solely on my father's face, the memories of his laughter and warmth swirling around me like ghosts in the air.

"Please, please," I whispered, desperation lacing my voice as Sam pressed his fingers against my father's wrist. "Don't leave us."

Then, in the tense silence, the house held its breath, waiting for the verdict that would change everything.

Chapter 10: Broken Bonds

The sun hung low, painting the sky in hues of gold and lavender, a canvas of warmth that contrasted sharply with the storm brewing inside me. I kicked at the dirt beneath my feet, watching as the particles danced and settled, a futile attempt to distract myself from the echoes of the fight with Sam that had reverberated through my mind for days. Every word exchanged, every accusation hurled, felt like a stone thrown into a still pond, creating ripples of doubt that threatened to drown me. My heart was a heavy anchor, tethering me to the guilt and confusion swirling around our fractured relationship.

The field stretched endlessly, a sea of waving wheat that whispered secrets only the wind could understand. I inhaled deeply, the earthy scent of tilled soil mixing with the sweet notes of sun-ripened grain. Nature's beauty felt almost mocking in its tranquility, a sharp contrast to the chaos swirling within me. I longed for clarity, for the certainty that had once defined my life, but all I had were these tangled thoughts that wrapped around my heart like thorny vines.

As I wandered, lost in my reverie, a familiar voice broke through the haze. "Hey! You're a long way from home." Luke's tone was teasing, but there was an edge of concern woven through it, a thread that tugged at my heartstrings. I turned to see him approaching, his silhouette framed against the sunset, a figure of strength and warmth that seemed to radiate a calm I so desperately craved.

He wore that infuriatingly charming half-smile, the one that always seemed to draw me in, as if he could see through the layers of my turmoil. I couldn't help but smile back, though it felt more like a reflex than a genuine reaction. Luke had this knack for making me feel like the world was still bright, even when I was engulfed in shadows.

"Thought I'd find you out here," he said, sliding down onto the weathered fence beside me. The wood was rough against my palms, a tangible reminder of the passage of time, much like the shifting currents of our lives. "You look like you could use some company."

"Yeah, company sounds great," I replied, my voice faltering as the weight of my emotions threatened to spill over. The last thing I wanted was to burden him with my chaotic thoughts, but the vulnerability in his eyes urged me to speak.

"Tell me what's going on," he prompted, his gaze steady, unwavering. The earnestness in his voice stirred something deep within me, pushing me to open up despite the knot in my stomach.

I took a breath, the warm air filling my lungs as I collected my thoughts. "It's just... Sam. We had this huge fight, and I don't even know why it escalated like that. It feels like everything is unraveling." My words tumbled out, desperate and unfiltered. "I keep thinking about what Dad built, how much it means to all of us, and I don't want to be the reason it falls apart."

Luke shifted closer, his fingers brushing against mine, sending a spark of comfort through me. "You're not going to be the reason for anything. Sam is just as responsible for the fight, and he knows it. He's your brother; you've been through so much together."

"Together, yes," I muttered, bitterness creeping into my voice. "But he feels so different now. Like a stranger. It's as if I've lost him to this... this rift that keeps widening." I looked out over the field, where the wheat danced in rhythm with the soft breeze, an illusion of peace that felt worlds away from the storm inside my chest.

Luke squeezed my hand, grounding me in the moment. "Relationships evolve, but that doesn't mean you can't find your way back to each other. Just because you're not on the same page right now doesn't mean you can't write a new chapter."

His words were simple yet profound, and I marveled at how effortlessly he seemed to untangle my chaotic thoughts. "You make it sound so easy. Like we can just patch things up with a few well-placed words and everything will be fine." The sarcasm dripped from my tone, a shield I often used to deflect the reality of my feelings.

"It's not easy. But nothing worth fighting for ever is," he replied, his voice steady as if he were recounting a well-known fact. "Look, I know Sam can be stubborn. Trust me, I've seen it. But you two have a bond that can withstand this storm. Just like you and me." His gaze locked onto mine, a spark of determination igniting between us.

The sincerity in his words warmed me, igniting a flicker of hope that had long been dormant. "What if I mess it up even more?" I whispered, the fear lacing my words heavy and thick. "What if he doesn't want to reconcile?"

"Then you keep trying. You don't give up on family." Luke leaned in closer, his breath warm against my skin. "You'd fight for your father's legacy, right? Well, Sam is part of that legacy. He's family, and families fight for each other, even when it's hard."

I chuckled softly, the sound laced with a bittersweet edge. "You're quite the motivational speaker, aren't you?" The moment felt lighter, the weight on my chest lifting just a bit under the warmth of his presence.

"Only for you," he said, flashing that disarming smile that made me feel like I was the only person in the world. "Now, how about we figure out a plan? You can't let this eat you alive."

The determination in his voice was contagious, and for the first time in days, I felt a sense of clarity. The shadows began to recede, replaced by the flickering candlelight of hope. Together, we could navigate the murky waters of familial ties, and somehow, we might just find our way back to the surface.

As the sun dipped lower in the sky, casting long shadows over the field, I felt a strange warmth bubbling up inside me, ignited by Luke's steadfast presence. It was as if he had drawn a line in the sand, separating my swirling fears from the promise of a brighter horizon.

I squeezed his hand back, the steady thrum of connection grounding me, reminding me that even amidst the turmoil, there was still light.

"Okay," I began, feeling emboldened. "Let's say you're right. Let's say Sam and I can work this out. What do I even say to him?" The uncertainty in my voice hung between us like a thick fog, clouding the clarity I'd started to feel.

Luke leaned back against the fence, his gaze thoughtful, as if he were measuring the words carefully before he released them into the air. "Just be honest. Tell him how you feel. Sometimes, the truth is all it takes to break down walls."

"Honest, huh?" I snorted, the skepticism lacing my voice. "Sam isn't exactly known for his receptiveness to feelings. He prefers to handle everything with a dose of sarcasm and a side of stubbornness." I could practically hear the sharp edge of Sam's retorts, a sound I once found comforting, now feeling like a weapon wielded against me.

"Sounds like he takes after someone," Luke said, a smirk tugging at the corner of his mouth. "You know, I could be mistaken, but I think that sarcasm might run in the family."

I rolled my eyes, but the warmth of his teasing broke through the tension. "Ha ha. Very funny. But seriously, do you think he'll even listen? I mean, we're talking about a guy who once tried to fix a leaky roof with duct tape and sheer willpower."

"Sounds like a solid plan," Luke said, winking at me. "If all else fails, you can always challenge him to a race up that hill." He gestured toward the distant rise, its grassy slope standing tall against the sunset. "It's hard to argue with someone while they're panting for air."

A laugh burst from my lips, the sound startling even me. The thought of Sam, too proud to back down from a challenge, stumbling over his own feet, was just ridiculous enough to lighten the mood. "Okay, maybe that's a solid tactic. If all else fails, I can always resort to embarrassing him in front of the cows."

"See? We're getting somewhere." He leaned closer, his voice dropping to a conspiratorial whisper. "I'm pretty sure the cows are great listeners. They could be your emotional support animals during this whole mess."

I nudged him playfully, the camaraderie between us a balm for my frazzled nerves. But beneath the laughter, a wave of anxiety washed over me. I was all too aware that, as much as I wanted to brush this off as a mere family squabble, it was more than that. Sam and I had navigated so many turbulent waters together; this felt like a fault line that could either tear us apart or bring us closer.

"You know, sometimes I think I'm just as stubborn as Sam," I admitted, my voice quieter, the weight of truth settling in. "I keep pretending like everything's fine, like I can hold the pieces of this family together, but inside, I feel like I'm falling apart."

Luke's expression softened, the teasing demeanor fading into something more serious. "You're allowed to feel that way. You're carrying a lot. It's okay to not have it all figured out." His thumb traced circles on my knuckles, an unspoken reassurance that made my heart flutter unexpectedly.

"Thanks, Luke," I murmured, glancing down at our hands. The juxtaposition of his warmth against my uncertainty felt like a lifeline, a reminder that I didn't have to navigate this alone.

The moment stretched between us, filled with unsaid words and lingering glances, a dance of intimacy that made my heart race. Just then, the distant sound of laughter broke the spell. A group of kids raced through the field, their carefree shouts ringing out like joyous bells, a reminder of the innocence we often lost in adulthood.

"Look at them," I said, pointing. "I can't help but feel a little envious. When did life get so complicated?"

"When you stopped wearing glittery butterfly clips in your hair and started worrying about bills and broken bonds," Luke quipped, his eyes twinkling. "But hey, maybe you just need a little glitter in your life again."

"Right! Let's throw caution to the wind and start a butterfly clip revival. I can see it now: 'The return of the glitterati,' starring us as the leading fashion icons of the countryside."

Luke burst into laughter, the sound bright and infectious. "I can see the headlines now: 'Local Farmers Turn Fashionistas, Ruin Entire Crop Season!'"

"Can you imagine? The horror!" I laughed along, the playful banter lifting my spirits higher than I thought possible.

But even as we shared this moment of levity, I felt the undercurrent of tension still lingering in the background. It was as if the universe was biding its time, waiting for me to make my move, to confront the storm that lay ahead with Sam. I had no idea how it would all unfold, but the thought of facing it alone felt infinitely more daunting than taking it on with Luke by my side.

The sun had begun its descent, casting a soft golden hue over the landscape. As the world around us transformed into a dreamy tapestry of colors, I felt a surge of determination welling up inside me. I would talk to Sam; I had to. It wasn't just about the family legacy or the past—it was about us, the bond we shared, and the possibility of healing.

"Okay," I said, straightening up, a newfound resolve blooming in my chest. "I'm going to do it. I'll talk to Sam, and I'll do it before the sun sets tomorrow."

Luke's face broke into a proud grin, and I could feel the warmth of his approval wrapping around me like a soft blanket. "That's the spirit! You'll crush it. Just remember: be the brave heroine of your own story."

"Or the slightly awkward sidekick who trips over her own feet at the most inopportune moments," I countered with a playful roll of my eyes.

"Hey, every good story needs a comic relief!"

We shared another laugh, and for a brief moment, I allowed myself to believe that maybe, just maybe, everything would work out. As the sun dipped below the horizon, painting the sky with shades of pink and purple, I felt a sense of hope blossom within me. Whatever lay ahead, I wouldn't have to face it alone.

The soft glow of dusk wrapped around us like a comforting shawl, yet my heart raced with the weight of the impending conversation with Sam. As I sat beside Luke, our laughter still echoing in the air, I couldn't help but feel that the world around us was holding its breath, waiting for something to break. I studied Luke's profile, the way the fading light danced over his features, illuminating the gentle strength in his jaw and the kindness in his eyes. It was a reminder of what I had to gain and what I stood to lose.

"Hey," I said, breaking the momentary silence, "if I chicken out tomorrow, can we blame the cows for eating all my courage?" The playful banter was my shield, the lightheartedness an armor against the oncoming storm.

"Absolutely," Luke replied, his voice dripping with mock seriousness. "Those cows can be quite persuasive. Especially if you dangle some hay in front of them." He leaned in, feigning deep thought. "We might need a whole herd to keep you from clucking out."

I laughed again, but the sound felt more like a nervous flutter than true amusement. The thought of facing Sam and all the unresolved tensions between us gnawed at my stomach. "You know, it's kind of ironic. I've spent my whole life navigating these fields, learning how to plant and harvest and tend to the land, but when it comes to my own relationships, I feel like a toddler in a minefield."

Luke turned serious, his expression shifting from playful to earnest. "You're not a toddler. You're a woman who cares deeply about her family. You're just trying to find your way through the chaos. And you've got more strength than you give yourself credit for."

The sincerity in his words melted some of the ice forming in my chest, but still, I felt the weight of the task ahead. "I just... I don't want to screw this up. I don't want to lose Sam."

"Then don't focus on what you might lose. Focus on what you want to rebuild. If there's one thing I've learned from you, it's that you're resilient." His words hung in the air, a promise wrapped in encouragement.

I nodded, absorbing his unwavering belief in me like a sponge. "Okay. Tomorrow it is. I'll talk to Sam." The resolve in my voice surprised even me, as if saying it aloud turned a nebulous thought into a tangible plan.

With the stars beginning to sprinkle the sky, we lingered on that fence, sharing our dreams and fears, the boundary between friendship and something more subtly shifting. The world outside faded, and for a moment, it was just the two of us, the scent of the earth beneath us and the warmth of his shoulder against mine. I wished it could last forever, but I knew the dawn would bring the reckoning.

The following morning dawned bright and clear, the air crisp and filled with the promise of a new beginning. My stomach churned with a mix of anxiety and determination as I stepped outside. The sun was a glowing orb, high and mighty, as I made my way toward the main house, where Sam was likely already plotting his day with all the fervor of a general strategizing a battle.

As I approached, I could see Sam working near the barn, his back turned to me. The familiar sight stirred a cocktail of emotions—nostalgia, resentment, love, and fear all twisted together like the knots in my stomach. Taking a deep breath, I crossed the threshold into what felt like a minefield of unspoken words and heavy silences.

"Hey, Sam," I called out, my voice sounding far more tremulous than I had intended. He turned, surprise flickering across his features before settling into something more guarded.

"What do you want?" he replied, the edge of defensiveness creeping into his tone. It stung more than I cared to admit.

"I want to talk." I stepped closer, unwilling to let his immediate reaction deter me. "Can we sit down somewhere? Just for a few minutes?"

He hesitated, the tension in the air palpable. "I don't really think there's anything to talk about. You said what you needed to say the other night."

"Yeah, but I didn't mean any of it! Well, I mean, I did, but—" I stumbled over my words, frustration boiling just below the surface. "Can't we just hit the pause button on the drama for a second?"

"Drama? Is that what you call it?" He crossed his arms, a defensive barrier that felt insurmountable. "Because it feels like you're the one throwing around accusations without thinking things through."

A wave of hurt crashed over me. "I wouldn't be so quick to dismiss everything we've been through. I just don't want to fight anymore, Sam." My voice wavered, betraying the vulnerability I was trying so hard to mask.

"Maybe I don't want to stop fighting," he shot back, his expression hardening. "Maybe this is all I have left, and if I give up, I lose everything. You don't understand."

"Maybe I do understand more than you think!" I snapped, the frustration boiling over. "I'm scared too, Sam. I'm terrified of losing you and what this family means to us. But we can't just keep clashing like this!"

The silence that followed felt heavy, thick with all the unspoken emotions swirling around us. Sam's eyes flickered, and for a brief moment, I saw the brother I had grown up with, the one who used to laugh and chase me around the fields, who stood by me through thick and thin.

"Fine," he finally said, his voice barely above a whisper. "Let's talk. But don't think this is going to magically fix everything."

We found a spot near the barn, the air still and heavy, as if the world itself was bracing for impact. As we sat on the wooden steps, I felt the weight of everything unsaid, of years of sibling rivalry and miscommunication pressing down on us like the humid summer air.

I took a deep breath, gathering my thoughts as I prepared to plunge into the depths of our shared history, to lay bare the fears and hopes I had clung to for so long. "I miss how we used to be," I said, my voice trembling slightly. "I don't want to lose that. I don't want to lose you."

But before Sam could respond, the distant sound of an engine revving broke the fragile moment. The rumble grew louder, cutting through the tension like a knife. We both turned, our conversation halted as a truck barreled down the dirt road, dust flying in its wake.

"Who the hell is that?" Sam muttered, a frown creasing his brow.

My heart raced as the truck pulled into view, my mind racing with possibilities. I scanned the dusty vehicle, but as it stopped and the door swung open, my breath caught in my throat.

Out stepped someone I hadn't seen in years, someone whose mere presence had the potential to unravel everything I had just tried to piece together. My pulse quickened, the air between us thickening with a sudden uncertainty that left me speechless.

"Sam," I whispered, my voice barely above a breath, the realization settling heavily in my stomach. "It's—"

But before I could finish, a shadow fell over us, and the world shifted, teetering on the edge of a cliff. The next few moments stretched into eternity as I braced for the impending impact, feeling the ground shift beneath my feet, a seismic change that promised everything would be different from here on out.

Chapter 11: Gathering Allies

The bell above the door jingled as I entered Rosie's Diner, a familiar sound that resonated like a warm greeting from an old friend. The place was alive with chatter and laughter, the clatter of dishes and the hiss of the grill blending into a comforting symphony. I took a moment to soak it all in—the sun filtering through the wide windows, casting a golden glow on the worn linoleum floors, and the cheerful checkered tablecloths that reminded me of simpler times. The walls were adorned with photographs of the town from decades past, a nostalgic gallery that felt like a testament to our shared history.

I spotted my favorite booth in the corner, the vinyl cracked and faded but inviting nonetheless. As I slid into the seat, I noticed a couple of locals exchanging glances, the kind that spoke volumes. Their smiles were genuine, but there was an undercurrent of curiosity, maybe even concern, swirling around the coffee mugs and plates of pancakes. I took a deep breath, the scent of bacon wafting through the air, and felt a flicker of determination ignite within me.

"Hey, Sam!" Rosie, the diner's owner and a force of nature wrapped in a floral apron, approached with her trademark enthusiasm. Her salt-and-pepper hair was pulled back into a neat bun, and her eyes sparkled with a mix of mischief and warmth. "What can I get you, sugar?"

I returned her smile, the warmth of her presence always grounding me. "Just a coffee for now, Rosie. I have a lot to talk about."

"Uh-oh. That sounds serious," she said, raising an eyebrow playfully. "You're not going to tell me you're selling the farm, are you?"

I shook my head, though a part of me flinched at the mere thought. "Actually, I'm hoping to rally the town. I want to revitalize the farm, restore my dad's legacy." The words tumbled out, filled with a passionate urgency that felt liberating.

Rosie's expression shifted from playful concern to fierce support. "That's the spirit! We need that farm, Sam. It's part of who we are." She leaned closer, her voice dropping to a conspiratorial whisper. "I'll get the coffee flowing and spread the word. You just wait."

With that, she vanished into the kitchen, and I sipped my coffee, the rich, dark liquid warming my hands. I could feel the anticipation building in my chest, a heady mix of fear and hope. The diner felt like the heartbeat of Riverton, and if I was going to pull off this monumental task, I needed to tap into that collective spirit.

Soon, the tables were filled with the familiar faces of my childhood—old Mr. Thompson, who always had a story about the "great storm of '82," and the Millers, their kids now teenagers towering over their parents. I caught snippets of conversations about the upcoming harvest festival, football games, and the usual gossip that knit the town together. It was all so wonderfully ordinary, and yet, it felt charged with potential.

As I stood to address the diner, I felt the weight of their gazes. "Hey, everyone! Can I have your attention for a moment?" The laughter died down, replaced by curious looks. I cleared my throat, the clinking of cutlery fading into a hush. "I've been thinking about the farm and what it means to us all. My father poured his heart into that land, and I want to do the same."

There was a murmur of agreement, and I pressed on, emboldened. "I'm hoping to restore the fields and bring back the community garden. It'll take work, and I can't do it alone. I need your help—your hands, your ideas, your support."

A ripple of excitement passed through the diner, and soon, hands began to rise. Clara, the local teacher, spoke up first. "I'd love to help with the garden! The kids could learn so much from it." Her enthusiasm was contagious, and I felt a surge of hope.

"Count me in too," chimed in Mike, the mechanic, his voice booming over the din. "I've got some spare tools and know how to fix just about anything. Just say the word, and I'm there."

With each declaration of support, my heart soared higher, buoyed by the community's willingness to rally behind a shared vision. Even the quietest patrons, usually content to stay in the background, leaned in, their expressions lit with a spark of interest.

"Let's not forget about the bake sale!" piped up Betty, the town's unofficial baker and champion of sweet treats. "I can whip up pies that'll bring folks from miles around. We could raise some funds for the project!"

Laughter erupted, and for a moment, it felt like we were a tight-knit family, a band of misfits united by a common cause. I couldn't help but smile, my cheeks flushed with warmth.

Just then, Luke pushed through the door, a whirlwind of energy and that effortless charm that always made my heart skip a beat. He spotted me, his eyes brightening, and sauntered over, exuding a casual confidence that both excited and grounded me. "What's going on? Did someone announce free coffee?"

"Close enough," I replied, unable to suppress my grin. "I'm trying to save the farm, and everyone seems on board."

"Are we really talking about a bake sale?" he asked, arching an eyebrow, a playful smirk tugging at the corners of his mouth.

I rolled my eyes, but my heart raced at his presence. "Well, if it helps get the farm back in shape, then yes!"

"Count me in," he said, his voice low and sincere. "I'm not leaving you to fight this battle alone."

As I looked around the diner, the warmth of the moment washed over me. This wasn't just about the farm anymore; it was about something bigger. It was about reclaiming my roots and weaving our stories together again. With newfound allies and a renewed sense of purpose, I felt the strength of the community bolstering my resolve, ready to face whatever challenges lay ahead.

The atmosphere in Rosie's Diner buzzed with an electric energy, a palpable sense of camaraderie that wrapped around me like a warm blanket. I glanced around at the faces that had shaped my childhood, their expressions reflecting an unspoken understanding of what the farm meant to each of us. There was an unmistakable magic in the air, an assurance that we were all in this together, no matter how steep the climb ahead might seem.

With coffee cups refilled and plates of pancakes devoured, plans began to take shape. The sound of enthusiastic discussions and laughter filled the room, a delightful cacophony punctuated by the clinking of cutlery and the sizzling of the grill. I felt buoyed by the weight of their support, a surge of hope flooding my veins. It was as if the diner had transformed into a war room, a hub of strategy and shared dreams.

"Okay, team," I said, attempting to channel my inner coach as I stood up once more, waving my hands like a conductor. "If we're going to make this work, we need to get organized. Who here can help with fieldwork?"

Hands shot up like eager students in a classroom, and I couldn't help but chuckle at the sight. "Alright, I'll take that as a yes! How about we do a Saturday workday? Bring shovels, rakes, and a can-do attitude!"

"Don't forget sunscreen!" hollered Mr. Thompson, his voice gravelly but kind, drawing laughter from the group. "And maybe some ice-cold lemonade! It gets hot out there!"

"Noted!" I laughed, grateful for his unwavering support. "And after the hard work, we can have a little barbecue. Nothing brings a community together like grilled burgers and homemade pie."

"Count me in for the pie!" Betty exclaimed, her eyes twinkling as if the mere thought of baking made her giddy. "I've been trying out some new recipes. There's this peach cobbler that'll knock your socks off!"

I grinned at her enthusiasm. "You had me at cobbler! We'll make it a potluck. Everyone can bring their specialty. Luke, you're on meat duty, right?"

"Meat duty? I didn't sign up for that!" he replied, feigning shock. But the corner of his mouth quirked up, and I knew he was already envisioning the sizzling steaks.

I shrugged playfully, folding my arms. "Oh, come on! I saw you grilling at the last block party. You can't hide your talent from me."

"Fine, but only if I get to taste test the pies first," he countered, his playful smirk returning. The laughter that erupted felt liberating, like the shackles of doubt were slowly being lifted.

As the conversation flowed, so did the ideas. We brainstormed ways to revitalize the community garden, discussed how to attract more visitors to the farm, and even considered hosting workshops to teach local kids about farming. I could hardly keep up with the enthusiasm; my heart raced with excitement at the thought of each new venture.

But just as the conversation reached a fever pitch, the front door swung open with a jingle, and in walked Sarah, my childhood rival. I had almost forgotten about her. With her perfectly styled hair and designer jeans, she stood out in stark contrast to the plaid shirts and worn sneakers of my friends. She surveyed the diner like a queen inspecting her kingdom, and for a moment, a hush fell over the room.

"Sam," she drawled, her voice dripping with feigned sweetness, "I heard you were trying to save the farm. How quaint." Her gaze flicked to Luke, and I could see her calculating whether he was a potential ally or a rival.

"Sarah," I replied, trying to keep my tone neutral, but the tightness in my chest betrayed my discomfort. "What brings you here?"

"Oh, just enjoying a lovely breakfast," she said, her smile too bright, too forced. "But I couldn't help overhearing your little plans. Isn't it adorable how you think the town will actually rally behind you?"

A ripple of tension swept through the diner, but before I could respond, Luke stepped in, his voice smooth and confident. "Actually, Sarah, it's pretty inspiring to see everyone come together. You might want to take notes. Community spirit can be quite powerful."

I could have kissed him in that moment. His defense of my ambitions made my heart flutter, and I could see Sarah's expression shift. The amusement faded from her eyes, replaced by a flicker of annoyance.

"Sure, Luke, but community spirit doesn't pay the bills or fix a dilapidated farm. Just remember, dreams don't pay taxes," she shot back, crossing her arms, her posture radiating disdain.

"Dreams don't pay taxes, but they do grow crops," I replied, my confidence ignited. "And crops feed families. So, while you may find my plans quaint, I believe they matter more than you realize."

Sarah's mouth twitched, her composure slipping. "Well, good luck with that, Sam. I'll be watching," she said, turning on her heel and striding out of the diner, the door slamming behind her.

The tension hung in the air like a storm cloud, but as the door closed, a collective sigh seemed to escape the townsfolk. Rosie, who had been quietly observing from the counter, poured herself a fresh cup of coffee and raised it in a mock toast. "To the dreamers! May they always outshine the cynics."

Laughter bubbled up again, lightening the mood, and I felt a surge of relief. "I guess we've got our first official naysayer," I said, shaking my head. "But let's not let her get under our skin. We're here to build something."

"Right," Clara said, her eyes sparkling with determination. "And if Sarah wants to doubt us, we'll just have to show her what we can do."

"That's the spirit!" I cheered, my heart racing. "Let's show Riverton what it means to come together."

With renewed vigor, the discussions resumed, and we began mapping out our plan. Ideas flowed freely, each one sparking another, as if a dam had burst open. It was no longer just about the farm; it was about reviving a sense of community that had faded over time, about breathing life into something that had once thrived.

As the sun dipped lower in the sky, casting a warm glow through the diner's windows, I felt the excitement shift to something deeper, more profound. We were weaving our lives together, creating a tapestry of shared hopes and dreams. There was no way I could do this alone, but with these wonderful people by my side, it felt not only possible but inevitable. I could almost see the fields bursting with crops, the laughter of children playing in the garden, and the smell of fresh pie wafting through the air. And in that moment, I knew we were embarking on a journey that would not only restore my father's legacy but build something even greater: a home where we all belonged.

With the vibrant energy of Rosie's Diner still humming in my veins, I stepped out into the crisp afternoon air, my heart light and buoyant. The sun cast a golden hue over Riverton, painting the familiar streets in warm colors that seemed to whisper promises of hope. I could almost feel the pulse of the town beneath my feet, a rhythm that synchronized with the beat of my heart. As I made my way down Main Street, the world felt alive with possibility, every rustle of leaves and chatter from neighbors reinforcing the bond we all shared.

Yet, the specter of doubt lingered in the back of my mind, reminiscent of Sarah's smirk as she'd walked out of the diner. Could I really pull this off? The questions danced like fireflies in my thoughts, but I pushed them aside, focusing instead on the faces of the people who had rallied behind me. Their belief in our cause sparked a new sense of determination that I couldn't easily dismiss.

"Where are you headed?" Luke's voice broke through my reverie, and I turned to find him strolling alongside me, hands shoved into his pockets, his expression casual but his eyes bright with interest.

"Just enjoying the day. You know, soaking in the fact that we're about to launch a community revolution," I replied, a teasing lilt in my voice. "What's the plan? Are we going to brainstorm ways to deal with Sarah's negativity or plot our revenge with baked goods?"

He chuckled, his laughter contagious. "Maybe a little bit of both? I could go for a good pie showdown. She wouldn't know what hit her."

"Exactly! Sweeten the deal with a slice of lemon meringue and let the baking do the talking," I said, nudging him playfully. "But seriously, we should probably start mapping out the details for the workday. I think if we could coordinate our efforts, we'd have a much better chance of success."

Luke nodded, his expression shifting to one of earnest contemplation. "How about we meet at my place tomorrow morning? I've got a whiteboard, and I'm not afraid to use it. We can lay everything out, make a schedule, figure out who's bringing what."

I raised an eyebrow, feigning seriousness. "A whiteboard? You really know how to woo a girl."

He smirked, his eyes twinkling. "What can I say? I aim to impress. I'll even let you draw diagrams. But first, we need to take a detour."

"A detour? To where?"

"Just trust me. It'll be worth it," he said, a mischievous glint in his eye.

Intrigued, I let him guide me off the main path, our footsteps echoing softly against the pavement. We walked a few blocks until we reached a small, overgrown garden tucked behind an abandoned shop. I had never noticed it before, its entrance hidden by a tangled mess of vines and weeds.

"What is this place?" I asked, peering through the dense foliage.

"This," Luke declared with a flourish, "is the Riverton Community Garden. Or what remains of it. It used to be vibrant—flowers, vegetables, everything you can imagine. But when the funding dried up, so did the enthusiasm. I thought maybe we could breathe some life back into it."

I stepped inside the garden, the scent of damp earth and wildflowers filling my lungs. "This is incredible! I had no idea it even existed."

"Exactly," he said, brushing aside a few wayward branches. "But it's not just about planting things. It's about reminding people that it was once a gathering place, a haven. We could host workshops here, classes for kids, even events. It would be an extension of the farm, a way to cultivate a sense of community."

As I looked around, the vision he painted began to materialize in my mind. I could see families gathered, children learning about nature, laughter and chatter mingling with the sound of bees buzzing from flower to flower. It felt like a chance to create something beautiful, something that could spark the same kind of passion that had thrived in my father's fields.

"I love it," I said, my heart racing with excitement. "We need to clean this place up and get the word out. We could even plan a reopening day—a festival! We can invite everyone!"

Luke grinned, his enthusiasm infectious. "Now that's what I'm talking about! Imagine the look on Sarah's face when she sees how much we're capable of."

Just as I was about to respond, a loud crash echoed from the nearby alleyway, jolting us both out of our daydreams. I exchanged a concerned glance with Luke, the atmosphere around us shifting from hopeful to tense.

"Did you hear that?" he asked, his expression turning serious.

"Yeah, it sounded like it came from over there." I pointed toward the narrow alley, my instincts kicking in. "We should check it out."

Cautiously, we approached the alley, its shadows looming ominously. As we rounded the corner, the scene unfolded before us: a group of teenagers were gathered around a broken sign, their laughter cutting through the air like a knife. But it wasn't their merriment that seized my attention; it was the defaced sign.

"Riverton's Farm: For Sale," it read, the words scrawled across the surface in what looked like red spray paint, as if someone had wanted to make a point—and a loud one at that.

"What the hell?" I breathed, my heart dropping. "Who would do this?"

Luke's jaw tightened as he stepped forward, his voice low and firm. "This isn't just vandalism; it's a statement. Someone wants to scare people away from the farm. It's almost like they want to push you out."

The implications crashed over me, the excitement from earlier dissipating like mist under the morning sun. "But why? This is more than just a piece of land; it's my home, my father's legacy. I can't let them win."

Suddenly, one of the teenagers caught sight of us, their laughter fading into an awkward silence. The atmosphere shifted again, this time laden with tension. "Hey, what are you doing here?" one of them challenged, stepping forward with a bravado that felt forced.

"What do you think you're doing?" I shot back, indignation rising within me. "This is vandalism, plain and simple."

"You don't know what you're talking about," another teen sneered, their tone laced with defiance. "The farm is a joke. You really think anyone cares about it? It's just an eyesore now."

Before I could retort, Luke placed a hand on my shoulder, grounding me. "This isn't going to solve anything. Let's just walk away."

But something in me snapped. "No! You can't just walk away from this. I'm not going to let you bully my home."

As the tension crackled in the air, I stepped forward, ready to defend what was mine, what was ours. The group of teens shifted, their bravado faltering for a moment, but the one who had first challenged us squared his shoulders, his eyes narrowing.

"You don't understand. You're not the only one fighting for this town. There are people who want change, and they're tired of looking at old reminders of the past."

"Change?" I echoed incredulously. "You think tearing down what's left of our history is progress?"

He shrugged, but his nonchalance didn't hide the simmering anger beneath. "Maybe it's time for you to move on, Sam."

My breath caught in my throat. They weren't just targeting the farm; they were targeting me. The stakes felt impossibly high, and suddenly, the vision of our community revitalization felt like a fragile dream teetering on the edge of a precipice.

With adrenaline coursing through my veins, I took a step closer, my voice unwavering. "You don't get to decide what's worth fighting for. This town belongs to all of us, and I'm not going anywhere."

A moment of silence stretched between us, heavy with unspoken challenges. Just then, a sharp voice cut through the tension, and we all turned to see Sarah, leaning casually against a brick wall, an amused smile playing on her lips.

"Looks like I arrived just in time for the fireworks. I told you it wouldn't be easy, Sam."

In that instant, the reality of our situation struck me like a lightning bolt. I wasn't just fighting for my father's legacy anymore; I was standing at the center of a brewing storm, surrounded by adversaries who wouldn't hesitate to take my dreams and tear them apart. I knew that the fight for the farm—and for Riverton itself—was just beginning, and suddenly, the stakes felt higher than ever.

Chapter 12: Secrets of the Past

The attic was a universe unto itself, cloaked in dust and shadows, where the air hung thick with the scent of aged wood and time forgotten. Climbing the rickety ladder, I felt the boards creak beneath my weight, echoing the unspoken secrets that whispered through the rafters. Each step carried the weight of anticipation, a pull that beckoned me into the depths of my family's history. As I pushed open the heavy door, sunlight spilled into the dim space, illuminating particles that danced like tiny stars caught in a celestial ballet.

In the far corner, cloaked beneath a heavy quilt, sat an old trunk, its surface marred with scratches and stories waiting to be told. My heart raced as I approached it, the thrill of discovery mingling with a twinge of trepidation. I knelt before the trunk, my fingers brushing against the worn leather, and felt a surge of emotion swell within me. It was a relic of my father's life, a tangible link to the man I had known only through fleeting glimpses and half-remembered conversations.

With a deep breath, I lifted the latch, the metallic click reverberating through the silence. The lid creaked open, releasing a musty breath that filled my lungs with the essence of nostalgia. Inside, layers of yellowed papers, brittle with age, lay stacked like the pages of a life unwritten. My fingers trembled as I reached in, pulling out a bundle of letters tied with a fraying ribbon. Each envelope bore my father's elegant script, a testament to his careful thoughtfulness.

Unraveling the bundle, I noticed the first letter addressed to someone named Sam. The name hit me like a thunderclap. My brother had always been the shadow I lived in, a specter of resentment and longing that loomed large in my memories. The letter began with an apology, words heavy with regret, and my heart stuttered at the raw honesty laid bare before me.

"Dear Sam," it started, the ink slightly smudged, as if my father had poured his heart onto the page without the luxury of reflection. "I've watched you grow, and it pains me to see the distance between us. You've always been my greatest joy and my deepest worry. I hope you can find it in your heart to forgive me for my shortcomings. I've made mistakes, but I love you, and that love has never waned."

I read on, feeling as if I were intruding on an intimate moment. The words flowed like a river, each sentence deepening my understanding of a man I had scarcely known. My father's dreams, fears, and hopes were laid bare, illuminating the darkness that had clouded our family's past.

As I leafed through the letters, photographs tumbled out, sepia-toned snapshots of laughter and warmth. There was a picture of a young Sam, his face alight with mischief, caught mid-laugh on the swing set in our backyard. I couldn't help but smile, remembering the way he used to challenge me to races, always pretending he'd let me win. In another, our father held a baby version of me, cradled in his arms, a look of adoration etched across his face. The image sent a pang through my heart—what had happened to that connection, that warmth?

The journals came next, pages filled with my father's meticulous handwriting, detailing everything from mundane daily routines to profound reflections on life and loss. He wrote about his dreams of adventure, of travels he never took and stories he never told. The words wrapped around me, pulling me deeper into his world, and I felt a strange mixture of love and sorrow for the man who had shaped so much of my life yet remained a stranger.

Suddenly, a thought struck me like lightning: how could I let Sam read this? Would he dismiss it as another feeble attempt at reconciliation? But I couldn't shake the sense that these letters might be the key to unearthing the chasm that had grown between us. Perhaps it was time to confront the shadows of our past.

I tucked the letters back into the trunk and left the attic, my heart racing with the weight of my discovery. The sun hung low in the sky, casting a warm golden hue over everything. I could see Sam sitting on the porch, his brow furrowed in thought, the weight of our family's history hanging over him like a storm cloud. The moment I stepped out, his gaze met mine, and I could feel the tension crackling between us like static electricity.

"Found anything interesting?" he asked, a half-hearted attempt at casualness that fell flat.

I took a deep breath, knowing that this moment could change everything. "I found some letters. They're... from Dad. To you."

His expression shifted, a mixture of curiosity and wariness flickering in his eyes. "What did he say?"

I hesitated, feeling the enormity of my father's words swirling in my mind. "He wanted you to know that he loved you. That he hoped for forgiveness."

Sam's jaw tightened, the flicker of hope quickly overshadowed by a wall of skepticism. "It's easy to say those things when you're gone," he muttered, his tone heavy with bitterness.

I stepped closer, determined to breach the barrier that had long kept us apart. "But maybe it's not about what he said. Maybe it's about what we can choose to believe."

He looked at me, uncertainty painting his features, and in that moment, I realized we were both still standing in the ruins of our childhood, haunted by ghosts of expectations and loss. Maybe these letters were a bridge—a chance to step into the light. And as the sun dipped below the horizon, casting long shadows across the porch, I knew that the secrets of our past could finally set us free.

As I stood on the porch, my heart thundering in my chest, I realized that the moment of revelation was upon us. Sam's gaze flickered from the fading light of the sun to my face, a complex tapestry of emotions etched into his features. I could see the gears of his mind turning, the familiar tension tightening the corners of his mouth. In that moment, the world around us faded, leaving just the two of us and the weight of our shared past hanging heavy in the air.

"Forgiveness, huh?" he finally replied, his tone sharp but not unkind. "That's a tall order. What do you think that looks like? A big hug and a 'thanks for the memories' card?"

I couldn't help but chuckle, despite the seriousness of the situation. "I think it looks more like awkward family dinners and too many silent car rides, but I'd take that over nothing."

Sam rolled his eyes but a smirk tugged at the corners of his lips. "Great, just what I've always wanted for Christmas—therapy in a box."

"Better than socks," I shot back, and we both laughed, a brief respite from the emotional whirlwind swirling around us. It felt like the briefest glimmer of light breaking through a thick fog, and I hoped it wasn't just an illusion.

"Look, I know it's easy to scoff at old letters, but Dad wrote these when he thought he had time to fix things. He wanted us to know he cared," I said, my voice softening as I gestured towards the trunk still resting heavily in the shadows. "This is a part of him we never got to see."

Sam looked at the trunk, a mixture of curiosity and wariness etched across his features. "Yeah, but maybe it's too late for all that. He's not here anymore to explain himself. It feels... unfair."

"It's not about fairness," I countered, stepping closer to him. "It's about understanding. We both deserve to know the truth, to figure out why he made the choices he did."

The silence that stretched between us was thick with unresolved tension, the kind that demanded a reckoning. Sam finally huffed out a breath, running a hand through his hair in that familiar gesture of exasperation. "Fine. Let's say I read the letters. What then? I'm not ready for a reunion of Hallmark proportions, you know."

"Neither am I," I replied, my heart pounding in my throat. "But I think we owe it to ourselves to try."

He crossed his arms, a defensive posture I recognized all too well. "And what if it doesn't go the way you want? What if it only stirs up more anger?"

"Then we'll deal with it. Together," I said firmly. "Just like we always should have."

Sam's eyes narrowed, weighing my words against a lifetime of disappointment. The tension in the air was electric, but I could see the flicker of something—curiosity, perhaps—behind the wall he'd built around his heart. It was a spark I clung to as I took a step back toward the trunk, heart racing as I unfolded the first letter.

"Here," I said, offering it to him. "Read it. Let's take the plunge together."

He hesitated, eyeing the letter like it might bite him. But after a moment, he reached out, fingers brushing against mine as he took the delicate paper. "You're a lot more optimistic than I ever remember," he said, a hint of admiration creeping into his voice.

"Well, someone has to be," I replied, my heart swelling at the moment. "Consider it my full-time job."

As he unfolded the letter, I watched his expression shift, the flickers of recognition and pain crossing his face like shadows flitting across the sun. I held my breath, feeling as though we were standing at the edge of a precipice, daring to leap into the unknown.

Minutes ticked by in a slow, agonizing crawl as Sam read the words penned so carefully by our father. I could see his brow furrow, lips moving silently as he absorbed each line. I fought the urge to reach out and touch his shoulder, to comfort him, but I knew this moment was his to navigate. The sunlight bathed us in a warm glow, contrasting with the chill of memories we both wished to forget.

Finally, he set the letter down, and the silence that followed felt profound. "He wanted me to forgive him," he murmured, almost to himself. "After everything, he thought that was possible."

I nodded, my heart aching for both of us. "He was human, Sam. He messed up, but he cared. He wanted to fix things."

"Did he? Or did he just want to absolve himself?" Sam shot back, a bitter edge creeping into his voice.

I could feel frustration bubbling beneath the surface. "You can't be serious. He loved you, even if he didn't know how to show it!"

"Love? Is that what you call it? A father who disappeared? A man who left us to pick up the pieces?" His voice cracked, the raw emotion spilling over, and for a moment, I saw the wounded boy he once was—the one who had never stopped longing for a father's approval.

"Sam, it's not that simple," I replied gently. "We can't change the past, but we can choose how to move forward. These letters, they might help us find a way through."

He exhaled sharply, his defenses slowly lowering as he contemplated my words. "Maybe I'm not ready to forgive. Maybe I don't even know what that looks like," he admitted, vulnerability creeping into his voice like a hesitant shadow.

"Then let's figure it out together," I said, the words spilling out with an urgency I could hardly contain. "Let's sift through the ashes and see if there's anything left to spark a flame."

For a long moment, Sam stared at me, his expression a cocktail of emotions—hurt, longing, uncertainty. "Okay," he finally said, a resigned acceptance settling in his tone. "But don't say I didn't warn you when this blows up in our faces."

I couldn't help but smile, relieved that we were taking a step toward healing, no matter how tentative. "I'll take my chances."

As we both turned back to the trunk, the sun dipped further beneath the horizon, casting our shadows long and intertwined—a silent promise that we would face whatever came next together.

The trunk lay open before us, a Pandora's box of memories and emotions, both exhilarating and terrifying. I watched Sam sift through the remaining letters, each one a delicate thread weaving together a tapestry of our father's heart. The dim light of the porch cast shadows on his face, emphasizing the flickers of recognition and confusion that danced across his features. It was as if each letter bore not just ink and paper, but the weight of our childhood, the laughter, and the lingering resentments, all jumbled together like a messy pile of laundry waiting to be sorted.

"Here's another one," Sam said, pulling out a letter marked with my name. I felt a flutter of apprehension in my stomach, an uncomfortable twist at the idea of being thrust back into a past I thought I had left behind. "You should read this one. It's dated just a few months before... you know."

My throat tightened as I accepted the letter, the familiar elegance of our father's handwriting bringing a wave of nostalgia crashing over me. I unfolded the delicate paper, its edges crisp and slightly worn, and began to read. The words danced on the page, as if my father's voice echoed in my mind.

"Dear [Your Name]," it began, the ink a deep blue that felt almost intimate. "If you're reading this, I can only hope that you are thriving, full of dreams and joy. I want you to know that my greatest regret has always been the time lost between us. Life has a way of slipping through our fingers, and I can't help but think of all the moments I took for granted."

My heart sank as I continued, each word a step deeper into the labyrinth of regret and longing. "You've always had such a bright spirit, and I see so much of your mother in you. It breaks my heart to think you may not understand how much you mean to me."

I paused, emotion clogging my throat, and glanced at Sam, who was watching me closely. "He was trying," I murmured, feeling the sting of tears threatening to spill. "He wanted to reach out."

"Yeah, but did he ever actually try?" Sam snapped, his voice laced with skepticism. "This is just words on a page, right? Talk is cheap, especially when you're not around to back it up."

I pressed my lips together, feeling the truth of his frustration. "I know. I feel it too. But maybe these letters can help us understand. Maybe they're not just empty words, Sam."

He huffed, running a hand through his hair in that familiar gesture of exasperation. "So what's next? We read through Dad's letters like it's some sort of book club? 'Chapter One: Regret; Chapter Two: More Regret'?"

I smirked despite myself. "What, you're not a fan of my riveting titles? I thought they really captured the essence of our family drama."

"Are we really joking about this?" he shot back, though a hint of a smile danced at the corners of his lips.

I sighed, the gravity of our conversation creeping back in. "No, we're not. But we can't let anger drown out everything else. Let's take a look at this letter together. It could give us both something to hold on to."

Sam relented, a slight nod indicating his willingness to dive deeper into our father's heart. As I continued reading, I felt Sam lean in, curiosity piquing in his eyes.

"Your laughter has always been my favorite sound," I read aloud. "It rings like bells on a spring morning, full of promise. I want you to remember that no matter where I am, I will always be cheering you on. Please, don't let the shadows dim your light."

The words hung in the air, a sweet yet bittersweet melody that filled the space around us. Sam's expression softened, and for a fleeting moment, I saw the glimmer of hope in his eyes. "He really wanted to be there for you," he murmured, almost as if trying to convince himself.

"I think he wanted to be there for both of us," I replied, feeling a surge of conviction. "This isn't just about forgiveness; it's about understanding who we are in the wake of his absence. We're not just his children; we're a part of his legacy."

Sam nodded slowly, and I could sense the walls around him cracking just a little. "I still don't know if I can just forgive him, but maybe I can understand him."

I smiled, feeling a warmth blossom in my chest. "That's a start."

Just then, a sudden noise shattered our fragile moment—an unexpected crash from inside the house. It echoed like a thunderclap, jolting us back to reality. Sam and I exchanged wide-eyed glances, confusion flickering across our faces.

"What was that?" he asked, shifting into a protective stance.

"I don't know," I replied, my heart racing as adrenaline surged through my veins. "Maybe a branch fell or something?"

Sam frowned, clearly unconvinced. "Yeah, right. Let's go check it out."

We both rose from the porch, the warm glow of the sunset replaced by the creeping chill of uncertainty. As we stepped inside the house, the shadows clung to us like old friends, and the atmosphere felt thick, charged with a sense of foreboding.

"Do you think someone's in here?" Sam whispered, the bravado in his voice wavering.

"Let's not jump to conclusions. It could just be a raccoon or—"

Before I could finish my thought, a second crash echoed through the hallway, louder this time, followed by a low groan that sent chills down my spine.

"Okay, that's not a raccoon," Sam said, his voice barely above a whisper.

We crept down the darkened hallway, every creak of the floorboards beneath our feet amplifying the tension. My heart raced, pounding against my ribcage like a trapped bird. With each step, the sense of unease grew, coiling tighter around us.

As we reached the living room, the sight that met us sent a wave of shock coursing through my body. The room was a mess, furniture overturned, books scattered like fallen leaves, and the old family portrait that had hung above the mantel lay shattered on the floor. But it was what lay in the center of the chaos that stole my breath—a figure slumped against the wall, half-concealed in shadows.

"Who the hell are you?" Sam demanded, taking a protective step forward, fists clenched.

The figure stirred, lifting its head slightly. "I—I'm sorry," it stammered, voice weak and trembling. "I didn't mean to—"

I gasped as recognition hit me like a bolt of lightning, my heart plunging into an abyss of confusion and dread. "Wait, is that...?"

But before I could finish, the figure spoke again, words tumbling out in a rush. "I need to explain! Please, just listen to me!"

The world around me spiraled as the figure leaned forward into the dim light, revealing a face I hadn't seen in years. A face that had been etched into my memory like a haunting melody, one that had lingered on the edges of my thoughts. And as my eyes widened in shock, a single thought raced through my mind, heavy and thunderous: sometimes the past doesn't just haunt you—it comes crashing back, uninvited, ready to rewrite everything you thought you knew.

Chapter 13: Unlikely Encounters

The air was thick with the sweet scent of ripe tomatoes and sun-warmed corn as I pushed my cart through the bustling local market, the hum of chatter and laughter creating a vibrant symphony around me. My mind was adrift in thoughts of the upcoming harvest festival, a flurry of to-do lists tangled with lingering worries about the farm. I had been so preoccupied with deadlines and dwindling funds that I almost didn't notice the familiar laughter rising above the din, a sound that threaded through the memories of sun-drenched summers and lazy afternoons.

And there she was. Emma, with her shock of curly hair catching the sunlight like a halo, stood at a stall, animatedly discussing heirloom tomatoes with an elderly vendor. My heart leapt, a jolt of nostalgia surging through me as I remembered the last time we'd shared a space like this—years ago, on the very same streets, before life swept us both in different directions. I hesitated, momentarily frozen in a swirl of uncertainty. Would she even remember me? The girl with dirt under her nails and an insatiable curiosity about the world beyond our small town?

"Lila!" Emma's voice rang out, cutting through my hesitation like a knife. She turned, her eyes widening in surprise and delight. "I can't believe it's you!"

Before I could muster a response, she had crossed the distance, enveloping me in a warm embrace that felt like wrapping myself in a familiar blanket. "How long has it been? Five years? Six?"

"More like eight," I replied, pulling back slightly to gauge her expression. "You've changed so much, but it's still you."

Her laughter was bright, and she waved away my comment. "Please, the city has a way of refining you. How about you? Still living the dream of farm life?"

I felt a flicker of unease at her question, the raw truth of my struggles looming in the back of my mind. "It's... been a challenge," I admitted, scanning her face for judgment, but finding only kindness. "The farm isn't what it used to be. My parents had their ways of doing things, and now it feels like I'm running uphill in a snowstorm."

"Running uphill, huh? That sounds exhausting." Emma smirked, her eyes glimmering with mischief. "How about we grab some coffee and you fill me in? I'm sure you have a lifetime of stories to share."

As we settled into a cozy corner of the market café, the clatter of cups and the aromatic blend of fresh coffee and baked goods enveloped us. The atmosphere buzzed with energy, yet it felt cocooning, like a protective bubble against the world outside. I recounted tales of the farm—its stubbornness, the weeds that seemed to sprout overnight, and the looming shadow of my family's expectations. Emma listened intently, her expressive brows knitting together in concern and laughter dancing in her eyes during lighter moments.

"You know," she said, leaning in as if sharing a secret, "you need to turn this around. What's stopping you from making the farm a destination? Think about it—a rustic retreat, local produce, maybe even workshops on canning or gardening. You have the land, and people crave authentic experiences."

I blinked at her, half in disbelief and half in wonder. "A destination? I can barely keep up with what we have now."

"Exactly!" she replied, a glint of excitement in her gaze. "But you could revitalize it. You need to share what you have with the world. I could help with marketing! I've learned a few tricks from my job in NYC."

I felt a spark ignite within me, a flicker of hope that had been dormant for too long. Emma's enthusiasm was infectious, weaving through my doubts like a thread of sunlight piercing through clouds. "You really think it could work?"

"Absolutely," she nodded fervently. "Imagine it—a weekend getaway for families, couples, anyone looking to escape the city. You could highlight what makes your farm special, the heart and soul you've poured into it. People love that."

Her words wrapped around me, tempting me with the possibilities. I pictured families meandering through sunflower fields, children giggling as they chased chickens, and couples lounging under the stars, savoring homemade preserves and fresh-baked bread. The image was intoxicating, and for the first time in ages, I felt a rush of inspiration that washed away the cobwebs of doubt.

"We could have a pumpkin patch in the fall!" I exclaimed, my voice rising with excitement. "And maybe even host workshops on making jams. My grandmother used to say every fruit has a story, and I'd love to share those stories."

Emma leaned back, a satisfied grin on her face. "See? You already have the beginnings of a plan. You just needed a little nudge."

As we mapped out ideas, sketching outlines of what could be on napkins stained with coffee rings, I realized how much I had missed this—someone to bounce ideas off, someone who believed in the possibility of dreams rather than the weight of realities. Emma's energy filled the space between us, a bridge from my worries to new hopes.

"I can't tell you how much this means to me," I said, my voice catching slightly as I fought the emotional swell. "It's like a breath of fresh air."

"Well, that's what friends are for, right?" she winked, her playful nature a balm to my anxious heart.

Our laughter echoed through the café, bright and buoyant, as the world outside continued to whirl around us. Little did I know, beneath the warmth of our reunion, the seeds of change were germinating, promising to alter the course of my life in ways I had yet to comprehend.

The morning sun climbed higher in the sky, pouring golden light over the market, illuminating the fresh produce and colorful crafts with an almost ethereal glow. The laughter of children bounced around me, mingling with the soft clinking of coffee cups and the chatter of vendors hawking their wares. Emma and I settled into a small table in the corner, surrounded by the vibrant energy of the market, our ideas spilling forth like the summer blooms that filled the nearby stalls.

"I mean, imagine the signage! You could have something quirky, like 'Get your hands dirty and leave with a smile!'" Emma exclaimed, her hands animatedly illustrating the point as if she were sketching the plans in midair.

I chuckled, the imagery tugging at a corner of my heart that craved that very sentiment. "And what would the locals say when they see that? 'Oh, look, Lila's finally lost it,'" I joked, taking a sip of my coffee. It was warm and comforting, much like Emma's presence.

"Who cares? If it makes people laugh and draws them in, that's what matters! You have to think outside the box, or, in this case, the barn," she quipped, her eyes sparkling with mischief.

"Thinking outside the barn might lead to some unexpected hayrides," I replied, grinning at the absurdity of it all. "But seriously, Emma, I'm all in for this brainstorming session. I've been so mired in the daily grind that I forgot to look up and see what could actually be done."

With every idea she tossed my way—her infectious enthusiasm wrapping around each suggestion—I felt the veil of doubt that had shrouded me start to lift. I began jotting down notes, my pen gliding across the paper as if it were channeling a long-buried ambition. "How about a petting zoo? You know how much kids love goats."

"Yes! Little fluffy things with tiny hooves. They'd be a hit! And think of the Instagram opportunities," she replied, her voice rising with excitement. "You could have 'Goat Yoga' on the weekends. It's all the rage in the city."

"Goat Yoga?" I echoed, laughter bursting from me. "Next, you'll tell me we should offer gluten-free, vegan pumpkin spice lattes made with locally sourced soy milk."

"Only if you promise not to roll your eyes at it!" she shot back, mock seriousness in her tone. "But seriously, why not play into those trends? It's all about creating an experience people will remember."

As we continued tossing ideas back and forth, a vision took shape. The farm could be more than a patch of land burdened with expectations; it could become a vibrant hub of community and creativity. The thought of people wandering through the fields, laughing and snapping photos, lit a fire inside me that had long been dormant. "Maybe we could host a 'Harvest Festival' with local musicians and food stalls," I proposed, warming to the theme.

"Yes! And you could have games, contests! Who can stack the highest hay bale?" she chimed in, her voice laced with playful competition. "I'll challenge you to a cornhole match."

"You're on!" I laughed, my heart swelling with camaraderie. It was the first time in ages that I felt the weight of responsibility lighten, the burdens momentarily slipping away.

Just as we began to lose ourselves in the excitement of our plans, an unexpected voice broke through the blissful bubble we'd created. "Lila? Is that you?"

I turned, only to find myself face-to-face with Blake, a childhood crush who had somehow managed to float back into my life at the most inconvenient of times. His tousled hair and warm smile made my stomach twist in a peculiar mix of anxiety and nostalgia. "Wow, it's been ages," he said, his voice smooth like the summer breeze.

"It has," I managed, feeling a blush creep up my cheeks. My mind was racing. The last thing I needed was a romantic distraction while I was trying to figure out my future.

Emma, ever the clever one, sensed the tension and quickly intervened. "Blake! What a coincidence. We were just discussing how to turn this farm into a must-visit destination."

"Are you? Sounds interesting." He leaned casually against the table, a devil-may-care attitude that only heightened my nervousness. "What's the plan? Goat Yoga?"

"Yes, actually!" Emma grinned, unabashed. "You could help us, right? You've always had a knack for marketing and charm."

I shot her a look that screamed "Not helping!" but she merely winked back at me. Blake's interest piqued as he leaned in closer, and I could feel the chemistry swirling, hot and undeniable. "I could throw in some ideas," he said, his gaze flicking between us. "But I'm not so sure about Goat Yoga. Seems a bit... odd."

"Odd can be good!" Emma declared. "Embrace the oddness; it's what makes it memorable."

Blake chuckled, clearly amused. "You're not wrong there. But, seriously, what else do you have planned? A corn maze? Pumpkin painting?"

My heart raced as I watched him interact with Emma. She was animated, her laughter ringing out like music, and for a moment, I envied the effortless ease between them. "Well, we thought about a Harvest Festival with music and local food," I jumped in, my voice slightly higher than usual. "And... other activities, of course."

"Sounds promising," he replied, his eyes sparking with interest. "I know some local bands who might be interested in playing, if you need them."

"Really?" I blurted, surprised and a little thrilled at the prospect. "That would be amazing!"

Emma nudged me with her elbow, a knowing grin on her face. "See? You're building a team here."

I couldn't help but smile, despite the swirl of emotions that threatened to overwhelm me. Suddenly, the notion of transformation seemed tangible. It wasn't just about the farm anymore; it was about the community, rekindling connections, and perhaps even confronting those unspoken feelings I had tucked away like last season's winter coats.

As our conversation flowed, I realized how much I needed this—new energy, fresh ideas, and yes, even a sprinkle of unexpected encounters. The market continued its lively dance around us, but for the first time, I felt as if I was truly part of something bigger than myself. It was the start of a journey I hadn't anticipated but now embraced wholeheartedly.

The lively chatter of the market wrapped around us like a warm hug, blending the scents of fresh-baked pastries and the crispness of early autumn air. I watched Blake and Emma interact, their banter flowing effortlessly, and it felt as though the whole world had narrowed to this little café corner, where dreams about the farm danced in the air like fireflies on a summer evening.

"So, if you're really serious about making this farm a destination," Blake said, leaning forward with a curious glint in his eyes, "you need to think about the overall experience. People love a story. What's the story of your farm?"

I hesitated, caught off guard by the weight of his question. "A story?" I echoed, my mind racing. "I mean, it's just... it's a family farm. We grow vegetables and fruits. It's not exactly a thrilling tale."

"Ah, but that's where you're wrong!" Emma interjected, a glimmer of mischief in her eyes. "Every farm has its own heartbeat. What if you leaned into your family history? The traditions, the struggles, the triumphs. The real, gritty stuff."

Blake nodded, his expression serious. "People connect with authenticity. They don't want cookie-cutter experiences. They want to feel something, to connect with a piece of someone's life."

I leaned back, contemplating their words. What was my farm's heartbeat? The struggles felt too personal, too raw to share with strangers, but perhaps the triumphs—the late nights spent canning peaches with my grandmother, the joy of watching my first crop of heirloom tomatoes flourish—those were worth telling. "I guess there are stories woven into the rows of corn and the apple trees," I mused, feeling a flicker of excitement.

"That's the spirit!" Emma beamed, her enthusiasm contagious. "Your farm can be a place where people can step back in time, savoring the simplicity and beauty of it all."

Blake grinned, the warmth in his eyes making my stomach flutter. "You could host storytelling nights by the firepit, complete with s'mores and local musicians. It'll create a cozy, inviting atmosphere that people won't forget."

"That sounds lovely," I said, imagining families gathered around a fire, their faces illuminated by soft flickering flames, laughter echoing into the twilight. But my excitement came crashing down as a twinge of doubt crept in. "But what if it doesn't work? What if nobody shows up?"

"Then we pivot," Emma replied, her tone unwavering. "But you won't know unless you try. This is your chance to breathe life back into the farm. Let it be a place of hope and community."

I nodded, a sense of determination swirling within me. I didn't want to let fear paralyze me any longer. "Okay. Let's do this. I'll embrace the stories, the traditions. We'll create something beautiful."

As I said those words, a sudden thought struck me. "Wait. Are you two serious about helping? I mean, you both have busy lives."

Emma waved her hand dismissively. "Please, my life is an endless cycle of spreadsheets and coffee runs. I could use some adventure. Plus, I'm excited to bring a slice of the city to the countryside!"

Blake shrugged, a teasing smile on his lips. "I can spare some time. Who wouldn't want to hang out on a picturesque farm? Plus, I'm intrigued by the prospect of Goat Yoga."

I laughed, the sound bubbling up like a rising tide. "You really are serious about that, aren't you?"

"Absolutely. I'm ready to embrace the oddness," he replied, his eyes sparkling with mischief.

Just then, my phone buzzed on the table, interrupting our playful banter. Glancing down, I saw a message from my mother: We need to talk about the farm. Urgent. My stomach dropped, the weight of her words settling like a stone in my chest.

"I, uh—" I started, my voice faltering as I looked up at Emma and Blake. "I need to take this."

I stepped away from the table, my heart pounding as I moved toward a quieter corner of the market. "What is it?" I answered, trying to keep my voice steady.

"Lila, we need to discuss the future of the farm," my mother's voice came through the line, clipped and tense. "There's a meeting with the bank next week. We need to present a solid plan."

"Mom, I'm working on something. I met with Emma, and she has great ideas—"

"Great ideas won't save us if the bank decides to pull funding," she interrupted, frustration seeping through the phone. "You need to take this seriously. We can't afford to lose it."

Her words hung heavy in the air, and I could feel the ground beneath me shifting. "I'm doing everything I can. Just give me a little time."

"Time is something we're running out of. Get your act together, Lila. We don't have the luxury of failure."

With that, she hung up, leaving me staring at the screen in shock. My stomach churned, a tight knot of anxiety forming as I rejoined Emma and Blake.

"Everything okay?" Emma asked, concern etched on her face.

I forced a smile, but the truth was tangled in my throat. "Yeah, just... family stuff."

Blake's expression shifted, and he leaned in closer. "You sure? You look a bit pale."

"It's nothing I can't handle," I said, brushing off their concern. But the weight of my mother's words loomed larger than I wanted to admit, threatening to overshadow the hopeful plans we had begun to build.

"Alright," Emma said, her voice gentle but probing. "But if you need anything, we're in this together."

I nodded, grateful for her support but feeling the burden of responsibility settle back onto my shoulders. As we began discussing the logistics of our new venture, the vibrant market continued to pulse around us, but I felt like I was standing at the edge of a precipice, my heart racing as I contemplated the fall.

Just as our conversation began to flow again, a familiar figure caught my eye across the market. A tall man, dressed sharply in a business suit, moved through the crowd with purpose, his gaze scanning the stalls. My breath hitched when I recognized him as Mr. Daniels, the local banker who had been eyeing our family farm for months.

What was he doing here? My heart raced with panic. Had he come to deliver bad news? I exchanged worried glances with Emma and Blake, and in that moment, I felt the delicate threads of our plans begin to fray.

Before I could act, he locked eyes with me, a knowing smirk playing at the corners of his lips. The world around me faded, the laughter and chatter replaced by the thundering of my pulse. I took a step back, feeling as if I were standing on the edge of a cliff with no safety net.

"Lila," he called, his voice cutting through the chaos. "We need to talk."

The knot in my stomach tightened, and I glanced back at Emma and Blake, who were watching with wide eyes. My mind raced with possibilities, each more dire than the last. I had fought so hard to breathe new life into the farm, but was it already slipping through my fingers? The weight of uncertainty pressed heavily on my chest, and as I took a deep breath, I knew that whatever he had to say would change everything.

Chapter 14: Storms of Emotion

Rain pounded the roof with a ferocity that felt personal, as if the heavens had turned against us. I stood by the window, my heart pounding to the rhythm of the storm outside. The fields we had nurtured, with their fresh greens bursting through the earth like hopeful promises, were now a patchwork of mud and anxiety. It was as if the sky itself was rebelling against our attempts at renewal. I could feel the weight of my brother Sam's gaze, a mix of frustration and worry, boring into my back. The air in the farmhouse crackled not just with static electricity but with unspoken words that begged for release.

"What were you thinking?" Sam's voice sliced through the noise, sharp and accusatory. "We could have prevented this. You and your dreams—always chasing something that doesn't exist."

I turned to face him, the flickering light of the candles casting shadows on his furrowed brow. "You think I wanted this?" I shot back, incredulous. "This wasn't some whimsical idea. I believed in our father's vision for this farm. I wanted to breathe life into it again. Is that such a crime?"

He took a step closer, and the space between us felt electric, charged with a mix of anger and grief. "You think that just because we've got a few crops sprouting, we're ready to take on the world? This storm—it's a reminder that we're not in control. Not anymore."

I swallowed hard, the lump in my throat reminiscent of the clouds overhead. It was a reminder, too, of the weight of our father's absence pressing down on us, straining our connection like the fraying edges of an old tapestry. We had both inherited his passion, but it was clear that we had channeled it in different directions. Where I saw potential, Sam saw recklessness. I could see the flickers of our childhood rivalry surfacing, the sibling squabbles over trivial matters morphing into this very real conflict rooted in shared loss and differing hopes.

"You think I'm the one ruining this place?" I felt a fire kindling within me. "What about you? You're stuck in this endless loop of despair, blaming me for everything that goes wrong. But you know what? I refuse to be your scapegoat!"

The wind howled outside, and I could almost hear our father's laughter mingled with the storm. He would have found humor in our spat, knowing how we could turn on each other like storms in the night, then reconcile with laughter just as quickly. But tonight, that laughter felt far away, drowned out by the relentless rain and our unresolved anger.

"I'm trying to protect this farm!" Sam shouted, his voice breaking slightly. "Can't you see that? Every time you throw yourself into another project, I worry you're just trying to escape—like you think you can replace him by working yourself to the bone."

His words stung, and I took a deep breath, forcing myself to ground my swirling thoughts. He didn't see it the way I did; to him, I was the reckless dreamer, blinded by visions of grandeur. But this place had always been my sanctuary. The memories of our father, the scent of fresh soil, and the thrill of planting seeds had woven themselves into the fabric of who I was.

As thunder cracked overhead, I turned away, unable to meet his eyes. "You don't know anything about what I'm feeling."

A heavy silence settled between us, thick and suffocating, punctuated only by the sound of raindrops hammering against the window. The storm outside mirrored the tempest within me, a swirling mix of fear, anger, and longing. I thought of Luke, his calming presence like a lighthouse in this turbulent sea of emotion. In the darkest moments, he'd been there, steady and reassuring, and I could feel the ache of missing him beside me now.

Just then, a sharp knock on the door startled us both. It was Luke, drenched but grinning, water cascading from his hair and splattering onto the floor. "Thought I'd find you two arguing instead of salvaging what's left out there," he said, shaking off like a wet dog, a playful twinkle in his eye.

"Now's not the time for jokes, Luke," Sam muttered, crossing his arms, clearly unimpressed by the interruption.

"Actually, I think it is," Luke replied, his voice lightening the tension like the first rays of sun breaking through the clouds. "You both look like you've just come out of a wrestling match. A storm can't stop us unless we let it." He stepped inside, shaking water from his boots. "Let's focus on what we can do rather than what we can't."

I couldn't help but smile, my heart warming at his unwavering optimism. "What do you propose? Build an ark?"

"Why not?" Luke chuckled, leaning against the doorframe, clearly unfazed by the argument. "We could take turns paddling around the fields. Just imagine the stories we could tell! 'The Great Flood of Mulligan Farm.'"

Sam rolled his eyes but couldn't suppress a grin. "Next you'll be suggesting we start a fishery."

"Not a bad idea, actually," Luke said, turning his gaze to me. "But for real, what if we go out and check the drainage? There's got to be something we can do before the crops drown. Teamwork, right?"

As the thunder rumbled softly in the distance, I felt the tension start to ease. The storm had brought us to a breaking point, but here was Luke, like a breath of fresh air, reminding us of what mattered. Maybe it was time to set aside the fighting and come together, not just as siblings grieving a loss but as partners in rebuilding something beautiful.

"Alright," I said, a tentative smile breaking through. "Let's do this."

As we donned our raincoats and gathered supplies, I caught a glimpse of Sam's hesitant nod. For the first time that night, I felt a glimmer of hope beneath the weight of our troubles. We were in this storm together, after all, and with Luke by our side, perhaps we could weather anything that came our way.

The rain beat down relentlessly, but there was a peculiar thrill in moving through the downpour. Luke had taken the lead, bounding ahead with an enthusiasm that would have been infectious even if I hadn't been drenched to the skin. Sam trailed behind, still wearing that stubborn scowl, arms crossed tightly over his chest. I could sense the gears turning in his mind, the lingering resentment tangled with concern for the farm.

"Didn't we just have a conversation about the dangers of waterlogging crops?" Sam muttered, struggling to keep his footing as the ground turned slippery beneath our boots. "You know, like, oh I don't know, five minutes ago?"

"Consider this a hands-on lesson in disaster management," Luke quipped, glancing back with a smirk that could warm a winter's day. "Besides, what's life without a little risk? Maybe we'll discover a whole new ecosystem down there."

"Yeah, maybe a swamp monster," Sam shot back, but I could see the edges of his lips twitching, just barely resisting the pull of laughter.

"Or an entire family of frogs just waiting to become our allies," I chimed in, my spirits lifting. "They'll help us battle the pests. It's all part of the grand plan."

With each step, I felt the tension that had knotted in my chest begin to unravel. Working side by side, even amid the chaos of the storm, shifted something in our dynamic. I caught a glimpse of Sam's profile, framed by the deluge, and I knew we were both yearning for the same thing—understanding.

As we reached the first field, the sight was heartbreaking. Water pooled in the low spots, threatening to swallow the young plants whole. I knelt down, fingers sinking into the saturated earth, feeling the pulse of life struggling beneath the surface. "We've got to divert the water," I said, urgency thrumming through my veins.

"Yeah, but how?" Sam sighed, surveying the damage with a frown that deepened with each passing second.

"Maybe we can dig a trench?" Luke suggested, his voice steady and focused. "If we channel the water away from the crops, we might save what we can."

"Right, let's just dig a trench in the middle of a storm," Sam muttered, sarcasm lacing his tone.

"Believe it or not, I've done crazier things," I replied, my heart racing as the idea took root in my mind. "Come on, we have to try. It's not like we have a choice."

With renewed purpose, we set to work, shoveling mud and debris, the rain mingling with our sweat and exhaustion. We moved in a rhythm that felt almost choreographed, the tension between us dissipating like mist in the sun. I couldn't remember the last time we had worked together so seamlessly, and even Sam began to crack jokes, mocking my over-enthusiastic shovel technique, which only fueled my resolve to prove him wrong.

"Maybe you should start your own YouTube channel: 'Shoveling with Sincerity,'" he teased, panting slightly as he plunged his own spade into the ground.

"Only if you're my first subscriber," I shot back, laughter bubbling up in spite of the rain.

But as we dug, a thought nagged at me, like a storm cloud refusing to dissipate. What if we couldn't save the crops? The possibility hung heavy in the air, stifling the laughter that had just begun to flow freely. I stole a glance at Sam, whose face was set in grim determination. It struck me then—this farm was more than just land; it was a legacy, a connection to our father that we desperately needed to preserve.

"Do you ever wonder if we're fighting a losing battle?" I asked, my voice barely audible over the wind.

"What do you mean?" Sam replied, not looking up from his work.

"I mean, every time we pour ourselves into this, it feels like we're just trying to hold back the tide. What if it's not enough?"

The question hung there, an unwelcome weight in the air. Sam paused, finally lifting his gaze to meet mine, vulnerability flickering in his eyes. "I think about that all the time. But if we give up, then what? We lose everything our dad worked for. I won't let that happen."

"And what if the world keeps throwing storms at us? Are we just supposed to keep building trenches forever?" I countered, my frustration spilling over. "Maybe it's time to reconsider what we're doing here."

"Reconsider?" Sam's brows knitted together, the storm outside reflecting the turmoil brewing within. "What are you suggesting? That we quit? That we just walk away?"

"No!" I exclaimed, my voice rising in pitch. "I want to find a way to adapt. Maybe we can rethink the crops, explore other ways to sustain the land."

Sam shook his head, disbelief etched across his features. "You want to abandon everything? Just like that?"

I let out a frustrated sigh, raking my hands through my drenched hair. "I'm not abandoning anything! I'm trying to save what's left. Can't you see that?"

Just as the tension reached a breaking point, Luke stepped in, holding up a hand as if to quiet the storm brewing between us. "What if we compromise?" he suggested, his calm demeanor like a lighthouse amidst choppy waters. "Let's not throw the baby out with the bathwater. We can brainstorm new ideas while still respecting your dad's legacy. There's strength in evolution, right?"

"Evolution, huh?" Sam crossed his arms, eyes narrowing slightly. "What are you thinking?"

"Maybe we diversify the crops," Luke suggested, his eyes lighting up with possibility. "What if we added some hardier plants? Something that could withstand storms better. We could research sustainable practices that our father didn't have time to implement."

I felt a rush of hope at the thought, my heart swelling with the idea of reinvention. "And we can still keep the core of what he wanted. We don't have to throw away the dream. We can just... reshape it."

"Yeah," Sam said slowly, his skepticism softening. "That could work. But it's going to take time, effort—"

"—and a lot of muddy boots," I chimed in, trying to lighten the mood.

Luke chuckled, the sound like a soothing balm to our frayed nerves. "I'll bring the snacks; you two bring the shovels. We're in this together."

The storm outside raged on, but in that moment, it felt like the clouds had lifted just a bit. The three of us stood together, soaked but united, ready to forge a new path. The journey ahead would be daunting, fraught with challenges and uncertainties, but for the first time in a long while, I believed we could weather any storm together.

We plunged into the depths of the mud with renewed determination, laughter now mingling with the splashing rain as we worked together to divert the water from our precious crops. I couldn't help but feel a sense of camaraderie building among us, a collective resolve to face whatever challenges lay ahead.

"Why do I feel like we're just reenacting a scene from a disaster movie?" I shouted over the howling wind, gripping my shovel with a sense of purpose.

"Because we're two seconds away from getting swept away into a watery grave," Sam quipped, his brows raised in mock terror. "I think I saw a shark fin back there."

"More like a catfish," Luke chimed in, laughter bubbling from him. "The only danger here is from all the laughter I'm holding back."

"Seriously, keep it down," I said, attempting to suppress a grin. "You're going to wake the swamp monsters."

As the rain poured harder, we dug deeper, feeling the weight of the situation with every shovelful of mud we shifted. Each scrape of the shovel against the earth felt like a small victory against the elements. But amid the lighthearted banter, a sliver of doubt crept in.

"What if it doesn't work?" I asked, my voice faltering slightly as I glanced up at the ominous clouds swirling above. "What if we just end up making things worse?"

"Then we'll just have to get creative," Sam replied, his tone steady, even if his eyes flickered with uncertainty. "If we mess up, we learn, right? That's how it works."

I felt a swell of gratitude toward him. It was almost ironic how a storm could bring us closer together, reminding me of childhood days spent mucking about in the rain, not a care in the world. But this was different; we were grown now, carrying the weight of our father's legacy on our shoulders, and that weight sometimes felt insurmountable.

As the rain finally began to ease, the air became charged with possibility. I was about to suggest we take a break when a sudden crack of thunder roared above us, louder than anything we'd heard all night. It sent a jolt through my body, and the ground trembled beneath our feet.

"Did that feel like an earthquake to anyone else?" Luke exclaimed, his eyes wide as he steadied himself against the wooden fence post.

"No, but I did feel a bit of my sanity shake loose," Sam said, grinning despite the tension.

Before I could respond, a bright flash lit up the sky, momentarily blinding me. I shielded my eyes, and when the light faded, I caught a glimpse of movement near the edge of the field. Something dark and looming rose against the backdrop of the stormy sky, and my heart raced as I squinted to see better.

"Did you see that?" I pointed toward the disturbance, dread pooling in my stomach.

"What? The rain? The mud? Or your rapidly deteriorating mental state?" Sam joked, but the smile faded as he caught the seriousness in my expression.

"No, really," I insisted. "Something's out there."

Luke took a cautious step forward, his face set in concentration. "Let's check it out," he said, his voice low and steady.

We waded through the soaked grass, mud sucking at our boots as we approached the shadowy figure that was becoming clearer. With each step, the air felt heavier, charged with a sense of impending doom that made my skin prickle.

As we drew closer, I could see that it was a large, toppled tree, its roots exposed like an angry fist raised to the heavens. But that wasn't what had caught my attention. Nestled amongst the roots was something glimmering—something metallic, partially buried in the mud.

"What the hell is that?" Sam asked, his brow furrowing as he knelt down for a better look.

I moved closer, my heart racing. "It looks like... a box?"

With cautious excitement, I began to dig around it, shoveling away clumps of mud, revealing more of the object. It was a small, weathered metal box, tarnished but intact, its surface etched with strange symbols that glinted in the dim light of the storm.

"What do you think is inside?" Luke asked, his voice barely above a whisper, as if he feared disturbing whatever mystery lay within.

"I don't know, but it looks like it's been here for ages," I replied, my fingers brushing against the cold metal. "Should we open it?"

"Is that really a question?" Sam shot back, his eyes wide with curiosity. "Of course we should!"

With a few more shovelfuls of mud cleared away, I managed to grasp the edges of the box, and together we pulled it free from its earthen prison. The rain had eased to a light drizzle now, but the air remained thick with tension as I lifted the lid, the hinges creaking ominously.

Inside lay a jumble of faded papers, their edges curling and stained. But what caught my eye first was a small, leather-bound journal, its cover embossed with intricate designs that echoed the symbols on the box. My fingers trembled as I reached in to grab it, the weight of history resting in my palm.

"What do you think it is?" Luke asked, leaning closer, the fading light glistening in his eyes.

"I don't know, but it looks important," I said, feeling a thrill of discovery coursing through me. "This could be something from our father's time."

As I opened the journal, a rush of musty air wafted up, carrying the scent of aged paper and forgotten memories. The pages were filled with notes, sketches, and observations that seemed to outline plans for the farm—crops, irrigation systems, even drawings of the layout. My heart raced as I scanned the pages, and then I froze.

"Wait..." I whispered, my voice barely audible above the gentle patter of rain. "This is more than just farming plans. He was talking about... something else."

"What do you mean?" Sam asked, peering over my shoulder, his expression shifting from excitement to concern.

I flipped through the pages, my pulse quickening as I read phrases like "hidden potential" and "future sustainability." But it was the last entry that made my blood run cold. "It's not just about the crops," I read aloud. "The true treasure lies beneath the surface—secrets waiting to be unearthed."

"What does that mean?" Luke asked, the unease palpable in the air.

"I don't know, but if there are secrets..." I trailed off, looking up at my brother and Luke. The storm seemed to retreat slightly, almost as if the world was holding its breath in anticipation of what we would uncover next.

Just then, a deafening crash echoed in the distance, and I felt the ground tremble beneath my feet once more. My heart pounded as I exchanged a glance with Sam. "We need to find out what else is buried here," I said, determination flooding my veins.

But before any of us could move, a loud rumble sounded from the edge of the field. We turned to see the last remnants of the storm swirling ominously, and then... something massive broke free from the trees, crashing toward us with an intensity that sent a wave of fear through my body.

"Run!" I shouted, adrenaline surging as I grabbed the journal, clutching it tightly to my chest.

The ground shook beneath our feet, and as we sprinted away from the chaos, I couldn't shake the feeling that this storm had only just begun. Behind us, the shadows of the forest loomed, ready to reveal secrets we weren't prepared to face.

Chapter 15: Unexpected Connections

The sun hung low in the sky, casting a warm golden hue over the freshly washed landscape. It was as if the world had taken a deep breath, inhaling the scent of wet earth and blooming wildflowers, then exhaling tranquility. I stood knee-deep in the remnants of what had once been an unruly fence, my fingers numbed by the chill of the wood, splintered but resolute against the recent storm. Luke approached, his silhouette framed by the light, and my heart fluttered at the sight of him, a welcome distraction from the weight pressing down on my chest.

"Thought you might need a little pick-me-up," he said, setting down a wicker basket with a flourish, the contents spilling out like a magician's final trick. Homemade sandwiches, neatly wrapped in parchment paper, glinted in the sun, along with a pitcher of lemonade that sparkled as if caught in a joyful dance. It was such a simple gesture, yet it felt monumental, a warm embrace in a world that had turned cold and gray.

"Where did you find all this?" I laughed, shaking my head in disbelief. "Did you raid the local bakery while I wasn't looking?"

He shrugged, a mischievous grin lighting up his face. "You underestimate my culinary prowess. It's all about using what you have, you know? Plus, I found this amazing lemon tree down by the creek." He gestured towards a distant cluster of trees, and I could already picture the hidden treasures he might have stumbled upon.

As we settled on a blanket laid out over the grass, I marveled at the effortless ease between us. The air buzzed with the gentle hum of insects, and I could almost hear the land sigh in relief, reclaiming its rhythm. The sandwiches were surprisingly delicious, the flavors a delightful medley of tangy mustard and fresh herbs. I found myself lost in the moment, laughing and teasing him about his culinary adventures, feeling lighter than I had in days.

"Do you remember that time we tried to make a campfire?" he asked, his eyes twinkling with mischief. "You nearly burned my eyebrows off."

I gasped, feigning offense. "That was not my fault! You're the one who thought using lighter fluid was a good idea!"

"I stand by my decision! It was a perfectly sound strategy at the time." He leaned back, arms behind his head, as he chuckled, the sound warm and inviting.

The laughter faded, and a comfortable silence enveloped us, the weight of unspoken words lingering in the air. I watched the clouds drift lazily overhead, and for a moment, I wished I could float away with them, far from the troubles that had settled like a storm in my heart.

"So," Luke began, breaking the tranquility, his voice suddenly serious. "What's really going on with you?"

The question caught me off guard, and I turned my head to look at him. There was a depth in his gaze, an earnestness that demanded honesty. I felt my walls begin to tremble, the instinct to shield myself fighting against the yearning to be vulnerable with him.

"It's just... everything has felt so heavy lately," I admitted, my voice softer than I intended. "The storm was a mess, but it was more than that. I've been carrying around a lot of things that I thought I could handle on my own. And maybe I can, but it feels different now."

He shifted closer, the warmth of his body radiating against my chill. "You don't have to go through this alone. You know that, right?"

I met his eyes, and in that moment, something shifted. The weight I had been carrying felt a little lighter, as if he had offered to shoulder some of it. "I know, but it's hard to open up. I feel like I'm always trying to hold everything together, and sometimes I'm terrified of what happens if I let go."

He nodded, a look of understanding etched across his features. "I get that. You should hear the expectations my family has for me. It's like they've set a blueprint for my life, and I'm stuck trying to color outside the lines."

The unexpected confession surprised me. Luke had always been the steady one, the anchor in the storm. "What do you mean?"

"It's like everyone expects me to follow a certain path—college, career, the whole shebang. But what if I don't want that?" He ran a hand through his hair, frustration creeping into his voice. "What if I want to be out here, living off the land, planting wildflowers, and just... being?"

The imagery he conjured up was so vivid it made me smile. "You'd make a great wildflower farmer," I teased, my heart lightening further at the thought.

"Maybe I should take it up as a side hustle," he replied, smirking. "I'd be the first person in history to make wildflower farming a career choice."

As our laughter filled the air once more, I couldn't shake the sense of camaraderie that had blossomed between us. It was a bond forged not just in the lighthearted moments but also in the heavy truths we had dared to share. Each word peeled back layers we had carefully constructed, revealing the rawness beneath.

"Do you think we're ever going to figure it out?" I asked, suddenly serious again. "All the things we're supposed to be?"

"Honestly? I think we're all just winging it," he replied, a lightness returning to his voice. "The trick is to find someone who makes the chaos feel like home."

His words lingered in the air, settling like a delicate whisper between us. I wanted to believe him, to lean into that feeling of connection, but my heart held onto the fears I had spent so long building. It was terrifying, exposing that vulnerability, yet here he was, a steady presence amidst the storm.

In that moment, I made a decision. Perhaps it was time to embrace the chaos, to step away from the blueprint, and instead, dance wildly in the unexpected. The path before us was uncertain, but with Luke beside me, it didn't feel quite so daunting.

The sun dipped lower in the sky, casting long shadows that danced across the field, where remnants of our makeshift picnic still lingered. The laughter faded, replaced by a comfortable silence that wrapped around us like a soft blanket. I watched Luke as he picked at the grass, a thoughtful expression crossing his face, and I felt a sudden urge to protect that moment, to freeze time right there.

"Do you think we're doing enough?" he asked, his voice breaking the quiet. There was a depth to his words, a hidden question that hung in the air between us, filled with a vulnerability I hadn't expected.

"Enough?" I echoed, tilting my head slightly. "In what sense?"

"Just... everything. The fence, the farm, our lives. Are we making a difference? Or are we just—" He paused, searching for the right words. "Spinning our wheels?"

I considered his question. "I think sometimes, doing enough looks like keeping your head above water. And right now, we're just trying to stay afloat."

He nodded slowly, the frustration etched in the lines of his brow. "I get that, but I can't help feeling like there's something more we could be doing—like we're meant for something bigger."

The idea resonated within me, reverberating through the chaos of my thoughts. I had felt it too, that gnawing sensation that life was meant to be more than this patchwork existence of chores and expectations. But what did 'more' look like?

"Maybe we're just waiting for the right moment," I suggested, the words tumbling out before I had a chance to consider them. "Or maybe we need to create our own moments."

His eyes met mine, a spark igniting between us, and suddenly I felt as if we were standing on the precipice of something extraordinary. "You might be onto something," he said, a grin spreading across his face, and I felt my own lips curl in response.

We began packing up the remnants of our picnic, the atmosphere shifting from pensive to playful. "Okay, how about this?" Luke said, his voice bright with mischief. "Let's make a list of things we've always wanted to do. A bucket list for our tiny corner of the world."

"A bucket list?" I raised an eyebrow, intrigued yet skeptical. "You mean like 'witness the world's largest cow' or 'become famous for our wildflower farming'?"

"Hey, don't knock it until you've tried it! But seriously, what if we did something wild? Something that scares us?" He leaned in closer, the challenge clear in his gaze.

I could feel my pulse quicken, an intoxicating blend of excitement and fear swirling in my gut. "Alright, let's start with something reasonable—like climbing to the top of that hill by the creek."

"Reasonable?" He laughed, the sound echoing in the open space. "That's the kind of thing they put on a list right after 'run away to join the circus.' We need to think bigger!"

"Okay, Mr. Adventurous, what do you have in mind?"

"Skydiving," he blurted out, his expression both earnest and ludicrous.

I gasped, pretending to be scandalized. "And here I thought we were just trying to fix a fence. Is skydiving really the next logical step?"

"Why not? It's the perfect metaphor for life—jumping into the unknown with reckless abandon!" He spread his arms wide, as if to embrace the very essence of spontaneity.

I chuckled, shaking my head. "Okay, maybe we should start with something a little less... life-threatening."

"Fine! But just know, I'm not letting you off the hook for skydiving." He winked, and I felt my heart race again, this time for an entirely different reason.

As we wrapped up our picnic, I couldn't shake the feeling that this was a pivotal moment for us. The laughter and banter felt like a safety net, weaving around our shared hopes and dreams. I could sense that beneath our playful exchange lay something deeper—a yearning to break free from the chains of expectation that had held us both captive for too long.

The next few days were filled with a newfound energy. We painted a bright blue on the fence, our laughter echoing through the fields, our shared mission morphing into an adventure of its own. We set about gathering materials for the garden, Luke's enthusiasm infectious as he recited plans for an herb patch and a wildflower section that would draw butterflies in droves.

"Imagine waking up to that every morning," he said, gesturing grandly as if it were the most splendid of castles. "A riot of color, a sanctuary of scents. It could be a haven!"

"And you could finally fulfill your wildflower farming dream," I teased, nudging him playfully. "Maybe even sell bouquets at the farmer's market."

"Just wait until the world sees my floral designs," he said with mock seriousness, striking a pose that made me laugh out loud. "I'll have a line of wedding bouquets named after our greatest adventures."

The days flowed seamlessly, each one blending into the next. Our conversations deepened, interspersed with lighthearted moments that seemed to bubble up effortlessly, yet beneath the surface, we both felt the currents of unspoken tension. I often caught Luke looking at me with a mixture of admiration and something else—something that sent a rush of warmth flooding my cheeks.

One evening, as the sun dipped below the horizon, painting the sky in hues of orange and pink, we sat on the porch, the weight of the day's labor slipping away. The air was thick with the scent of freshly turned soil, and the sounds of crickets serenaded us.

"Do you think we'll ever leave this place?" Luke asked, breaking the stillness that had settled between us.

"Leave?" I repeated, considering his question. "I don't know. Sometimes I dream about moving away, exploring cities and finding new adventures. But then I think about all the memories here, the comfort of home."

He nodded, his expression contemplative. "It's like we're stuck in this bubble, but maybe it's a bubble we can shape ourselves."

"Shape it how?"

"By doing what we want. Not what's expected." He leaned forward, his voice barely above a whisper. "And I want you to be a part of that. I want to explore, take risks, and I want to do it with you."

My heart raced, and the weight of his words hung in the air, laden with possibilities. I glanced away, unsure of how to respond, the enormity of what he was suggesting crashing over me like waves against the shore. Did I dare to step outside the confines of my comfort zone, to venture into the unknown with him by my side?

"Luke," I began, the words feeling heavy on my tongue. "What if we dream too big? What if it doesn't work out?"

"Then we'll just have to find a way to make it work," he said, his gaze unwavering. "You've taught me that life isn't just about safety nets; it's about taking chances, and sometimes, the biggest risks lead to the greatest rewards."

In that moment, the tension transformed into a different kind of energy—a mix of anticipation and fear, laced with the intoxicating thrill of the unknown. As the sun surrendered to twilight, I realized that it was time to embrace the chaos, to weave our dreams into a tapestry of adventures, regardless of what lay ahead.

The twilight air held a crispness that promised change, weaving a sense of anticipation into the very fabric of our small world. After our conversation, the weight of unspoken dreams felt lighter, as if we had loosened the bonds that had tethered us to our predictable lives. I could still hear Luke's voice echoing in my mind, the sincerity of his words wrapping around me like a warm quilt against the chill of uncertainty.

We spent the next few days transforming the farm, each task fueled by an exhilarating mix of newfound purpose and the sweet thrill of rebellion against the expectations that had long dictated our lives. We planted seeds of wildflowers that danced in the wind, a riot of color destined to sprout and blossom in ways we could hardly imagine. The energy between us crackled with a playful intensity, and every shared glance felt charged with possibilities.

One morning, we set out to explore a hidden trail I had stumbled upon last summer, just past the old oak tree, where the sunlight spilled onto the path like honey. The promise of adventure hung in the air as we ventured deeper into the woods, laughter spilling forth like the bright stream beside us. Luke stepped ahead, the sunlight highlighting the way his shoulders moved with purpose.

"Do you ever feel like we're just walking in circles?" I asked, pushing a strand of hair behind my ear as I hurried to catch up.

"Maybe," he mused, glancing back with a smirk, "but circles can be pretty fun if you're with the right person. Plus, it's a good workout!" He flexed his biceps dramatically, pretending to strain against the weight of an invisible burden.

I laughed, the sound echoing through the trees. "Oh yes, my heart is racing from all this rigorous exercise!"

The path twisted and turned, revealing patches of vibrant ferns and wildflowers peeking through the underbrush. With each step, I felt the weight of my old life fade further into the background, the colors of the forest pulling me into the present moment. The chatter of birds above felt like a soundtrack to our unfolding adventure, their songs weaving through the rustling leaves.

As we reached a small clearing, my breath caught in my throat. Before us lay a hidden pond, glistening like a polished jewel under the sun's warm embrace. The surface rippled gently, mirroring the sky, and I could hardly believe we had stumbled upon such a secret place.

"Wow," I breathed, taking in the breathtaking sight. "This is incredible!"

"Almost as incredible as my ability to find delicious picnic spots," Luke quipped, his voice laced with pride as he set his backpack down. "How about another round of lemonade? We might as well make this our second picnic."

"I'm not sure it can compete with the first one," I teased, but I was already reaching for the basket, excitement bubbling inside me.

As we settled beside the pond, sipping lemonade and soaking in the serenity of our surroundings, a comfortable silence enveloped us. I stole glances at Luke, his features softened by the sun's glow, and felt a rush of something unnameable, a swell of warmth that coursed through my veins.

"Do you ever think about where we'll be in five years?" he asked suddenly, breaking the stillness with a serious tone that took me off guard.

"Five years?" I pondered, furrowing my brow. "That seems so far away. I barely know what I want for lunch half the time."

"But seriously," he pressed, his expression earnest. "Do you think we'll still be here? Still doing... this?" He gestured to the tranquil surroundings, the idyllic life we'd carved out.

I took a moment, letting his words settle. "I guess it depends on what 'this' means, doesn't it? If 'this' means working the farm, then maybe, but if it means being stuck in the same routine, I can't see myself doing it forever."

Luke nodded, contemplating my response. "You're right. Maybe it's time we figure out what our 'this' really is. We could explore more, go places we've never seen. Experience life."

"Like a road trip?" I suggested, my heart racing at the thought. "Or... I don't know, traveling the world?"

"Why not both? We could hit the open road and see where it takes us!" He leaned back, a grin stretching across his face, as if he had just unveiled the greatest plan ever conceived.

I couldn't help but laugh at the infectious enthusiasm radiating from him. "And how would we fund this grand adventure? Last I checked, our bank accounts are less than impressive."

"Details, details," he waved away my concern. "We'll figure that out later. Think of the stories we could tell, the memories we'd make!"

The thought was intoxicating, and for a moment, I was swept away by the daydreams of faraway places and adventures. But then reality clawed its way back in, reminding me of the responsibilities waiting for me back home. "Luke, I can't just abandon everything. I have obligations."

He sat up, a hint of frustration flaring in his eyes. "You deserve to live for yourself too. Just because you have obligations doesn't mean you have to let them suffocate you."

"Wow, such wisdom from a self-proclaimed wildflower farmer," I shot back, unable to hide my amusement.

"Hey, I'm a philosopher at heart," he replied, crossing his arms defensively. "But really, think about it. What do you want?"

"I want..." I hesitated, searching for the right words. "I want to feel free, to make choices that aren't dictated by anyone else."

"Then let's do it. Let's find that freedom." His voice was steady, urging me to believe in the possibilities we were crafting together.

The air around us crackled with energy, and as we laughed and tossed ideas back and forth, I felt a shift within me—a crack in the façade of my fears. Maybe I could take a leap of faith. But just as I began to entertain the thought, a sudden rustling in the bushes behind us made me jump.

"What was that?" I whispered, instinctively leaning closer to Luke.

"Probably just a deer," he assured me, though his brow furrowed, revealing his own unease.

As if to prove him wrong, a figure stepped into the clearing, shadowed and ominous against the backdrop of the sunlit pond. My heart dropped, and I instinctively reached for Luke's hand.

"What are you doing here?" the newcomer demanded, his voice low and menacing, sending chills racing down my spine.

"Who are you?" I managed to stammer, heart racing as I clung to Luke, who shifted protectively in front of me.

The figure stepped closer, and with each step, the sun dipped further behind the clouds, casting the clearing into a shadowy gloom.

"I'm here for something you both have, and you need to hand it over."

Panic surged through me, and I felt the warmth of Luke's hand squeeze mine tightly. The weight of uncertainty loomed, threatening to shatter the fragile world we had begun to build. The idyllic pond, once a sanctuary, now felt like a stage for the chaos about to unfold. I could barely catch my breath as I looked into Luke's eyes, searching for reassurance, but all I found was the same flicker of fear mirrored back at me.

"Now," the figure insisted, his gaze piercing through the haze of disbelief. "It's time for you to decide how far you're willing to go to protect what's yours."

The words hung heavy in the air, a storm brewing on the horizon of our peaceful lives, and in that moment, I knew everything was about to change.

Chapter 16: The Weight of Choices

The air was thick with unspoken words, the kind that hung in the silence like a dense fog, blurring the line between what was and what could be. I stood outside Sam's office, my heart thumping like a drum echoing in a quiet room, each beat urging me forward while simultaneously tethering me in place. The community's support had wrapped around me like a warm blanket, but with it came the chill of Sam's threats, those bitter seeds of discontent planted deep within him. The promise of conflict loomed over me, palpable and ominous.

Pushing the door open, I stepped inside, the scent of old paper and faint coffee intertwining with the musty air, a strange comfort in this war-torn sanctuary. Sam sat hunched over his desk, shoulders stiff, eyes glued to the pile of paperwork that seemed to have accumulated since the dawn of time. For a fleeting moment, I thought about turning back, but I squared my shoulders, steeling myself for the confrontation that awaited.

"Sam," I began, my voice softer than I intended, as if afraid to disturb the delicate equilibrium of the moment. His head snapped up, and I saw the momentary flicker of surprise before his expression hardened into a mask of indifference.

"Here to talk about Dad again?" he replied, his tone dripping with sarcasm. "How novel."

"Actually, I'm here to talk about us," I shot back, a flash of irritation sparking in my chest. "This isn't just about Dad anymore."

"Isn't it?" His eyes narrowed, and I could feel the distance between us stretching, a chasm that had been years in the making. "Everything always comes back to him, doesn't it? The great David Mallory, who never had a flaw in his life, who built this place from nothing while I just... sat in his shadow."

The accusation hung between us like a physical entity, heavy and suffocating. I took a step closer, trying to bridge that gap. "You're not in his shadow, Sam. You're your own person. Just look at what you've accomplished with this office."

"Accomplished?" He scoffed, a bitter laugh escaping his lips. "Is that what we're calling it now? I'm a glorified paper pusher. It's a far cry from saving the world like our father did."

I clenched my fists, feeling the weight of my frustration surge. "You think I haven't felt the pressure? The expectations? Just because I'm his daughter doesn't mean I'm not struggling too."

His gaze softened for a fleeting moment, and I caught a glimpse of the hurt lurking beneath his bravado. "What do you know about struggle? You waltzed in here, a little princess, looking for love letters and nostalgic stories."

"Do you think it's easy for me?" My voice rose, echoing against the walls. "I've spent my entire life trying to figure out who I am outside of his legacy, outside of your shadow. I didn't come here just to dig through dusty boxes. I came to understand—"

"To understand what?" he interrupted, his tone sharp. "To understand that you're destined to inherit the throne? That you'll be the next beloved figure in this town, and I'll be left to watch as everyone fawns over you?"

I took a breath, letting the air fill my lungs, calming the storm that threatened to erupt. "I don't want that. I never asked for that. I just want to find some piece of him that connects us, that reminds us we're family. I thought you'd want that too."

A silence fell over the room, thick and uneasy. Sam ran a hand through his hair, frustration palpable in every line of his face. I could see the conflict warring within him, the vulnerability peeking through the cracks of his bravado. "You don't get it. You've always been the favored one, the one everyone believed in. I was just... there."

"You weren't just there!" I exclaimed, the desperation creeping into my voice. "You're so much more than that! You're brilliant, Sam!

You've built this place from the ground up. People respect you. I respect you."

He met my gaze, and for the first time, I saw a flicker of uncertainty in his eyes, as if my words were shifting something within him. "You really think that?" The hardness in his voice wavered, and my heart raced with a glimmer of hope.

"Of course I do. I've been watching you, trying to figure out how to break through. I thought maybe if I could find something meaningful, something from Dad, it could help us both."

His expression turned contemplative, and the weight of my confession settled between us like an uninvited guest. "You think a few letters will fix everything? Make me feel like I'm not just a second-rate version of him?"

"No, but they might help us understand him better. And maybe, in doing so, we can understand ourselves." My words hung in the air, an invitation wrapped in vulnerability, and the silence stretched, ripe with possibility.

"I found some letters, Sam," I continued, my voice softer, more deliberate. "They weren't just about his accomplishments; they were about his dreams, his fears. He wrote about you, about how proud he was of you, how he never wanted you to feel overshadowed." I stepped closer, willing him to see the truth behind my words. "I believe he loved us both in ways we couldn't even fathom."

He turned away, staring out the window, where the sunlight poured over the town like a gentle embrace, illuminating the imperfections in the glass. "Maybe you're right. But I'm not sure I can forgive him. Or myself."

In that moment, I understood the complexity of our struggle, the tangle of resentment and longing that bound us. We were both lost, adrift in a sea of expectations and grief, searching for a lifeline that might lead us back to one another. The path forward felt uncertain, and yet, as I stood there, I sensed a shift, a glimmer of hope threading through the jagged edges of our fractured relationship.

The sunlight streaming through the window painted the room in warm hues, a stark contrast to the chill of our conversation. As I watched Sam wrestle with his thoughts, I noticed the way his brow furrowed, deep lines etching themselves into his forehead. The air felt electric, thick with possibilities, as if we were teetering on the edge of something monumental. I could sense his internal battle, the reluctance to let go of the anger that had become a part of him like a second skin.

"Look, I don't want to argue about our childhood," I said, trying to find the right words, the magic combination that might crack through his hardened shell. "What I want is to understand why you're so angry. I need to know what's behind all this."

He sighed, a sound that seemed to carry the weight of the world, and ran a hand through his hair. "It's not just about being angry, you know. It's about feeling like I'm not enough. Not for him, not for you, not for anyone."

His admission hung in the air like a lead balloon. I could feel the heat of it, the intensity of his vulnerability. "You are enough, Sam. In ways I can't even begin to express. You've taken on so much, and you've done it with grace. I just wish you could see that."

He met my gaze, skepticism shadowing his features. "Grace? You think there's grace in drowning in a job that feels more like a trap than a career? That's rich coming from the daughter of the man whose footsteps I'm constantly trying—and failing—to follow."

My heart ached for him, for the burden he carried. "I don't want you to drown. I want you to rise above it, to step into the light you've created for yourself. There's more to you than just being David Mallory's son."

His jaw tightened, and I could almost hear the gears turning in his mind, wrestling with the truth I'd laid bare. "Maybe it's easier for you to say that, but you don't know what it's like to be constantly measured against someone else's greatness."

"Do you really think that?" I asked, incredulous. "Do you think I've floated through life untouched by comparison? I spent years trying to carve out my own identity, always in the shadow of what my father built. I didn't choose this life, Sam. None of us did. But we can choose how we respond to it."

Silence engulfed us, thick and heavy. I took a step closer, my voice barely a whisper. "I've seen the way people look at you, how they admire you for what you've accomplished. Maybe you don't see it, but you're inspiring them in ways you can't even imagine."

"Maybe," he muttered, staring at his desk, a pile of papers littering the surface like abandoned dreams. "But it still doesn't change the fact that I feel like a fraud. I'm not Dad; I never will be."

"Neither am I," I replied, the words spilling out before I could think them through. "I don't want to be. I just want to be me."

He finally looked up, the flicker of vulnerability in his eyes replaced by something sharper, more dangerous. "And who is that, exactly? Do you even know?"

"Maybe I'm still figuring it out," I admitted, a tinge of frustration creeping into my voice. "But I refuse to let our father's legacy dictate who I am. And you shouldn't either."

Sam's expression shifted, the storm within him momentarily quieting as he processed my words. "What if we're both just trying to live up to an impossible standard? What if we keep pushing each other away instead of leaning on one another?"

The thought struck me like a lightning bolt, illuminating the tangled web of emotions that bound us together. "What if we stopped letting his memory drive a wedge between us?"

The challenge hung in the air, and I could see the gears shifting in Sam's mind, as if he were reconsidering everything he'd ever believed about himself and us. He took a deep breath, his posture relaxing slightly. "And how do you propose we do that?"

"By starting here," I said, gesturing between us. "We're not our father. We need to stop comparing ourselves to him and instead focus on what we can build together. You have so much to offer, and I can't be who I need to be without you."

A small, reluctant smile tugged at the corners of his mouth. "You're more optimistic than I am, you know."

"Or maybe I'm just better at seeing the bright side," I replied, my own smile creeping onto my face. "You've been carrying this for so long, and I'm not saying it'll disappear overnight, but maybe we can help each other lighten the load."

He nodded slowly, as if testing the idea in his mind. "I suppose it's worth a shot. But don't be surprised if I still throw a few punches along the way."

"Trust me, I'm prepared for that," I said with a smirk, relieved to see a glimmer of the brother I'd known before all the heartache. "Just promise me you won't throw anything too heavy."

The laughter that erupted between us felt like the first cracks in a wall that had loomed between us for years. I had missed this connection, the shared humor that often danced on the edge of our conversations, and as the tension eased, I felt a sense of hope blossoming in the pit of my stomach.

But as quickly as the moment arrived, it dissipated into the air, leaving behind an undercurrent of anxiety. "What about the letters?" Sam asked, suddenly serious again, his brows knitting together as he leaned forward. "What did Dad really say about me?"

I hesitated, the weight of the words heavy on my tongue. "He spoke about his fears, how he worried you'd feel overshadowed. He wanted you to know that you were more than his legacy—that you had your own path to carve."

Sam's expression shifted, a flicker of surprise crossing his face. "He really thought that?"

"Yes," I affirmed, my heart racing with the thought of revealing this hidden piece of our father's love. "He wrote about how proud he was of you, about your strength and your passion for this community. He believed in you, Sam."

"Then why didn't he say it to my face?" His voice trembled slightly, a vulnerability peeking through the layers of his defenses.

"Because it's hard," I said, my voice steady. "We're all flawed, Sam. Sometimes the hardest words to say are the ones that matter most. But we can change that for each other. We can be more open, more honest."

He mulled over my words, the shadows lifting from his eyes as understanding began to dawn. "You might be onto something there. I guess it's time I let go of the anger. It hasn't done me any favors."

"It's a start," I said, the warmth between us igniting a flicker of something that felt almost like reconciliation. "Let's figure this out together."

"Together," he echoed, a hint of resolve settling in his voice. "I can work with that."

In that shared moment, with all our unspoken fears lingering in the air, we began to weave the frayed strands of our relationship back together, no longer defined by our father's legacy but by our shared experience, our hopes, and the love that still existed, waiting patiently beneath the surface.

The air was lighter now, buoyed by the tentative truce we'd brokered. I could feel the edges of the past softening, the jagged pain slowly rounding into something more manageable. Sam and I exchanged glances, a silent acknowledgment passing between us, as if we'd both taken the plunge into the murky depths of our shared history and emerged, breathless, into a fragile but welcoming light.

"Okay, so let's say I'm willing to work on this," Sam said, leaning back in his chair, a hint of mischief dancing in his eyes. "What's our first step? More therapy sessions? Group hugs? Perhaps a weekend retreat to find our inner peace?"

I laughed, the sound breaking the tension that had clung to us like an unwelcome guest. "I'm thinking more along the lines of brunch. You know, something that involves coffee and maybe a side of your infamous eye rolls."

"Ah, yes, my eye rolls are legendary," he replied, pretending to be impressed as he arched an eyebrow. "And let me guess, we'll be discussing how you'll continue to be the golden child while I remain the lovable rogue?"

"More like we'll talk about how I can help you recognize your worth without comparing it to our father," I corrected playfully, and his smile faded slightly, replaced by a more serious expression. "Sam, you're brilliant. You need to see that for yourself."

"And you're annoying," he shot back, but the warmth in his voice was undeniable. "Fine, brunch it is. But I want mimosas. The good stuff."

"Deal." I raised my imaginary glass, a triumphant grin breaking across my face. "Here's to new beginnings and not letting Dad's ghost suffocate us any longer."

We spent a few more moments in easy banter, the conversation flowing more freely now, a river of shared memories and jokes that had once been dammed up. It felt good, like shedding a layer of skin that had grown too tight, but in the back of my mind, I knew we weren't entirely out of the woods yet. There were still the letters—the ones that held secrets and perhaps answers we hadn't yet uncovered.

Just as I was about to mention them again, the sharp ring of my phone sliced through the moment, jarring me back to reality. I glanced at the screen and felt my stomach drop. It was a call from the community center. My mind raced as I answered, hoping for news that wouldn't complicate our fragile peace.

"Hello?" I said, trying to keep my voice steady.

"Is this Clara Mallory?" The voice on the other end was professional but held a hint of urgency.

"Yes, that's me."

"Clara, we need you to come down to the center. There's been an incident. It involves your father's legacy project."

The words hit me like a punch to the gut, slicing through the warm moment with Sam. "What kind of incident?"

"There's been a breach, and we believe someone may be trying to sabotage the project. We need your input as soon as possible."

"Is everyone okay?" Panic surged within me, and I could almost hear the frantic beating of my heart in my ears.

"Yes, everyone's fine for now, but we need to act quickly. Can you get here?"

I nodded, even though the person on the other end couldn't see me. "Yes, I'll be there as soon as I can."

I hung up, the reality crashing down around me like a wave. "What's wrong?" Sam asked, concern etching itself into his features.

I took a deep breath, the remnants of our earlier conversation slipping away like sand through my fingers. "There's been an incident at the community center. Something's gone wrong with the legacy project."

"What kind of incident?" he pressed, his eyes narrowing with worry.

"I don't know yet. I need to go and find out."

His expression shifted, a mix of determination and concern flashing across his face. "I'm coming with you."

I opened my mouth to protest, to say that this was my responsibility, but the thought of facing whatever chaos awaited me alone felt unbearable. "Okay, but let's keep our heads cool. We can't afford to make this about... well, everything else."

He nodded, a steely resolve taking hold. "Right. Cool heads, warm hearts. Got it."

We headed out of his office, the air buzzing with the electric charge of uncertainty. As we walked side by side, a comfortable silence fell between us, but it was punctuated by the underlying tension of what lay ahead. Sam's presence was grounding, a reminder that we were no longer fighting our battles alone.

When we arrived at the community center, the atmosphere was fraught with anxiety. People moved hurriedly, whispers trailing in their wake, and I could feel the weight of their eyes on us, a mixture of expectation and fear. I scanned the room, my heart racing as I searched for any sign of trouble.

A familiar face broke through the crowd—Lily, the center's director, her usually bright smile replaced by a grave expression. "Clara! Sam! Thank you for coming. We really need your help."

"What happened?" I asked, urgency coloring my voice.

Lily gestured for us to follow her to a side room where a group of volunteers had gathered, their faces lined with worry. "It's about the funding for the legacy project. Someone hacked into our system, and they've been sending out false reports claiming that the project has been mismanaged. We think it's sabotage."

"What?" Sam exclaimed, disbelief etched across his features. "Why would anyone do that?"

"I don't know, but if this gets out, it could ruin everything your father worked for." Lily's eyes locked onto mine, pleading for reassurance I wasn't sure I could give.

I felt my chest tighten, the panic rising once again. "We need to find out who did this and stop them before it spirals out of control."

As we huddled together, discussing possible next steps, I couldn't shake the feeling that we were being watched. The weight of unspoken tensions hung in the air, thickening the atmosphere. And then, just as the plan started to form, my phone buzzed again, this time a text.

I pulled it out, my heart plummeting as I read the message: "I know what you found. If you don't want the truth to come out, you'll do exactly as I say. Meet me where it all began. —S"

The blood drained from my face, the implications of the message crashing down like a tidal wave. I turned to Sam, panic flooding my voice. "It's from someone who knows about the letters. They're threatening me."

"What do they want?" he demanded, his protective instincts kicking in.

"I don't know," I whispered, fear twisting my stomach. "But if I don't meet them, they might expose everything."

"Clara, you can't go alone." Sam's voice was firm, laced with concern.

"I don't have a choice," I replied, determination rising. "I have to protect us—protect what we've started to build. If this person knows about the letters, they could destroy everything."

"Then I'm going with you," Sam insisted, his eyes fierce with resolve.

I shook my head, torn between gratitude and fear. "I can't put you in danger. I can't risk—"

"Stop. You're not doing this without me." His tone brooked no argument, and I could see the unwavering support beneath his bravado.

As the walls closed in around us, I felt the weight of the moment settle deep in my bones. Choices loomed ahead, their consequences both enticing and terrifying. Together, we stood at the precipice of a decision that would change everything, teetering on the edge of the unknown, just as a shadow flickered at the corner of my vision—a figure watching, waiting.

And suddenly, the air crackled with anticipation, as if the world itself was holding its breath for what would come next.

Chapter 17: A Fork in the Road

The farmhouse loomed ahead, its silhouette softened by the twilight glow. As I stepped onto the creaking porch, the familiar scent of cedar and earth enveloped me like a long-lost embrace. The day's warmth lingered in the air, mingling with the faint whisper of the wind that rustled the leaves of the surrounding trees. Yet, the inviting atmosphere did little to ease the tempest brewing within me. The confrontation with Sam replayed in my mind, a relentless loop of anger, frustration, and regret.

Sinking into the worn wicker chair beside Luke, I let out a breath I hadn't realized I was holding. He turned to me, his deep-set eyes reflecting a warmth that contrasted sharply with the chill of my turmoil. "What did he say?" he asked gently, as though probing a bruise still fresh. I hesitated, feeling the weight of my words as I considered how to share the depth of my frustration without burdening him.

"He thinks I'm wasting my time," I finally managed, my voice taut like a bowstring ready to snap. "He sees the farm as a relic, something to be tossed aside for... I don't know, city life? Something shiny and new." I shrugged, bitterness dripping from my tone. "He doesn't understand what this place means to me. It's not just land; it's our history, our father's dreams."

Luke squeezed my hand, his touch igniting a warmth that felt almost rebellious against the cold realization that my brother and I were miles apart, both physically and emotionally. "You know he's scared, right? Scared of what might happen if you fight for something he wants to let go of. You're both losing something, but in different ways."

His words hung in the air, heavy and unyielding. I turned to look at the sprawling fields that had once been vibrant with crops, now cloaked in shadows. They felt like a reflection of my heart—overgrown, neglected, yet somehow still alive with possibility. "I'm terrified too, Luke," I admitted, my voice barely above a whisper. "What if I'm fighting a losing battle? What if I can't hold on to what's left?"

He tilted his head, the setting sun casting a warm glow over his face, accentuating the crinkles around his eyes that formed when he smiled. "But what if you can? What if this fight brings you closer to the memories you cherish, to the dreams your dad had for this place? You have to ask yourself what you're willing to sacrifice."

The question struck me like a lightning bolt, illuminating the dark corners of my mind where doubt thrived. Sacrifice. What was I willing to give up to save the farm? The thought of losing Luke gnawed at me, a relentless creature with sharp teeth. Could I keep pursuing my dreams and maintain our fragile relationship? As if reading my mind, Luke leaned closer, the warmth of his body seeping into mine. "We're in this together," he murmured, his breath warm against my skin. "Just don't lose sight of why you started this fight in the first place."

I could almost hear my father's voice, the way he'd say, "Every seed you plant is a testament to hope." Those words had been my mantra, yet here I was, caught in a web of familial tension and despair. The sun dipped lower, and with it, a sense of urgency seeped into the air, punctuated by the distant call of a whippoorwill, echoing the questions in my heart.

The air grew cooler as we fell into a contemplative silence, the occasional creak of the farmhouse settling echoing around us. A part of me longed for the simplicity of the days spent planting seeds, laughing in the fields, feeling invincible alongside Sam. But those days felt like fragments of a long-lost fairy tale, overshadowed by the looming reality of what the farm was becoming—a battleground for our conflicting desires.

"What do you think he'll do?" I finally broke the silence, my voice a fragile thread weaving through the quiet. "If I push him, if I stand my ground?"

Luke sighed, running a hand through his tousled hair, the evening breeze tousling it further. "Sam is stubborn. He might lash out, but deep down, he loves you. He just needs to see how much this means to you. Maybe he needs a reminder of the good times."

I sighed, the weight of his words settling heavily on my chest. "It's hard to remember when it feels like the good times are buried under resentment."

"Then dig them up," he challenged softly. "Show him why this matters, why you matter. This is as much about your father's legacy as it is about your relationship with Sam."

His words sparked something deep within me. "You're right," I said, feeling a flicker of determination ignite in my chest. "I need to show him what we can do together instead of pushing him away. But how?"

"Start with a plan," he said, his gaze piercing yet supportive. "Maybe a family dinner. Get everyone together, share stories, remember what made this place special. Appeal to his heart, not just his mind."

As I contemplated his suggestion, I felt a newfound clarity. I had been so focused on defending the farm that I had forgotten to celebrate what it represented. It was time to remember, to share the laughter and love that had once echoed through its walls. I took a deep breath, the air filling my lungs with a sense of resolve that surged like the night sky above us, dotted with stars flickering with promise.

"Okay," I said, squeezing Luke's hand tighter. "I'll do it. I'll reach out to him. We'll talk, and maybe we'll find common ground again."

Luke smiled, a glimmer of pride shining in his eyes. "That's the spirit. I'm here every step of the way."

As the first stars began to twinkle in the deepening blue of the night sky, a sense of possibility replaced the weight of dread that had hung over me like a storm cloud. The path forward was uncertain, but with Luke by my side, I felt fortified, ready to face whatever awaited me at the crossroads of my family's legacy and my own dreams.

I awoke the next morning to a soft golden light streaming through the slats of the window, illuminating the dust motes swirling lazily in the air. It felt like a new day, but the remnants of the previous night's conversation lingered like the scent of fresh coffee. I sat up, stretching my arms above my head, the muscles in my shoulders protesting with a dull ache. Today was the day I had chosen to bridge the chasm between Sam and me. With a sigh, I tossed off the covers, the cool air sending a shiver down my spine.

In the kitchen, the aroma of bacon sizzling in the cast-iron skillet filled the air, a comforting ritual that always welcomed me home. Luke stood at the stove, a spatula in hand, flipping strips of crispy goodness as if he were a maestro conducting a symphony. The sight made me smile. "What's the occasion?" I asked, leaning against the doorframe, crossing my arms and trying to suppress the grin that was threatening to break free.

He glanced over his shoulder, his face breaking into a mischievous smile. "Well, I figured you could use a little fuel for the emotional gymnastics you're about to perform." He winked, and I chuckled, the tension in my chest easing slightly.

"Is that what this is? Emotional gymnastics?" I mused, stepping closer to the stove. "More like a high-stakes game of Jenga. One wrong move, and it all comes crashing down."

"Let's just hope you're more coordinated than a toddler on a balance beam." He raised an eyebrow, and I rolled my eyes, snatching a piece of bacon from the plate. The crispy texture burst in my mouth, a small comfort against the anxiety swirling in my stomach.

Once breakfast was over, I felt a mix of resolve and trepidation coursing through me. "Okay, I should probably get this over with," I said, pushing my chair back with determination. "Sam's probably already avoiding me like I'm carrying a rabid raccoon."

Luke followed me to the door, his expression shifting to something more serious. "Just remember, be honest with him. Sometimes the hardest conversations lead to the best outcomes."

I nodded, grateful for his unwavering support. Stepping out into the crisp morning air, I inhaled deeply, the scent of pine and earth invigorating my senses. I walked down the familiar path toward the barn, the gravel crunching underfoot like popcorn in a quiet theater, punctuating my thoughts.

As I approached the barn, I spotted Sam leaning against the weathered wooden frame, arms crossed, his expression a mix of defiance and weariness. He looked like a statue carved from stone, immovable and unyielding. The memory of our last confrontation rushed back, making my heart race, but I pushed forward, driven by the hope of rekindling the bond we once shared.

"Hey," I called out, my voice steady despite the fluttering in my chest.

He turned, his brow furrowing slightly, as if processing my presence was akin to deciphering an ancient text. "What do you want?"

I took a breath, steeling myself. "I wanted to talk. I think we need to clear the air."

"Clear the air? That's a nice way of saying you want to convince me that clinging to this old place is a good idea." His tone dripped with skepticism, and I felt the familiar stir of frustration bubbling just beneath my skin.

"Maybe it is! Have you even considered why this matters to me?" I shot back, the words spilling out before I could temper my emotions. "This isn't just about the farm. It's about our family, our memories. You know that, right?"

He shifted, pushing himself off the barn with a grunt, his shoulders tense. "Memories don't pay the bills. This place is a sinking ship, and you're the one trying to patch the holes with nostalgia."

"Is that really how you see it?" I challenged, stepping closer, my voice rising with the intensity of our exchange. "You think I'm just being sentimental, but this place is our history! It's where we grew up, where Dad dreamed big dreams for us. You can't just toss it away because it's easier."

"Easier?" he scoffed, throwing his hands up in exasperation. "You think I want to walk away? I'm trying to be practical! It's not like we can just wish away the debt or the crumbling walls. It's not all sunshine and rainbows, sis."

A silence hung between us, thick with unspoken words. I glanced at the barn, the once-vibrant red paint now faded and peeling, mirroring the weariness I felt in my heart. "Maybe we can find a way to make it work. Together," I offered, my voice softer now. "We could fix it up, revitalize the farm. I know it sounds crazy, but we owe it to ourselves to try."

Sam's gaze softened, the hard lines of his face easing just a fraction. "You really think we could do that?"

"Why not?" I pressed. "We could bring in fresh ideas, maybe even some new crops. There's so much potential here. And if we pull together, I believe we could turn it around."

He stared at me for a long moment, and I could see the wheels turning in his mind. "And what if it fails? What if it doesn't work out? I'm not sure I'm ready to take that risk."

"Then we learn from it," I replied, my heart pounding with urgency. "Isn't that what growing up is about? Taking risks, learning, failing, and trying again? I can't let this place go without a fight, Sam. It means too much to me."

He ran a hand through his hair, his expression shifting as the weight of my words settled in. "You really believe in this, don't you?"

"I do," I said, my voice unwavering. "I believe in us. We can be more than just siblings divided by resentment. We can be partners, even if it means making mistakes along the way."

There was a flicker of something in his eyes, a glimmer of hope beneath the layers of doubt. "Fine," he said, a reluctant smile creeping onto his lips. "But if we're doing this, we're doing it right. No half measures."

I felt the tension dissolve, replaced by an exhilarating rush of possibility. "Absolutely. Together," I affirmed, my heart swelling with the weight of new beginnings.

"Okay then, partner," he said, extending his hand. I took it, and the grip felt solid, a promise sealed in the dust of our shared past and the potential of our future.

With the morning sun climbing higher in the sky, a wave of optimism washed over me. Together, we would not only revive the farm but perhaps also the bond we had almost lost.

The following days were a whirlwind of planning and preparation. Sam and I dove headfirst into the challenge of revitalizing the farm, an effort that felt like piecing together a jigsaw puzzle whose picture remained stubbornly hidden. We spent hours in the barn, surrounded by dusty boxes filled with remnants of our childhood—old toys, faded photographs, and letters written in our father's looping script. Each find pulled at my heartstrings, urging us to forge ahead.

"You know," I said one afternoon, holding up a weathered baseball glove that had belonged to Sam, "if we really want to do this, we're going to need more than just nostalgia to fuel our dreams."

He smirked, leaning back against a stack of crates. "Ah, yes, the mythical fuel of dreams. Is it a special blend of fairy dust and ambition?"

"Something like that," I shot back, laughing as I tossed the glove into the pile. "Maybe we should brew a potion and call it 'Hope.'"

"Perfect. I'll grab the cauldron," he quipped, his eyes dancing with mischief. The banter eased the tension that had once crackled between us, replacing it with a camaraderie I thought we had lost forever.

We decided to start small. Sam suggested clearing out the old greenhouse, which had been overtaken by weeds and broken glass, an ugly remnant of what once was a sanctuary for our father's prized plants. Armed with gloves, shovels, and a heavy dose of determination, we got to work. The sun beat down on us, turning the task into a sweat-drenched affair that soon turned into a competition of sorts.

"Whoever pulls out the most weeds gets to choose the next movie for movie night," I declared, wiping the sweat from my brow.

"Consider it a challenge. You'll regret this," Sam shot back, determination flooding his features.

We dug, pulled, and tossed the stubborn roots aside, but with every weed uprooted, the undercurrent of tension seemed to dissipate. With each laugh, every shout of mock victory, I could almost hear the echoes of our childhood, the laughter that used to bounce off these walls. Yet, just as the air felt lighter, a sense of impending dread lingered at the edges of my mind.

After a grueling afternoon, we stood at the greenhouse's entrance, gazing at the fruits of our labor. The glass panes, though shattered and grimy, caught the late afternoon sun in a way that made them twinkle like tiny stars. It felt like a victory.

"See? This wasn't so hard," I said, glancing over at Sam, who had taken a moment to wipe his forehead with the back of his hand.

"Yeah, I mean, if we ignore the fact that I nearly severed my hand on that glass." He held up his hand, revealing a minor cut. "You owe me a Band-Aid and a celebratory pizza for this."

"Deal. But only if I get to choose the toppings."

"Absolutely not. We're going classic—pepperoni."

We both laughed, but the moment was short-lived as a familiar shadow passed over Sam's face. "What about the debt?" he asked, suddenly serious. "No matter how much we clean or plant, it doesn't erase the fact that we're still in over our heads."

I felt the wind in my sails falter. "I know. But we'll figure it out. I can look for grants or community support. This town is built on family farms. There has to be something."

"Sure, and I can see if there's a knight in shining armor who wants to buy us a new tractor," he replied sarcastically.

"Hey, you never know. I've heard there are angels out there with deep pockets," I said with a wink, trying to lighten the mood.

Just then, my phone buzzed in my pocket, breaking the tension like a sudden clap of thunder. I pulled it out and felt my heart leap into my throat. It was a message from Luke: Can you meet me? Important.

"Everything okay?" Sam asked, noticing the shift in my expression.

"I don't know. Luke just texted me. He wants to meet."

"What do you think it's about?"

I shrugged, unease curling in my stomach. "I have no idea, but it feels... urgent."

"I'll come with you."

"Sam, it might be something personal."

"Right. Because I wouldn't want to intrude on a deep conversation between you and your boyfriend." His tone was playful, but the underlying seriousness was evident.

"Fine. But if he starts getting all mushy, you've got to promise to keep your eye-rolls to a minimum."

"Cross my heart," he said, putting his hand over his chest dramatically.

As we made our way to the local café, the atmosphere shifted from lighthearted to something heavy, as if the sky had thickened with dark clouds. I glanced over at Sam, who walked beside me, his expression unreadable.

Arriving at the café, I spotted Luke sitting at a corner table, his hands wrapped tightly around a steaming cup. When he looked up and met my gaze, something in his eyes sent a shiver down my spine.

"Hey," I said, settling into the chair across from him, trying to gauge the tension in the air.

"Thanks for coming," he replied, his voice steady but laced with an undercurrent of something—concern, perhaps.

I gestured to Sam, who perched himself on the edge of the chair like a hawk ready to swoop down. "This is my brother, Sam. What's going on?"

Luke glanced at Sam before returning his gaze to me, the gravity of the moment intensifying. "I received a call this morning from a financial advisor I've been working with. It's about the farm."

My heart dropped. "What do you mean?"

He took a deep breath, the weight of his next words hanging heavily in the air. "They're considering foreclosing."

The room seemed to spin as the words hit me like a physical blow. I glanced at Sam, whose expression mirrored my shock. "But we're working on it! We've just started cleaning things up. We can make it work!"

Luke shook his head. "I know, but time is running out. We need to act fast if we want to save it. They want a meeting... and it's happening tomorrow."

The weight of the news settled heavily between us, like an anchor pulling us down into a dark abyss. I felt my heart race, my mind racing ahead to all the possibilities.

"Tomorrow?" Sam echoed, incredulity coloring his tone. "That doesn't give us enough time."

"We can't let it end like this," I insisted, desperation creeping into my voice. "There has to be something we can do."

Luke looked at me, determination sparking in his eyes. "We can gather our resources, reach out to the community. Maybe rally some support. But we need to act quickly."

"Okay," I said, a surge of resolve washing over me. "We'll make calls, talk to everyone we know. This farm means too much to let it slip away."

"Right," Sam said, nodding slowly as if trying to grasp the enormity of our situation.

But as I looked into Luke's eyes, the looming uncertainty in the air felt palpable, a storm brewing on the horizon. Before I could voice my next thought, the door swung open, a gust of wind billowing through the café, catching my attention.

A figure stood in the doorway, silhouetted against the sunlight. My breath caught in my throat as recognition dawned, an icy dread settling in my gut. There stood someone I hadn't seen in years, someone whose very presence threatened to unravel everything I had fought for.

"Surprise," they said with a smirk that sent shivers down my spine, stepping into the café as if they owned the place. "I heard you could use a little help."

The air crackled with tension, and the weight of unspoken history hung heavily over our table, pulling me into a confrontation I wasn't ready to face.

Chapter 18: A New Beginning

The sun dipped below the horizon, casting a warm golden hue over the farm as I stood at the edge of the field, feeling the crisp autumn air swirl around me. I had always loved this time of year—the way the leaves transformed into a riot of colors, vibrant against the fading light, and how the earth seemed to hold its breath in anticipation. It felt like nature's own way of reminding us that change, even in its most chaotic forms, could be beautiful. Today, however, was not about the beauty of the seasons. It was about the change I was determined to bring to our community.

I had arranged for everyone to gather at the old barn, a place that had witnessed laughter, tears, and the relentless passage of time. It was a familiar setting, yet it felt brand new, infused with the hope of reconciliation. My heart raced with both excitement and dread as I prepared to share my vision—a vision for revitalization, a path toward healing. The air buzzed with the scent of freshly baked pies and roasted vegetables, wafting through the open doors, inviting the townsfolk in. I could hear snippets of laughter and the shuffle of feet as familiar faces began to fill the space, their warmth a comforting presence.

As I looked around, I felt a swell of emotion. Each person who walked through those barn doors carried a piece of the past, a story interwoven with my own. I spotted Mrs. Thompson, her silver hair glinting in the soft light, her arms laden with a basket of her famous apple turnovers. She had a knack for making everything feel just a bit brighter, as if her mere presence infused the air with the aroma of cinnamon and nostalgia. Nearby, the Williams twins—who were no longer toddlers but strapping young men—chattered excitedly as they stacked chairs, their laughter reminiscent of summers spent racing through fields.

It was then I noticed Sam hovering at the entrance, his frame backlit by the fading light. He looked out of place, like a lone cloud on a clear day, unsure whether to stay or drift away. My stomach flipped at the sight of him, a combination of longing and anxiety swirling within me. Sam and I had once shared everything—the whispered dreams, the late-night confessions, the plans for a future that now felt like a distant memory. But our paths had diverged, leaving an uncomfortable tension between us that I desperately wanted to dissolve.

Taking a deep breath, I stepped toward him, my heart pounding like a drum in my chest. "Hey, you made it!" I said, trying to infuse my voice with casual cheer. He looked down for a moment, shuffling his feet, and I wondered if he felt as fragile as I did. "You should come inside. We're just getting started."

He hesitated, a shadow flickering across his features. "I'm not sure if this is my thing," he replied, his voice a low rumble, filled with uncertainty.

"Maybe it could be," I countered, letting a playful smile tug at my lips. "You know, I hear there's pie. And Mrs. Thompson's turnovers could resurrect the dead. Seriously, they're that good."

Finally, he chuckled—a sound that felt like music to my ears. "Fine, you win. I'll brave the pie." And with that, he stepped into the barn, and the air shifted slightly, as if the world had tilted just enough to change the perspective.

The moment he entered, I felt an invisible thread pulling us closer, even as I tried to ignore the past that loomed like a specter between us. I moved toward the center of the barn, the space decorated with strings of fairy lights that twinkled above us like stars captured in glass. As I glanced at the faces surrounding me—friends, neighbors, and the few who had once turned away—I sensed the collective breath, a moment of shared anticipation.

"Thank you all for coming," I began, my voice steady despite the fluttering nerves. "This farm has always been more than just a piece of land. It's a part of our community, a part of our history." I gestured to the wooden beams overhead, worn and beautiful in their imperfections. "It's time we breathed new life into it, just as we breathe life into each other."

The crowd murmured their agreement, a chorus of voices weaving a tapestry of support. I spoke passionately about the potential for community gardens, shared workshops, and cultural events that would not only honor my father's legacy but also foster connections among us. With each word, I felt the walls around my heart begin to crack, revealing the hope that had long lain dormant within.

When I finally paused to look around, I caught Sam's gaze. He was leaning against a wooden post, arms crossed but a flicker of interest sparked in his eyes. I could see the gears turning in his mind, weighing the possibilities. The sight filled me with a warmth I hadn't anticipated, a reminder that perhaps we could still find our way back to each other amidst the chaos of everything we had endured.

As I continued to share stories about the farm and my father's dreams, the atmosphere shifted from uncertainty to camaraderie. Laughter erupted as we shared memories, and soon the barn was filled with the sound of connection, the kind that only comes from shared experiences and open hearts. I could feel the acceptance washing over us, like a balm soothing old wounds.

And then, unexpectedly, someone raised a hand—a gesture that felt bold yet inviting. It was Clara, a woman known for her fierce spirit and candid opinions. "What if we make this a monthly thing? A way to keep the momentum going?" Her eyes sparkled with mischief, as if she were ready to take on the world, one gathering at a time.

"Yes!" a voice called from the back. "Let's bring back the potlucks! It's been too long!" The suggestion sparked enthusiasm, and soon the room was abuzz with ideas, voices overlapping in a delightful cacophony of plans.

Amidst the rising tide of hope and excitement, I caught Sam's eye again, a silent conversation passing between us. Maybe this was the moment we needed, not just for the community but for us as well. Perhaps, just perhaps, this gathering would be the first step toward mending what had once been so beautifully whole, or at least a way to rediscover the pieces we had lost along the way.

As the evening unfolded, the barn transformed into a sanctuary of laughter and stories, illuminated by the soft glow of twinkling fairy lights strung above our heads. The clinking of glasses mingled with the aromas of homemade dishes wafting through the air, filling my heart with warmth. I reveled in the sounds of my community finding their rhythm, the way they congregated around tables piled high with food, their faces lighting up with each shared anecdote.

I leaned against the wooden railing, watching the scene unfold. There was Clara, her laughter infectious as she playfully elbowed her husband, Tom, who had been tasked with the dubious honor of serving the punch. Tom, clearly overwhelmed, looked like he was trying to manage a storm in a teacup, spilling a few drops as he juggled cups and ladles. "Clara, if you keep making me laugh like that, I'm going to need a mop," he quipped, shaking his head dramatically.

"Don't worry, honey. Just think of it as me keeping you on your toes!" Clara shot back, her eyes sparkling with mischief. Their banter felt like a breath of fresh air, grounding me in the moment and reminding me of the love that existed in the simplest exchanges.

The warmth of connection wrapped around me, but a flicker of unease lingered. Sam was still standing off to the side, engaged in quiet conversation with Mrs. Thompson. I could see the way she animatedly gestured, her hands painting pictures in the air, her voice full of passion. It was both a relief and a frustration; I longed to draw him into our circle, to feel that spark of familiarity reignite, but it seemed a delicate dance between pushing too hard and allowing him the space to breathe.

Taking a deep breath, I wandered over, drawn by the magnetic pull of our shared history. "So, Mrs. Thompson, are you convincing him to try one of those legendary turnovers?" I asked, adopting a playful tone, hoping to lighten the mood.

Sam turned, his brow arching in mock surprise. "I thought I was being stealthy. How did you find me here?"

"You forget," I said with a teasing grin, "I have a radar for delightful baked goods and handsome, brooding men standing in corners."

Mrs. Thompson chuckled, her laughter like the soft ringing of a bell. "He needs to try one of my turnovers, Sam. It's practically a rite of passage around here."

I felt a spark of hope as Sam's lips twitched upward, a flicker of his old self shining through. "Alright, I suppose I'll brave the turnover," he conceded, looking at me as if searching for confirmation.

"You won't regret it. Just think of it as diving into the deep end of the pool. You'll either float or come up gasping for air," I replied, injecting a bit of playful drama into the moment.

With a reluctant smile, he followed me to the table, where Mrs. Thompson had set out a colorful array of baked goods. I picked up a turnover, the crust golden and flaky, glistening with a dusting of powdered sugar. "This one's a classic," I said, handing it to him like a prized trophy. "You have to promise to give an honest review. If it's terrible, I'll personally take the blame."

As he took a bite, his eyes widened in delight. "Okay, you might be onto something here. This is exceptional. How do you even make something taste like a hug?"

Mrs. Thompson beamed, clearly pleased with his compliment. "It's all in the love, dear. And a little cinnamon doesn't hurt!"

Laughter erupted around us as we delved into the delicious spread, the atmosphere thick with camaraderie. I felt the tension ease between Sam and me, like the fragile tendrils of a spider's web slowly unwinding. We exchanged quips, our old rhythm creeping back, teasing each other like we used to. It felt familiar yet charged with an energy that was foreign and exciting.

"I remember the last time you tried to bake, Sam," I teased, leaning closer. "You almost burned down the kitchen."

"Hey, I still maintain that the fire department was just being overly cautious," he shot back, a playful gleam in his eye. "Besides, I thought I was going for that charred, rustic look."

"You could have just asked for a smoke signal instead," I replied, grinning widely.

As we bantered back and forth, I noticed the way the atmosphere shifted, drawing in those around us, laughter mingling with shared memories. It felt almost magical, weaving us all together like the intricate stitches of a quilt. Each story shared was a thread binding us closer, and I reveled in the warmth that enveloped the barn.

Yet, amidst the laughter, a flicker of concern nagged at the edges of my mind. The revitalization of the farm and the reconciliation of our community felt like a daunting task, one that had been overshadowed by past grievances and old wounds. I glanced at the faces around me, each one reflecting the weight of our shared history, and wondered if we were ready for the change I envisioned.

Suddenly, Clara's voice broke through my thoughts, commanding attention. "Alright, everyone, we're not just here for the food! Who's ready for some real fun?"

The crowd buzzed with anticipation, shifting from their tables, eager for whatever Clara had in store. "Let's play some games! We can relive our youth—trust me, it'll be a blast!"

Sam chuckled. "Games? I'm not sure I'm ready to embarrass myself just yet."

"Oh, come on, Sam. You can't hide behind those brooding good looks forever," I teased, elbowing him playfully. "What's a little embarrassment compared to the joy of victory?"

With a mock sigh of resignation, he relented. "Fine, but only if I get to choose the game."

"Deal. As long as it doesn't involve fire," I replied, my heart racing with a mix of anticipation and excitement.

We joined the throng of townspeople moving toward the open space in front of the barn, laughter bubbling like champagne as we formed teams for the first game—an absurd yet entertaining combination of charades and scavenger hunt. The rules were simple: act out various tasks while your teammates guessed what they were. As Sam and I teamed up, I felt an electric thrill course through me, a reminder of the connection we once had.

I watched as he dramatically mimed a chicken laying an egg, his movements exaggerated to comedic perfection. "No one can resist the charm of a poultry performance!" he declared, striking a pose as the crowd erupted in laughter.

"Clearly, you've found your calling," I shot back, and we both burst into laughter, the sound mingling with the night air, an echo of everything that had led us to this moment.

As the game continued, I felt the fragile threads of our past beginning to weave together again, the laughter binding us as we moved through the games, fueled by camaraderie and the shared joy of being together. The evening was a delightful dance, one where old wounds began to heal under the gentle warmth of acceptance and understanding.

And just as the night began to settle into a comfortable rhythm, a flicker of unease crept back in, tugging at the edges of my joy. I couldn't shake the feeling that this sense of connection, this fragile new beginning, was standing on the precipice of something unforeseen, a truth yet to be revealed that could change everything. But for now, I allowed myself to bask in the warmth of the moment, the laughter echoing in my heart, each shared smile a promise of hope in a world that felt ready to embrace the possibilities ahead.

The games rolled on, the laughter mingling with the crisp night air, weaving a tapestry of joy that enveloped us all. I had lost track of time, swept away in the laughter and the easy camaraderie that had formed like a second skin. Each round of charades brought fresh guffaws, old stories, and new inside jokes. Sam had surprised me with his ability to morph into a variety of characters, from a dramatic diva to a clumsy bear, capturing the spirit of each with an enthusiasm that felt infectious.

At one point, Clara, always the instigator of fun, decided to ramp things up. "How about a dance-off? Who's brave enough to show their moves?" she shouted, eyes sparkling with mischief.

"Oh no," I muttered to Sam, "that's a death sentence for dignity."

"Don't worry; we'll just blame it on the punch if we embarrass ourselves," he quipped, his smirk teasing at the corners of my heart.

The challenge hung in the air, crackling with anticipation. I could feel the collective hesitance; everyone knew they had two left feet just like me. But that spark of competition ignited, and one by one, pairs began to step into the makeshift dance floor, laughing as they twirled and stumbled. Clara, always the bold one, kicked off with a spontaneous shimmy that was so absurdly charming, even the most reluctant were pulled in by the energy.

"Alright, I guess we can't let the world see us hiding in a corner, right?" I said, nudging Sam. "Let's give them a show they'll never forget."

"Or regret," he countered, rolling his eyes but not hiding the grin spreading across his face.

We made our way to the center, the wooden planks creaking beneath our feet as the crowd began to cheer us on. I could feel the heat rising in my cheeks, both from embarrassment and the thrill of being the center of attention. Sam grabbed my hand, and we started with a simple sway, moving in sync as I found myself lost in the moment, the music enveloping us like a cozy blanket.

"Just follow my lead," he said, his eyes sparkling with mischief. I nodded, attempting to mimic his rhythm as he spun me around. We twirled and laughed, our movements growing bolder with each beat.

And just like that, the atmosphere shifted again. The weight of the past began to lift as the music intertwined with our laughter, becoming a bridge that spanned the gaps between us. For a moment, it felt like all the heartache and confusion melted away, leaving just the two of us dancing under the starlit sky.

Yet, just as I was beginning to feel invincible, the music abruptly stopped. A heavy silence fell over the crowd, the energy shifting like the wind before a storm. I glanced around, puzzled, and my heart sank when I saw Clara's face, which had turned pale as she looked toward the entrance.

"Is everything okay?" I asked, my voice barely above a whisper.

Then I saw him—Jim, the town's unofficial troublemaker and self-appointed moral compass, striding in with an air of indignation. He was the kind of guy who could turn a peaceful gathering into a courtroom drama with a single glare. The moment he stepped into the barn, the atmosphere soured like spoiled milk.

"Are we seriously celebrating?" Jim's voice sliced through the air, his words dripping with disdain. "Celebrating what? A plan to throw good money after bad? This place is falling apart, and you want to make it a party?"

I could feel the weight of the room shift, a collective intake of breath as he laid down his gauntlet. "We're supposed to be mourning what we've lost, not acting like everything is fine."

The energy crackled with tension, and I felt Sam tense beside me. "Jim, we're not just celebrating the farm," I said, trying to keep my voice steady. "We're celebrating the community. This is about coming together, not tearing each other apart."

"Coming together? You mean like you and Sam?" Jim sneered, pointing an accusatory finger in our direction. "Everyone knows the two of you were supposed to be the perfect couple. And look where that got you—back together for a night and about to fall apart again."

Heat flooded my cheeks as I realized everyone's eyes were on us, and I could feel the judgments forming like clouds above. "That's not fair," I retorted, anger bubbling just beneath the surface. "You don't know anything about us or what we've been through."

"Or what you'll drag this town through next," he shot back, his tone harsh.

The crowd murmured, some people shifting uncomfortably, while others looked intrigued, caught in the clash of wills. Sam took a step closer, a protective stance enveloping us both. "You can't just come in here and ruin what we're trying to build. This night is about hope, not fear."

"Hope?" Jim laughed, a hollow sound that echoed in the suddenly tense silence. "You think you can rebuild this place with optimism? You're just burying your heads in the sand while the world crumbles around you!"

I clenched my fists, frustration mounting. "We're trying to do something meaningful, to make a difference. Maybe it's not perfect, but it's a start. Isn't that worth celebrating?"

As the words left my mouth, the tension coiled tighter, a spring ready to snap. Sam's expression was a mix of frustration and determination, and I could see the wheels turning in his mind.

Jim shook his head, a smirk creeping across his lips. "You want to build something? Then you better be ready for what comes next. I'm not done yet."

The air felt electric, heavy with unspoken challenges as Jim turned on his heel and stormed out of the barn, leaving behind a swirling cloud of uncertainty. The laughter and camaraderie that had defined the evening began to dissipate, replaced by a gnawing anxiety that echoed in the silence.

"What just happened?" I whispered, feeling the color drain from my face as I turned to Sam.

"Just a bit of typical Jim drama," he said, but his tone was far from lighthearted. The tension between us returned, thick and unsettling.

The crowd started to murmur, uncertainty rippling through them like a wave. Clara stepped forward, trying to regain control. "Alright, let's not let one sour grape ruin our harvest! We can still enjoy the evening. Who's ready for another dance?"

But the laughter was quieter this time, hesitant. I could feel Sam's hand slip away from mine, the warmth that had enveloped us moments ago now a distant memory.

Then a loud crash echoed from the back of the barn—a sound that sent a chill through me. My heart raced as I turned to see the shadows shifting, and just as I was about to say something, a figure burst through the barn doors, breathing heavily, eyes wild with fear.

"I saw something in the fields! Something's wrong!"

The words hung in the air like a damning declaration, and suddenly, all eyes turned toward the entrance, the room frozen in a moment of collective dread. I could feel the ground shift beneath me, the laughter evaporating into an unsteady silence, leaving only the pounding of my heart as a reminder that perhaps this night, meant to spark a new beginning, was only the precursor to something far more complicated and terrifying.

Chapter 19: An Invitation to Dance

The air shimmered with the remnants of a hot summer day, the kind where the sun hesitated to retreat, lingering in the sky like a guest who had overstayed their welcome. The backyard was a tableau of colors, string lights draped like lazy fireflies above the heads of my friends, illuminating the faces that sparkled with mirth. Laughter rang out, bright and infectious, mingling with the tantalizing aroma of barbecued burgers sizzling on the grill. The sight made my heart swell, a potent reminder that sometimes joy comes unexpectedly, tucked away in the moments we dare to embrace.

I stood at the edge of the crowd, my fingers fidgeting with the hem of my sundress, a soft fabric that danced around my knees. I could feel the anticipation building within me, a cocktail of nerves and excitement that bubbled just below the surface. The music pulsed, a rhythmic heartbeat that reverberated through my chest, coaxing me to step closer to the dance floor, where a few brave souls had already surrendered themselves to the beat.

Across the yard, Luke's smile shone brighter than the twinkling lights above. His dark hair tousled in that effortlessly handsome way, like he had just rolled out of bed and stepped into a scene from a movie. When our eyes locked, my breath hitched, as if he had plucked the very air from my lungs. He tilted his head, a playful grin spreading across his face, urging me to join him. With a deep inhale, I pushed the doubts aside. Tonight, I was determined to be bold, to seize the moment, and maybe, just maybe, find a part of myself I had lost along the way.

I stepped into the thrumming heart of the gathering, the warmth of bodies pressing together in joyous abandon. With every step, the vibrant colors of the world seemed to intensify, igniting my senses. The music wrapped around me, each note a gentle nudge to let go of my inhibitions. As I approached Luke, he held out his hand, fingers long and inviting. I took it, feeling the heat of his skin seep into mine, and in that fleeting touch, a current of electricity jolted through me, igniting a spark that threatened to light up the night.

"Are you ready to show these folks how it's done?" he teased, his voice smooth like honey as he pulled me closer, our bodies swaying gently to the rhythm. I couldn't help but laugh, the sound bubbling out of me with an ease I hadn't anticipated. "Show them? I barely know what I'm doing!" I shot back, but there was no mistaking the thrill in my voice. He just chuckled, the warmth of his laughter wrapping around me like a cozy blanket.

As the music shifted, a lively beat took over, and Luke twirled me with a flair that sent me spinning, my laughter bursting forth in a cascade of unfiltered joy. The world spun around us, a dizzying mix of colors and sounds, but all I could focus on was the way his eyes sparkled under the fairy lights, the way the world faded into a blur, leaving just the two of us standing at the center of something wonderfully profound.

"See? You've got it!" he exclaimed, effortlessly matching my rhythm, his movements fluid and confident. It was as if he could read my mind, sensing my hesitation and gently coaxing it away with every step we took together. I felt lighter, as though the weight of my worries had been lifted, replaced by an intoxicating blend of freedom and connection.

"Okay, okay," I laughed, my cheeks flushed with exhilaration, "but what happens if I trip over my own feet?"

"Then I'll catch you," he promised, a teasing glint in his eye. "And I'll make sure you don't land too hard."

His confidence was infectious, and with every twirl and dip, I surrendered a little more, my inhibitions dissolving like sugar in water. I hadn't danced like this in years, not since before life became a series of cautious steps and calculated moves. Here, under the starlit sky, I felt the past melt away, replaced by a vibrant present that enveloped me in its embrace.

"Let's make a deal," he said suddenly, leaning in closer, the scent of his cologne wrapping around me like an unexpected warmth. "If you trip, I'll get you an ice cream. But if you don't, you owe me a dance-off later."

I raised an eyebrow, a playful challenge flickering between us. "A dance-off? You're on, but I warn you, I might just embarrass you."

"Bring it," he shot back, his competitive spirit igniting the atmosphere between us. The stakes were set, and the air crackled with anticipation. With each turn, our laughter intertwined with the music, creating a melody that was uniquely ours, a song that seemed to promise endless nights of dancing beneath the stars.

As we lost ourselves in the moment, I felt a connection blossoming between us, a delicate yet potent thread woven through every glance, every shared laugh. It was a stark contrast to the mundane struggles I had faced earlier. The ache of loneliness that had once weighed heavily on my heart began to lift, revealing a landscape of possibilities I hadn't dared to imagine. In that dance, surrounded by friends and the glow of string lights, I could see a future illuminated by hope, glittering just beyond my reach.

But as the night wore on, shadows flickered at the edges of my mind, reminding me that happiness was often fleeting, a butterfly that danced just out of grasp. Just as I began to forget, the world surged back, sending tendrils of doubt wrapping around my heart. What if this was just an illusion, a moment suspended in time that would vanish with the dawn? But as Luke pulled me closer, our laughter ringing out against the backdrop of the stars, I found myself wondering if perhaps, just perhaps, I could learn to hold onto this joy a little longer.

The music surged, wrapping around us like a soft embrace, and with each turn, I felt my heart race, not from exertion but from something far more thrilling. Luke's laughter bubbled through the air, a sweet melody that beckoned me to join the rhythm of the night. As we danced, his hands anchored firmly on my waist, I was struck by how perfectly he fit into this moment—his warmth grounding me while the world around us spun in a dizzying array of colors and sound.

"Is it just me, or do we look ridiculously good together?" Luke leaned in, his breath warm against my ear. There was a playful challenge in his tone that made me giggle. "I mean, if we were a couple on a rom-com poster, I'd say we'd sell tickets."

"Right? The tagline would be 'Two Idiots, One Dance Floor,'" I shot back, unable to suppress a grin. The banter was easy, natural, and it made me feel light, as if I could float away if I didn't keep my feet planted on the ground.

The twinkling lights above us dimmed, creating a cozy cocoon that felt detached from the outside world. It was as if the universe conspired to keep this moment suspended in time. I glanced around, spotting our friends swaying, their faces illuminated by the golden glow of the bulbs. Someone had taken charge of the playlist, and a familiar tune began to pulse through the speakers—a classic, something we all knew by heart. Instinctively, I began to sing along, my voice mixing with the chatter and laughter around us.

"Oh, a serenade! Now I'm really impressed," Luke teased, his eyes sparkling with mischief. "I didn't know I was dancing with a pop star. Should I be getting your autograph now or later?"

"Only if you promise to frame it. I hear it boosts resale value," I quipped back, relishing the banter. But the playful jabs weren't merely a diversion; they were a lifeline. With each exchange, I felt the walls I had built begin to crumble. The fears that loomed over me—fear of rejection, fear of inadequacy—faded, replaced by something undeniably sweet: connection.

As the song shifted, Luke pulled me closer, our bodies swaying in sync. It felt both intimate and exhilarating, the kind of closeness that made my pulse quicken. I could feel the warmth radiating from him, a tangible energy that drew me in. "You know, you're surprisingly fun to dance with," he remarked, a smirk playing on his lips.

"Surprisingly?" I feigned offense. "What does that mean? You thought I'd be a wallflower?"

"Not at all! You've got the moves," he said, his gaze intense as it locked onto mine. "It's just... I wasn't expecting you to enjoy it this much. I mean, look at you! You're practically glowing."

His compliment sent a rush of warmth through me, igniting my cheeks. "Well, it helps when you've got a dance partner who knows what he's doing. So, teach me your secret," I shot back, tipping my head playfully.

"Ah, the secret is simple: confidence and a healthy dose of not caring what anyone thinks." He winked, twirling me again, this time faster, and I laughed as the world spun in a kaleidoscope of laughter and color.

Then, in a moment of perfect serendipity, a sudden shift in the atmosphere pulled me back to reality. I spotted an old friend of mine, Sophie, lingering at the edge of the dance floor. She had a familiar smile, one that could light up a room, yet now it faltered, her brow furrowing as she glanced around. I felt a pang of unease ripple through me. She was alone, and there was a heaviness in her expression that spoke volumes.

"Hey, is everything alright?" I asked Luke, my smile faltering as I pointed her out.

"Should we go check on her?" he suggested, his tone shifting from playful to concerned.

"Yeah, I think we should," I replied, suddenly aware of how quickly the night could turn from joy to something far more complicated. As we approached Sophie, the music faded into the background, and I could see the telltale signs of distress—her arms crossed tightly, fingers tapping nervously against her skin.

"Hey, you!" I greeted her, trying to infuse warmth into my voice. "What's going on?"

"Oh, nothing. Just enjoying the ambiance," she replied, her words forced, each syllable laced with tension.

"Right. Because who doesn't love a party while simultaneously appearing like they're about to be swallowed by the ground?" I quipped, attempting to lighten the mood, but it fell flat.

Her eyes darted away, tracing the perimeter of the yard. "I just... I didn't expect to see him here," she admitted, a tremor in her voice. "It's kind of overwhelming."

"Who? Is it—" My words caught in my throat as I followed her gaze, landing on a figure across the yard, unmistakable and striking. Jake. The ghost of my past had appeared, and with him, a wave of nostalgia crashed over me, bringing with it a tumult of unresolved emotions.

"Jake's here? Are you serious?" I asked, my voice barely above a whisper, my stomach twisting in knots.

"Yeah. I didn't think he'd come," she murmured, her eyes glassy as if bracing for something painful.

In that moment, I was torn between my instinct to comfort her and the raw tide of memories flooding my mind. Jake had been my first love, the one who had taught me the intricacies of romance, and also the one who had shattered my heart into a million pieces. Seeing him now, years later, rekindled old wounds I thought had healed. The cocktail of emotions—resentment, nostalgia, and lingering affection—swirled within me, threatening to pull me under.

"You know you don't have to face him alone, right?" I reassured Sophie, glancing back at Luke, whose expression mirrored my own concern. "We can get out of here if it's too much."

"No, I'll be okay. I just need a moment," she said, forcing a smile that didn't quite reach her eyes. "It's just... complicated."

Complicated didn't even begin to scratch the surface. In the fleeting seconds that followed, I watched as Jake's laughter rang out, a sound that used to send shivers of joy down my spine. But now, it echoed like a distant memory, a reminder of both what was and what could have been.

"I'll be right here," I promised Sophie, watching as she took a deep breath, summoning the strength to face her past. And though my heart raced, caught between the warmth of Luke's presence and the cold shadow of Jake, I realized that this moment would be a defining one—not just for Sophie, but for me as well.

The air grew thick with tension as I watched Sophie wrestle with her emotions, her eyes fixed on Jake, who appeared all too comfortable in the chaos of our gathering. I felt a strange mixture of sympathy for her and something deeper, more unsettling—an instinctual urge to protect my own heart from the past that had tried to break me. Luke stood beside me, a steady presence, but even his easygoing demeanor couldn't dispel the heaviness in the air.

"Hey," I murmured to Sophie, my voice barely cutting through the ambient noise of laughter and chatter. "You want me to talk to him? I can distract him while you slip away."

She shook her head, a hint of defiance creeping into her expression. "No. I need to do this. I just... need a moment." Her voice trembled, but I admired the bravery in her eyes. There was a strength in her vulnerability that reminded me of the way I felt with Luke—invincible, even when fear loomed.

"Alright, but I'm right here if you need anything," I said, offering her a reassuring smile before reluctantly stepping back. I turned my gaze back to Luke, who seemed to sense the shift in the atmosphere. His brow furrowed, concern clouding his usually bright expression.

"What's going on?" he asked, his voice low, almost protective.

"Just... old drama," I replied, my tone light, though I felt the weight of my own history pressing against my chest. "Sophie has some unfinished business, and I think it's going to get messy."

"Do you want to step away?" he suggested, his eyes scanning the crowd, assessing the situation as though he were gauging the risk of a tightrope walk.

I took a deep breath, trying to mask my apprehension with a smile. "No, I want to stay. I want to be here for her. But can we agree that if things go south, you'll whisk me away to an ice cream shop?"

He chuckled, his laughter a balm against my unease. "Deal. But I'm holding you to that dance-off later, too."

"Only if you promise to wear your best dancing shoes." I nudged him playfully, grateful for his attempt to lighten the mood.

As we stood there, the music shifted once more, and I found my eyes drifting back to Sophie, whose expression had morphed from anxiety to determination. It was both inspiring and terrifying. I watched as she squared her shoulders and began to walk toward Jake, her stride steady despite the tremors that echoed through me. The crowd seemed to thin around them, a hush falling over the party as if the universe itself held its breath.

"Here we go," Luke murmured, the tension palpable. I glanced up at him, searching for a hint of reassurance, and found his eyes locked on the scene unfolding before us.

Sophie approached Jake, her chin tilted defiantly, and for a fleeting moment, I wondered if perhaps she would rise above the pain. But just as she opened her mouth to speak, a shadow flickered at the edge of my vision—a flash of movement that caught my attention.

It was Jake's friend, Eric, who burst into the circle like a whirlwind, arms flailing as he shouted something that was instantly swallowed by the noise. The commotion drew my attention away from Sophie, and I watched as Eric's face twisted in panic, his eyes wide as he scanned the crowd.

"Everyone! There's an emergency! Someone's hurt!" The words sliced through the air like a knife, sending a ripple of alarm across the yard. Laughter ceased, and whispers of confusion began to swirl among the partygoers. I felt my stomach drop, the joy of the evening evaporating in an instant.

Luke's grip tightened on my hand, and we both instinctively stepped closer to the chaos. "What happened?" he asked, his voice steady even as uncertainty flickered in his eyes.

"I don't know!" I responded, my pulse racing. "I think someone collapsed or—"

Before I could finish my sentence, the throng began to shift, everyone moving toward the commotion. I caught sight of Sophie and Jake in the crowd, their confrontation forgotten, both turning toward the growing cluster of concerned faces. My heart pounded in my chest as dread washed over me.

We squeezed through the crowd, weaving past familiar faces now painted with worry. As we approached, I caught glimpses of panic—the flurry of movement, a figure crumpled on the grass. My breath hitched, and I fought the rising tide of fear. "Who is it?" I whispered, desperately searching for a familiar face among the chaos.

"Hang on!" Luke shouted, pushing ahead, his protective instinct kicking in. I followed close behind, trying to shake off the suffocating dread coiling in my stomach. When we finally broke through to the front, my breath caught in my throat at the sight before us.

There, sprawled on the ground, was Clara, a girl from our friend group known for her infectious laughter and boundless energy. She was unconscious, her friends hovering around her like moths to a flame, worry etched across their faces. Someone was kneeling beside her, checking her pulse, while others fumbled with their phones, desperate for help.

"What happened?" I gasped, my heart racing as I crouched down, trying to assess the situation. Luke knelt beside me, his expression shifting from concern to alarm.

"She just... collapsed. We were dancing, and then she just fell," one of her friends stammered, tears glistening in her eyes. "We don't know what to do!"

"Is anyone calling for help?" Luke asked, his voice firm, cutting through the rising panic.

"I'm on it!" another voice shouted, fingers flying over a phone screen. I felt a surge of helplessness, a knot of fear tightening around my throat. I reached for Clara's hand, squeezing it gently, hoping she could somehow feel my presence.

"Clara, can you hear me? It's me, Emily. Please wake up." My voice was shaky, but I forced it to be steady, as if my words could bridge the gap between consciousness and the void.

Seconds stretched into what felt like hours, and the world around us faded into a blur of urgent whispers and flashing lights. The music had stopped, replaced by the chilling sound of anxiety rising among our friends. Luke's hand brushed against mine, an anchor in the storm, reminding me I wasn't alone in this chaos.

But just as I thought we might have a moment of clarity, I heard a shout from the back of the crowd. "Wait! Is that...?" A voice rose above the din, drawing our attention away from Clara.

And there, emerging from the shadows, was Jake, his face pale, eyes wide as he took in the scene. "I didn't mean to—" he started, but the words died on his lips as the chaos unfolded around him.

A collective gasp rippled through the crowd, and I felt the air grow heavy with a tension that crackled like electricity. My heart raced, knowing that whatever had just happened was only the beginning, and the night's revelations were yet to unfold, pushing me into a spiraling abyss of uncertainty.

Chapter 20: Fractured Trust

The twilight sky had draped itself in hues of indigo and blush, the kind of beauty that wrapped around the world like a cozy shawl. The sun dipped low, casting long shadows across the old barn, its weathered wood and peeling paint whispering tales of summers past. I had thought the gathering would smooth the edges of the jagged tensions that had settled like dust on the farm, but as I stepped outside, the warmth of the fading light turned to a chill that gnawed at my insides.

The argument floated through the open window like a sinister wisp, pulling me closer against my better judgment. Sam's voice, usually so steady, now cracked with accusation, slicing through the calm evening air. "You think you know what's best for this place, but you're just a distraction, Luke! You've always been looking out for yourself." His words were heavy, saturated with an anger that felt foreign yet familiar, like the distant rumble of thunder before a storm.

I hesitated at the threshold, my heart racing as if it could sense the brewing tempest. Sam, my steadfast brother, the anchor to my swirling thoughts, was unraveling before my eyes. Luke's response was measured, a contrast to the heat of Sam's fury, yet it had an edge that hinted at the storm brewing beneath his calm facade. "I've given everything to this farm, Sam! Everything! I believed in our vision, in what we can build together." There was a desperation in his voice that sent a shiver down my spine.

The air crackled with tension, and I could feel it pulling me closer, urging me to intervene. The thought of Sam and Luke at odds was a fracture I never wanted to see, a crack in the very foundation of what we were trying to build. I pushed open the door, the creaking hinges echoing like a warning bell in the charged atmosphere.

"Hey!" I called out, my voice cutting through the thick air. Sam turned, his expression morphing from anger to surprise, and in that split second, I saw the vulnerability that lay beneath his tough exterior. Luke stood rigid, his arms crossed defensively, a frown marring his handsome features. I stepped further outside, the cool breeze wrapping around me like a soft embrace, but the chill I felt inside was far more biting.

"What's going on?" I asked, forcing myself to keep my tone neutral, even as my heart raced. Sam's shoulders slumped, and I knew that my presence had shifted the atmosphere, if only slightly.

"Just a little disagreement," Sam said, his voice thick with sarcasm, though the fire in his eyes remained unquenched.

"Disagreement? It sounded more like an explosion," I shot back, crossing my arms as I attempted to be the mediator I had hoped I could be. The tension shifted, and I could feel the eyes of both men boring into me, each with their own unspoken words hanging in the air like heavy fog.

"I'm trying to protect what we have, Em," Sam said, his voice softening just enough to remind me of the brother who had always had my back. "I don't want Luke to come in here and take control like he knows better."

I could see the hurt in Luke's eyes as he braced himself against Sam's words, as if they were physical blows. "You think I want to take control? I want to work together. I thought that's what we all wanted." His voice was raw, the layers of emotion peeling back with each word.

A silence fell, thick and suffocating. I could feel my heart pounding in my chest, the reality of the situation weighing down on me like lead. This was about more than just a disagreement over the farm; it was about trust, loyalty, and the fragile threads that tied us together.

"Look," I said, my voice steadier than I felt. "We all care about this place. We've poured our hearts into it. Sam, you've always been the protector, but Luke is part of this too. You need to see that." I stepped closer to Luke, feeling the warmth radiating from him, a stark contrast to the icy atmosphere. "He's not your enemy."

"Isn't he?" Sam countered, the hurt in his eyes flickering like a candle threatened by the wind. "What if he's here to pull you away from me, from us?"

I inhaled sharply, the accusation cutting deeper than I expected. "Sam, don't you see? This isn't about me choosing between you two. I want both of you in my life. I want us to build something together, but it can't happen if we're at each other's throats."

Luke's gaze flicked between us, his expression shifting from defensive to contemplative. "Sam, I'd never do that to you. I've been here, fighting for this place, fighting for us. I thought you believed in me."

The rawness of his words hung in the air, and I could feel the intensity of their conflict pressing down on us. I could see the walls around Sam beginning to crack, the stubbornness that had always defined him wavering ever so slightly.

"Maybe it's not just about believing in each other," I offered, my voice softer now. "Maybe it's about learning to trust again." The words echoed in the stillness, heavy with the weight of unspoken emotions.

Sam turned away, looking out at the sprawling fields bathed in the fading light. I watched as he wrestled with his thoughts, the tension in his shoulders easing just a fraction. I took a step closer to him, my heart pounding with a mixture of hope and fear.

"I need you to trust me, Sam. I love you, and I want you to be happy. But I also love Luke, and I want him to be a part of our family. Can't we find a way through this?"

A long moment passed, the weight of my words lingering in the air. The crickets began their nightly serenade, a soft backdrop to the uncertainty that hung between us. Sam's jaw clenched as he took a deep breath, his gaze still distant, wrestling with his emotions.

"I don't want to lose you," he finally murmured, vulnerability creeping into his voice.

"And you won't," I replied, stepping closer, my hand finding its way to his arm, grounding him. "We can navigate this together."

The silence stretched on, filled with a fragile hope that shimmered in the twilight. The path ahead was shrouded in uncertainty, but maybe, just maybe, we could find our way back to each other without losing ourselves in the process.

The night wore on, a heavy blanket of darkness settling over the farm, but the tension lingered like the last light of dusk refusing to fade. I could hear the distant rustle of leaves as the wind whispered secrets through the fields, but my heart was too tangled in the chaos between Sam and Luke to heed the call of nature. I stood there, caught in the crossfire of emotions, feeling as if I were about to step onto a tightrope with no safety net.

"Why don't we just talk about this?" I suggested, trying to pull the pieces back together like a patchwork quilt, but the words felt weak against the unresolved anger still crackling in the air. Sam turned to me, a flash of frustration in his eyes, the kind of look that warned me I might be stepping into a minefield.

"Talking hasn't exactly worked, has it?" he shot back, his voice a taut string threatening to snap. I knew my brother well enough to recognize the storm brewing in his heart. He was stubborn as a mule, the kind of steadfastness that had always been both his strength and his flaw.

Luke, still standing with a calm that belied the turmoil within him, stepped forward. "I'm not the enemy here, Sam. You're just making it impossible for us to move forward." His tone was level, but there was a fierce intensity in his eyes, a fire that begged to be acknowledged.

"Maybe you should have thought about that before you got cozy with my sister," Sam retorted, the barb slicing through the air. I could feel the heat of embarrassment creep into my cheeks, and a pang of disappointment lodged in my chest. How had we arrived here, with love twisted into a weapon?

"Cozy? Really?" I interjected, unable to contain my frustration. "Is that what you think this is? A game? Luke isn't here to steal me away; he's trying to help us. Help this place!"

"Help us or help himself?" Sam's skepticism poured forth, each word dripped with suspicion. "I want to know that you're not going to lose sight of what matters. This farm, our family—"

"Your family? Or your idea of family?" Luke cut in, the tension sparking anew between them. "I'm trying to be part of that family, but you're acting like I'm a threat."

My heart raced as I watched them, two men who mattered deeply to me locked in a battle of wills that felt as senseless as it was inevitable. "Can we stop with the blame for a second?" I pleaded, desperation slipping into my voice. "What happened to being partners? We can't build anything if we're tearing each other down."

Sam's jaw tightened, and I caught a flicker of vulnerability in his eyes that made my heart ache. He was grappling with so much—his fear of losing me, his fear of change, all wrapped in that fierce loyalty he felt towards our family.

"Maybe I'm just tired of feeling like I'm the only one who cares about this place," he finally admitted, his voice softer, the anger simmering down to embers.

"You're not alone, Sam," I urged, my own emotions flaring like wildfire. "We all care. Luke has given so much to this farm—"

"And yet you think I'm trying to take something away?" Luke asked, frustration spilling into his words. "I'm trying to lift it up. If you'd let me, we could actually do something amazing together."

I could see the challenge in Sam's eyes, the way he weighed Luke's words against the backdrop of his own doubts. The silence stretched between them, an unseen force that seemed to hold the world in place, and I couldn't help but feel the weight of the moment.

"Fine," Sam said at last, his voice rough but quieter. "Then prove it. If you're really in this for us, show me."

"I can do that," Luke replied, his gaze steady and unwavering. The challenge had shifted, and I could sense the tension transforming into something more constructive, a fragile thread of possibility woven through their words.

"Just so we're clear," Sam added, crossing his arms as he stood tall, his demeanor still brimming with the remnants of defensiveness. "You pull any funny business, and I'll be right there to put you in your place."

"Funny business? Seriously?" Luke chuckled, the tension lightening as he shook his head. "I'm here to help, not to make things weird. You're the one making it weird."

With that, I couldn't help but laugh, a breath of relief bursting forth. "Oh great, now we're fighting about who makes it weird."

The air felt lighter, the storm clouds momentarily parting to let a sliver of understanding through.

"I'd like to see you both work together without me in the middle, but I know that's asking for a miracle," I said, a grin playing on my lips. "But let's at least try not to go for each other's throats over it."

The chuckle that escaped Luke was warm, genuine, and I couldn't resist the spark of hope that flickered within me. "Okay, maybe we can put our heads together, but I can't guarantee I won't give Sam a hard time about his control issues."

"Control issues?" Sam exclaimed, mock outrage spilling from him. "I prefer to think of it as 'leadership'!"

"Of course you do," I teased back, feeling the tension continue to ebb away, replaced by the comforting banter that had always characterized our relationship.

As we stood there, an unlikely trio against the backdrop of the sprawling fields, I felt the connection strengthen, woven together by our shared dreams for the farm and the undercurrents of our complex relationships. There was still a long way to go, still bridges to mend and wounds to heal, but in that moment, the air was filled with the unmistakable scent of possibility.

"We'll figure it out," I said, a sense of determination settling over me like a familiar blanket. "We have to."

The last remnants of daylight faded, and the first stars began to twinkle overhead, like tiny beacons of hope. We had all been fractured, but perhaps, just perhaps, we could begin the slow, painstaking process of putting the pieces back together—stronger and more united than before.

The laughter lingered in the air like the fading notes of a well-loved song, and for a brief moment, it felt like we had stepped back from the brink. Luke and Sam exchanged reluctant smiles, the tension still crackling between them but softened by our shared camaraderie. It was the kind of laughter that hinted at old friendships, one where past grievances could be brushed aside—if only for a night. The warmth of that camaraderie, however, was undercut by the unsettling knowledge that the shadows of doubt were lurking just out of sight.

"Okay, let's be real," I said, trying to keep the mood buoyant. "If we're going to tackle this, we need a plan. And by 'plan,' I mean something more than standing around glaring at each other." I gestured to the barn, where the faint smell of hay mingled with the cool evening air, a backdrop to the chaos swirling in our hearts.

Sam rubbed the back of his neck, a gesture I recognized as one of his telltale signs of anxiety. "What's your brilliant idea? A circle of trust? We can sit around a campfire and roast marshmallows while we talk about our feelings?"

"Hey, that sounds oddly therapeutic," Luke quipped, a playful glimmer in his eyes. "I can already envision us singing 'Kumbaya.'"

"Please, let's not make this worse," I replied, rolling my eyes. "No one needs to hear that rendition."

We shared a laugh, the warmth bridging the gap between our misunderstandings, and I felt a flicker of hope ignite within me. "Seriously though, let's think about what we need. This farm isn't just about us; it's about the future. And it's going to take all of us pulling in the same direction."

Sam leaned against the barn door, a thoughtful look crossing his face. "Okay, fine. We can start with the crops. We've got that planting deadline coming up, and I want us all on the same page before we start digging."

Luke nodded, his brow furrowed in concentration. "Agreed. And maybe we can divide up responsibilities so it doesn't feel like I'm intruding on your territory, Sam. I'm here to collaborate, not to take over."

As we discussed the ins and outs of our plans, the darkness of the night deepened around us, the stars twinkling overhead as if cheering us on. It was hard to ignore the thrill of possibility as we strategized, the air buzzing with an electric energy that made me feel alive. I wanted this to work; I wanted us to be a team.

After what felt like hours, we finally wrapped up our brainstorming session. I felt a sense of camaraderie blooming like wildflowers in spring. "See? Not so hard," I said, my heart light with the sense of progress we had made.

As we began to disperse, I noticed Sam's shoulders still tensed, a storm brewing beneath the surface. "Hey, Luke," he said suddenly, his tone shifting from camaraderie to something more serious. "I know we're on the same team now, but I can't shake this feeling that something's off. I just... I need you to understand what this means to me."

Luke's expression shifted, his easygoing demeanor replaced by something more serious. "I get it, Sam. This is your family, your legacy. But I'm not trying to replace you. I'm here to build something with you, for all of us."

The sincerity in Luke's voice hung in the air, and I could see the two of them trying to navigate the uncharted waters of their relationship. I was reminded of how fragile trust could be, yet here we were, navigating it together.

"Just don't forget that this is my home too," Sam replied, his eyes narrowing slightly as he crossed his arms, a habit of his when he felt threatened. "I won't let anyone come in and take it away from me."

"I'm not here to take anything, Sam. I promise," Luke replied, the tension rising again, but I sensed the sincerity in his words.

Before I could intervene to diffuse the growing pressure, the barn door creaked open behind us, a shadow sliding across the wooden floor. My heart dropped as I turned, the familiar face of our neighbor, Mr. Hargrove, stepping into the soft light spilling from the barn.

"Sorry to interrupt," he said, his voice gravelly and low, sending a shiver down my spine. "I didn't mean to eavesdrop, but there's something you all need to know."

A knot formed in my stomach as the tension in the air thickened once more. "What is it?" I asked, stepping forward, my heart racing.

"There's been some talk," he said, his brow furrowed in concern. "Rumors swirling about the land. The developers are circling like vultures, and they're looking to make an offer. I thought you should hear it from me before things get out of hand."

"What?" Sam's voice was sharp, a blade cutting through the night air. "You can't be serious. We've worked too hard for this!"

Luke's expression hardened, and I could see the gears turning in his mind, the weight of the news settling like a rock in his stomach. "Are they trying to push us out?"

"It sounds like they're willing to do whatever it takes," Mr. Hargrove replied, his tone grim. "I wanted you to know that you have allies in this. We can't let them take what's rightfully yours."

A heavy silence enveloped us, the implications of his words sinking in. The air buzzed with a different kind of tension now, one that came with the threat of losing everything we had worked for. I glanced at Sam and Luke, their faces reflecting shock and determination, and I could feel the world around us tilting on its axis.

"What do we do?" I whispered, the weight of the unknown pressing down on me.

Mr. Hargrove stepped closer, his voice low and steady. "You fight. You come together. And you don't let them tear you apart."

The night seemed to stretch endlessly as we processed this new reality, the stars above us twinkling like distant fires, while below, the ground felt unsteady, fraught with uncertainty. As the first hint of dawn began to break, casting a faint glow over the horizon, I knew that we were standing on the precipice of a battle far greater than any of us had anticipated.

I looked at Sam and Luke, and something unspoken passed between us—a shared resolve, a determination that we wouldn't back down. But just as hope began to weave its way through the uncertainty, a sound pierced the stillness: the distant rumble of engines approaching, loud and threatening, like a dark storm rolling in.

"What now?" Sam muttered, his eyes narrowing.

And just like that, the shadows returned, lurking at the edges of our fragile alliance, ready to unleash a storm that none of us could see coming.

Chapter 21: Seeds of Doubt

The sun hung low in the sky, a molten ball of amber casting long shadows over the fields. Each beam felt like a gentle caress, yet the warmth that enveloped me was belied by a chill that had taken root in my chest. It whispered doubts, like dark tendrils curling around my heart. I knelt in the soil, my hands working through the earth, yet my thoughts were elsewhere, spiraling into the abyss of uncertainty. Sam's words, with their sharp edge, replayed in my mind like a relentless record, filling the air with a tension I couldn't shake.

"You're too soft for this, Amelia. It's not just about pretty vegetables and smiling faces at the market. You'll drown in all of it," he had said, his voice low and heavy with a mix of concern and something darker.

As I dug my fingers into the cool, rich soil, I could almost feel my father's spirit beside me, a reassuring weight against the burgeoning doubt. I remembered his hands, calloused and strong, guiding mine as he taught me the intricate dance of planting seeds. "Each one carries the promise of life," he would say, his voice tinged with a warmth that always made the world feel brighter. "But you have to believe in their potential, Amelia. Just like you must believe in yourself." The thought brought a flicker of comfort, yet it was quickly snuffed out by the encroaching shadows of my anxiety.

"Are you planning to plant those seeds or just worry them into the ground?" Luke's voice broke through my reverie, a lighthearted jab that had me looking up. He stood there, leaning against the wooden fence, a grin splitting his face, dust motes swirling around him like tiny stars in the golden afternoon light. There was a rugged handsomeness about him, the kind that felt both familiar and refreshing. His plaid shirt was rolled up at the sleeves, revealing sun-kissed arms, a testament to long days under the sun, and his dark hair tousled just enough to look like he had a perpetual wind behind him.

"I was just... contemplating the mysteries of life," I replied, unable to suppress a smile as I straightened up, brushing the soil from my knees. "You know, the usual."

He laughed, a deep, rich sound that settled warmly in my chest. "Right, of course. Mysteries like why you always choose to plant carrots when you're obviously much better suited for broccoli?"

"Broccoli?" I feigned offense, waving a hand dismissively. "Broccoli is so... boring."

"Boring?" He stepped closer, his brow arched in mock disbelief. "I don't think you know how to make broccoli exciting. You should try adding garlic and lemon zest next time. Maybe even a bit of feta."

"Oh, now we're getting fancy," I shot back, unable to hide my laughter. "I could take my broccoli game to the next level, just for you. If that's all it takes to impress you, I might start a vegetable revolution."

"Now that's the spirit," he said, crouching beside me, the warmth of his presence chasing away the lingering shadows. "Let's plant these together. I'm sure we can make broccoli worthy of a Michelin star."

We worked side by side, our hands moving in a synchronized rhythm, loosening soil, placing seeds with care, and patting the earth back into place. Every now and then, our shoulders brushed, sending sparks of warmth through me. With each seed nestled into the ground, I felt a small part of my doubts peel away, replaced by an exhilarating sense of possibility.

"Do you ever think about how much we have to learn from these plants?" I mused, my voice a soft murmur. "They grow despite the odds. Storms, droughts, pests—yet they keep pushing through. It's like they know they belong."

Luke paused, considering my words as if he were unraveling a profound mystery. "Maybe that's what we should do too. Just keep pushing through the doubt and uncertainty, like stubborn weeds."

"Exactly," I said, encouraged by his insight. "It's almost poetic, really. I wish I had your confidence to just... be."

"Confidence isn't always a choice. Sometimes it's about accepting the messiness of life," he said, his voice steady yet layered with something unspoken. "Like this farm. It's chaotic, but that's where the magic is."

Magic. The word hung between us, thick with unfulfilled potential. My heart fluttered with unspoken thoughts as I searched his gaze. There was an openness there that hinted at understanding, a connection that was becoming increasingly difficult to ignore. But a nagging voice, small but persistent, whispered of Sam's warnings. Could I truly carry the weight of this farm? Could I lean on Luke without losing myself in the process?

As the sun dipped lower, painting the sky with hues of pink and purple, I felt the weight of the day settle over us, a comfortable silence enveloping our shared space. Luke reached over, brushing a stray lock of hair behind my ear, his touch light yet electrifying. "You're doing better than you think, you know. This place needs you."

A flutter of uncertainty stirred in my chest. "But what if I'm not enough? What if I fail?"

"Then you fail," he said simply, the corners of his mouth twitching into a smile that was both reassuring and mischievous. "But it'll be an epic failure. One for the books. And you'll have me right beside you, probably failing spectacularly too."

I couldn't help but laugh, the sound breaking free like a breath I didn't know I was holding. "Epic failures? I guess I could use a partner in crime for that."

"Exactly," he replied, his eyes sparkling with mischief. "And who knows? Maybe we'll even invent a new way to make broccoli exciting along the way."

In that moment, with the weight of my worries momentarily lifted, I realized how much I craved this connection—the lightness of his laughter, the reassurance of his presence. Together, we weren't just planting seeds in the soil; we were sowing hope, courage, and a hint of something more that lingered in the air, tantalizingly close, like the sweet scent of blooming flowers on the horizon.

The days melted into a routine, a comforting rhythm punctuated by the sounds of rustling leaves and the distant clucking of chickens. Yet even amidst this tranquility, unease lingered like a stubborn shadow. I'd risen early that morning, the golden sunlight spilling through the window, stirring me from dreams filled with half-formed worries. I glanced around my small kitchen, taking in the familiar clutter—the drying herbs hanging from the rafters, the array of mismatched mugs lined up like soldiers waiting for coffee.

But as I ground the coffee beans, the rich aroma filling the air, my thoughts drifted again to Sam's words. "You're playing a losing game, Amelia." The phrase played on repeat, each syllable a fresh reminder of the insecurities I thought I had banished. What if I was indeed setting myself up for failure? I shook my head, trying to dispel the cloud hanging over me.

The garden was calling, a vibrant canvas waiting for my touch. I stepped outside, inhaling the earthy scent of freshly turned soil mixed with the sweetness of blooming zinnias. As I began to prune the flower beds, I could feel the sun warming my back, urging me to let the doubts dissipate with each snip. I lost myself in the colors, the textures, and the tiny, optimistic buds peeking through the earth. But no amount of gardening could entirely keep Sam's voice at bay.

"Amelia, you have to listen to me," I muttered to myself, frustration boiling beneath my calm façade. "You are capable. You can do this."

But deep down, the nagging voice countered, reminding me of every misstep I'd made in the past.

Just then, a light tapping on the garden gate pulled me from my spiral. Luke stood there again, a friendly giant with a playful smile, holding a basket of fresh strawberries as if they were the answer to all my worries. "Thought you could use a snack. And maybe a distraction from your existential crisis," he said, arching an eyebrow.

"Isn't it too early in the day for existential crises?" I replied, taking the basket from him, our fingers brushing momentarily. A jolt of electricity shot up my arm, and I quickly hid my reaction behind a chuckle. "I thought we save those for late-night conversations over wine."

He stepped into the garden, his hands finding a spot on his hips as he surveyed my work. "Only if you promise to keep the broccoli in line," he teased, leaning over to inspect a few of the plants I had put in the ground just days before.

I tossed a strawberry his way, which he caught effortlessly. "If I keep the broccoli in line, you have to promise to help me with the carrots next week. I'm convinced they're plotting against me."

His laughter was rich, and I found myself grinning despite my earlier doubts. "Deal. But you have to show me your secret carrot-rearing techniques first."

With the sun high above us, we settled into a rhythm, sharing stories as we munched on strawberries, their sweetness bursting in our mouths. "Did I ever tell you about the time I tried to make strawberry jam? I nearly turned the kitchen into a science experiment," I confessed, wiping juice from my chin.

Luke leaned back against the fence, laughter dancing in his eyes. "Do enlighten me. Did the jam survive?"

"Let's just say the jam was a casualty. I may or may not have added salt instead of sugar. It was a taste sensation that could only be described as... tragic."

"Salted strawberry jam? Now that's a bold choice. I'm surprised you didn't get a call from the culinary police."

His playful banter soothed the growing tension within me, a reminder that maybe I wasn't navigating this journey entirely alone. Each joke and story built a bridge across the chasm of uncertainty that had been threatening to swallow me whole.

But as our laughter faded, a slight shift in the air replaced the lightness with a gravity I couldn't ignore. "You know," Luke said, his tone suddenly serious, "you've been working so hard on this farm, but you can't forget to take care of yourself, too. I see you out here all the time, pushing yourself. It's okay to ask for help."

A wave of warmth spread through me, tinged with embarrassment. "I appreciate that, really. But asking for help feels like admitting defeat, and I've got this weird stubborn streak in me." I laughed, but it felt more like a mask than a genuine response.

"Stubbornness has its perks," he admitted. "But you're not weak for wanting support. Even the strongest roots need a little assistance to grow."

His gaze held mine, earnest and unyielding, and I felt the walls I'd built around my vulnerability begin to crack. I glanced down at the strawberries, their glossy red surfaces reflecting the light, their sweetness a stark contrast to the bitterness of my thoughts.

"I guess I just don't want to let anyone down," I admitted, the confession tumbling out before I could reel it back. "I've always felt like I had to prove myself, especially now that I'm carrying this farm on my shoulders."

Luke nodded, the weight of my words settling between us like a shared secret. "But who are you proving it to? If it's to Sam, I don't think he's worth it. You know what he did, right? He left. And here you are, making this place bloom."

"Easier said than done," I murmured, my heart thudding in my chest. "What if it all collapses? What if I can't do this?"

"Then we'll build it back up again," he said, his tone unwavering, as if he'd made a promise to the very earth beneath our feet. "You're not alone in this. And if you ever need a hand—or a laugh—well, you know where to find me."

His words washed over me, soothing the frayed edges of my anxiety. I smiled, a genuine warmth spreading through me as I looked at him, really looked at him. "Thank you, Luke. For... everything."

He shrugged, a small smile playing at his lips. "What can I say? I'm a sucker for adventure—and if that adventure involves broccoli, then count me in."

Just as I was about to respond, a loud clattering sound from the direction of the barn startled us both. We exchanged wide-eyed glances, our laughter fading into a shared uncertainty. My heart raced as I stood, instinctively moving toward the noise, with Luke at my side. Whatever awaited us, it was yet another reminder that this farm held both beauty and chaos, and I was still learning how to navigate it all.

The clatter echoed through the barn, a jarring sound that sliced through the afternoon stillness. I froze mid-step, my heart racing as adrenaline kicked in. Luke's hand rested gently on my back, a reassuring weight that pushed me forward even as uncertainty gnawed at my insides. Together, we exchanged a glance, the kind that speaks volumes without uttering a single word.

"Should we investigate?" he asked, his eyes dancing with curiosity, or perhaps mischief. "Or do we pretend we didn't hear anything and just blame it on the chickens?"

"Considering the state of the chickens lately, that might be our best bet," I replied, attempting to mask my own unease with a laugh.

But as we stepped toward the barn, the sound of muffled clucking and the occasional crash drew us in like moths to a flame. I pushed the large wooden door open, the creak echoing like a warning. Inside, the afternoon light streamed through the slatted windows, illuminating a chaotic scene. Hay was strewn across the floor, the chickens flapping their wings in a frenzy as they scuttled about like tiny, feathered tornadoes.

And then I saw it. A large, stubborn goat, one I had thought securely tethered outside, was evidently on a personal mission to wreak havoc. It stood proudly amidst the chaos, munching on what appeared to be a bundle of freshly harvested herbs I had left on a nearby table, utterly unfazed by the disarray it had caused.

"Basil and thyme for breakfast?" Luke said, his voice dripping with amusement. "I see we have a culinary goat on our hands. Quite the ambitious palate."

"Very ambitious," I said, my heart racing from a mix of laughter and disbelief. "Maybe it's time for us to implement some strict dietary guidelines around here."

The goat looked up at us, its beady eyes sparkling with mischief as it chewed, completely unaware—or perhaps uncaring—of its egregious behavior. I let out a chuckle, the absurdity of the moment grounding me, a reminder that even in the most chaotic times, there were pockets of joy to be found.

"Let's corral it back outside before it develops a taste for my entire herb garden," I said, already stepping forward, ready to retrieve the rogue creature.

Luke moved beside me, his laughter blending with mine as we devised a plan. "How about I distract it with some leftover strawberries while you do the actual wrangling? That way, we can both claim victory."

"Strawberries? You really know how to sweeten the deal," I quipped, eyeing the goat as it took another triumphant bite of my herbs. "Deal."

With a quick hand gesture, Luke brandished a handful of strawberries, holding them like a magic wand as he approached the goat. "Hey there, gourmet! You want some real food?"

The goat paused, its ears perking up as if it had just been offered the world's greatest delicacy. With a few quick moves, I sidled behind it, and as Luke dangled the fruit, I managed to secure a rope around its neck. The goat bleated in protest, but I tightened my grip, feeling a rush of triumph.

"We've got you now," I said, laughing as I led the reluctant creature out of the barn.

"That was impressive!" Luke remarked, a sparkle in his eyes. "You should consider adding 'goat wrangler' to your resume."

"Right under 'expert in vegetable warfare' and 'proficient in existential crises,'" I shot back, the playful banter lifting my spirits further.

We managed to tether the goat back to its pen, and for a moment, as we leaned against the fence, catching our breath, it felt like we had accomplished something monumental. Maybe wrangling a goat wasn't exactly akin to saving the world, but it was a much-needed reminder that laughter and teamwork could be the salve for a restless heart.

But as I turned to Luke, I noticed a slight shift in his expression. The playful glint faded, replaced by something deeper. "You know," he began, his tone more serious, "I'm really impressed with how you handle everything. This place—it's more than just a farm to you, isn't it? It's your home. Your heart."

His words struck a chord, resonating within me. The weight of the farm—the responsibility of it all—settled like a blanket over my shoulders. "It is," I said softly, vulnerability creeping into my voice.

"Sometimes I wonder if I'm enough to make it thrive. I mean, I grew up here, and I always thought I would do great things with it. But... what if I'm just chasing shadows?"

Luke's gaze held mine with an intensity that sent my heart racing. "Amelia, you've already done great things. Look at the garden! Look at how you've brought this place back to life. You're not just trying to save it; you're creating something new. That's incredible."

His sincerity washed over me like a warm wave, filling the cracks of self-doubt that had formed over time. "Thank you," I murmured, unsure how to respond to such earnestness.

Just then, a loud crash erupted from inside the barn again, jolting us back to reality. We exchanged incredulous glances before racing back inside, our previous moment of connection shattered by the chaos.

Inside, I was met with a scene that was surprisingly worse than before. The shelves had toppled, spilling tools and buckets of paint everywhere. The chickens had discovered an escape route, flapping frantically around the barn as if auditioning for an avian circus.

"What the—" Luke started, his eyes wide. "How is this even possible? We just fixed this place!"

I shook my head, half-laughing and half-pulling my hair out. "Maybe we have a poltergeist? Or a goat army? Honestly, at this point, anything seems possible."

"Or maybe your farm is just trying to remind you that it's a living, breathing entity," he mused, grabbing a broom from the scattered tools. "I'd say it's more demanding than a toddler on a sugar high."

"Exactly!" I said, grabbing another broom. "We're literally fighting chaos with chaos."

As we set to work clearing the debris and trying to corral the now-rambunctious chickens, I caught glimpses of Luke's laughter echoing through the disarray. Somehow, amidst the madness, our earlier connection reignited, fueling a shared determination to restore order.

But just as we began to feel a semblance of control returning, a sudden, startling sound ripped through the barn—the unmistakable roar of a truck engine. Confusion settled over us as we exchanged glances, the energy shifting into a tense undercurrent.

"Who could that be?" I wondered aloud, the previous laughter evaporating. The sound grew louder, drowning out the chaos of the barn.

Luke's expression hardened. "I don't know, but we should find out."

As the engine roared to a halt outside, I felt my heart thump in my chest. I wiped my hands on my jeans, a surge of adrenaline pushing me toward the barn door. "Let's go check."

We stepped outside together, uncertainty thick in the air. The truck door swung open, and a figure stepped out, silhouetted against the setting sun. My breath caught in my throat as recognition hit me hard, a wave of mixed emotions washing over me. The figure stood tall, dust swirling around them as they approached, the weight of their presence sending a shiver down my spine.

The unmistakable outline of Sam.

Chapter 22: Cracks in the Foundation

The sun hung low in the sky, spilling its golden hues over the fields, casting elongated shadows that danced across the fresh soil. I inhaled deeply, the rich scent of tilled earth mixing with the sweet aroma of the nearby wildflowers, a bittersweet reminder of the beauty surrounding me even as my heart felt burdened. The farm was finally coming alive; rows of vibrant crops stretched across the land like a patchwork quilt, each swath of green a testament to our labor and resilience. I should have felt proud, buoyed by the thought of what we had achieved together, but an unseen tension loomed between Sam and me, suffocating the joy that should have been blossoming in this newly thriving sanctuary.

As I stirred the simmering pot of tomato sauce, the comforting scent wafted through the kitchen, grounding me in the familiar routine. Cooking had become my refuge, a way to navigate the chaos that had invaded my life. But today, even the clattering of pans and the rhythmic chopping of vegetables did little to ease the knot tightening in my stomach. The clamor from the barn pierced the evening calm like a crack of thunder, and I dropped my knife, the blade clattering against the wooden board as I dashed outside.

The sun dipped lower, painting the sky in streaks of orange and violet, but my heart raced not with awe but dread. I found Sam standing toe-to-toe with one of the local farmers, a burly man whose face was flushed with anger. Their words were sharp, cutting through the air with a bitterness that churned my stomach. "You've got no right to claim this land, Sam! Your father may have handed it down, but it was never his to give!" The farmer's voice echoed against the barn, each syllable dripped in contempt.

"Don't act like you own the whole county, Rick! We're not selling. You need to back off!" Sam retorted, his jaw clenched tight, muscles in his neck tensing like steel cables. He had always been the fierce protector, the one who would stand up to anyone, but today, it felt different—more desperate, more fractured.

I stepped forward, my heart pounding, and called out, "Sam! Let's talk about this." But the moment my words broke through the tension, Sam's eyes flared with something akin to rage or perhaps just an overwhelming sense of helplessness.

"Why are you even here?" he shot back, his voice sharp enough to cut. "You don't get it, do you? This is between me and Rick."

The pain in his tone pierced through me. It was as if a chasm had opened between us, a rift that had been widening for weeks now. "I do get it, but fighting won't help. Let's just—"

"Just what?" he interrupted, hands gesturing wildly as if trying to grasp at something intangible. "Pretend everything is okay? Pretend you didn't bring this all on yourself?"

I felt my breath hitch, the words striking a nerve deep within me. Was I really to blame for everything that had gone wrong since Dad died? Sure, I had pushed for us to take over the farm, to honor our father's legacy, but I'd thought we were in this together. My gaze dropped to the ground, an instinctual shield against the sharpness of his accusations. The weight of his words settled heavily on my shoulders. I was losing him—losing my brother.

Rick, sensing the tension between us, stepped back with a smug look, arms crossed over his chest as if he were watching a show. "I'll let you two work this out. But you know I'll take what's rightfully mine, Sam." With a final sneer, he turned, leaving us standing amidst the remnants of his challenge, the air thick with unresolved conflict.

The barn door swung shut behind him, leaving an uncomfortable silence that stretched painfully between us. I looked up, trying to find the brother I once knew in the depths of Sam's stormy eyes, but the flicker of recognition seemed lost. "What's happening to us?" I whispered, my voice barely a breath.

He scoffed, running a hand through his tousled hair, a gesture I had once found charming but now seemed to radiate frustration. "What's happening is that you can't keep ignoring the reality of this place. You're trying to turn a profit like it's some hobby, while I'm out here fighting for what's ours!"

I took a step back, his words hitting me like a punch. "It's not just a hobby to me! I care about this farm, about us! I thought we were rebuilding together."

"Rebuilding?" he echoed, disbelief lacing his tone. "What have you done but drag me back into a life I didn't want?"

Each accusation twisted the knife deeper. The farm had been our father's dream, a place where laughter and hard work intertwined, yet here we were, unearthing wounds instead of planting seeds. I had hoped this endeavor would draw us closer, but instead, it was tearing us apart. "I'm not trying to replace Dad, Sam. I'm trying to honor him!"

A flicker of something—was it regret?—passed across his face, but it was gone in an instant, replaced by an iron mask of resolve. "I don't need your version of honor. I need you to get out of my way."

The air was thick with resentment, and my heart felt heavy, burdened by the realization that my brother, my friend, was slipping through my fingers like sand. The vibrant world around us faded, leaving only the echo of our words hanging in the dusk. I turned, retreating toward the house, the warm light spilling from the kitchen a stark contrast to the chill that settled over my heart. The sunset was beautiful, but its splendor felt cruel, illuminating the cracks in my foundation while shadows loomed, waiting to swallow us whole.

Inside the house, I could still feel the weight of Sam's words clinging to me like a shadow. I leaned against the kitchen counter, the cool granite grounding me as I absentmindedly stirred the sauce, its rich red hue now reminding me more of anger than of warmth. The rhythmic simmering had become a ritual of solace, but today it offered no comfort. I tried to focus on the tasks before me—chopping basil, grating cheese—but my mind was a whirlwind, and each slice of the knife felt like a futile attempt to cut through the tension gnawing at my insides.

The shadows stretched long across the floor as the sun dipped lower, retreating behind the hills that cradled our farm. Outside, the distant sounds of cows lowing and chickens clucking felt almost mocking, a stark contrast to the storm brewing within the walls of our home. I should have been savoring the quiet moments, appreciating the beauty of the evening, yet all I could think of was the gulf growing wider between Sam and me. I remembered the evenings we used to spend out on the porch, teasing each other under the stars, laughter spilling into the night. Now, those memories felt like remnants of a dream, hazy and unreachable.

As I plated the dinner, a mixture of spaghetti and the sauce that had turned an unwelcome shade of crimson in my mind, I could hear the faint clattering of hooves against the barn floor. I set the table with deliberate care, hoping to spark some semblance of normalcy, but as I poured a glass of wine, the familiar sound of Sam's boots on the porch announced his return. The door creaked open, and he stepped inside, his shoulders hunched, a worn-out figure engulfed in exhaustion and irritation.

"I'm not hungry," he said, brushing past me with a resolute air, as if the mere act of eating were a betrayal of our discord.

I blinked, a surge of frustration mixing with the sorrow in my chest. "You can't avoid me forever, you know. And you can't ignore your own hunger."

He stopped, turning to me, the dim light casting sharp angles across his face. "Is this about the dinner, or is it about the farm? Because I'm more than willing to talk about how you're making everything worse."

The accusation hung in the air like a storm cloud, ready to unleash its fury. "I'm trying to make it better, Sam! This isn't just about land or legacy; it's about us! It's about honoring Dad's memory!"

"You think that making spaghetti is going to solve our problems?" His tone dripped with sarcasm, and I could feel my resolve beginning to crack under the pressure of his words.

"Making spaghetti is just a dinner, Sam. It's what happens at the dinner table that matters. I want us to talk!" My voice rose, echoing off the walls, the intensity of the moment pushing me to the edge of my composure.

"Talk?" He scoffed, and for a moment, the anger in his eyes flickered with something softer—perhaps regret? "What is there to talk about? You're just pretending everything is fine, but it's not."

In that moment, my heart clenched. "I'm not pretending, and I'm not going anywhere. This is my home too. We have to find a way through this together."

Sam rubbed the back of his neck, a telltale sign that I was reaching him, even if just a little. "Together? It doesn't feel like we're together at all. It feels like you're on one side and I'm on another, fighting against you."

"Then let's change that," I said softly, taking a step closer, the air between us thick with unspoken emotions. "Let's not make each other the enemy."

He hesitated, his gaze drifting to the table, where the spaghetti sat waiting, untouched. "You really think we can just sit down and pretend we're a happy family again?"

"I think we can start by sharing a meal," I replied, my voice steady, hopeful. "Just like we used to. You know I've always been better at talking over food. Or at least eating it."

A reluctant smile tugged at the corners of his mouth, the tension around his eyes easing ever so slightly. "You always did have a knack for making food seem more inviting than it actually was."

"Hey, it's a talent!" I grinned, trying to lighten the mood, the warmth of nostalgia sweeping through me. "Plus, the sauce is a family recipe. I think Dad would have appreciated the effort."

"Fine," he relented, the softness creeping back into his voice. "But only if I get to drown it in cheese. You know how he liked it."

I laughed, feeling a small glimmer of hope bloom in my chest as I dished out a generous helping onto his plate. "Deal. But only if you promise not to throw the fork at me later when I insist on a bite of your garlic bread."

The moment felt fragile, like the first fragile shoots of spring peeking through winter's lingering frost. We settled at the table, the sound of our forks clinking against the plates punctuating the heavy silence. The food was delicious, or so I hoped, but it was hard to taste anything past the bittersweet flavor of our strained conversation. As we ate, the initial tension began to ebb, but the undercurrents remained, threading through our words, silent yet insistent.

"Rick's a real piece of work," I ventured, hoping to stir the conversation toward less incendiary territory.

"He's not wrong about the land, though." Sam's brow furrowed, his expression serious again. "I just don't want to lose it. It's all I have left to hold onto."

"Losing it doesn't mean losing him," I said, daring to reach out across the table, my hand brushing against his. The contact felt electric, a reminder of the bond we still shared. "We'll figure this out. Together."

He met my gaze, a flicker of vulnerability dancing behind the walls he had erected. "You think we can? You think we can find a way back to each other through all of this?"

The air felt charged, ripe with possibilities, and I nodded slowly, my heart brimming with determination. "We have to try. Because if we don't, we'll end up like Rick—bitter and alone."

For a moment, the storm clouds seemed to part, revealing a glimpse of the sky beyond, where hope flickered like distant stars. In that shared silence, the weight of our unspoken fears began to lift, and perhaps, just perhaps, we were on the cusp of rediscovering the family we once were—battered but not broken, forged anew in the fires of our struggles.

The clinking of forks against plates faded, replaced by a cautious silence that lingered between us like a half-remembered melody. As we finished dinner, the remnants of the meal lay untouched on the table, a bittersweet reminder of the tension that had both separated and tethered us. Sam stared into his glass, swirling the dark liquid as if searching for answers in the depths of the Merlot. His brow furrowed, and I could almost see the gears turning in his mind, the way they used to when he was trying to solve a puzzle or figure out the most efficient way to herd the cattle.

"Do you ever think about leaving?" he asked suddenly, his voice barely above a whisper. It was as if he had pulled a thread, unraveling a tapestry of thoughts I hadn't realized he was weaving.

"Leaving? Why would I want to leave?" I countered, feigning lightness as I pretended to be busy clearing the table. "This is home, Sam. I have roots here."

"Roots can strangle you if you let them." He placed his glass down with a quiet thud, the sound reverberating between us. "What if this place isn't what we thought it was? What if it's just a glorified prison, tying us to memories we can't escape?"

The words hung in the air like a bitter fruit, ripe for plucking but laden with the risk of sourness. I paused, the weight of his statement pressing against my chest. "You think that's what it is? I see it as our future."

"Do you?" His gaze pierced through me, searching for sincerity. "Or is it just a refuge from the storm?"

I opened my mouth to respond, but the words caught in my throat. Maybe it was a refuge—a sanctuary from the chaos of grief and uncertainty. But was that enough? "You're talking about leaving, but what would that even look like? We can't just throw everything away."

Sam leaned back in his chair, a sigh escaping his lips as he ran a hand through his hair. "I don't know, Elise. I really don't. It just feels like we're trapped in this endless cycle of fighting and avoiding each other. Maybe it's better to cut ties before we get hurt more."

I felt a stab of anger mixed with sadness. "Cut ties? With each other? With the farm?" The frustration spilled over, my voice rising again. "Do you think that's what Dad would have wanted? To just give up?"

For a moment, he looked vulnerable, the lines on his face softening as he considered my words. "I don't want to give up, but it's like I can't breathe here anymore."

Before I could respond, a loud crash echoed from the direction of the barn, jolting us both. Instinctively, we shot up from our seats, the tension between us momentarily forgotten. I exchanged a glance with Sam, uncertainty flashing in his eyes, and together we moved toward the door, stepping into the cool night air. The stars sparkled above us, indifferent to the turmoil below, as we hurried down the path.

The barn loomed ahead, its silhouette dark against the twilight sky, but it was the clamor of voices that drew us closer. "What the hell is going on?" I murmured, half to myself, as we reached the entrance.

Peeking inside, I was met with a startling scene: Rick, the farmer from earlier, was inside with another local, both of them shoving crates of supplies and equipment around. "You can't just come in here and take what you want!" Sam yelled, stepping into the barn, a protective instinct flaring within him.

Rick turned, a smug grin plastered across his face. "Oh, but I can. This is all part of your father's deal, remember? You're just too blinded by your own pride to see it."

"Get out!" I shouted, the urgency of the moment pulling me forward. "This is private property!"

"Oh, is it? It doesn't feel that way when I can waltz in and grab whatever I need," he taunted, his voice dripping with contempt. The other farmer chuckled, a harsh sound that grated against my nerves.

Sam stepped forward, tension radiating off him like heat from an open flame. "You need to leave. Now."

The room thickened with animosity, and I felt the air grow colder, the shadows closing in around us. "You really think you can scare me off this land? Your father was weak, and you're just as weak." Rick's laughter echoed, a taunting sound that sparked fury in my brother's eyes.

"Don't talk about him like that!" I interjected, anger bubbling up inside me, mixing with the fear of what this confrontation could lead to.

"Or what? You'll throw more spaghetti at me?" he sneered, and suddenly, it was too much. I stepped between them, my heart pounding. "This isn't a game, Rick! This is our home!"

He rolled his eyes, stepping closer, invading my space. "You're just a little girl playing dress-up on a farm. You think you can keep up with the big boys?"

Sam's fist clenched at his side, and the tension in the room crackled. "You're outnumbered," he warned, eyes narrowing. "And if you don't leave, I'll make sure everyone knows what a pathetic coward you are."

The threat hung heavily in the air, and for a moment, it felt like a dare. The other farmer, sensing the shift, looked uneasy, but Rick just laughed again, unbothered by the gravity of the situation. "Go ahead. Do your worst. But know this: I'm not going anywhere. This land belongs to me too."

"What are you talking about?" Sam barked, the frustration boiling over. "It's been in our family for generations!"

"Isn't it funny how quickly things can change?" Rick stepped back, his eyes glinting with something sinister. "You don't know what kind of game you're playing, do you? This isn't just about land; it's about control. And I intend to take back what was stolen."

I felt a chill run down my spine, an unshakeable fear gripping me. "What do you mean?" I asked, my voice steady despite the trepidation pooling in my gut.

Rick leaned closer, his breath hot against my ear. "You'll find out soon enough. Just remember, every storm leaves behind a wreckage." With that, he turned on his heel and strode toward the exit, leaving us in the suffocating silence of the barn.

As he stepped outside, the door slammed shut behind him, the finality echoing in the stillness. My heart raced, confusion and fear intertwining, while Sam stood rigid beside me, his expression a mixture of disbelief and fury. "What the hell just happened?"

"I don't know, but I have a bad feeling about this." I glanced at Sam, whose jaw clenched in anger.

Before he could respond, a loud thud resonated from outside, followed by the unmistakable sound of shattering glass. "What now?" he muttered, dread creeping into his tone.

"Sam, we need to check on the house!" I urged, urgency flooding my veins.

As we sprinted back, the unease coiling tighter around us, a thought struck me. "Do you think he's going to do something reckless?"

"I wouldn't put it past him," Sam replied, his voice grim.

Rounding the corner, the sight that greeted us stopped us dead in our tracks. The front door of our house stood wide open, and inside, chaos reigned. Furniture was overturned, papers strewn about like autumn leaves in a windstorm. My heart sank as I realized: Rick wasn't done with us yet.

"Get back!" Sam shouted, and instinctively I stepped behind him, my breath caught in my throat. The world around me dimmed, shadows growing longer, and as we took our first cautious steps into the chaos, I sensed something darker looming, waiting just beyond the threshold.

A voice echoed from the darkness within, low and dangerous. "Welcome home."

Chapter 23: Shadows of the Past

The coffee shop buzzed with a familiar hum, a chorus of clinking mugs and low conversations that wrapped around me like a warm blanket. I settled into our usual nook, a plush red velvet armchair that had seen better days but still offered a comforting embrace. The aroma of freshly ground coffee beans danced through the air, mingling with the sweet scent of cinnamon rolls and scones. Emma arrived just as the barista placed my steaming cappuccino on the table, the froth swirling into whimsical patterns that reminded me of the chaos swirling in my mind.

"Okay, spill it," she said, her bright eyes gleaming with curiosity as she slid into the chair opposite mine. Her dark hair fell in soft waves, framing her face and accentuating the freckles that dusted her cheeks. Emma had a knack for making me feel seen, even when I was drowning in my own thoughts. "What's eating you?"

I took a sip, allowing the rich, velvety liquid to settle my nerves. The warmth coursed through me, but my heart raced with the weight of everything unsaid. "It's Sam," I confessed, my voice barely above a whisper. "I just... I don't know how to fix this."

Her expression shifted, morphing from casual interest to earnest concern. "Still stuck in that endless loop, huh?" She leaned forward, elbows resting on the table, her gaze steady. "What did he do this time?"

I ran my fingers over the chipped edge of my cup, feeling the small imperfections that seemed to mirror the fractures in my life. "It's not just him. It's our entire history, Emma. The things we've buried, the arguments we've had... they're all piling up like storm clouds. I feel like I'm standing in the eye of a hurricane, and I don't know how to get out."

Emma nodded, absorbing my words as if they were a puzzle she was determined to solve. "What if we had a family meeting? You,

Sam, and maybe even your parents? Lay it all out there. You can't move forward without facing the past, right?"

The thought sent a chill down my spine, a cold rush of anxiety that settled deep in my stomach. "A family meeting?" I echoed, my voice tinged with disbelief. "You mean, drag everyone into a room and air our dirty laundry? That sounds like a recipe for disaster."

"Or a breakthrough," she countered, her tone laced with unwavering conviction. "Sometimes you have to break things to build them back better. You're not alone in this. You need to confront it, not just for yourself but for Sam too."

I bit my lip, contemplating the idea. The notion of facing my brother, of unearthing everything we'd kept buried, felt like standing on the precipice of a cliff, staring down into the abyss. But as I looked into Emma's encouraging gaze, I realized she might be right. What choice did I have? The ghosts of our past needed to be confronted, or they would continue to haunt us.

By the time I returned to the farm, the sun was beginning its descent, casting long shadows that stretched across the fields like fingers reaching out for something lost. I parked my car by the barn, the familiar creak of the door echoing in the stillness as I stepped out. The air was crisp, carrying the earthy scent of damp soil and the sweet notes of autumn leaves beginning to fall. It was beautiful, yet it felt heavy, burdened with the weight of unsaid words.

As I walked toward the house, my heart pounded in my chest, an unsteady rhythm that matched the anxiety coursing through my veins. I found Sam sitting on the porch, a battered guitar resting against his leg, strumming absentmindedly. His head was bowed, and for a moment, I hesitated. He looked so lost in thought, so far removed from the brother I remembered—the one who could make me laugh even in the darkest of times. But that laughter felt like a distant echo now, buried under layers of resentment and misunderstandings.

"Hey," I said, my voice cutting through the silence, feeling like a lifeline tossed into a turbulent sea.

He looked up, surprise flickering across his features before settling into something more guarded. "Hey." The word was flat, a neutral tone that made the air between us feel like a taut wire ready to snap.

"Can we talk?" I took a deep breath, the words tasting foreign yet necessary.

He studied me for a long moment, his expression unreadable. Finally, he nodded, setting the guitar aside and gesturing for me to sit on the step beside him. "Sure. What's up?"

I swallowed hard, feeling the weight of my decision pressing down on my shoulders like a heavy cloak. "Emma and I were talking today, and... well, we think it's time we had a family meeting. Lay everything out on the table."

A flicker of surprise danced in his eyes, quickly replaced by a shadow of apprehension. "A family meeting? You really think that'll help?"

"It might," I replied, forcing the words past the lump in my throat. "I don't want to keep pretending everything's fine when it's not. I want to confront our past, all the hurt and misunderstandings... and maybe find a way to move forward."

He rubbed the back of his neck, his gaze drifting to the horizon where the sun was a fiery orange, setting the sky ablaze with its brilliance. "You think Mom and Dad are ready for that? They've got their own stuff to deal with."

"Maybe that's the point," I said softly, the truth hitting me with startling clarity. "We're all tangled up in this together, and we can't untangle it unless we confront it."

Sam exhaled slowly, the tension in his shoulders easing just a fraction. "You're right. But it's going to be messy, you know that?"

"Life is messy," I replied, a hint of a smile breaking through the heaviness. "But it's also beautiful. And if we're going to heal, we have to start somewhere."

He looked at me then, and for a fleeting moment, I saw a glimmer of the brother I missed—the one who shared secrets under the stars and made me believe in endless possibilities. "Alright," he said, determination creeping into his voice. "Let's do it. Let's face this together."

I felt a rush of relief wash over me, a small spark igniting the hope that had flickered dangerously close to extinguishing. Maybe, just maybe, we could find our way back to each other, even amid the shadows of the past.

The days crept by, each one dragging the weight of unspoken words, yet somehow the anticipation of that family meeting flickered with an undeniable energy. I spent hours imagining how it would unfold, scenes playing out in my mind like a movie I couldn't pause. Would Mom cry? Would Dad lose his temper? And what about Sam? Each possibility wove a tangled web of anxiety and hope.

As I prepared for the meeting, I turned to my ritual of baking, a soothing balm for my racing thoughts. The kitchen filled with the scent of vanilla and melting butter, a delicious distraction as I mixed flour and sugar with deft precision. I decided on a batch of chocolate chip cookies—the kind that had always drawn my family together, a sweet reminder of simpler times. I could almost hear Sam's laughter echoing in the background, teasing me about my overly enthusiastic use of chocolate chips.

The sun was beginning to set, casting a warm, golden glow through the kitchen window, when I heard the familiar rumble of tires on gravel. I glanced outside to see Sam's truck pulling up, the engine sputtering to a halt as he emerged, hands shoved deep in his pockets. He looked different, somehow, as if the weight of our impending confrontation had pressed down on him in a way I hadn't anticipated. The shadows of the evening danced around him, but I saw the resolve in his stance.

"Hey," he called out, forcing a casual tone that didn't quite mask the tension beneath.

"Hey yourself. You hungry?" I motioned toward the cooling rack, where the cookies were still warm and the chocolate chips glistened like tiny jewels.

He grinned, a flash of his old self surfacing. "Are those fresh? Because I might just consider sticking around if there's chocolate involved."

"Good thing I made a double batch. Grab a plate," I said, my heart swelling at the hint of normalcy. As we stood side by side in the kitchen, a comforting familiarity enveloped us, making it easier to ignore the storm clouds swirling above.

We filled our plates and settled at the kitchen table, the rhythmic crunch of cookies punctuating our silence. I savored the moment, allowing the sweetness to seep into the corners of my mind, wrapping me in a layer of nostalgia that felt almost safe.

"Do you remember when we used to make these after school?" Sam asked, his voice softening as he took a bite. "We'd pretend we were on a cooking show, and you were always the star chef while I was the hapless sous-chef who couldn't get anything right."

A chuckle escaped me, the warmth of his memory easing some of the tension in the air. "You were the best sous-chef! Except for that one time you tried to bake a cake without reading the recipe. I still can't believe we ended up with a gooey mess instead of a masterpiece."

"Hey, in my defense, I was trying to impress you!" he said with a mock huff, rolling his eyes playfully. "Clearly, I had a crush on my sister's cooking skills."

"Clearly," I teased, unable to resist the urge to poke fun. "But seriously, what were you thinking? Baking a cake is a science, not an art."

"Maybe that's why I've always stuck to guitar," he shot back, his smile fading slightly as he strummed an imaginary chord on the table. The laughter hung in the air, suspended like the moment itself, but the reminder of our shared past only intensified the burden of the truth looming over us.

As the sun dipped below the horizon, casting a dusky hue across the room, I felt the gravity of our upcoming meeting settle heavily on my chest. "Sam," I said, my voice faltering slightly. "About the family meeting... I know it's going to be tough. I just want us to be honest with each other."

His expression shifted, the laughter fading as he met my gaze with a seriousness that made my stomach churn. "Yeah, I know. But we've been avoiding it for too long. I just hope Mom and Dad are ready for what's coming. I don't want to make things worse."

I nodded, my heart racing at the thought of all the buried truths we would unearth. "Neither do I. But I think we owe it to ourselves to try. To not carry this weight any longer."

He leaned back in his chair, a thoughtful look crossing his face. "You really think talking is going to change anything? What if it just opens old wounds?"

"Maybe that's the point," I said, feeling the conviction in my words. "We can't heal what we refuse to acknowledge. It'll be messy, but it might also be liberating."

Sam studied me, a flicker of respect flashing in his eyes. "You've thought this through, haven't you?"

"I've had a lot of time to think," I admitted, the truth hanging heavily between us. "And I want us to be able to breathe again, without this heaviness pulling us down."

His gaze softened, the corners of his mouth turning up in a hint of a smile. "Alright, sis. I'm in. Let's face the music together, no matter how off-key it might be."

As we finished our cookies, an unexpected lightness settled over us, an unspoken bond strengthening in the face of uncertainty. I felt a flicker of hope igniting within me, a fragile flame flickering against the darkness that had loomed for too long.

The following day was our family meeting. I woke up early, my heart racing as the morning sun poured through my bedroom window, igniting the room in a warm glow. I spent extra time preparing—choosing my outfit carefully, a comforting sweater paired with my favorite jeans. I needed to feel grounded, a pillar of strength amid the turmoil that awaited us.

The kitchen buzzed with a nervous energy as I set the table with a mixture of resolve and trepidation. The aroma of brewing coffee filled the air, mingling with the sweet scent of cinnamon rolls I had prepared as a peace offering, a small token of hope to cushion the blow of our impending conversations.

Mom was the first to arrive, her brow furrowed with worry as she stepped through the door. "What's going on, sweetheart? You seem... tense."

I managed a smile, though it felt like a fragile mask. "Just wanted us all to come together for a family meeting, that's all."

Dad joined us moments later, his usual stoic demeanor replaced with a rare hint of concern. "Is everything alright?"

"Everything's fine," I said, my voice steadier than I felt. "But I think we need to talk. About us. About everything."

As we settled around the table, the weight of unsaid words hung in the air, thick and palpable. I glanced at Sam, who sat across from me, his jaw set in determination. The time for avoidance was over; we were ready to dive into the murky waters of our past, and there was no turning back now.

The table was set, its surface adorned with an array of comforting breakfast items, each one a silent offering for the difficult conversation that lay ahead. The cinnamon rolls, their icing glistening in the morning light, seemed to taunt me with their sweetness, a stark contrast to the heaviness in my chest. I could hear the clock ticking, each second echoing in my mind like a countdown to an uncertain fate.

Mom poured herself a cup of coffee, the rich aroma mixing with the scent of baked goods, but her hands trembled slightly as she lifted the mug. "This looks wonderful, sweetheart," she said, attempting a smile that didn't quite reach her eyes. "Did you make all this?"

I nodded, grateful for the distraction. "Just thought we could use some comfort food today." The attempt at levity fell flat, as I could sense the underlying tension tightening the air around us.

Dad settled into his chair, his expression serious but concerned. "So, what's the deal? You said you wanted to talk about something important?"

"Yes," I replied, taking a deep breath that felt like it could shatter the fragile atmosphere. "I think it's time we had an honest conversation. About our family. About us."

Sam shifted in his seat, his posture tense, the previous ease from our cookie baking now replaced by an unspoken dread. He caught my eye, and I offered him a reassuring nod. This was it—the moment where we would open Pandora's box.

Mom exchanged glances with Dad, her worry deepening. "Is this about the argument you had the other day, Sam? Because I—"

"No, it's bigger than that, Mom," Sam interjected, his voice firm. "It's about everything we've been avoiding. We can't keep pretending that everything's fine when it's not."

"Are you sure this is the right time?" Dad asked, his brow furrowing as if he were trying to piece together an intricate puzzle. "We've had a lot on our plates lately. Maybe we should—"

"Maybe we should stop pretending!" I burst out, the frustration spilling over like the foam of an overfilled coffee cup. "We can't keep shoving everything under the rug. I'm tired of feeling like we're all just strangers living in the same house."

The room fell silent, the tension thickening like fog settling over a quiet town. My heart raced as I felt the weight of every unresolved issue pressing down on us, and I feared I had pushed too hard. But the truth needed to be spoken, even if it came out jagged and raw.

"What do you mean, strangers?" Mom asked softly, her voice trembling slightly. "We're family, of course we're not strangers."

"But are we really?" Sam challenged, his gaze steady on our parents. "When was the last time we really talked? About how we feel? What we want? We've become this...this caricature of a family, filled with smiles and laughs, but it's all a mask. I'm done with masks."

"Sam, that's not fair," Dad shot back, his voice tinged with frustration. "You think we don't care? That we haven't tried?"

"Maybe you've tried to hold it all together, but it's falling apart," I added, my voice gaining strength. "I love you both, but it feels like we're just going through the motions. We need to talk about what happened last summer. About what we've lost. About how it affected all of us."

Silence enveloped the room, thick enough to suffocate. The tension seemed to pulse in the air, a living thing waiting to strike. Mom's eyes glistened, and I could see the realization wash over her, the memories surfacing like a tide.

"I think we all feel it," she finally whispered, her voice barely audible. "We've just been afraid to face it. I didn't want to drag anyone back into that pain."

"What pain?" Sam pressed, his brow furrowing in confusion. "What are we all tiptoeing around?"

"Last summer was... catastrophic," Dad admitted, his voice low and heavy. "We lost your grandfather, and it shattered us in ways we still don't understand. But we didn't talk about it. Instead, we buried ourselves in distractions—work, chores, anything but the truth."

"What truth?" I urged, feeling my heart thud in my chest. "We can't keep avoiding it."

"Fine," Sam said, his frustration palpable. "Let's just say it—Grandpa's death hit us hard, and none of us are okay."

A heavy pause lingered before Mom spoke again, her voice trembling with emotion. "It's more than just his passing. There were... things left unsaid. Regrets. And it's affected how we relate to each other, how we cope."

My heart raced, the pieces of a long-buried puzzle beginning to shift in my mind. "What do you mean? What regrets? You've never told us what he meant to you. To you both."

Dad sighed, a deep weariness settling in his shoulders. "He was my father. I never told him how proud I was, how much he taught me. I thought I had time to say all those things. But now—"

Mom's voice broke, and she pressed her hand to her mouth as if to stifle the pain. "We always thought there would be time. Time to mend things, time to say everything. But now... it feels like we're drowning in what-ifs."

Tension rippled through the room, a shared understanding settling in like a thick blanket. It was in that moment, as we sat in silence, that the enormity of the conversation began to crash down on us. The truth was a tidal wave, threatening to pull us under, and I wasn't sure any of us were prepared to face it.

"I wish I had said I loved him," Dad murmured, staring down at the table, his fingers tracing the grain as if trying to grasp something lost. "I wish I had told him how much he meant to me. I should have done better."

Sam's eyes glistened, the anger melting away to reveal raw vulnerability. "We're all struggling, and it's okay to admit it. It's okay to say that we're not okay."

My heart raced as we began to peel back the layers of grief and regret, the heaviness lifting just enough to allow hope to seep in. We were finally getting somewhere, finally digging into the heart of what had driven us apart.

Just as I was about to speak, the front door burst open with a loud bang, and my younger sister, Lily, rushed in, her face flushed and her breath coming in ragged gasps. "You guys! You need to see this! It's bad!"

Her words hung in the air, sharp and cutting through the moment we had built. The raw emotion faded for an instant, replaced by a jarring sense of urgency. We exchanged glances, confusion swirling in our eyes.

"What's going on?" I asked, rising from my seat, the warmth of our conversation eclipsed by dread.

"There's something out by the barn. You won't believe it!" Lily's eyes were wide with fear, and a chill crept down my spine as I felt the darkness close in once more.

With one last glance at my family, I bolted toward the door, the remnants of our fragile connection shattering against the looming unknown. The moment of truth we had just begun to unravel seemed to hang in the balance, overshadowed by whatever lay waiting for us outside. My heart raced as I followed Lily, dread mixing with anticipation, knowing that whatever awaited us would force us to confront not only our past but perhaps a darker truth we had yet to uncover.

Chapter 24: Ties That Bind

The table gleamed under the afternoon light, its polished surface reflecting the memories that lingered within the grooves of my father's old dishes. Each plate, chipped yet charming, bore witness to countless family meals, arguments that echoed across the table, and laughter that danced around the edges like fireflies in twilight. Today, it was more than a simple gathering; it felt like an act of defiance against the chasms that had formed between us over the years. The gentle clink of the silverware was a hesitant prelude to the confrontation that loomed on the horizon.

As I placed the final dish—a steaming casserole that had been my mother's go-to for family dinners—Sam walked in. He had always possessed a presence that could fill a room, though at that moment, he seemed to drag in an invisible weight. His shoulders were stiff, and his gaze flickered over the table before settling on me, a mix of wariness and resentment swirling in his dark eyes. I tried to smile, a simple gesture meant to ease the tension, but it felt as fragile as the porcelain beneath my fingertips.

"Is this supposed to be some kind of peace offering?" he asked, his voice flat, lacking any semblance of warmth. The air between us thickened, and I could almost hear the crackling of past grievances clawing at the edges of our tentative peace.

"It's just dinner," I replied, though my heart raced at the implied accusation. "I thought it might help us... talk."

"Talk," he echoed, a sardonic twist to his lips. "That's rich. When was the last time we actually talked?"

The words hung in the air like a lead balloon, heavy and suffocating. I gestured towards the table, my hands trembling slightly. "We can start now, if you want."

He hesitated, the wall he had built around himself seeming impenetrable. "You think this is going to solve anything? A few dishes and a casserole?"

"No, but it's a start," I insisted, my voice rising slightly, tinged with frustration. "I'm trying to reach out, Sam. I miss you."

A flicker of something—surprise, maybe, or irritation—crossed his face. For a brief moment, the mask slipped, and I saw a glimpse of the brother I once adored, the one who would make me laugh until my sides hurt, the one who would share his secrets late at night when the world outside faded into a comforting silence. But that spark was quickly doused, replaced by a steely resolve.

"Miss me?" he scoffed. "You didn't seem to miss me much when you moved away. You chose your life over this family."

I felt my heart sink at the accusation. "It wasn't like that! I needed to find my own way. You know that."

"Sure, but you could have at least kept in touch. It's like you vanished. You left me here to deal with everything alone."

The memory of our childhood flashed in my mind, vivid and chaotic—the two of us running through the backyard, dodging the demands of our parents, the bond we shared through laughter and unspoken promises. It was as if a part of me ached for that lost connection, the one I could sense slipping through my fingers like sand. "You weren't alone, Sam! You had Mom and Dad."

"Right, and that turned out great, didn't it?" he shot back, the bitterness in his tone like a dagger. "You don't know what it was like after you left. You have no idea what I went through."

My breath caught in my throat, a mixture of regret and defensiveness bubbling to the surface. "What do you want me to say? I can't change the past, but I'm here now. I want to help."

Silence engulfed the room, thick and suffocating. I could see the myriad emotions flashing in Sam's eyes—hurt, anger, disappointment, but buried beneath that tumult was a glimmer of longing. It was an unspoken plea for reconciliation, though he seemed unable to voice it.

"Help? You think you can just waltz in here and fix everything with a casserole and some half-hearted apologies?" he asked, a wry smile curving his lips but not reaching his eyes. "It doesn't work that way."

"No, it doesn't," I admitted, my voice dropping to a whisper. "But I want to try. I'm willing to fight for us."

"Fight for us?" he echoed, incredulity lining his tone. "Where were you when things started falling apart?"

I could feel the air growing heavier, each second stretching out painfully. "I was trying to find my place in the world. I thought... I thought you'd understand."

He shook his head, a bitter laugh escaping his lips. "Understand? You mean you thought I'd sit back and cheer you on while I was left here to deal with everything on my own? You've changed, you know that?"

"Maybe I have," I replied, my heart racing. "But that doesn't mean I don't want to reconnect. I want to be part of this family again. Can't you see that?"

The storm brewing in Sam's eyes shifted slightly. For a fleeting moment, I thought I might have pierced through the armor he had wrapped around himself. The air between us crackled with unresolved tension, a fierce need for honesty and vulnerability battling against the years of hurt and betrayal. Just when I believed we were teetering on the brink of a breakthrough, his expression hardened once more.

"You say that now," he said, his voice low and edged with frustration, "but how long until you decide this is too much work?"

"It's worth it," I insisted, fighting to keep my voice steady. "You're worth it."

He looked away, the weight of unspoken emotions heavy between us. The world outside continued its chaotic dance, unaware of the fragile thread weaving itself between two estranged siblings. I sensed the winds of change, a stirring hope whispering through the air, yet doubt clawed at my heart like a persistent shadow.

The casserole, once a symbol of my intent, now sat uneasily between us, cooling in its own tension. As Sam leaned against the doorframe, arms crossed defiantly, I felt the stirrings of an old wound—one that refused to heal. The initial hope that flickered in the warmth of the afternoon sun was now choked by the weight of our unspoken words. I took a deep breath, trying to steady myself against the gale force of his discontent.

"Do you really think this is going to change anything?" he asked, the bite in his voice sharp enough to cut through the tension.

"I'm not expecting miracles, Sam," I replied, the words coming out more firmly than I intended. "But can we at least try to communicate?"

"Communicate?" His laugh was hollow, devoid of humor. "You mean, like the way you communicated when you packed up your life and left? The way you dropped off the map without so much as a text?"

"Enough!" I burst out, feeling the anger bubble over. "I'm here now! I've been back for months! Can't we just... start fresh?"

"Start fresh?" he echoed incredulously. "You mean pretend like the last five years didn't happen? I can't just forget that I was left to fend for myself while you played house in some fairy tale!"

The accusation felt like a punch to the gut. "I didn't play house, Sam. I was trying to find myself. I thought you would understand that. We both needed space."

"Space?" He shook his head, his expression a blend of disbelief and scorn. "That's rich coming from you. Space is what you took, while I was here, holding everything together. Do you know what that's like?"

I swallowed hard, a bitter lump forming in my throat. "I can't change the past, and I can't rewrite the mistakes I made. But I want to be part of your life again. Isn't that worth something?"

As if weighing my words, he fell silent, the flicker of conflict warring with something softer beneath the surface. I dared to hope that maybe—just maybe—we could dig through the rubble of our shared history and find something salvageable. But with every beat of silence, I sensed the anger still simmering beneath the surface, just waiting for an excuse to erupt again.

"I don't know if I can do this," he finally said, his voice softer now but laced with uncertainty. "I don't know if I can let you back in after everything."

"I'm not asking you to forgive me overnight," I said, feeling a pang of desperation. "But can we at least talk about it? Talk about what really happened?"

He shifted, his body language tight as he processed my plea. "What's the point? We can talk until we're blue in the face, and it won't change anything."

"But it can!" I leaned forward, earnestness spilling out of me. "Talking can help us understand each other. It can help us heal."

He rolled his eyes, but the tension in his jaw eased slightly. "Fine. What do you want to talk about?"

I hesitated, choosing my words carefully as if walking through a field of landmines. "How about the last time we actually enjoyed each other's company? Remember that trip we took to the lake when we were kids? You, me, and that awful tent we fought over?"

A flicker of amusement danced in his eyes, but it quickly vanished. "You mean the one that collapsed on us halfway through the night?"

"Yes! And we ended up sleeping in the car, all because you insisted we take the tent instead of the camper." I smiled at the memory, warmth creeping in as I relived the joy of those innocent days. "We spent the entire night laughing at how ridiculous we were. We were a team, Sam."

"We were kids," he shot back, but his tone was less harsh, a hint of nostalgia creeping in. "Things were simpler back then."

"Exactly," I pressed, my heart racing at the small breakthrough. "We were so close. We can be like that again, can't we?"

He leaned back against the counter, the tension in his body softening just a bit. "You really think it can go back to that?"

"Not exactly back, but forward," I said, the determination in my voice growing stronger. "We can create new memories, ones that don't carry the weight of the past."

"Easy for you to say." He sighed, raking a hand through his hair. "You don't know what it was like for me. You don't know how lonely it was without you."

My heart ached at the vulnerability in his voice. "You're right, I don't. But I want to understand. I want to know what you went through."

He looked away, his gaze fixed on something beyond the window, as if searching for answers in the swirling leaves outside. The silence stretched, filled with the ghosts of our childhood and the hurt that lingered like an unwelcome guest. I dared to hope that maybe this was the moment we could push through the barriers that had grown between us.

"You want to know?" he finally said, his voice steady but quiet. "I spent nights staring at the ceiling, wondering what I did wrong. Why you chose to leave. Every birthday, every holiday, I'd look at the empty chair where you should have been. It felt like I was losing a part of myself."

The raw honesty of his words cut through the air, a moment of clarity piercing through the fog of our misunderstandings. "I never wanted to hurt you," I whispered, my own emotions spilling over. "I was trying to find myself, but I never stopped caring about you."

"I know," he said softly, the edge of bitterness fading slightly. "But it still hurt. And now, here you are, expecting everything to just... change."

"I'm not expecting anything," I said earnestly. "But I want to try. For us."

He paused, the weight of my words settling between us like a fragile truce. "Okay," he said finally, the word hanging in the air like a tentative promise. "Let's try. But I can't guarantee it'll be easy."

"Neither can I," I replied, a small smile tugging at my lips. "But then again, nothing worthwhile ever is, right?"

A flicker of a smile broke through his serious facade, and I felt a rush of warmth. Maybe we were on the brink of something new, a fragile thread pulling us back into each other's lives. The past might never fully fade, but I believed we could build a future, one awkward conversation at a time.

The awkward silence that followed our fragile truce was a strange mix of relief and uncertainty. The familiar tension hung in the air like an unwelcome guest, but I felt the possibility of something new blossoming between us. It wasn't a miracle or a grand revelation, but perhaps it was enough. I stood at the kitchen counter, wiping my hands on a dishtowel while stealing glances at Sam, who still leaned against the counter, arms crossed. The stubborn set of his jaw indicated that the conversation was far from over.

"Okay," I said, summoning every ounce of courage. "What do we do now?"

"Now?" he echoed, tilting his head slightly, a challenge gleaming in his eyes. "Now, we figure out how to get through this without killing each other."

A half-laugh escaped my lips, the tension easing just a bit. "Good plan. I'll try to keep my casserole-flinging to a minimum."

Sam chuckled, the sound surprising us both. It was a brief respite, a moment that felt almost sacred amidst the ruins of our relationship. "Right. Let's start there."

I gestured toward the table, the remnants of our previous argument still evident in the air, but somehow, it felt lighter. "Want to eat first? I promise it's not poisoned."

"Fine. But if I end up in the hospital, I'm blaming you," he quipped, moving to take a seat.

As we dished out the food, I couldn't shake the feeling that this was a new beginning, however tentative. The casserole, a dish laden with memories of family gatherings past, seemed to carry its own weight, as if it knew it was meant to bridge the gap between us. We ate in silence for a few moments, the clinking of forks against plates filling the void that words had yet to bridge.

"This isn't half bad," he said, raising an eyebrow as he took another bite. "You might be onto something here."

"I've had a lot of practice pretending to be a domestic goddess," I replied, a playful smirk dancing on my lips. "Just don't tell anyone; I've got a reputation to uphold."

He laughed again, the sound echoing in the kitchen like music. "Don't worry; your secret's safe with me. Just as long as you promise to teach me your ways. I can barely boil water."

"Deal," I said, feeling the warm glow of camaraderie beginning to thaw the icy resentment that had built up between us. "But you'll have to promise to try not to burn down my kitchen."

"Only if you promise to be less dramatic," he shot back, his tone teasing yet sincere.

We exchanged playful banter, the weight of our shared past receding, even if just for a moment. Each laugh felt like a step closer to healing, a gentle reminder of the brother I once knew. But as the meal wore on, I could see Sam's expressions shift from humor to thoughtfulness, as if the conversation was gradually steering back toward the deeper waters we had both been avoiding.

"Seriously, though," he said, his voice losing its playfulness, "how do we even begin to rebuild? It's not like we can just pretend everything's fine now."

A shadow fell over my heart, but I knew he was right. "I guess we start with honesty. We talk about what happened. We admit our mistakes."

"Admitting mistakes is easy when they're not your own," he replied, his tone turning serious. "What about the stuff I messed up? I didn't handle things well, either. I kept everything bottled up. I thought if I didn't show it, it wouldn't hurt so much."

"Didn't work out so well, did it?" I said softly, the weight of understanding settling between us. "You can't carry that alone. I should have been there."

"And I should have reached out," he admitted, his gaze dropping to his plate. "But I was angry. And I didn't know how to fix it."

"Neither did I," I confessed. "I thought leaving would help, but all it did was create distance."

He looked up, eyes searching mine as if trying to gauge whether I truly understood the labyrinth of feelings we were wading through. "What if we end up hurting each other again? What if trying to fix this makes it worse?"

"Then we'll deal with it together," I replied, my voice steady despite the anxiety churning in my stomach. "But we can't let fear dictate our choices. That's how we lose each other."

Sam's expression softened, and for a moment, I thought I caught a glimpse of hope in his eyes. "You really think we can make this work?"

"I do," I said firmly. "It's going to be messy and complicated, but we're family. We owe it to each other to try."

"Family." He echoed the word softly, almost reverently. "I haven't felt like we were a family in a long time."

"Neither have I," I admitted, feeling the sting of unacknowledged pain. "But it's not too late to change that."

As we sat there, a fragile connection forming between us, I couldn't shake the sense that we were on the precipice of something significant. I was finally opening up to my brother, peeling back layers of hurt and resentment, and it felt both exhilarating and terrifying.

Just then, a loud knock on the door shattered the fragile moment. Sam and I exchanged startled glances, our conversation hanging in the air like an unfinished sentence.

"Who could that be?" he asked, frowning as he rose from the table.

"I have no idea," I replied, my heart racing. "Maybe the casserole police are coming to get me."

"Or an angry mob," he joked, though the smile didn't quite reach his eyes.

As he approached the door, I felt a sense of foreboding creep in. My gut twisted with anticipation, an instinct that told me this was no ordinary visitor. Sam opened the door, revealing a figure silhouetted against the late afternoon sun.

"Sam!" The voice was sharp, filled with urgency. "We need to talk. Now."

My breath caught in my throat, my heart pounding against my ribs. The tension returned, wrapping around us like a noose. As I glanced at Sam's stunned expression, I realized that whatever this visitor had to say would change everything we had just begun to build.

Chapter 25: A Heart Divided

The stars twinkled like scattered diamonds against a velvet sky, their brilliance overshadowed only by the tempest brewing in my heart. I leaned against the worn wooden railing of the porch, my fingers tracing the intricate carvings worn smooth by years of weather and touch, each groove holding a memory of laughter and tears. The cool night air was infused with the earthy scent of freshly turned soil and the faintest hint of lavender from the garden, reminding me of the home I fought to preserve. But with every breath, I felt the weight of uncertainty settle over me like a heavy quilt, smothering the warmth of familiarity.

Luke emerged from the shadows, his silhouette outlined by the soft glow of the porch light, and for a moment, he looked like a guardian of my fragile heart. The corners of his mouth curved into that lopsided smile that could banish the clouds swirling in my mind. "Looks like the stars are putting on a show tonight," he said, sliding onto the railing beside me, his elbow brushing against mine.

I chuckled softly, the sound surprising me as it broke through the heavy silence that had enveloped me since our family meeting. "If only they could solve my problems," I replied, glancing sideways at him. His gaze held a depth I had come to rely on—a mixture of empathy and genuine concern.

"What's on your mind?" he asked, tilting his head slightly as if he were waiting for the clouds to clear.

I hesitated, the words tangling in my throat. The struggles with Sam felt like a weight I had carried alone for too long. "It's just... everything's a mess. I never thought I'd have to choose between two people I care about so deeply. Sam's my brother, and I want to help him, but he's pushing me away. And then there's you," I admitted, the admission sliding from my lips like a forbidden secret. "I don't want to lose you either."

Luke's expression shifted, the smile fading into something more serious, more earnest. "You don't have to choose between us, you know. Your heart can hold more than one love."

"Is that really true?" I asked, the incredulity spilling out in my voice. "It feels like I'm standing at a crossroads, and every direction feels like a step towards heartbreak."

He turned to face me fully, his eyes sparkling with determination. "It's okay to feel torn. Love isn't linear; it's messy and complicated, like this farm we're fighting to save. You're battling for what you believe in, and that's something to be proud of."

His words wrapped around me, grounding me like the roots of the ancient oak tree swaying gently in the breeze. I leaned into his warmth, my heart fluttering like the leaves rustling above us. "But what if I make the wrong choice? What if I choose the wrong path?"

"Then you learn from it. You're brave enough to face the consequences, whatever they may be. You're a fighter." The passion in his voice ignited a spark within me, reminding me of the fire I thought I had extinguished in the wake of family drama.

The silence enveloped us again, but this time it felt charged with something electric, a pulse of shared understanding and unspoken promises. I inhaled deeply, the night air filling my lungs, and felt the tension in my shoulders ease slightly. "You're right. I can't let fear dictate my choices. I just wish Sam could see it that way."

"He might surprise you," Luke said thoughtfully, his brow furrowing as he considered my brother's turbulent spirit. "Sometimes, it takes the right moment for people to realize what they need. Give him time."

A laugh bubbled up from my chest, surprising us both. "Time? I've run out of time. We're all on borrowed time with this farm." The words fell out with a bitterness I hadn't intended. I looked away, swallowing the hurt that had clawed its way up my throat.

Luke's hand found mine, warm and steady. "Then fight for it. Fight for him. Fight for the farm. And if you need help, I'm right here." His thumb brushed over my knuckles, a soothing gesture that made me want to believe.

"I just wish it didn't feel so heavy," I confessed, squeezing his hand as if it were a lifeline. "It's like the weight of the world is on my shoulders."

"And yet, here you are, standing tall." He held my gaze, unwavering. "You're stronger than you know. Every choice you make leads you to where you're meant to be. Embrace that uncertainty. Lean into it."

His words wrapped around me like a protective cocoon, and for a fleeting moment, I let the fears dissipate like fog under the sun. It felt freeing to share my burden, even if just for a little while. "You always know just what to say," I said, a smile tugging at my lips.

"That's the plan," he replied, his eyes sparkling with mischief. "But I can't take all the credit; your charm is contagious. Anyone would want to help you."

I rolled my eyes, laughter bubbling to the surface again. "I'd like to think it's my incredible cooking skills that seal the deal. Have you tried my lasagna?"

"Touché. But I'm still convinced it's the way you light up a room." He grinned, and I felt the heat rise in my cheeks. "And the way you talk about this place. It's like you see magic in it."

The magic, I thought, had begun to feel like a distant dream, overshadowed by reality's relentless grip. Yet, as we sat there, our hands entwined and the stars shining above us, I couldn't shake the feeling that maybe, just maybe, the spark could be rekindled. And perhaps the crossroads before me held more than just heartache; they offered a chance for growth, understanding, and a love worth fighting for.

The quiet that enveloped the porch felt different now, a delicate blend of tension and hope. I pulled my knees up to my chest, letting my chin rest on them as I stared into the depths of the night sky. The stars seemed to pulse with life, twinkling with a kind of energy that made my heart race. Luke leaned back on his hands, his silhouette outlined against the moonlight, a vision of calm amidst my swirling thoughts.

"What if we take a night off?" he suggested suddenly, his voice a playful whisper. "Let's leave the farm behind for just a bit. I know a place where the stars shine even brighter."

I raised an eyebrow, skepticism woven into my expression. "Are you trying to escape the chaos, or are you just trying to lure me away with the promise of heavenly bodies?"

He laughed, the sound rich and genuine, washing over me like a gentle wave. "Why not both? We can pretend for a few hours that we're not tangled in family drama, that the weight of the farm isn't pressing down on our shoulders. Just you and me, the stars, and a thermos of mediocre coffee."

The idea hung in the air like a sweet fragrance, teasing me with the allure of simplicity. I considered it for a moment, the thought of slipping away from the stress that had nestled itself deep in my bones. "Okay, you've convinced me. But only if you promise not to let me fall asleep while stargazing. I need to soak up every moment of this escape."

"Deal," he replied, rising to his feet with a playful flourish. "Prepare to be amazed by my impeccable driving skills and my mediocre playlist."

With a shared chuckle, we made our way to his truck, the gravel crunching beneath our feet a soundtrack to the impromptu adventure. As he opened the door for me, the light from the interior cast a warm glow on his face, illuminating the excitement in his eyes.

I climbed in, the scent of leather and the faint hint of his cologne wrapping around me like a cozy blanket.

"Prepare for the ride of your life," he declared, turning the key in the ignition, the engine roaring to life. "Just hold on tight."

"Is this how you win over all your dates? By taking them on reckless adventures?" I teased, my heart racing not just from the thrill of the moment but from the magnetic energy sparking between us.

"Only the special ones," he shot back, his grin widening as he shifted into gear. The truck jolted forward, and I couldn't help but laugh, the sound mingling with the rush of the wind whipping through the open windows.

The road twisted and turned, a ribbon of asphalt leading us away from the farm and into the embrace of the surrounding countryside. The familiar sights faded into the backdrop of our shared escape, replaced by stretches of open fields glistening under the moonlight. As we drove, I felt the tension that had clung to me like a second skin begin to dissipate, replaced by the exhilaration of the unknown.

"What's your ideal star-gazing setup?" Luke asked as he navigated the curves of the road, his focus unwavering.

I pondered for a moment. "A blanket, some snacks, and a killer playlist would do. Oh, and a telescope, of course, for some serious star scrutiny."

"A telescope, huh? You're making this sound way too sophisticated. I was thinking more along the lines of the backseat and a thermos of coffee."

"Ah, the classic approach. Perfectly romantic," I replied, stifling a laugh. "Do you have a secret stash of snacks in this thing, or do I need to pack my own?"

"Why do you think I asked you to come along? I'm all out of snacks, and I was hoping you'd be my personal snack guru," he teased, shooting me a sidelong glance.

"Just wait until you taste my homemade trail mix. It's practically gourmet," I quipped back, the playful banter igniting a warmth in my chest that I couldn't ignore.

After what felt like mere moments but was likely an hour, we reached a small clearing, far from the distractions of everyday life. Luke parked the truck, and we climbed out, the night air crisp against my skin. The stars loomed overhead, magnificent and unfiltered, like a blanket of diamonds scattered across the infinite black.

"Wow," I breathed, unable to contain the awe that bubbled up inside me. "This is breathtaking."

"Right? The world feels different out here," he said, laying out a thick, plaid blanket on the ground. "Just nature and us. No distractions."

We settled in, and I poured us each a cup of lukewarm coffee, the smell rich and comforting. "You might want to take your caffeine with a splash of milk next time," I suggested, passing him a cup. "Or perhaps with a bit more skill."

"Hey, I'm trying to add a touch of adventure here," he replied, taking a sip and grimacing playfully. "What do you think the secret ingredient is? Chaos?"

"Definitely chaos," I laughed. "But it's also the warmth of your company that makes this perfect."

As we reclined on the blanket, staring up at the stars, I felt a wave of peace wash over me. I pointed out constellations, my enthusiasm bubbling over as I shared bits of lore I'd collected over the years. Luke listened, occasionally chiming in with his own insights, and I was struck by how easy it felt to connect with him—like we were two pieces of a puzzle that fit together effortlessly.

"This one's my favorite," I said, pointing to a cluster of stars that twinkled brightly against the vastness of the sky. "It's called

Cassiopeia. She was a queen in Greek mythology, known for her beauty and her... questionable decisions."

"Ah, a queen with a flair for drama," Luke mused. "Sounds like you should keep an eye on her. You might end up with a bit of chaos in your life too."

"Perhaps," I replied, a glimmer of mischief in my eyes. "But at least I'd have a loyal companion in you."

He turned to me, the weight of the night settling in his gaze. "You know, no matter what happens with Sam or the farm, I'll always be here for you. You're not alone in this."

His sincerity wrapped around me, comforting yet unsettling, like a warm blanket that somehow felt too heavy. "Thank you, Luke. It means more than you know," I whispered, my heart racing as the truth of his words seeped into my bones.

The moment hung between us, charged with unspoken emotions. I couldn't shake the feeling that something was shifting, that we were teetering on the edge of a precipice, the uncertainty of what lay ahead both thrilling and terrifying. The stars above us shimmered, seemingly aware of the tension that lingered in the air, a witness to our delicate dance between friendship and something deeper.

The stars shimmered above us like secrets waiting to be uncovered, each one a story tethered to the earth by invisible threads of longing. The night air wrapped around us, fragrant with the scent of damp earth and blooming wildflowers, a reminder of life's persistent beauty even amidst the chaos swirling within me. Luke shifted beside me, propping himself up on one elbow, the moonlight casting soft shadows across his features.

"I'm pretty sure we just discovered a whole new constellation," he declared with mock seriousness, pointing at a cluster of stars that had begun to twinkle more brightly as if responding to his bold claim. "That one right there? Clearly a toaster. I name it... Toasterius!"

I burst into laughter, the sound breaking the stillness of the night. "Toasterius? Really? How about we go with something more original? Like... The Breakfast Hero!" I shot back, shaking my head as I fought to suppress my giggles.

"Fine, fine, but only if you promise to add a bagel to the constellation," he replied, feigning defeat while maintaining that charming grin. The warmth of our shared laughter settled over me like a favorite sweater, easing the tension that had wound itself around my heart.

"Alright, deal. But you know, all this star-gazing could lead to some serious philosophical discussions." I turned serious, gesturing toward the sky. "Like why the universe chose to give us both so many messes to sort through at once. Like a cosmic joke, perhaps?"

"Maybe it's to keep us on our toes," he said, his tone suddenly reflective, as if contemplating the weight of my words. "Or maybe it's because the universe knows we can handle it. You've got fire in you, and it shines brighter than any star up there."

His gaze held mine, the intensity of his sincerity wrapping around me like a warm embrace. In that moment, the distance that had lingered between us felt like it was collapsing, drawn into a singular focus. I opened my mouth to respond, the fluttering in my chest escalating, but before I could speak, the peace of the night was shattered by the blaring of a horn.

We both jumped, heads snapping toward the direction of the sound, and my heart raced as I realized it was coming from the direction of the road. "What was that?" I asked, panic edging into my voice.

"Sounds like trouble," Luke replied, his brow furrowing as he stood and peered into the darkness. "Let's check it out."

We hurried back to the truck, and as I climbed inside, I felt a chill creeping up my spine. The sudden shift from light-hearted banter to concern was jarring, but I followed Luke's lead, trusting in his instinct. He fired up the engine, and we sped toward the sound, the gravel crunching beneath the tires like whispers of impending chaos.

As we rounded the bend, the headlights illuminated a scene that stole the breath from my lungs. There, on the side of the road, was a car, the hood crumpled like an empty soda can, steam rising from the engine in thick white clouds. A figure was bent over, struggling to pull something from the wreckage.

"Pull over!" I shouted, my heart racing as Luke maneuvered the truck to the side. I jumped out before he could fully stop, adrenaline coursing through my veins. "Are you okay?" I called, rushing toward the figure.

The person turned, revealing a familiar face, smeared with dirt and panic. It was Sam.

"What the hell, Sam?" I exclaimed, rushing to his side. "What happened? Are you hurt?"

He looked disoriented, eyes wide as he took in my presence. "I... I don't know. I was just driving, and then the brakes... they just failed! I couldn't stop!" His voice cracked, the raw fear beneath his bravado seeping through.

"Did you call for help?" Luke asked, his voice steady as he approached, keeping a safe distance yet exuding calm.

"I didn't think about it! I just—" Sam's voice broke, and he raked a hand through his hair, clearly agitated. "I thought I'd get home and sort it out. I didn't want to bother anyone."

"Bothering? You could've gotten killed!" I shot back, my concern morphing into anger. "You need to call someone, and we need to get you checked out."

Before Sam could respond, a distant siren echoed through the night, drawing closer. "It's too late," he muttered, looking defeated, and I could feel my heart plummeting. The frustration I felt for him was eclipsed by the fear of what would happen next.

"Let's just wait for the police," Luke said, trying to diffuse the tension. He stepped forward, placing a hand on Sam's shoulder. "But first, we need to make sure you're okay. Can you stand?"

"I think so," Sam replied, though his voice was shaky. He pushed himself upright, wincing slightly as he straightened. I could see the shadow of pain flicker across his features, and it hit me like a punch to the gut.

"Let's sit you down," I urged, helping him toward the back of the truck, where the tailgate awaited. I was torn, my heart split between relief at seeing him safe and the wave of anger that swelled with each passing second.

"What were you thinking?" I asked, unable to hold back. "You can't just take risks like this. You could have hurt someone else!"

"I was trying to get away!" he snapped, the tension crackling like electricity between us. "From everything! You have no idea what I'm dealing with!"

"I'm right here, Sam!" I countered, frustration spilling over. "You don't have to do this alone! You're scaring me!"

Before he could reply, the police car pulled up, its lights flashing ominously against the darkness. The officer stepped out, scanning the scene with a keen eye, and my stomach dropped. Just when I thought things couldn't get more complicated, they did.

"Is everyone alright?" the officer called, moving toward us. "What happened here?"

The weight of the situation felt heavy in the air, pressing down on us like a storm cloud threatening to burst. I glanced between Sam and Luke, the tension palpable. My heart raced as I prepared to speak, my mind racing with thoughts of how to protect Sam, to shield him from the consequences of his recklessness.

But just as I opened my mouth, a second, more familiar vehicle pulled up behind the police car. My breath caught in my throat, recognition flooding through me. It was my father, his face tight with worry, the lines of his age etched deeper than I remembered.

He stepped out, looking between the three of us, and in that moment, I realized that whatever had been brewing in the quiet of the night was about to boil over into chaos. The impending confrontation loomed ahead like an insurmountable wall, and I was left standing on the brink, uncertain of what would happen next.

Chapter 26: The Harvest Festival

The sun hung low in the sky, casting a warm golden hue across the sprawling fields of Riverton, where the vibrant colors of autumn began to flirt with the horizon. The Harvest Festival wasn't just an event; it was a riotous celebration of community, a canvas painted with laughter, music, and the sweet, earthy scent of freshly turned soil. As I walked through the town square, the air buzzed with anticipation, every corner adorned with scarecrows sporting mismatched clothing and pumpkins boasting cheeky grins. The scent of caramel apples wafted through the crowd, mingling with the rich aroma of roasted corn, filling my lungs with the promise of indulgence.

Luke and I had been prepping for weeks. Our booth would be a tribute to our farm—the rich soil that cradled our produce, the hands that toiled to nurture it. We had stacked baskets high with glossy red apples, their skins gleaming like freshly polished rubies under the sunlight. There were jars of homemade preserves, glistening like jewels, and a selection of freshly baked breads, their crusts golden and inviting. I could practically hear them whispering, "Pick me, pick me!" as we arranged them, the sweet and savory aromas blending into an irresistible invitation.

"Do you think we should have made more pies?" Luke asked, glancing nervously at our setup. His sandy hair glowed in the sunlight, and I could see the faintest hint of worry etched on his brow.

"Relax," I said, nudging him playfully with my elbow. "People will devour anything with the words 'fresh' and 'homemade' in front of it. Besides, I've heard that pie-making is practically a competitive sport around here." I smirked, recalling last year's festival, where Mrs. Henderson had gone toe-to-toe with the town's new baker over a pecan pie.

As the festivities kicked off, laughter erupted like fireworks, filling the air with a jubilant cacophony. Children dashed between booths, their faces painted like woodland creatures, while local musicians strummed guitars and fiddled as if coaxing the very notes out of the crisp autumn air. It was a scene that felt like it had leaped out of a storybook, each detail more delightful than the last.

As we mingled with the crowd, greeting neighbors and friends, I felt a warmth swelling in my chest, a sense of belonging I hadn't truly experienced in a long while. "There's something about this place," I murmured to Luke, my voice barely above the cheerful din. "It just feels right."

"It does," he agreed, his eyes scanning the crowd. "I think it's because everyone pitches in. It's like one big family reunion without the awkward conversations."

With the sun dipping lower, casting long shadows across the stalls, I caught sight of Sam, a figure who seemed both familiar and distant, standing by the cider booth. His demeanor had softened, the corners of his mouth curving slightly as he interacted with a group of children, their laughter mingling with his own. For a moment, the heaviness that usually clung to him lifted, revealing a glimpse of the man I used to know.

"Do you think he'll come over?" I asked, my heart suddenly racing. The hope that flickered within me felt like a fragile candle, teetering on the edge of a gusty wind.

"Why wouldn't he? It's a festival, not a funeral," Luke chuckled, but there was a hint of concern in his voice. "You want him to, don't you?"

I nodded, suddenly conscious of the butterflies swirling in my stomach. My relationship with Sam had always been complicated—filled with unspoken words and lingering glances that often drifted into misunderstandings. But seeing him now, free from the burdens he typically wore like a cloak, sparked a flicker of nostalgia and longing.

Before I could second-guess myself, I took a step towards him, drawn like a moth to a flame. Just as I reached the edge of the crowd, Sam turned, and our eyes met. His expression flickered between surprise and something deeper, something that made my heart skip. "I didn't expect to see you here," he said, his voice a blend of warmth and cautious curiosity.

"I was hoping you'd stop by our booth. We've got fresh apples and—" I gestured vaguely behind me, feeling a little foolish for my sudden nervousness, "—other stuff."

"Apples, huh? I hear they're good for making pies," he replied, a teasing lilt in his tone, and I couldn't help but grin.

"Only the best! But if you're looking for someone to compete with Mrs. Henderson, you might want to look elsewhere," I shot back, my confidence rekindled by the banter.

Our conversation flowed like the cider being poured in the booth nearby, light and bubbly, yet rich with undertones. We laughed, reminiscing about the absurdities of previous festivals, the time when I accidentally tossed an entire pie into the pond thinking it was an empty basket. Sam's laughter rang like a melody, drawing me deeper into the moment, warming me against the chill of autumn that began to creep into the evening air.

"Have you tried any of the baked goods yet?" he asked, glancing over his shoulder toward the booth. "You know, just in case they need a judge."

"Funny you mention that," I replied, leaning closer, conspiratorial. "I've been told my pumpkin bread is award-worthy."

"Is that a challenge?" he quipped, a glimmer of mischief dancing in his eyes.

I took a breath, my heart dancing to its own rhythm. "Only if you're brave enough to accept it."

As the sun dipped below the horizon, painting the sky in hues of purple and gold, I realized that perhaps this festival was more than just a celebration of harvest—it was a chance for new beginnings, a tapestry woven from threads of laughter, friendship, and perhaps, something deeper that lingered just beneath the surface.

With the sun now sinking beneath the horizon, a tapestry of stars began to twinkle against the deepening blue sky, casting a soft glow over the festival grounds. The music from the local band swelled, a lively rhythm punctuated by the laughter of children darting between stalls, clutching sticky candy apples and oversized balloons. My heart felt light, buoyed by the sense of connection that wove itself through the fabric of Riverton, a place where even the air seemed to hum with unspoken camaraderie.

As the festival reached its peak, I was startled by the sudden rush of visitors at our booth. It was as if an invisible switch had been flipped, and suddenly, everyone decided they needed their fill of fresh apples and baked goods. I smiled as I handed out jars of apple butter and slices of pumpkin bread, reveling in the moment. "One taste, and you'll be hooked," I declared with a wink to a customer who looked skeptical. He hesitated before taking a bite, and his eyes widened in surprise.

"Okay, I might need a whole loaf," he admitted, laughter dancing in his voice as he reached for his wallet.

"See? I told you!" I replied triumphantly, feeling like a contestant on a cooking show where I was winning the crowd over with each bite. Luke worked alongside me, his easy laughter echoing mine, and it felt as if we were in our own little world amid the bustling crowd.

Just as I handed over the last of the pumpkin bread, my gaze wandered back to Sam. He was now surrounded by a small group of friends, animatedly recounting a story that made everyone burst into laughter. The way his eyes sparkled in the soft light made my breath hitch. I wanted to capture that moment, to bottle it like the preserves on our table, so I could savor it whenever I felt lost in the weight of the world.

"Hey, don't just stand there daydreaming," Luke said, nudging my shoulder as he noticed my gaze. "Go talk to him. I'll hold down the fort."

"Are you sure?" I asked, glancing back at our bustling booth. The last thing I wanted was to leave him to manage it alone, especially when I knew how much he despised being in the spotlight.

"Trust me. I can sell a thousand loaves of bread with my charm. Just go." He grinned, giving me an encouraging shove in Sam's direction.

With a hesitant breath, I made my way through the crowd, weaving past familiar faces. The chatter swelled around me like waves, but my focus remained on Sam. As I approached, his laughter floated through the air, wrapping around me in a comforting embrace. The moment I reached him, he turned, and our eyes locked. The world around us faded, leaving just the two of us in a bubble of warmth and possibility.

"Looks like you're having fun," I said, unable to suppress my smile.

He chuckled, the sound deep and genuine. "It's hard not to with this crowd. They could make a funeral feel like a carnival."

"Or a family reunion," I added, recalling our earlier banter. The air between us felt charged, like we were both aware of the unspoken words lingering just beneath the surface.

"I think you're the real star of the show, though," he said, nodding toward the bustling booth where Luke stood, juggling orders like a circus performer. "I had to remind myself to not be too distracted by all that homemade goodness."

"Homemade goodness? That's just my fancy way of saying 'overly ambitious baker,'" I quipped, my cheeks warming under his gaze.

"I wouldn't call it overambitious; I'd say you're just passionate." His expression was earnest, and my heart fluttered at the compliment. It was refreshing, this back-and-forth of lightheartedness, the way we could effortlessly slip into an easy rhythm.

Before I could respond, a little girl with pigtails and a face smeared with caramel approached, her eyes wide and pleading. "Can you help me get some apples?"

"Of course! I'm basically an apple expert," I said, kneeling down to her level. "What kind do you want?"

"Red ones!" she squealed, clapping her hands in delight. I couldn't help but laugh, the sheer joy radiating from her infectious.

As we made our way to the booth, I caught Sam watching me, a knowing smile playing on his lips. It felt as if we were on the cusp of something significant, an uncharted territory teeming with potential. I handed the girl an apple, and she beamed, running back to her parents, her laughter trailing behind her like a melody.

"See? You're a natural," Sam said, leaning against the booth, arms crossed. "You should add 'apple whisperer' to your résumé."

"Right next to 'overly ambitious baker,'" I replied, my playful tone masking the fluttering in my stomach.

As the night deepened, the band struck up a slower tune, inviting couples to the dance floor. The twinkling lights strung above cast a soft glow, transforming the festival into a magical realm. I felt a longing to join them, to be swept up in the rhythm of the evening, but my feet felt rooted in place, caught between the familiar comfort of our booth and the allure of what could be.

"Do you want to dance?" Sam's voice cut through my thoughts, an unexpected invitation wrapped in uncertainty.

"Dance? Me?" I stammered, caught off guard. My heart raced at the thought, a mix of exhilaration and trepidation.

"Unless you prefer critiquing my dance moves from a safe distance," he teased, a playful glint in his eyes.

"I can't let you hog all the fun," I replied, feigning bravado. "Lead the way."

We navigated through the throng of festival-goers, and I felt the warmth of his presence beside me, steady and reassuring. When we reached the dance floor, the world around us faded, leaving only the sound of the music, soft and enveloping. As we swayed, I could feel the pulse of the festival surrounding us, yet it felt like we were suspended in our own universe. His hands found my waist, and I placed mine on his shoulders, a simple touch that sparked an undeniable chemistry between us.

"Who knew you had such moves?" I quipped, forcing myself to relax into the rhythm.

"I'll have you know I was the reigning champion of the middle school dance-off," he replied, a mock-serious expression crossing his face.

"Reigning champion, huh? Impressive," I laughed, feeling lighter than I had in ages.

As we twirled and spun, I became acutely aware of the way our laughter intertwined with the music, creating a melody all our own. The festival was a canvas painted in memories, each laugh and glance a stroke of brilliance, and as I looked up at Sam, I saw more than just a friend; I saw someone who could become a part of my future if I dared to let him in. The night shimmered with the promise of new beginnings, and with each step, the weight of the past began to lift, carried away by the warmth of shared smiles and the joy of connection.

The music wrapped around us like a soft embrace, each note inviting and rich as we danced, swaying gently beneath the twinkling lights strung above. The laughter and chatter of the festival swirled around us, yet it felt as though we were in a bubble, cocooned in our own world of shared smiles and unspoken connections. Sam's hands were warm on my waist, steady and reassuring, grounding me in this moment that felt suspended in time.

"You know, for someone who claims to be a former dance champion, you're surprisingly good at this," I teased, trying to mask the fluttering in my stomach as I looked up into his hazel eyes.

"I had to practice somewhere. Middle school dances were the proving grounds. If you could survive those awkward encounters, you could handle anything," he replied, his expression shifting from playful to serious in an instant. "Besides, it's not just about the moves; it's about the company."

My heart quickened at his words. "Flattery will get you everywhere, you know."

As the song drew to a close, Sam leaned in, his breath warm against my ear. "Maybe I just want to make sure you keep coming back to the booth. It's hard to run a one-woman show."

With the last notes fading, we reluctantly stepped back, a lingering connection sparking between us that felt both thrilling and terrifying. But the moment didn't last long. A sudden shout from across the dance floor pierced the air, drawing our attention.

"Hey, Sam! There you are!" A tall woman with flowing dark hair came barreling through the crowd, her voice booming with enthusiasm. "I've been looking everywhere for you!"

Sam's expression shifted instantly, a flash of uncertainty flickering across his face. "Jess," he said, his tone slightly strained as he stepped away from me. "What are you doing here?"

"I came to surprise you! I thought we could hang out tonight. We haven't seen each other in ages!" she exclaimed, her eyes darting between us with curiosity.

I could practically feel the air in the vicinity shift, and suddenly the warmth that had wrapped around me like a soft blanket felt more like an unwelcome chill. Sam's smile faltered, the easy laughter we'd just shared now replaced by something more complex, a tension weaving its way into the atmosphere.

"Uh, this is Claire. She's... she's been helping out at the farm," Sam introduced, his voice a touch awkward, as if he were trying to keep things light despite the weight that suddenly loomed over us.

"Nice to meet you!" Jess beamed, extending her hand. "You must be a miracle worker. I've seen Sam dance, and trust me, that's not easy."

"Miracle worker?" I echoed, forcing a laugh while taking her hand. "I think that might be a stretch."

"So, you're really into apples then?" Jess continued, glancing at the booth behind us. "Sounds delicious. But I don't blame you for pulling him away from his responsibilities. We could use a good break from work, right, Sam?"

He hesitated, his eyes darting back to me. "Yeah, I guess. But—"

"But nothing," she interrupted, her tone light yet insistent. "Come on, let's go check out the pie-eating contest. I heard it's a mess, and I can't miss that!"

With that, she tugged at his arm, clearly not taking no for an answer. My heart sank as I watched them drift away, a dissonance forming in the rhythm we had just shared. I felt the laughter from the dance floor fade into the background as I stood there, caught between the remnants of a beautiful moment and the abruptness of an unwelcome distraction.

"What just happened?" I whispered to myself, the lingering warmth of the dance now feeling like a distant memory.

"Hey, you okay?" Luke's voice broke through my thoughts as he reappeared, slightly out of breath but grinning, holding a tray of caramel apples. "You looked like you were having a moment there. And not the good kind."

"I think I just got blindsided," I admitted, running a hand through my hair. "Sam's friend, Jess, just showed up out of nowhere and took him away. It was like watching a scene from a rom-com where the best friend swoops in and steals the spotlight."

Luke raised an eyebrow, his expression shifting to one of understanding. "I can see how that would throw you off. Do you think there's something more between them?"

I sighed, crossing my arms as I glanced at Sam, who was now chatting animatedly with Jess, their laughter echoing across the festival. "I don't know. They seem... comfortable. But it felt different with us, you know? There was something there, something real."

"Maybe it's just a friendship," Luke suggested, but the doubt in his voice mirrored the uncertainty twisting in my stomach. "Or maybe it's more complicated. Either way, you need to decide if you want to fight for your place in that equation."

"Fight? I didn't know we were in a competition," I replied, trying to sound lighthearted, though the reality felt heavier.

"Life is a competition, Claire," he said with mock seriousness. "Just look at Mrs. Henderson's pie. She's ready to take on anyone who dares to challenge her throne."

"True," I chuckled, but my heart wasn't in it. I turned back to the dance floor, trying to shake off the unease curling within me. "I guess I just thought things would be clearer after tonight."

"Clarity often comes with a side of confusion," Luke replied wisely. "But you've got to be true to what you want. So, what's it going to be?"

Before I could formulate a response, another shout from the pie-eating contest erupted through the square, momentarily distracting me. I couldn't help but chuckle at the spectacle of people smeared with whipped cream and pie filling, faces painted with a mix of determination and defeat.

"See? There's your distraction!" Luke said, nudging me. "Why don't we go join the chaos? Who knows? You might even find your place in the spotlight again."

I laughed, but the knot in my stomach tightened. "Alright, but I'm not getting pied in the face."

"Famous last words," he grinned, taking my hand and pulling me into the crowd.

As we approached the contest, the tension around Sam and Jess began to dissipate, replaced by the infectious laughter of festival-goers eager to watch the hilarious showdown. But just as I began to immerse myself in the laughter, I felt a hand on my shoulder.

"Claire!" Sam's voice broke through the noise, and I turned to find him standing there, Jess lingering nearby. The warmth in his eyes had returned, but this time, it was laced with urgency. "I need to talk to you."

My heart raced as I met his gaze, caught off guard by the intensity of his expression. Before I could respond, a deafening cheer erupted from the contest area, drawing our attention for a fleeting moment. But all I could focus on was Sam, his words hanging in the air like an unspoken promise.

"I think we need to clear the air," he said, and the seriousness in his voice sent a thrill of apprehension coursing through me.

"Sure, but maybe not here?" I suggested, glancing at Jess, who seemed oblivious, still cheering for a contestant. "This isn't exactly the most private place."

He hesitated, then nodded, his brow furrowed with thought. "Let's step aside for a moment."

As we moved away from the crowd, the world around us began to blur, the laughter fading into an indistinct hum. My heart raced, anticipation thrumming beneath my skin. Whatever conversation lay ahead felt like the turning point, the moment where everything could shift into something new.

"Claire," he started, and the way he said my name sent butterflies swirling in my stomach. But just as he began to speak, a loud crash echoed from behind us, followed by a collective gasp from the crowd. We turned in unison, confusion etched across our faces, and I felt a surge of anxiety as the festival lights flickered ominously.

"What was that?" I asked, my voice rising slightly above the din, but before Sam could respond, another shout rang out, cutting through the buzz of the crowd like a knife.

"Fire! Fire in the barn!"

In an instant, panic erupted around us. The warmth of the festival faded into a cold rush of adrenaline, and my heart pounded wildly as I grasped Sam's arm. "What's happening?"

His expression mirrored mine, a mix of concern and determination. "We need to find out. Come on!"

As we rushed back toward the chaos, a sense of dread curled in my stomach, intertwining with the thrill of uncertainty that had shadowed the evening. The laughter faded, replaced by the urgent cries of townspeople rushing toward the source of the commotion.

With every step, I felt the weight of the moment, the possibility of change looming over us like a storm cloud. And as the bright lights flickered overhead, illuminating our path through the darkening festival, I couldn't shake the feeling that whatever happened next could alter the course of everything I thought I understood.

Chapter 27: An Unforgettable Evening

The golden hues of twilight bathed the Harvest Festival in a warm glow, casting long shadows and painting the hay bales in rich shades of amber and mahogany. I stood with Luke at the edge of the dance floor, our fingers entwined, hearts drumming a rhythm that echoed the lively tunes played by the local band. The scent of caramel apples mingled with the earthy aroma of freshly tilled soil, a combination that wrapped around us like a familiar embrace. Each twirl and sway felt as if the world outside had melted away, leaving just the two of us, suspended in time beneath a canopy of stars that seemed to wink knowingly at our burgeoning romance.

"Do you think they ever get tired of playing 'Cotton Eye Joe'?" Luke quipped, his voice barely above the music but thick with that playful charm that made my heart flutter. His eyes sparkled with mischief, and I couldn't help but laugh, shaking my head as if to say, impossible.

"I think it's part of the contract," I replied, tilting my head back to catch a glimpse of the band. They seemed blissfully unaware of the monotony, lost in their own revelry as they strummed their instruments with wild abandon. Just as I felt myself relaxing into the moment, letting the strains of the fiddle wash over me, a jarring shout punctured the air, slicing through the atmosphere like a cold gust of wind.

I turned sharply, my stomach tightening instinctively at the sound. Sam was at it again, his voice rising above the cheerful cacophony of laughter and music. "You don't know what you're talking about! This is our land, and I'll be damned if I let you take it!" The confrontation unfolded in a swirling cloud of indignation and pride. My heart sank as I caught sight of the neighboring farmer, a hulking figure with arms crossed over his chest, face set like granite. Tension crackled in the air, and I could feel the eyes of festival-goers turning toward the fray, their cheerful smiles dimming in the face of discord.

"Sam, wait!" I called, urgency slipping into my voice as I pushed through the crowd, my heart racing. Each step felt heavy with the weight of familial obligation and the desire to protect the fragile peace we'd fought so hard to maintain. The festival had always been our sanctuary, a place where laughter could drown out the bitterness lurking just beneath the surface, but tonight it felt as if that delicate balance was about to shatter.

"Step away from him, Sam! This isn't the time!" I urged, finally breaking through the throng to reach my brother. He looked at me, eyes wild, a flash of surprise breaking through his stormy expression.

"Stay out of this, Mira. He's trying to cheat us out of the land!" Sam spat, his voice low and furious, almost a growl. My heart ached at the sight of him so agitated, his fists clenched tightly at his sides, the veins in his neck throbbing with emotion.

"Is that what you think?" The farmer retorted, his tone incredulous. "I came here to negotiate, not to steal. But if you want to turn this into a brawl, I can make it easy for you."

"Enough!" I shouted, stepping between them, feeling as if I was standing on a tightrope, trying to balance the weight of both sides. The crowd murmured, the lively music fading into a dull thrum in the background. The eyes of neighbors and friends bore down on us, judging, whispering, waiting for a resolution that felt impossible.

"Sam, let's just go back to the booth. We can talk about this—"

"No! I'm not backing down," he snapped, glaring at the farmer as if he could will him into submission. A flicker of pain crossed his face, a crack in the armor he wore so fiercely.

"What if he's right?" I ventured softly, desperate to reach him. "What if this is about more than just us? You know the land is important, but so are our relationships. Can we really afford to fight like this?"

For a moment, silence enveloped us, a fragile bubble that held my words like a prayer. Sam's expression shifted, confusion mixing with anger. I could see the battle within him, a tempest of loyalty and pride. "You don't understand, Mira. It's not just about the land. It's about standing up for what's ours, for what our family has built."

"And we're on the brink of tearing it all down," I replied, my voice breaking slightly as I stepped closer, reaching out to touch his arm. "This isn't who we are. We're supposed to be united, especially here, at the festival."

The corners of his mouth twitched, a flicker of uncertainty flashing in his eyes. Just then, the farmer took a step back, breaking the tautness that had coiled around us. "Look, I don't want any trouble. I just want what's fair," he said, his voice losing some of its bite.

"Then let's talk," I urged, hoping to cool the flames. "No more shouting. Just words."

Gradually, the energy in the air shifted. The crowd, sensing the tension dissipating, began to murmur amongst themselves, their curiosity morphing back into the festive spirit, laughter bubbling up once more like champagne uncorked. I held my breath, watching as Sam's shoulders relaxed just a fraction, the fire in his eyes dimming to embers.

"Fine," he muttered, though I could tell he was still grappling with his frustrations. "Let's talk."

As we stepped away from the throng, the music swelled around us again, wrapping us in its embrace, but I couldn't shake the lingering sensation that tonight had changed something fundamental in our family dynamic. The festival that had once felt like a blanket of warmth now seemed to drape heavy over my shoulders, each stitch woven with unspoken tension.

Luke caught my eye from the sidelines, a look of concern clouding his features, but he gave me a small nod of encouragement.

I turned back to Sam, my heart racing with the realization that while we may have staved off disaster for the moment, the roots of our conflicts ran deep, and we were only beginning to unearth them.

The moment Sam finally relented and agreed to talk felt like a fragile truce, one that could shatter at the slightest provocation. I led him toward the edge of the festival grounds, where the sounds of laughter and music began to fade, replaced by the distant hum of cicadas and the rustle of leaves overhead. The air was thick with the sweet scent of fried dough and the earthy tang of freshly turned soil, a reminder that we were anchored in this land that had been home for generations.

"Why do you always have to be so stubborn?" I asked, breaking the silence as we reached a small clearing lit by strings of fairy lights, casting a soft glow over our faces. Sam crossed his arms, the lines of tension still etched into his brow.

"I'm not being stubborn," he shot back, his voice tinged with frustration. "I'm standing up for what's ours. You're too busy playing peacemaker to understand what's at stake."

"I understand perfectly well what's at stake, but you can't just bulldoze over people to prove a point," I replied, my tone sharper than I intended. "This isn't just about the land; it's about the people we're fighting with. You're not just making enemies; you're pushing away allies."

Sam ran a hand through his hair, the movement fraught with the kind of exasperation that made it clear he was teetering on the edge of a precipice. "So what? Just let them walk all over us? Just because they've been here longer doesn't mean they have the right to dictate what we can do with our land."

"Sometimes it's not about rights, but relationships," I countered, softening my voice in an attempt to bridge the widening gap between us. "This festival is supposed to celebrate our community, not turn it into a battleground. We can't afford to burn bridges. Not now, not ever."

He stared at me, his expression a mix of defiance and uncertainty, and for a heartbeat, I thought I might reach him. Then he shook his head, the resolve returning to his posture. "You don't understand, Mira. You've always been the diplomat, the one who keeps the peace. But what happens when that peace comes at the cost of our family's legacy? What if we lose everything?"

Before I could respond, a sudden burst of laughter erupted from the nearby dance floor, drawing my attention momentarily. I watched as Luke twirled a little girl, her pigtails bouncing with each spin, her laughter ringing like chimes in the air. It was a simple joy, but in that moment, it felt like a poignant reminder of what we had to protect—our family, our community, our shared history.

"Look at him," I said, nodding toward the dance floor. "That's the kind of spirit we need to keep alive. If we get mired in this anger, we risk losing it all. It's not just about us; it's about the future."

Sam's shoulders sagged slightly, as if my words had found a small crack in his armor. "I just... I don't want to see our family lose what Mom and Dad built."

"Neither do I," I said gently, my heart aching for him. "But fighting like this will only tear us apart. We need to find a way to make our voices heard without losing our connections. I refuse to let the bitterness of one argument define who we are."

His expression shifted, and for the first time, I saw a flicker of understanding in his eyes. "Maybe I've been too intense about it all," he admitted, his voice quiet. "But when you're raised in a family that fights tooth and nail for everything, it's hard to turn that instinct off."

"Believe me, I get it. But sometimes the loudest voices in the room aren't the ones that bring about real change. Sometimes, it's the quiet negotiations that do," I said, an idea forming in my mind.

"What if we invite that farmer to join us for dinner after the festival? A chance to sit down and actually talk things through. No shouting, just conversation."

The idea hung in the air, and I watched as Sam considered it, his brow furrowed in thought. "Dinner, huh? That's... different. You think he'll agree?"

I shrugged, a smile creeping onto my lips. "I don't know. But I'm willing to bet that a home-cooked meal has more power than all the shouting in the world. Besides, it might just surprise you how much common ground can be found over a plate of mashed potatoes."

Sam chuckled, his tension easing just a little. "Only you would think of using food to broker peace."

"Food is universal. Plus, if I burn the roast, at least we'll have something to laugh about," I added, lightening the mood. "And if all else fails, we can always throw in a dessert to sweeten the deal."

He shook his head, a reluctant grin breaking through the seriousness that had hung over us moments before. "Okay, let's give it a shot. But if he shows up with an attitude, I'm not above pulling out my famous glare."

"Fair enough," I said, clapping him on the shoulder as I felt the weight of our earlier confrontation begin to lift. "But we're both going to have to keep our cool. After all, it's all about the future of the family, right?"

"Right," he agreed, his gaze softening as he glanced back toward the festival. "I just hope it doesn't end in disaster."

With that, we headed back to the heart of the celebration, the music wrapping around us once more like an old friend, while the laughter of children echoed through the night. But as I caught sight of Luke again, standing with an easy smile on his face, I felt a stirring in my heart that reminded me of the unpredictability of family life. Each moment we shared was woven with complexities, laughter, and the occasional rift that needed mending.

As I stepped onto the dance floor beside him, Luke took my hand and pulled me close. "You okay?" he asked, his brows knitting with concern as he scanned my face.

"Better now," I replied, and I could feel the weight of the evening begin to lift. "We had a breakthrough of sorts. Sam's willing to talk."

Luke's expression brightened, the warmth in his gaze igniting a spark of hope. "That's great news! I know how much that means to you."

"Let's just say it's a step in the right direction," I replied, my heart lighter as I surrendered to the rhythm of the music once more. The twinkling lights above us began to fade into the background as we lost ourselves in the dance, surrounded by the laughter and joy of those who cared most about us.

The festival swirled around us, a kaleidoscope of colors and sounds that reminded me how easily joy could rise from the ashes of conflict. Each spin, each twirl felt like a promise—a promise that we could come together, that we could heal, and that our family could still thrive amidst the uncertainty. And as I leaned into Luke, feeling his warmth seep into my skin, I knew that whatever lay ahead, we would face it together, armed with the strength of love and the bonds of family.

The music pulsated around me, a heartbeat that matched the ebb and flow of emotions swirling beneath the surface. As Sam and I returned to the dance floor, I could feel the lingering tension in the air, crackling like static before a storm. Luke had fallen into easy conversation with a few friends, but I could see the question in his eyes, a silent plea for reassurance. I smiled, hoping to mask the chaos still rumbling within me, but I knew he could see through the façade.

"Hey," he said, pulling me aside, his voice low but firm. "You look like you've just wrestled a bear. What's going on?"

I chuckled, though it came out more like a nervous laugh. "Just a little family drama. Nothing I can't handle."

"Are you sure?" His brow furrowed with concern, a crinkle appearing between his eyes. "You know I'm here for you, right? You don't have to pretend everything's fine."

I glanced back at Sam, who was now engaged in conversation with a couple of festival-goers, his demeanor relaxed, the tension easing as the evening wore on. "It's complicated," I said, my voice barely above a whisper. "But I think I can talk him into a dinner with the farmer. If we can sit down together, maybe we can start to heal some of this."

Luke's lips curved into a smile, and the warmth in his eyes made me forget about the shadows lurking at the edges of the night. "That's a solid plan. You always know how to cut through the chaos."

"Only because I've had plenty of practice." I couldn't help but tease, feeling lighter, even if just for a moment.

"Want to take a break from the dance floor? Grab a funnel cake?" he suggested, his grin wide and infectious.

"Only if you promise to share."

"Deal." He winked, and I felt a flutter of excitement as he led me away from the dance area, the music fading into a distant hum.

The aroma of fried dough and powdered sugar wafted toward us, mingling with the scents of warm cinnamon and crisp apples. The line at the funnel cake stand snaked through a cluster of festival-goers, but it didn't bother us. We shared jokes and laughter, the kind that poured out of us like old friends reuniting after years apart. Just as I was about to lean in to tell Luke about the time Sam tried to bake a pie and ended up with a kitchen disaster, a loud crash interrupted our moment.

I turned sharply, heart racing. A few stalls down, the bright lights flickered as a wooden display collapsed, sending pumpkins rolling across the ground like errant children fleeing a scolding. In the chaos, I spotted Sam, his expression twisted in shock and frustration, as he knelt to help the vendors gather their scattered goods.

"What the hell?" I muttered under my breath, hurrying toward the scene.

"Stay here," Luke said, but I didn't want to be left out of the action.

"I need to check on him," I insisted, darting away before he could protest.

As I reached the commotion, the neighboring farmer stood, hands on his hips, jaw set tight. The vendors scrambled, trying to recover their merchandise, but Sam remained kneeling, fuming.

"Just when we thought this festival couldn't get any worse," he grumbled, shooting a glare at the farmer.

"Did you trip over your ego this time?" the farmer snapped back, eyes glinting with irritation.

"Why don't you keep your mouth shut and help them instead of making it worse?" I interjected, stepping between them. The tension was palpable, each word like a lit fuse, waiting to ignite a firestorm.

"Here we go again," Sam muttered, glancing up at me, frustration simmering beneath his surface.

"Can we not do this now?" I pleaded, gesturing to the scattered pumpkins and the anxious vendors. "Let's just help them out. We can argue later."

The farmer seemed to relax a bit, and his posture softened as he crouched down to help gather the pumpkins. Sam followed suit reluctantly, but I could see the irritation still flickering in his eyes.

"This festival is supposed to be about community," I said, trying to keep my tone light even though I could feel the weight of the situation pressing down on me. "Let's show that we can work together instead of tearing each other apart."

The farmer nodded slowly, and after a moment, Sam sighed, the tension in his shoulders easing just a fraction. "Fine," he said, sounding defeated but willing to cooperate. "I'm in. Let's just get this cleaned up."

As we worked together, the warmth of the festival began to seep back into the atmosphere. Vendors laughed nervously, thankful for the helping hands. I found myself glancing at Luke, who stood off to the side, arms crossed, wearing an expression that was half amusement, half concern.

"What do you think?" I mouthed at him, hoping for a bit of encouragement.

He grinned and nodded, the corner of his mouth quirking up as he caught my eye. It felt like a small victory, like we were making progress despite the turmoil.

Once the pumpkins were back in place and the vendors were ready to continue selling, I took a deep breath, the tension dissipating as laughter returned to the air. "See? Not everything needs to end in a fight," I said, glancing between Sam and the farmer.

"Let's just hope it stays that way," Sam muttered, eyeing the farmer warily.

"Can we put the past behind us?" the farmer asked, looking at Sam directly. "No more fighting over who gets to farm which plot. Let's figure this out like adults."

"That sounds nice in theory, but we all know how these things go," Sam replied, crossing his arms defensively.

"Let's give it a shot, huh? You never know until you try." I smiled at the farmer, hoping to smooth the ruffled feathers. "Dinner at our place? I promise we won't serve pumpkin."

The farmer looked surprised but nodded slowly, a grin creeping onto his face. "Alright, I'll take you up on that. You cook, and I'll bring the drinks."

I turned to Sam, who was still a little guarded, but I could see the wheels turning in his mind. "What do you think?" I asked, urging him to meet my gaze.

"I suppose it's worth a try," he finally conceded, albeit reluctantly.

Before I could respond, the festival's main stage erupted with applause and the lively sounds of a local band announcing their next performance. Luke sauntered over, his expression bright, and I felt a rush of warmth as he took my hand, intertwining our fingers.

"Is it safe to say we're out of the woods?" he asked, teasingly lifting an eyebrow.

"Only if you promise not to let me go wandering off again," I shot back, feeling a sense of camaraderie blossom between us.

As the band began to play a catchy tune, we fell back into the rhythm of the festival, the earlier chaos fading into the background. But as we danced, a chill crept up my spine. The feeling lingered, as if a shadow had passed overhead, an unsettling thought prickling at the edges of my consciousness.

The music played on, vibrant and full of life, but I couldn't shake the sense that this was merely a temporary calm before a much larger storm. I caught sight of the neighboring farmer whispering something to Sam, a flicker of concern crossing Sam's face.

"What's going on?" I asked, a sense of unease settling in my stomach.

"I... I don't know," Sam stammered, his eyes darting to the farmer before he shrugged it off. "Probably nothing."

The moment felt like a puzzle piece that didn't quite fit, a twist in the tale I hadn't anticipated.

And just as I turned back to Luke, my breath caught in my throat. Across the dance floor, a figure emerged from the shadows, moving toward us with purpose, a familiar face that shouldn't have been here, not tonight, not ever.

"Surprise!" the figure called out, and the world around me tilted dangerously on its axis.

"Why are you here?" I whispered, heart racing, as reality blurred and shifted beneath the weight of their presence.

Chapter 28: A Moment of Truth

The barn felt like a sanctuary, with the scent of hay mingling with the earthy aroma of wood and the faint trace of the summer rain outside. The sun was slipping away, casting a golden glow that filtered through the slats of the weathered barn door, illuminating the dust motes dancing in the air. I leaned against a stack of straw bales, my heart racing, each beat echoing the chaos of the festival that had just unraveled in the fields beyond. The laughter and joy of the day felt worlds away, replaced by the heavy silence that wrapped around me like a too-small blanket.

My thoughts darted through my mind like startled sparrows. What if Sam didn't come back? What if the farm, our family legacy, was lost to us forever? Each question spiraled deeper into despair, gnawing at my heart with a relentless hunger. Just as I was about to drown in my fears, the door creaked open, and Luke stepped inside, his silhouette framed against the fading light.

"Hey," he said softly, taking a step forward, concern knitting his brows. The warmth in his voice pierced through the fog of my anxiety, grounding me. I wiped away a few rogue tears that had slipped down my cheeks, unsure how much I wanted to reveal. But in that moment, the dam inside me broke. I rushed forward, my voice thick with emotion, the words tumbling out in a frantic rush.

"Luke, I'm scared. What if Sam doesn't come back? What if I lose everything?" Each word was heavy, weighted with the rawness of my fears. I could see his expression shift from concern to a deep understanding, as if he could see right through the mask I wore, straight into the core of my worries.

"Hey, hey," he said gently, stepping closer, closing the distance between us. His hand found mine, warm and steady, and it felt like a lifeline in the storm that was my mind. "We'll figure this out. You're not alone in this."

His grip tightened slightly, and I felt the warmth of his skin seep into my trembling fingers. In that instant, the weight of my worries began to lift just a little. "I don't know how to keep this place afloat," I admitted, my voice barely above a whisper. "My family is depending on me, and it feels like the ground is crumbling beneath us."

Luke took a deep breath, his eyes locking onto mine with an intensity that made my stomach flip. "You're stronger than you think. I've seen you handle worse. Remember last summer when the cows got loose? You rallied the whole town to help you round them up."

"Barely," I scoffed, a small smile breaking through my despair. "And you nearly fell into that mud pit."

He chuckled, the sound rich and infectious, easing some of the tension in my chest. "Okay, maybe that wasn't my finest hour. But the point is, you've got people who care about you. We all want to see this farm thrive."

I felt the warmth in his words wrap around me like a soft blanket, but the nagging fears clawed back into my mind. "And what if that's not enough? What if I can't save it?" The vulnerability in my voice hung between us, heavy and real.

"I wish I had all the answers," Luke confessed, his own vulnerability laid bare. "But I can tell you that I'm in this too. I can't stand by and watch you struggle alone. You're important to me, Alex. This farm, it's important to you, but so are you." His words washed over me, soothing the raw edges of my anxiety, even as they ignited a flicker of something deeper within me.

The tension in the air shifted, and I could feel the weight of unspoken words lingering between us. "You've been such a constant for me," I said softly, my heart pounding in my chest. "But what about you? How do you feel about all this?"

Luke paused, a flicker of uncertainty crossing his face. "Honestly? I've been trying to figure that out too. I'm caught between wanting to support you and my own... feelings. I care about you, Alex. A lot." The sincerity in his voice sent a shiver down my spine, a rush of warmth flooding my cheeks.

"You do?" The surprise in my tone was unmistakable. It was a truth I hadn't dared to hope for, yet here we were, standing in the barn's embrace, teetering on the edge of something new and frightening.

He nodded, taking a step closer, our bodies now inches apart. "It's complicated. I don't want to add more weight to your shoulders, especially now, but I need you to know."

"What if we decided to share the weight instead?" The words slipped from my lips before I could reconsider, bold yet hopeful. "What if we faced this together?"

The vulnerability in the air thickened, and for a heartbeat, it felt as if the universe itself held its breath, waiting for his response. His expression softened, and I could see the gears turning in his mind. "You really mean that?"

"I do," I replied, feeling an exhilarating mixture of fear and excitement surge through me. "We could be a team. I'm not asking for a miracle. Just someone to stand beside me, to figure this out together."

A slow smile spread across his face, transforming the tension into something electric and palpable. "Then we'll figure it out. Together." In that moment, a weight lifted, replaced by a sense of clarity and purpose that surged through me like sunlight breaking through the clouds.

The barn, once a shelter for my worries, felt like a canvas for new beginnings.

The warmth of Luke's promise hung between us like the sweet scent of blooming wildflowers, filling the barn with a sense of possibility. I glanced out through the cracks in the wooden walls, watching as the sun sank lower in the sky, painting everything in hues of orange and pink. It was the kind of evening that could easily distract you from the world's troubles, yet my heart still raced, the tension bubbling just beneath the surface.

"So, what's the plan?" I asked, trying to shift my focus from the looming uncertainty of the future. "We're going to save the farm with a motivational speech and a few Pinterest ideas?" I attempted a playful smile, though the flutter of anxiety in my stomach suggested I wasn't quite pulling it off.

Luke chuckled, the sound deep and infectious. "Well, I was thinking more along the lines of an elaborate scheme involving some friendly competition with the neighboring farms. Maybe we can host a harvest festival, charge admission, and have a pie-eating contest?" His eyes sparkled with mischief, and for the first time that day, I felt a genuine smile break across my face.

"Pie-eating? Count me in!" I responded, laughing lightly. "That sounds like a surefire way to ruin our chances at saving the farm. But if we can make the best apple pie in town, maybe we can attract a crowd."

"Exactly!" Luke exclaimed, his enthusiasm infectious. "We'll be the talk of the county! 'Alex and Luke, the pie power duo!'" He struck a ridiculous pose, puffing out his chest as if we were already standing in front of a crowd, and I couldn't help but burst into laughter.

"Now that's a title I could get behind," I said, shaking my head at his theatrics. "But you do realize we'll need actual pies, right? You can't just charm the apples into the crust."

His mock-serious expression faltered for a moment before he broke into another grin. "Fair point. So, how about we start with a baking lesson? I'll make the crust. You can be the official apple chopper."

"Chopping apples? That sounds dangerously close to actual work." I raised an eyebrow, pretending to consider the proposal.

"What if I get distracted by the shiny peeler and end up missing half the apples?"

"Then we'll just have to make a second trip to the orchard. I've been meaning to spend more time there anyway," he replied, his gaze turning a bit wistful. "It's beautiful this time of year, especially as the leaves start to change. We can pick a few and just... talk."

The warmth of his suggestion wrapped around me, igniting a flicker of hope that perhaps we could really do this. Maybe we could wrestle our way through the trials ahead together, armed with humor and a few stolen moments among the apples.

"Okay, Luke," I agreed, my heart swelling with a newfound sense of purpose. "Let's start planning this harvest festival. We'll turn this place around if it kills us." I punctuated my determination with a mock glare, but there was a spark of seriousness in my words, a promise to fight for what mattered most.

As the evening deepened, we shared ideas, each one leading to another, creating a vibrant tapestry of possibilities. The atmosphere lightened, our laughter filling the barn like music, mingling with the rustling of hay and the gentle sounds of the farm settling down for the night. We were in this together, a duo forged in the fire of uncertainty but tempered with hope and connection.

But just as we began to feel the swell of excitement over our plans, the peaceful ambiance shattered when the barn door swung open with a loud creak. The figure silhouetted against the dusky sky sent a jolt of anxiety through me. It was Sam, his face shadowed by the brim of his cap, but the tension in his posture was unmistakable.

"What are you two up to?" Sam asked, his voice laced with suspicion. There was a guarded edge to his words that instantly doused the warmth in the barn.

"Just brainstorming some ideas for the harvest festival," I replied, my voice steady, though my heart raced. "We want to attract some visitors and generate interest in the farm."

Sam stepped further inside, and I could see the confusion on his face turning to irritation. "Is that what you call it?" he shot back, crossing his arms defensively. "Because it sounds more like a distraction than a solution."

Luke stiffened beside me, the air thickening with an unspoken tension. "We're trying to make this work, Sam. We can't just sit back and wait for things to get better. We have to act." His tone was calm but firm, an anchor against the rising storm.

"Act? You mean pretend everything's fine?" Sam's voice was sharp, laced with frustration. "You're both acting like this is some kind of game. This is our livelihood we're talking about, not a school project."

"Believe me, I know how serious it is," I interjected, struggling to keep my composure. "But if we don't find a way to bring in income, we might lose everything. And I won't just stand by and let that happen."

"You don't understand," Sam replied, his voice dropping, revealing a hint of vulnerability. "This is all I have left. I can't afford for us to fail." The words hung in the air, heavy with desperation.

The room fell silent, tension coiling like a spring ready to snap. I glanced at Luke, who was watching Sam with a mixture of sympathy and frustration. I could feel the weight of the unspoken truths pressing down on us all, and suddenly the laughter from earlier felt like a distant memory.

"Sam, we're all in this together," I said softly, hoping to bridge the gap between us. "We're family. Let's figure this out, not fight about it."

For a moment, the barn felt smaller, the walls closing in with the gravity of the situation. Sam's expression softened, the hardness of his eyes giving way to a glimmer of something else—perhaps hope, perhaps fear.

"Fine," he sighed, the weight of defeat heavy on his shoulders. "But I want in on this festival planning. We can't just wing it. We need a solid plan."

Relief washed over me, tinged with the lingering tension that still crackled in the air. "Absolutely. Together, we'll make it happen," I said, my heart swelling with determination.

As we began to discuss ideas, Luke's presence beside me felt like a steadying force, a reminder that even in the face of uncertainty, we were not alone. The road ahead was far from clear, but for the first time in a long while, it felt like we were heading toward something worthwhile. And that was enough to light the way forward.

The barn was alive with a newfound energy, the air crackling with potential as we dived into the logistics of our makeshift harvest festival. The idea of gathering the community, of turning the tide, felt like a lifebuoy tossed to a drowning ship. Sam, his brow furrowed with determination, began jotting down notes on the back of a hay-strewn flyer, a makeshift clipboard in a sea of straw.

"Okay, so we need food, activities, and a way to get people to show up," he said, his tone shifting from defensive to pragmatic. "I think we should focus on things people love—corn mazes, pumpkin carving, maybe even some local music."

"I can handle the pies," Luke piped up, excitement shining in his eyes. "And maybe we can have a bake-off? Get some locals involved, get their competitive spirits riled up."

"Great idea, but I'll need to supervise those pies," I shot back with mock seriousness. "The last thing we need is you burning down the barn."

Luke feigned shock. "Burning down the barn? Me? I'll have you know I have a perfectly clean record when it comes to baked goods!"

I raised an eyebrow, smirking. "Unless you count the time you tried to make bread and ended up with a rock-solid loaf that could double as a doorstop."

"Okay, that was one time!" he protested, laughter dancing in his eyes. "But I've learned since then. Consider my skills upgraded."

The playful banter filled the barn, creating a comforting rhythm as we worked through the details. Even Sam, who had initially come in with a storm cloud over his head, started to crack smiles between his serious comments. For a fleeting moment, the heaviness of the world outside felt manageable.

As we brainstormed ideas, I couldn't help but notice how natural it felt to work alongside them. Luke's easy confidence complemented Sam's practicality, and I found my own enthusiasm blossoming amid their energy. I was reminded of simpler times when we'd all spend summer evenings together, sharing dreams and laughter without the weight of expectations hanging over us.

But as the sun dipped lower, the shadows in the barn began to stretch ominously. Just then, Sam's phone buzzed on the makeshift table. He grabbed it, glancing at the screen, his expression suddenly shifting from engagement to concern.

"Uh, I need to take this," he said, stepping outside, leaving Luke and me in the barn's comforting embrace. I exchanged a glance with Luke, curiosity flickering in the air.

"Wonder what that's about," I murmured, trying to shake off the sudden unease that prickled at the back of my mind.

Luke shrugged, leaning against a nearby hay bale, his fingers brushing the edges of the rough straw. "Probably just the usual farm stuff. It's never quiet around here for long." He flashed a reassuring smile, but I could sense the tension beneath it.

As the minutes ticked by, I found myself wandering toward the barn door, peering outside at the fading light. Sam stood with his back to us, speaking in hushed tones, his shoulders rigid. I couldn't catch his words, but the way he rubbed his forehead suggested the conversation wasn't about anything mundane.

"Everything okay?" I called out, attempting to keep my voice light, but the anxiety bubbling in my stomach made it come out more strained than I intended.

Sam turned, his expression grim, and I felt a ripple of apprehension travel through the barn. "It's... well, it's not great," he replied, his voice tight.

"What do you mean?" Luke straightened, the playful energy dissipating.

Sam stepped back inside, glancing around as if the walls themselves could listen. "It's Dad. He... he's been talking about selling the farm."

The words hung in the air like a thunderclap, jolting us both into silence. The playful camaraderie we'd built just moments ago crumbled into shards of uncertainty, sharp and piercing.

"No," I said, shaking my head, my heart racing. "That can't be right. He wouldn't just give up on this place."

"Apparently, he's been thinking about it for a while," Sam continued, his voice low, tinged with an edge of anger and hurt. "He says it's not worth the struggle anymore, that we should let someone else take it over."

"What? This farm has been in our family for generations!" Luke interjected, his voice rising with disbelief. "He can't just throw it away!"

"I know! But it's like he's resigned himself to the idea," Sam replied, frustration spilling over. "He thinks we can't handle the pressure, that we're all just wasting time."

The betrayal lanced through me, sharp and unforgiving. "He can't really think that," I said, my voice barely above a whisper. "We're trying to save it! We can turn things around!"

"We need to show him that we can," Sam replied, determination sparking in his eyes. "We need to make this festival happen. It's our best shot at proving we can keep the farm alive."

"Then that's what we'll do," I declared, the urgency igniting a fire within me. "We'll throw the best harvest festival this town has ever seen. We'll make him see what this place means to us."

Luke nodded, a steely resolve taking over his features. "Absolutely. We can't let him give up without a fight."

The three of us stood in a tight circle, a bond forged in shared purpose, yet the specter of doubt loomed large. What if our efforts weren't enough? What if we failed?

But there was no room for hesitation. We dove back into the planning, discussing how we would spread the word, decorate the barn, and prepare for the festivities. The night wore on, our voices growing animated as ideas flowed freely, but beneath the excitement lurked an ever-present anxiety—a ticking clock counting down the days until the festival, until we had to confront our fears head-on.

Finally, just as we were wrapping up for the night, Sam's phone buzzed again, pulling his attention away. This time, his face paled, a sheen of sweat breaking out on his forehead.

"Sam?" I asked, concern creeping back into my voice.

He held up a hand, motioning for silence. "It's... it's about the farm."

A chill raced through the room as we leaned in closer, the air thick with tension. "What did they say?"

His voice trembled, laced with dread. "They're sending someone out to inspect it... tomorrow."

The gravity of the situation crashed down like a heavy storm, the reality settling in with a terrifying finality. If the inspection went poorly, everything we'd worked for could slip through our fingers like grains of sand.

I could feel my heart hammering in my chest, a fierce determination rising within me. "Then we need to pull everything together tonight. No more delays."

But even as the words left my mouth, a nagging doubt flickered in my mind. Would our efforts be enough? Or were we racing against an inevitable tide, fighting to save something that was already slipping away?

With the clock ticking and stakes rising, the tension hung thick in the air, a prelude to an uncertain tomorrow. I locked eyes with Luke and Sam, an unspoken agreement hanging between us. We would fight. We had to. But as the shadows deepened around us, I couldn't shake the feeling that a storm was brewing, and the real battle was just beginning.

Chapter 29: The Road Ahead

The warmth of the farmhouse enveloped us like a well-worn quilt as I stood at the head of the old wooden table, the scent of freshly baked apple pie mingling with the crisp autumn air that wafted through the open windows. A gentle breeze tugged at the edges of the tablecloth, reminding me of the fleeting days of summer, while the promise of a vibrant fall stretched ahead, full of potential. Sam leaned against the wall, his arms crossed, a skeptical look shadowing his face. But then again, skepticism was part of his charm, the spark that often ignited our debates into friendly banter.

"Let's just hope you don't set fire to the place this time," he quipped, breaking the tension that seemed to cling to the air. His eyes danced with mischief, the kind that made me want to roll my own eyes and laugh all at once. I could always count on Sam to find the humor, even in the weighty moments.

"Please, that was one time," I replied, playfully exasperated. "And besides, the only thing I plan to ignite tonight is enthusiasm for our future."

The neighbors gathered around the table, their faces reflecting a mixture of curiosity and concern. Martha, a formidable woman with silver-streaked hair and a no-nonsense attitude, took her usual seat, her gnarled hands clutching a mug of herbal tea. Her eyes sparkled with an energy that belied her age, a living testament to the resilience of our community. Beside her sat Frank, his lanky frame draped in a plaid shirt, his enthusiasm for farming outmatched only by his tendency to recount every crop failure of the past decade in painstaking detail.

"Let's get on with it, shall we?" Martha said, breaking the silence that had settled like dust. "I didn't come here to reminisce about burnt pies and crop failures."

Her straightforwardness served as a grounding force, reminding me that our purpose tonight wasn't merely to reminisce but to forge a path forward. I cleared my throat, feeling the weight of my father's legacy on my shoulders. "I've called you all here tonight because I believe we have a real opportunity to come together," I began, my voice steady despite the quiver of nerves that danced at the edges of my confidence. "The farm is facing challenges—financial strain, the unpredictable weather. But we're not just fighting for the land; we're fighting for each other."

A murmur of agreement rippled through the room, a mixture of apprehension and hope. Luke shifted beside me, his presence a steadying anchor. I could feel the warmth radiating from him, like sunlight filtering through the autumn leaves. "We need a plan," he added, his voice low yet resolute. "Not just for the farm but for all of us."

"Plans are nice and all," Frank interjected, scratching his chin in thought, "but they're only as good as the people behind them." His eyes darted from me to the others, as if searching for validation. "We need to know that we can trust each other."

"Trust is built, Frank," Sam replied, the smirk never leaving his lips. "And what better way to build trust than to plant seeds together?"

"Seeds, huh?" Martha chuckled. "Better not make any more pie references unless you want the whole town buzzing about your kitchen disasters again."

The laughter that erupted felt like a balm over the tension that had threatened to seep into the corners of the room. I took a breath, seizing the moment to channel our lighthearted banter into a serious dialogue. "What if we organized community work days? We can help each other with the harvest, share resources, and skills. If we all pull together, we can weather whatever storms come our way—figuratively and literally."

"Like a neighborhood watch for crops?" Sam mused, a gleam in his eye. "Only instead of patrolling, we'll be planting and picking."

"Exactly!" I replied, buoyed by the unexpected momentum. "It's not just about the harvest; it's about building a support system. If we lean on one another, we can make sure that no one falls behind."

The discussion flowed like a river, ebbing and surging with excitement and skepticism alike. Some voiced concerns over logistics and availability, while others offered ideas about pooling resources and shared equipment. I could feel the energy shift, the room filling with a sense of camaraderie that had been absent for far too long. It was like the first flickers of dawn breaking over a long, dark night.

As the conversation swirled, I caught Luke's eye and couldn't help but smile. He returned it, a subtle nod of encouragement that made my heart flutter. Perhaps I wasn't as alone as I had felt when I first inherited the farm. We were not just fighting for our own futures; we were investing in something greater—a tapestry woven from the threads of our collective stories.

Then came the unexpected. Just as I felt the air around us lighten, a loud bang echoed from the direction of the barn. The cheerful ambiance shattered as we all turned, startled. "What was that?" Martha exclaimed, her eyes wide as she shot up from her chair.

"I'll check it out," Luke said, moving quickly toward the door. I hesitated, the warmth of our gathering dissipating into the cool air.

"No, wait," I called after him, but he was already striding out into the evening twilight. I felt a surge of unease tighten in my chest. What could have happened?

"Do you think it's the old tractor?" Frank speculated, glancing nervously at the door.

"I hope it's nothing serious," I muttered, but dread settled over me like a heavy cloak. I could sense a shift in the room, the laughter replaced by hushed murmurs, as we all exchanged worried glances.

Minutes felt like hours as we waited, the excitement of our plans suspended in uncertainty. Just then, Luke burst through the door, his expression a mix of confusion and urgency. "You all need to come quickly!" he called out, and I felt a chill race down my spine as I followed him outside, the vibrant colors of autumn suddenly dimming in the shadows of something I couldn't yet name.

The air outside was thick with anticipation as I followed Luke into the barn, my heart racing like a child on a sugar high. I had half-expected to find a wayward raccoon or maybe a stray sheep that had gotten itself into trouble, but as the barn doors swung open, the sight that greeted me was far more chaotic.

The barn was in disarray; hay bales lay scattered across the floor like the aftermath of a tornado. A curious cluster of neighbors had followed us, their expressions a mix of worry and intrigue. My eyes widened at the sight of a few of our farm tools strewn haphazardly, a wheelbarrow tipped on its side, and an enormous ladder leaning precariously against the wall. But that wasn't what had captured everyone's attention. No, the real spectacle was the colossal wooden beam that had come crashing down from the loft, right where the old feed sacks had been stored.

"Is everyone alright?" I shouted, rushing to inspect the scene.

"Seems like the barn is more fragile than my mother's confidence in my cooking," Sam chimed in, trying to lighten the mood. "Who knew wood could have such a flair for drama?"

Luke shook his head, his expression grim. "No one was underneath it when it fell, thank God, but we've got to get this cleaned up before someone gets hurt."

The gravity of the situation wasn't lost on me. We all felt it—the collective relief that no one was injured mingled with the urgency of the moment. "Let's move these hay bales first," I suggested, rallying the troops. "If we clear the way, we can figure out how to lift the beam back up."

Martha stepped forward, her demeanor shifting from spectator to leader. "Everyone grab a hay bale. And for goodness' sake, someone check the ladder before we use it. We don't need a second accident tonight."

With everyone working together, the atmosphere began to shift. Laughter bubbled up amidst the chaos, the sound like music after the earlier tension. I could hear Frank muttering about the safety of wooden structures while wrestling with a particularly obstinate bale.

"This is why I prefer my office," he grumbled, puffing out a breath as he heaved the bale toward the exit. "No falling beams, just the soft glow of a computer screen."

"Ah, but where's the adventure in that?" Sam shot back, lifting a bale over his head like a trophy. "This is what real life feels like! Plus, I'm pretty sure a computer screen can't give you splinters."

"True," Frank replied, rolling his eyes. "But I'm still taking my chances with it."

With the hay bales cleared, we gathered around the fallen beam, our breaths mingling in the crisp air, a symphony of shared exertion and camaraderie. "On three," Luke instructed, his brow furrowed in concentration. "One... two... three!"

With a collective grunt, we lifted the beam, the rough wood pressing against our palms, the weight a testament to the years it had supported our family's dreams. As we maneuvered it back into place, a rush of adrenaline coursed through me, along with a sense of unity that felt palpable.

"Now, if only I could lift the weight of my mortgage like that," I joked, trying to ease the strain in my arms.

Frank snorted. "You might need a stronger crew for that."

The banter eased the tension, and for a moment, it felt like we were all just friends working on a project together instead of neighbors united by circumstance. Once the beam was secured, we stepped back to survey our handiwork.

"I'd say that's a win," I declared, wiping the sweat from my brow. "Teamwork at its finest."

"Right, but now we have to clean up this mess," Luke said, glancing around at the scattered tools and debris. "And then maybe we can discuss a backup plan for future structural integrity."

"Like hiring a structural engineer?" Martha suggested, hands on her hips.

"Or a miracle worker," I added, grinning. "Because apparently, this barn is full of surprises."

As we tidied up, the conversation shifted back to our earlier meeting. Luke and I exchanged glances, the earlier sense of camaraderie lingering, as though we had forged an unbreakable bond in the chaos. I could see the wheels turning in his mind, and I suspected he was brewing up ideas about how to rally our community, not just for the farm but for something greater.

"Maybe we should host a barn-raising event," he suggested, turning to the group. "Get everyone involved and fix up this place once and for all."

Martha nodded, her expression thoughtful. "I like that idea. We can throw in some food and music—turn it into a real community affair."

"A dance party in the barn? Now you're speaking my language," Sam added, a mischievous glint in his eye. "Just imagine the dancing, the hay flying everywhere. It'd be an autumn spectacle!"

I laughed at the imagery, feeling the earlier tension ebb away. "Just no one in the loft this time. We don't need any impromptu acrobatics."

As we finished cleaning up, I felt a surge of gratitude for this motley crew of neighbors who had come together. Each one of them was a thread in the fabric of our community, and I could see that their hearts were willing to mend what had been frayed.

The evening settled into a comfortable quiet as the sun dipped below the horizon, casting a golden glow over the fields. I stood outside the barn, watching as the stars began to twinkle overhead.

"What do you think?" Luke asked, stepping beside me. "Are we ready to take this leap?"

I looked at him, the weight of the world momentarily lifted. "I think we've just started. But if tonight was any indication, we're more than ready."

He smiled, a genuine warmth in his eyes that made my heart flutter. "Good. Because I think we're onto something special."

In that moment, I felt a flicker of hope, a spark of something that promised to grow. As the crisp air wrapped around us, I knew that whatever challenges lay ahead, we would face them together. The road was still winding, but with the support of my neighbors and the steadfast bond of family, I believed we could pave a way forward—one filled with laughter, hard work, and perhaps a dance or two among the hay bales.

The air outside had turned crisp, the fading sunlight painting the sky in breathtaking strokes of orange and purple, as if even the heavens were celebrating our small victory. I felt a buzz of exhilaration, the kind that often follows a storm. The barn stood sturdy against the twilight, a testament to the teamwork that had woven us closer together, and as I turned to Luke, I couldn't help but smile.

"Think we can get everyone on board for the barn-raising?" I asked, the enthusiasm bubbling up again.

He grinned back, a look of determination lighting his features. "If tonight's any indication, I'd say we're already halfway there. Everyone is eager to pitch in, and we can turn this into something memorable."

Martha, still wiping her hands on a dish towel, chimed in. "Memorable is one word for it. Just don't expect me to lead a conga line while balancing hay bales."

"Challenge accepted!" Sam retorted, feigning a dramatic stance as if he were already choreographing our future dance-off. "We'll call it the 'Bale Boogie.'"

The laughter rolled around us, wrapping us in a comfortable cocoon. The bond we had forged was still fresh and fragile, like a newly woven tapestry. I could see the changes etched on everyone's faces—hope, excitement, and a flicker of trust where skepticism had once reigned.

As the sun sank below the horizon, I suggested we gather for a quick planning session in the kitchen, where I could pull together a few snacks. The idea of our gathering transforming into something more festive felt like the right way to keep the momentum going.

"Don't forget the apple pie!" Frank called out, his eyes sparkling with mischief. "You know that's the secret ingredient for success."

I laughed. "I'll have you know I've improved since the last pie incident. This one is foolproof."

"Foolproof? Please," Luke teased, stepping closer to me, his shoulder brushing against mine. "You might want to define 'foolproof' for the guy who ended up in the middle of that pie disaster."

I rolled my eyes, remembering all too well how I had ended up with more filling on my face than in the crust. "I assure you, it'll only be a culinary disaster if you eat it first," I shot back, savoring the playful exchange.

Once inside the kitchen, the scent of cinnamon and apples filled the air, mingling with the warm glow of the lights. The neighbors filed in, eager to help. We divided tasks like a well-oiled machine, chatting and laughing as we prepared to map out our barn-raising extravaganza.

"Should we include a rain date?" Martha suggested, stirring a pot of cider. "Or is that tempting fate?"

"Let's just not mention rain," Sam interjected, standing by the open window and gazing out at the sky. "I'm already envisioning soggy hay and a mudslide of epic proportions."

"Great, now you've cursed it," Luke said with mock seriousness, shaking his head. "Next, you'll be telling us to wear rubber boots and bring a kayak."

We all chuckled, the camaraderie making the kitchen feel warmer than the cozy fire crackling in the living room. In the midst of it all, I felt a sense of contentment wash over me—a promise of a future built not just on soil but on shared laughter and determination.

As we sipped cider and plotted out our plans, the atmosphere turned to one of genuine excitement. We sketched out ideas on napkins, mapping everything from food stations to entertainment options, debating whether we needed a DJ or just a good old-fashioned playlist.

"And for entertainment, how about a scarecrow contest?" I suggested, envisioning the laughter as we all tried to outdo each other with our creations.

"Only if you promise to make a scarecrow version of yourself," Luke joked, leaning against the counter with that infuriatingly charming smile. "I can already picture it—sunflower head, plaid shirt, and a permanent smirk."

"Great idea! Just what I need, a straw version of my more successful self," I retorted, unable to hide my grin.

As the ideas bounced around, I suddenly felt a pang of nostalgia for the way my father had rallied people together, turning mundane moments into lasting memories. I wanted that for us, to create our own legacy intertwined with laughter and joy, much like the memories of my childhood.

Yet, just as I was getting lost in this reverie, the door burst open with an unexpected crash, and we all turned as one, the sudden noise cutting through the warmth of our gathering. A gust of wind swept in, sending napkins and papers flying, creating a whirlwind of chaos that mirrored my heart's sudden skip.

"Not another falling object!" Frank exclaimed, eyes wide as he clutched his cider like a shield.

"Everyone stay calm!" I called, moving toward the door to see what had happened. But before I could reach it, a figure stumbled in, muddy and breathless.

It was Toby, the local mechanic and friend, his shirt clinging to him, streaked with dirt and a look of sheer panic on his face. "You need to come quick! There's a fire—down by the south field!"

The room fell silent, the jovial atmosphere evaporating in an instant, replaced by a sense of urgency that thickened the air.

"Fire? How bad?" I asked, heart pounding as dread settled in my stomach.

"Bad enough that you can see it from the road. I thought you should know. Grab the others!"

I felt the world tilt on its axis, the flicker of warmth and laughter extinguished. "Let's go!" I yelled, adrenaline rushing through my veins as I rushed to gather everyone, our plans for the barn-raising slipping into the background.

As we raced outside, the twilight deepened around us, the first stars beginning to peek through the canvas of night, oblivious to the chaos unfolding below. I could already smell the smoke as we hurried to the field, the shadows growing longer with each hurried step.

"We need to get the tractor!" Luke shouted, his voice cutting through the growing panic.

"Right! And the fire extinguisher!" I added, my mind racing as I grasped for clarity in the whirlwind of chaos.

But as we reached the edge of the property, the sight before us sent a chill down my spine. Flames danced in the distance, flickering like malevolent spirits amidst the dry grass, casting eerie shadows across the field. My heart sank as I realized that this was no ordinary fire; it had a hunger that threatened to consume everything in its path.

And just as we stood, frozen in shock, I saw movement at the edge of the flames—dark figures darting around, their intentions unclear, their faces obscured by smoke. My breath caught, a cold knot forming in my stomach. The night was far from over, and the real fight had only just begun.

9 798227 353429